Winchinchala

a Little "City Indian" in the 1950's

Winchinchala is the daughter of Seawolfe, Sagamore of a Wôpanâak (Wampanoag) Indian tribe of Massachusetts and Joy of Austrian descent. Studies, work and curiosity have taken her around the world. Its history, peoples, their myths and her life experiences inspire her stories. Many of her characters' psyches have been affected by familial dysfunction and trauma, areas she confesses she is "sadly too familiar with."

Winchinchala is a graduate of Columbia University in the City of New York where she earned her MFA in Film/Writing and B.A. in social anthropology. She won the Warner Brothers' Award for *The Tea Party*, a screenplay. In the decade prior to one as a professor at Berklee College of Music in Boston, she spent another teaching at Boston University. Currently she writes full time.

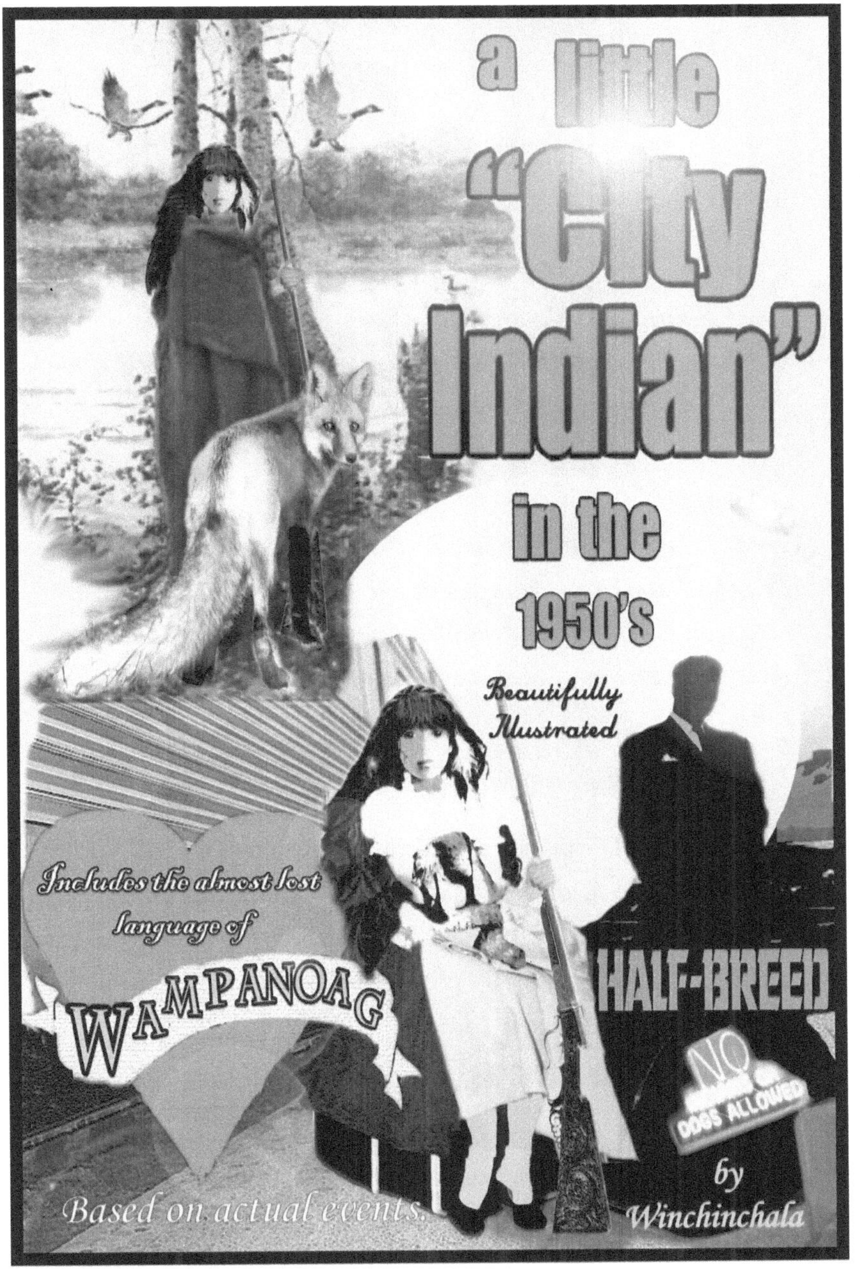
a little
"City
Indian"
in the
1950's
Beautifully
Illustrated
Includes the almost lost
language of
WAMPANOAG
HALF-BREED
NO
DOGS ALLOWED
by
Winchinchala
Based on actual events.

Also by *Winchinchala Winchinchala*

FICTION/ NON-FICTION

The Life and Loves of Mariner Jackie Vik (2012)
Only Human Short Stories (2011)
Seinfeld & Neeneemoosha Sweetheart (2013)
Hope, Between the Wolf & Long-Night Moon (2013)
Derriere: Premiere Seat to Writing (2014)

POETRY

*Sexy Solitary Suicide & That Beat-Hippie Indian Chick, a trip
thru the Racism & Changes of the 50's & 60's to Overcome
Depression*, a tripartite self-help, novella, poetry *(2011)*
Novelty Series: Sexy Red/Crazy Yellow/Bohemian Blue (1992)

TV /SCREENPLAYS

SEINFELD Episode: "Schleppen Feathers" (1997)
Remote Man, a play ©1990/publication 2002
SAVING GRACE (1982)
THE TEA PARTY (1979) Winner of Warner Bros. Award

SELECTED VIDEOS (writer/producer/director)

The Empress Dowager's Robe (2001)
Reflections of an Evening (1999)
Young Lovers' Christmas Cowboy Caviar (1999)

Winchinchala Winchinchala
2013 Edition

a Little "City Indian" in the 1950's

People With Wings Illustrated Books

Since 1992

Boston -- Denver -- Amsterdam – Paris

People With Wings Illustrated Books, 2013 Edition

a Little "City Indian" in the 1950's

This book is a work of fiction inspired by the life of the author. With the exception of iconic celebrities and political figures who are part of the historical backdrop of the 1950's, any resemblance of characters in this book, their names or lives to actual people is entirely coincidental.

Printed in the United States of America.
Library of Congress Cataloging-in-Publication Data
96070538

ISBN 9781889768366

Front Cover Art: UPPER: Collage by Winchinchala. Face photograph of Winchinchala as a child, ©Seawolfe 1955, Background illustrated by John Rae American Indian Fairy Tales 1921. Front Cover Art LOWER: Collage art by Winchinchala.

In Loving Memory of
Joy, my beautiful mother;
Grandma, Aunt Naomi & Aunt Ida, all
shining, strong, wise women.

– Contents –

Acknowledgements

Who among artists: singers, dancers, sculptors, painters or writers can create without love, support, some kind of help? Not I and luckily, I receive all from several. The lion's share comes to me from Wechêkum, Mukquoshim, Seawolfe, my father whose longevity is due in part to his adoring wife, M.A. We also need a bit of humor so as not to take ourselves so seriously. My dear friend Frank has plenty that has helped keep my head out of the oven. He is himself an artist, a crooner. *Take One*, is his inaugural CD[1])

Other friends offer kind encouragement and knowledge of the times and places: Patricia Dwyer; Robert G. Gardner, Cambridge, MA; George Peabody Gardner, Brookline, MA; Mr. William Morris Hunt, Boston, MA; Bill and Francesca Shakespeare, Brookline, Ma.

Reference librarians, our indispensable finders: Linda Mac Iver, the Boston Public Library in Copley Square and its Social Science Reference staff; Derek Moses, the San Diego Central Library who also generously shared first hand knowledge; Faith Yoman, Librarian of the Southwest Collection, New Mexico State Library; The Massachusetts Historical Society; The 1997 President of the Myopia Hunt Club, Northampton, MA.

Institutional archivists and historians who have been equally helpful: Victoria Kasstner, Historian of the Hearst Castle "San Simeon"; Ben Lippincott, Newport Historic Society; Mark S. Young archivist and historian of the Tennis Hall of Fame; Gino Francesconi, Historian Carnegie Hall; Loren Schoenberg, Artistic Director, The National Jazz Museum in Harlem; Mary Jo Mc Nally, Pierre Hotel, NY; Terry at Collectors' Firearms[2]; Attorney Diane W. Spears, Boston, MA.

---

[1] http://www.cdbaby.com/franktabata (All profits are donated to Doctors without Borders.)
[2] http://www.collectorsfirearms.com

Special Thanks to:

Thornton D. Barnes, T.D., Hypersonic Flight Specialist, CIA (RET) and Executive Director Nevada Aerospace Hall of Fame[3], who most light-heartedly listened to and answered my questions about the top secret, Air Force culture and operations of Groom Lake, "Area 51" in the 1950's. I must confess, I was intimidated by the idea of interviewing a CIA operative no matter what his title, but he broke down all the "men-in-black stereotypes" I had. The insight he offered into the culture of the organization added tremendously to the story's authenticity. Furthermore he allowed me access to the site of his comprehensive and period specific photo collection. His book is sure to be fascinating.

Strong Woman, Dr. Julienne Jennings & Waabu, Dr. Francis Joseph O'Brien Jr. for their generosity of spirit and help with Algonquian languages, their writings[4] in particular proved crucial in including the Wampanoag – Wôpanâak language.

I am grateful to Mary Deane of course for her masterful manuscripts skills but also for her prodding me toward the completion of this task I long wanted to do.

Yianni Courduvelis provided patient assistance in helping me navigate software programs professional and simple with their many challenges. As a keenly talented lyricist and avid reader, he offered personal critiques and encouragement which I very much appreciated.

José Gurria (Gurri) enthusiastically translated the colorful, time period and situation-specific Mexican Spanish.

Lauren Ash Donhaho, and Judith Bond (RIP) who was so generous in giving me the extended personal historical tour and private time to create memories of the Hotel Del Coronado, San Diego, CA.

---

[3] http://nvahof.org/
[4] http://www.docstoc.com/docs/23970980/Understanding-Algonquian-Indian-Words-New-England-(rev.-ed)

Notes to the reader:

Language: Words herin are reflect the era and are not meant to offend.

Wampanoag - Wôpanâak. The latter from the 17th century is closer to the original Native Indian word. The former is the modern spelling.

Italics: Used to emphasize a word or sentences of character's thoughts.

Arrow parentheses « » Signals French.

Illustrations: "Illustrated literature is typically, and sadly, only associated with children. We all loved those pictures, didn't we? But when we leave grammar school, they disappear from our books. There is a nasty myth running around unchallenged in the world suggesting that minimizing their number in fiction magically elevates stories in depth and complexity and better challenge readers' imaginations. The very opposite is true. An author's rendering of a character or a scene doesn't stop a reader from creating one or serve as a substitute for descriptive passages. Images bolster the mind, exemplify or authenticate precisely what the writer is communiating. For example in *The Life & Loves of Jackie Vik,* I mentioned a wooden ice-chest which baffled a few of People With Wings feedback readers whose minds, despite my mention of wood, could only conjure up a Styrofoam cooler, so I drew one and put it in. Also in that book, I included images of documents specific to the 1940's such as ration cards, an induction letter etc. Most readers have told me they enjoy the illustrations, so I hope what's old will become what's new again."

In the 19th and early 20th century, much of fiction was illustrated. One edition of *Tom Sawyer* boasts 175! Interesting pairings were born of the practice. Henry Matisse sketched works for James Joyce's 1935 limited edition of *Ulysses,* Noel Sickles for the 1952 edition of Ernest Hemingway, *The Old Man and the Sea* etc. The practice required extra time for formatting which added the expense of commissions, so it was phased out.

Electronic technology has made including images affordable which is why we are People With Wings *Illustrated Books.*

Preface

★★★★★ FULL OF LOVE, 50'S HISTORY & MANY CULTURES. MARVELOUS!

Once I started reading I was eager to find out what would happen to Hebe, the charming, young "half-breed" girl and all the wild people she meets. How would she deal with her mother? Would she keep drinking herself? Winchinchala's writing is magical.

★★★★★ HEBE IS SURE TO BE AN EPIDEMIC

Hebe Jeebie is the most engaging book I have read in a long, long time. Winchinchala plays hardball with the human psyche, and just when you think you have run the gamut of all possible human emotions, bang zoom…another kidney punch sends you careening into the next chapter. Get a good HMO and get a copy of *Hebe Jeebie*.

★★★★★ ABSOLUTELY TOUCHING BRILLIANCE

There seem to be only a few authors who can write about life with passion and wonderment and actually put it into a coherent and wonderful story. Winchinchala has written a piece full of emotion expressed right from her heart. *Hebe Jeebie* explores the many subjects life brings about. As a motherless daughter, I was enticed by the powerful and complex, mother-daughter relationship and touched by Winchinchala's observations, absolutely touching brilliance.

★★★★★ WINCHINCHALA: AN INCREDIBLE AUTHOR

This is the most amazing book I have ever read. It echoes all the childhood pain I went through albeit in a different way, but you relive through Hebe. She touched your heart, all of the characters are written so real. You can't believe it when the book is over. I really hope there is a sequel. I can't imagine what it would be like but with Winchinchala, I get the impression anything could happen. I cannot stress enough how much you need to read *Hebe Jeebie*.

★★★★★ A THOUGHT PROVOKING MASTERPIECE

Hebie Jeebie is both entertaining and very real, a treat to anyone who loves a good story. I cannot praise Winchinchala enough for her entertaining yet thought provoking masterpiece.

One of my favorite expressions is "the only thing that is constant is change." It is applicable to much of my life and that includes writing, *a Little "City Indian" in the 1950's*. It began as *Hebe Jeebie (*1997) and was slated for editing as the publisher's note mentioned those many years ago. The book, as also stated at that time, was added to the list of unedited published manuscripts such as Jack Kerouac's first draft of *On the Road, The Scroll* (1957) and Alan Ginsberg's *Original Draft Facsimile, Transcript, and Variant Versions of Howl, Fully Annotated by Author* (1956). Initial feedback was positive, and I was, of course, flattered but dissatisfied with the work. I had written neither the character nor her journey as I truly wanted. Doing so require lengthy revisitations to the scary, dark, confusing days in my personal life and the society of the 50's, and I never seemed to be able to find the necessary moxie. I vowed to get it done "by January," then by "Native American New Years," and then by "the summer." The days appeared on the calendar but not the spirit to write.

An invisible fault line under the sea of my life had opened. My career and all but one cardboard box of my worldly possessions had tumbled irretrievably into it. A dock strike and a postal mishap delivered the latter to the Pacific Ocean floor and parts unknown. As a refugee from disaster, I searched for a new home and position, but the economy, my age and even experience worked against me. Author, James Baldwin's description of his state of mind before he left for Paris summarizes mine so well, I would like to offer it. "Looking for a place to live, looking for a job, you begin to doubt your judgment, you begin to doubt everything. You become imprecise. And that's when you're beginning to go under. You've been beaten, and it's been deliberate. The whole society has decided to make you nothing." [5]

I was in the depths of the fault, and it was pitch black. Palming at the wall for an exit, my fingertips came across the same two-thousand-five-hundred-year-old-truth Siddhartha Gautama Buddha had found. "There is no knowledge won without sacrifice. Looking back, I see that

---

[5] *The Paris Review*, Spring, 1984, No 91, James Baldwin, "The Art of Fiction," No. 78, Interview by Jordan Elgrably.

mantra and an experience with a Holy Bible got me through. Light dawned again in my life, and what I saw was my manuscripts, new and old, were all around me, so I set about editing them, saving *Hebe Jeebie* (1997) for last. Eventually, I arrived at a confluence of available time and spirit to tacle it. Rereading the book revealed recent experiences had changed me so completely that I could not edit or rewrite it. The options were do nothing or start over which I did and wrote, *A Little "City Indian," in the 1950's.* The protagonist, Hebe/Nuttah, has a new personality with which to face familial dysfunction, questions of race[6] and her search for identity and home, though she never had one.

The tale predates my life, but much of what happens to the character happened to me, being a child at large in the openly racist world of the 50's, confronting its physical dangers and battling dark secrets, the soul-sucking beasts of abuse, neglect and rejection. Adults often automatically employ avoidance tactics to deal with them and simply stuff them into the farthest storage bin in their heads which plants the fear of someone, anyone, finding these things out. Hiding dark secrets can make a host suspicious, paranoid, somber or silent and turn one to methods of forgetting, lying, drinking and taking drugs. Dark secrets make navigating life's waters damn difficult because they are pernicious whether hidden or confronted. No one is eager to drag them out of storage to do combat, but one must to have peace of mind

My dark secrets came about in the 50's when I was born. WWII was over, and "the boys" were home. Employment was high. The suburbs were booming; rock 'n roll was blasting from cars as long as eighteen feet! The decade is often referred to as the "Great Time," which it was but only for some. Laws and social attitudes about the mythical concept of race made it much less than a "Great Time" for most non-Whites. In the 85 years since the Civil War, discrimination toward non-Whites had diminished but not disappeared. In 1948, "equality of treatment and opportunity for all persons in the armed services without regard to race, color, religion, or national origin," was ordered by President Truman, but real Civil Rights was years away. White society had been

---

[6]   Dr. Spencer Wells, Geneticist and Explorer in Residence at National Geographic, and other renowned geneticists, have proven race biologically non-existent to my satisfaction. No bibles, to my knowledge, tell of more than one Adam and Eve.

infused with Sir Francis Galton's pseudo-scientific theory of Eugenics which, supposedly, proved them biologically superior to other "races." The discrimination that ensued threatened me and many non-Whites across our county. Virginia's Racial Integrity Act of 1924 only acknowledging the existence of two races: White and Colored. Determining who was what, as it were, was a complex political matter which shocked immigrant Slavs, Italians and Greeks who arrived in the New World to be labeled as Colored, second-class citizens.[7] "Coloreds" were denied rights, property, education, opportunities and even love by the law or the self-righteous discriminatory actions of others.

National polls and statistics show marriages between Whites and all other races at a weak 5%[8] in the 1950's. It was, after all, illegal in most states. As a result, "mixed-race" couples endured intense discrimination from all sides. Even one non-White neighbor was thought to devalue neighborhoods which made renting or buying difficult. They were basically banned from socializing publically. The White spouse was often shunned by his/her own racial circle, and s/he was often maligned by the minority group for having "stolen" one of their men or women. Perhaps the children suffered the most because they did not understand the skin-color based hostility of the world into which they were born. The ridiculous question: "What are you?" was asked on government forms and by the curious and ignorant. Laws surrounding identity drove a wedge between them and the White parent whose race a child could not claim and the non-White parent whose race was responsible for a child's perceived lowly status. A child should not have to battle discrimination, but I and my peers did. Decades later Civil rights movements by minorities helped to relieve some of that pressure, but growing up in its midsts was horrible. Self doubt, insecurity, feelings of inferiority and a fear of being judged, for what I am or what I am not, had infiltrated my psyche so deeply; I could not be true to myself, my own Native American identity in writing. I fabricated someone else in the initial story attempt in 1997. In the 1980's I had wanted to pursue a doctorate in anthropology focusing on my people; I was told I could

---

[7] John Tehranian, "Performing Whiteness: Naturalization Litigation and the Construction of Racial Identity in America," *The Yale Law Journal*, Vol. 109, No. 4. (Jan., 2000), pp. 825-827.

not study my own because I "would not be objective." And in 1997, when I consulted others about using our "sleeping" Wampanoag language, the remark came that "To use a dead language is pretentious." Hmpf. Eventually reading, living and breathing in the changed world, defeated the beasts within and the deep-seated insecurities connected to my identity and writing came undone. Stronger now, I poked Wampanoag.

"Tokish Tokêtuck." (Let's wake up.)

Miles from pretension, my intent is to let my 1950's characters speak as they did, make Wampanoag language, at least some words, accessible. Most importantly, I want to honor our Wampanoag ancestors by removing the silencing earth shoveled into their mouths by cultural imperialism. Our people came perilously close to total extinction. First we were ravaged by smallpox; the fatality rate was 90%! Then the Europeans broke the peace treaties which gave rise to Metacom's War 1675-1678 between the British and the Wampanoag. Captured Native Indians were killed, and their families sold to merchants from as far away as Spain and the Caribbean. The Colonial leaders fought on. Land was sold out from under tribes. Indian children were forced to relocate to "schools," mandatory indoctrination centers where the threat of harm to their parents, beatings and rape were used to encourage them to denounce their religions, deny their cultures and stop using their languages, but we survived and by the 1950's a great wave of Red Power began to swell. The battle for rights continues, but I have slain at least one beast. I believe I have achieved my goal of long ago, to write about the 1950's world of prejudice and dysfunction from a child's perspective.

Happy Reading!

Winchinchala,
Boston, Massachusetts,
December 21, 2013

a Little "City Indian" in the 1950's

Pocahontas & her husband, John Rolfe in Englan

I

A "City Indian"

Brookline, Massachusetts, January 1959

In the midst of an out-of-body experience, Hebe, a twelve-year-old girl pondered the nature of reality.

Who told me we leave our bodies under stress? Rem? Bob? Hans? Whoever may be right, but leaving my body and floating around like this doesn't relieve me of stress any more than closing my eyes leads to falling asleep or falling asleep leads to dreams. Suddenly, here I am ghosting around the bathroom at the top of the stairs watching myself trying to pee in a big, fat wedding gown. And all my friends are here. 'I hope this is the last time,' one of them said. How many times have I been up here? What is going on? I guess, as always, I have to wait and see.

She watched herself hop from foot to foot while her bridesmaids lifted her voluminous gown and she positioned herself, but she no longer had to go. For more than fifteen minutes, they bent awkwardly and knelt uncomfortably beside her, their arms and sometimes mouths full of dusty pink, ruffled tulle. The first clue she had that she might be dreaming was when she saw a memengwe because she knew the ball was December 31st, and the chances of a butterfly having survived that far into the cold were unlikely. Perhaps she was dreaming about earlier in the year when she was trying on dresses? Humid fog from the hot water running to help her pee made determining the correct season momentarily impossible. She guided the fragile wilting insect toward the opening in the window and he flew into the arms of Wuttootchìk-kìnneasin Nippawus, Grandfather Sun. Her fancy feather adornment dangled by her ripe, young cheek, and she prayed silently.

Nuppeantam. Kiehtanit, Ohke, Okummus nepauzshad, Wuttꝏtchìk kìneasin nippawus, Taubot neanawayean. Taubot neanawayean ne-wutche wame netomppauog: neg pamunenutcheg, neg pamom pakecheg, puppinashimwog mehtugquash kah moskeh-tuash namoh-sog. Kiehtanit, taubot neanawayean. Nuppeantam, Let me know I am doing the right thing marrying this man, losing my identity in his name and going abroad. It's as if I am dying. Don't let Nuttah die," she demanded and then asked herself, *Why can't I pee?*

Below was one of her favorite spots at the Birches, the cloistered garden where, in blissful, verdant solitude, she had often sat reading. In her mind's eye, she saw herself there in the dead of winter, in her sensible winter clothes, while Jack Frost tried to send her inside by biting her cheeks and nose. She stayed to watch the busy chipmunk moving surreptitiously among the bushes. He was warmly dressed too in his snug tan-striped coat which stood out against the sparkling white snow while he scampered industriously to and fro. Beneath winter's quiet sky, she almost wished for the vivacious, squawk and ruckus of crows among summer's high dense leaves. Eventually they dropped and flurried down to protect the roots from troublesome Jack, to reenter the ground and emerge again as they did now in new, green life. For the moment, the garden provided a respite for guests seeking refuge from the clamorous New Year's Ball on the lower floors. Alone and in pairs they drifted out; most smoked; a young couple kissed with passionate abandon and an elderly gentleman relieved his flatulence in loud trumpeted bursts, but they all admired the greenery, glanced up at the sky and strolled along the ancient stones. Centuries of infidels and holy men, enemies and friends, corpses and mourners had taken the path they formed in front of the village church in France. During the war, a bomb turned its insides into a weighty downpour of chards, broken relics, splintered pews, shattered stained glass and fragmented roof shingles landed on the path, and for years it led to ruins. Assessed as destroyed beyond resurrection, the church was understandably slated for removal but, to Rem's dismay, so was the path. On their behalf, she argued "they had served beneath millions and witnessed the birth of the village, the church and each and every one of them." When no one agreed, she shipped them to Massachusetts and her sanctuary at the Birches.

She imports everything from Europe. Hebe thought, *preserves, coffee, perfume, cars, even my intended.*

He was a lean, attractive sandy-haired nobleman two and a half times her age. On the few occasions they had met, including a brief trip to New York, she found him good-natured, sensitive and thoughtful; nevertheless, he was a stranger, a stranger who would soon be waiting for her with all the others in the chapel.

Preparing had been so much fun, especially selecting clothes for the trousseau and of course the gown, all graciously provided by Rem. As an active socialite and triple divorcée, who changed two or three times for each of her own weddings, her collection was enviably luxurious. Her lady's maid dressed a dozen headless mannequins in a viewing salon. Soft silks in brilliant whites or muted to shades of ivory billowed from the forms, but Hebe was disinclined to try them. "White will be for my real wedding," was her reason which Rem thought "precious." The mannequins were redressed in gowns blushing pastels which, Rem was glad to learn, were more to Hebe's taste; she encouraged her to "choose one as soon as you can." To that end, Hebe enlisted her nearby friends who hindered more than helped the process because each time she emerged in a different gown, they spoke in unison, "This is the one."

"But no feathers," Bozena suggested, and reached for her hair.

"No," the other girls sang out in a collective chorus.

"I thought everyone knew feathers are Nuttah's signature."

"Scuze me, Missus Countess Rem, but in Poland chickens are for food, not accessories. I do like the feathers Hebe, very pretty," she added in a flat tone which came across as insincerity.

"Not a chicken, a red tail hawk. Wénise, made it for me."

Bozena rolled her eyes in disapproval. The girls saw but ignored her; they knew wearing a feather made her feel close to Wénise, who had first tied one in her hair.

"What a mosunnoquat teag," a pretty thing, Hebe's father said when he came to pick her up those many years ago.

The compliment doubled her delight in wearing the feather; even though, her mother was of the opinion that "Parading your identity among regular people is asking for trouble."

Her father argued that, "The child should be encouraged to be herself," which entitled her to the feathers for a while. Her great grandmother wove a headband into which the feather was stuck and stood up straight from Hebe's head, but within a few months she had outgrown it. When her parents delivered her to Wénise's house in the summer, her first words requested a new one.

"No Wénise. She doesn't need it. Hebe is not going to be at home all day with me but at school where feathers are not worn," Gaye-Lee bit out, in her hybrid, British-bent, Boston-Vienna accent.

"Don't speak to her in that tone," Kutty told his wife.

Wénise chuckled and touched his arm. "It doesn't mean anything, that tone. They all talk to each other that way. You should know that by now," but she did not disagree with her daughter-in-law. She knew that an American Indian girl would have an easier time in the churning belly of the Whites' city if she conformed but thought Nuttah could wear the feather, see what happened and then decide for herself if she wanted to hide or broadcast her identity.

"Skinny walks around town in his breechcloth, and…"

"Gets pulled in for indecent exposure Wénise."

"Just like he wants," she quipped.

With slim rawhide strip, she created an adornment with red-tail hawk feather with a clip, so Nuttah could reveal or conceal it among her hair. Today it was prominently displayed and hung over the shoulder of her gown. She had selected it because when she emerged from the dressing area, Nell exclaimed, "You look just like Princess Pauline." Hebe was impressed by her, not because the princess was a raving beauty; she was not, but because she was so feisty. The Viennese and Parisian socialite Princess Pauline Clémentine von Metternich-Winneburg zu Beilstein née Countess Pauline Clémentine Marie Walburga Sándor de Szlavnicza was an impressive lady. Hebe had to examine it closely two or three times to believe her eyes when she saw *The Naked Duel* which was prominently displayed in the Birches print

The Emancipated Duel

room. The princess had crossed swords with Countess Sophia Kielmannsegg on a hill in Verduz, Liechtenstein. Their bodies were fully clothed in their riding habits and hats, but they were nude from their waists to their shoulders.

"That's spunk," Rem noted, winked and tapped her finger on the woman 'whose shapely breasts were visible, "von Metternich- Winneburg, my mother's branch of the family."

"Are they fighting for love?" Hebe asked inciting a lyrical laugh.

"Oh no. It was much more important."

"Oh, you mean honor."

Rem shook her head and corrected her. "Flower arrangements."

"Flower arrangements?! I would not stab anyone for flowers."

"Perhaps not, but that doesn't mean others would not. I have known people to do harm for the most mindless reasons my dear."

Rosalita brought Hebe back to the stuffy bathroom by ordering her to, "Go already," in her rapid Mexican-Spanish, "the humidity is shrinking me. I can't afford to get any smaller. "

She held up her left arm which was a quarter length shorter than her right. The girls laughed, accustomed to her self-deprecating jokes.

"Yes, go, or tell your Grandfather Sun to dry the air?"

"Wuttootchìkkìnneasin Nippawus?"

"Whichever god is available."

To distract themselves from the clammy climate in the small space, they talked about marriage. Nell the impossibly pretty, nineteen-year-old honey-blonde sylph from an aristocratic Belgian family was extremely interested in finding "a proper husband, a good match, to please mother."

"Picky picky gonna leave you with no body. What is a girl with no husband?" Rosalita asked and answered, "Old maid, a lonely old maid."

A reply danced in Holly's eyes, but she kept it to herself and scratched at the stray drops of oil paint near the hem of her gown. The fibers from which she was woven had been spun from propriety and that prevented her from sharing unless no one else had anything to say. Then, and only then, providing, it would not provoke disharmony, she put her thoughts forth, softly and femininely. When no one responded to Rosalita's remark Holly did.

"What is a girl with no husband? She repeated. "She is herself. That is what a girl is with no husband—herself.

She retreated behind her mousy brown hair to resume cleaning her hem.

Bozena, a hearty helping of beet-tinted Polish potatoes, was already married and in a family way at sixteen. She chimed cheerily that "Marriage is to make babies," and added with a kittenish twinkle, "to make sexy and to make babies."

Embarrassed titters erupted.

"Amor!" Rosalita belted out, "is the most important. I almost forgot amor."

"Amor? Amor is usually an illusion."

"S'cuse me Mrs. Rem, but Adam and Eve disagree with you," Rosalita countered.

"And Lilith would disagree with you," Rem quipped and confounded the Catholics, Rosalita and Bozena.

"Who?" they asked together.

Holly waited, and then clarified, "Lilith was Adam's first wife. She left. God grew weary of his whining and created Eve."

"¿Qué? Todos ustedes están locos. Dios hizo a Adán y Eva, y todos en el mundo...You are estupid if..."

"Rosa!" Hebe scolded.

"Sorry Hebita, but that is craziness."

"I told you our creator, Kiehtan made a man and woman out of stone, but he didn't like them, so he made more from a tree. You didn't call me stupid."

"You were telling me an Indian story. They are talking about the Holy Bible. I didn't mean you are estupid Holly."

"How did we get on religion? Love is love, but marriage is an institution to protect women and families' wealth and to save us from a preponderance of bastards."

The sharp point of Rem's perspective closed the topic.

"Faire pipi Hebe. 'Faire pipi pour paix d'esprit' the nanny used to tell me," Rem muttered.

"It's true. Peeing does give one peace of mind." Nell agreed and asked, "Are you sure this wedding is legal?"

Rem cut a what-do-you-think glance at her. The girls bantered while Hebe plummeted into the depths of anxiety. Broken tears splattered on her naturally tanned cheeks, and her body trembled.

"I am not getting married today. Rem, feel like I am dead" she bawled.

"Dead? That's ridiculous. You are only twelve," Rem remarked half to herself, and realized she had to have a private chat with Hebe. "Wedding day jitters," she announced and shooed the girls out.

Henry, the estate manager, buzzed on the intercom.

"Madam, the activities in the upper reaches have found passage to the first floor via the vent."

"I have every confidence in your problem solving abili…A song should do the trick just fine."

Before she had hung up, the musicians played "Swing Low Sweet Chariot," and a chorus of guests joined in.

Certainly now, no one can hear me us here, she thought.

"The plan was for you to leave in the carriage drawn by Lightning, not a hearse. Death? What a silly thing."

"No. I just mean…I will only be Hebe now, not Nuttah, just like Pocahontas. The English kept her away from her father and her tribe and married her to that John Rolfe to get her land. They put her in those stiff clothes and renamed her Rebecca, you know? Pocahontas was nowhere except in her own memories or dreams. Maybe she was the first city Indian," she concluded and at long last relieved herself.

Rem felt no more qualified to address Hebe's comments on identity today than she had the many months ago when they first met, especially as she had begun the morning with celebratory champagne.

"Would you like to speak to Skinny or… Rains Fire?" She burst out laughing. "I never imagined I would know people with such unusual names. I can not believe the diverse array of people I have met through you Hebe. Oh your Filipino friend Joe arrived last night…and Anders," she lifted Hebe's veil. "I think everyone noticed how he makes you smile." At the mention of his name, a glimmer of light sparkled on Hebe's face, but she didn't say anything. "Well, what does that even mean, 'city Indian,' is it an insult?"

"Sure. It's like saying you are not really Indian because, you don't live in the Indian way."

"How can they in the thick of White society?"

"Exactly," Hebe nodded, scooped up her dress and lay on the counter in a despondent pink chiffon heap.

Rem felt helpless, and she questioned the wisdom of having recruited her charge to her cause.

What is wrong with me thinking a child could make such a decision? Based on what? She has no experience. She was probably afraid if she declined, I would send her away. Such a sweet and dear girl didn't ask for anything, not like Nell. She—well that mother—wanted everything just as we predicted, and she wanted it written in stone, but not Hebe. All she wanted was to belong, a bit of love.

Hebe's profoundly deep attachment to Rem was obvious to everyone; she would have done anything, including marrying a man, simply because she had asked. The wedding masquerading as a New Years Ball was supposed to help them, and a few weeks ago Rem was sure it would "blow over like a harmless spring breeze." Instead it gusted balefully through the Birches' many rooms?

With a gentle tug on the bell pull, her lady's maid promptly arrived and hustled away with her instructions. They sat in contemplative peace punctuated with "Swing low, sweet chariot." Rem's own first marriage at eighteen flooded into her mind. She was madly in love, or thought she was, and while she didn't think it forecast death, she was losing part of herself, leaving her family and France to live in her husband's country, Italy.

"Who calls you Nuttah?" Rem asked Hebe, "Wénise and your father's people, right? Don't use Hebe anymore, use Nuttah. There are no laws against that. What is my name?"

"Rem," Hebe replied befuddled.

"Right, nothing to do with the name my parents gave me, and I am French, but I speak English here. In Italy, I speak Italian, mais I—am— French! Ask anyone; they will tell you,"

"And anyone will tell you, I am Mexican or Italian, a city Indian with a White mother."

"Alors, you are White."

"Not according to the law. I can not be White."

The word "law" tapped into the dark days Rem recalled of Hitler's insanity that had infused sorrow and disharmony into France and into her personal circle. There were those few who were neither whole-heartedly opened to his beliefs nor opposed to them which she found most callous and disconcerting. Some comments were so painfully ignorant; she found it increasingly difficult to remain neutral. Religion had never been an acceptable topic, but eventually circumstances divulged to her who among her friends was Jewish. Rachel, the scholar insisted on being called Marika, left university and then disappeared. Judith, who always departed with, "À la prochaine mes amis," a little too loudly, but ever so entertainingly, in the salon, stopped. One evening, seemingly out of the blue, by her car, flung her arms around her and wept. When Rem asked what was wrong, she simply shook her head, claimed she had too much to drink and delivered a sentimental thank you for all the years of their friendship. It was the last time Rem saw her and others who had left similarly. To protect themselves and Rem, all refused the connections, foreign residences or manufactured documents, she eagerly offered to help, and with dreams of "getting together when it is all over," they disappeared with astonishing success. How was a mystery which remained unsolved until this day and which filled her with curiosity as to who had survived and where and how they were. Expecting German Occupation to be a nightmare, Rem along with her family slipped into the Hong Kong contingent of their extended social circle until, hopefully, "France was herself again." So many lives in the world had been sacrificed to eradicate what she considered the Nazi's absurd and inhumane ideas.

The American troops came to help us get rid of the evil spreading thinking that race or beliefs make one person better than another. Now, fourteen years later, I learn, U. S. law does not allow people to be themselves! Their leaders didn't believe their mission in their hearts. They stopped the Germans while they were doing exactly the same thing against the Indians, and the Blacks and the Chinese. What a world.

An "Argh," of displeasure released more memories of days gone by and tears pooled in her eyes. The tender vision of Hebe trying on gowns for the ball touched her heart, for on that day, Hebe had mistakenly called her "mother." She corrected herself and then, in the sweetest and most sincere tone added, "But if a person could choose a mother, I would have chosen you."

The maid returned with a bottle of champagne, Hebe's bird-wing fan, dried sage and abalone shell, so she could smudge. It always seemed to calm her. She lit the sage, poured herself a glass of champagne and toasted Hebe.

"Santé! Hebe my dear, sweet girl. Look there's your....how do you say papillon?" she snapped her fingers, "...memengwe, that's it." Rem picked up Hebe's rifle and aimed it at herself in the mirror. "Pow. You picked this up very quickly Hebe...Nuttah... such a character. I will never forget you, none of us will."

""Rem?" the girls called impatiently and tapped on the door.

The Palace

II

"There but Not There"

Early 1950's, Cape Cod and Cambridge, Massachusetts

Indulging in the cottony limbo between slumber and wakefulness, Hebe postponed the arrival of another day by holding her eyes closed. It had been the best summer she could remember on the Cape. After a brief sojourn to see Oma, her mother's mother, Mrs. Livingston in her rambling Victorian home along Nantucket Sound, she spent two months with her father's grandmother, Wénise. Passersby and a few relatives referred to her house as a "little old shanty-shack." It was one room, but Wénise consider it small because to her the land was part of her home. She and her husband, Neesneéchag Skeétompauog, Twenty-Men, a Passamaquoddy, were married in 1899 up north, and they relocated to the Cape to live and work at the Ochre family villa. They could have stayed on, but they wanted their own property on which to plant trees and watch them grow old with them. As soon as they had the money, they bought the place which had Indian neighbors in three directions. Twenty-Men's blacksmithing and carpentry and Wénise's agricultural endeavors kept them outside most of the time; a cozy cabin was fine with them, and they jokingly called it the Palace. All who visited were impressed to learn they had raised seven children there which she mentioned to her family members whenever they complained about too little money or space. After Twenty-Men passed from this world to Kiehtan's, her siblings and children began bothering her about moving into town to live with one of them. They harped on the dangers of being "way out there." To stem their loving nagging, she asked a series of questions in the gentle, mellifluous manner for which she was known.

"Is my husband's spirit all around me there? What about nunnau-monog, my sons, taken by the war? Can I light my fire? Catch I catch fish and smoke it? Give you gladiolas and green beans and strawberries if I don't have my garden? Can our people gather and sing under the trees and the stars? What about talking to my animals?"

Hebe had seen Wénise hold her shotgun by her side and talk to a bear as calmly as she spoke to Wohwohkau, Mr. Joseph's dog. She ordered him to go. "Mat. Mat mosk. Mat. Admish. Admish. Hawúnshech, now." He looked right at her, sniffed and moaned and waddled disappointedly away; she didn't even raise the gun. Hebe wanted to talk to them too, to do everything Wénise did from pumping water and growing food to weaving baskets and sewing to shooting and taking care of her guns. Wénise had an attractive collection hidden from view on the racks in the wardrobe doors, but two were visible, the ancient Winchester, engraved with a dainty scroll and rose design, belonged Twenty-Men. He had made its buckskin sheath. It was stored under the bed during the day, but at night, Wénise loaded it and laid it on top of the case within arm's reach. In the summer heat, the skins odor and that of Twenty-Men rose from it which is why Hebe assumed her great grandmother kept it there.

Wénise took the shotgun outside where she worked all day. The scarecrow and the jingling cones which she and Hebe had tied on short stakes scared the birds and most of the critters, but not all. If her great-grandmother saw any in the garden, she used the shotgun to shoot them. "Cheer up. That didn't hurt the wuhtokquas, just dusted their fluffy tails," she told Hebe. "I didn't grow those vegetables for you," she would say and send them scampering with a spray from the shotgun. Hebe was eager to grow strong enough to do it, to "handle the kick," but for the time being, she was satisfied with slipping in the cartridges.

She placed her finger close to the barrel. "Ahque!" Wénise warned her, "Don't touch. Guns are for bad business."

"Bad business?" Hebe echoed.

"I mean killing Nuttah."

"Oh no. No killing please. No dying."

"Dying is unavoidable we all leave this earth. If we are kind, we go to live with Kiehtan. Death is part of life," her joints reminded her because they had lost most of their elasticity when she arose and moaned involuntarily. "But not today. We have too much to do."

Wénise & Nuttah in the Cornfield

Wénise could have said that about every day, for her life was chores, mostly outside. The usual routine began when they opened the windows to let the fresh air in. They hung the bedding on the line to air, and out there, they offered prayers. Repeating "Nuppeantam Kiehtanit" words branded in Nuttah's mind long ago. After they washed and ate they replenished the water supply from the pump. The leaf-scented air and dew on her ankles refreshed her, and she went with Wénise even before she was able to carry the heavy buckets. Pump water had a unique fragrance and sweet taste; she always drank a little from her cupped hands. Together, they weeded the garden, collected acorns or ground corn. For that they went into the clearing on the hill to the big stone where Wénise had pounded grain for years and years which created a smooth hollow in the center. Before they offered prayers at sunset, they sewed, wove cattail mats or any of a number of tasks; they were never ending. Except for her instructions or answers to Nuttah's questions, they didn't say much.

Every now and again, Nuttah raised her eyes to Wénise's glittering in her warm reddish-brown face. When she went into town, she puffed her skin with powder, put her hair up, traded her moccasins with a pair of hard, lace-up shoes and put on gloves. In a certain light she could have been mistaken for a White woman, but she was so fiercely proud of being Indian, Nuttah doubted that was her intention. With or without powder, men lit up when Wénise, her great-grandmother passed, everyone did. The sight of her instantly stole her woes and wrapped them in ribbons of rainbows that little white swallows winged into the infinity beyond Wuttootchìkkìnneasin Nippawus shining in the sky. Her disarming presence dispelled her parent's disharmony which may have lasted for an hour on the way to the Cape. As soon as they saw her, they grinned and one of them.

"There she is!"

Nuttah particularly liked Wénise slowness to anger, almost nothing bothered her. Once Nuttah's blithe, young spirit danced her into a meadow where she paid more attention to a memengwe flitting from flower to flower than where she was stepping, and she sank into mud up to her ankles. Sheepishly, she returned to the Palace trying to come up with an excuse; none was needed.

"Dirty shoes? You know what that means, Nuttah?" Wénise asked with a smile.

"Nìtchwhaw is going to yell."

"What? Why do you think your mother will yell because you had a good time?"

They washed the shoes in a bucket, set them in the sun until they had dried, and then polished and buffed them to good-as-new. Evenings, Wénise told the history of King Philip or "Weetamoo," 'lady Sachem' and warrior, and if Hebe asked, she read about Kit Carson. Kuttiomp didn't care for the frontiersman who had a reputation as an Indian killer.

"I showed her my woodcut of Weetamoo in the river."

He was interested in Nuttah's response to the British "cutting off Weetamoo's head, impaling it on a post and displaying it in town until the flesh rotted off." His venom-laced tone amused Wénise because it was identical to Twenty-Men's. In their veins, flowed a rankling resentment for the lies, broken promises and atrocious acts carried out on their people in the name of imperialism that began "the day the first European, put his loud, hard, ugly-ass, buckle-shoe on our soft, quiet sand," as Twenty-Men used to say. Wénise missed their boisterous irresoluble venting about the evil which Kutty noted, "continues to this day."

"What did she say," he asked again and brought Wénise back to the room.

She imitated Nuttah's small voice.

"'I want my hair to grow long too,' is all. Why do you want to teach her to hate? I don't have to tell her gruesome tales. We have Skinny Iroquois for that."

"He knows the history. And he is well-informed."

"True. But at our last gathering, his details of guts and gore and mutilation and killing made a girl sick, and others wanted to leave. No need to shock us or Nuttah. Gives bad dreams. Today it was Kit Carson."

Hebe, who had been listening, brought the book and opened it to the picture of Carson with one of his Indian wives.

"There he is again, that bastard," Kutty snapped under his breath.

"Daddy, her name is Grass-Singing. I like that name. Kit Carson loved her," she stated as if she knew it for a fact.

Suspecting Wénise to have put the suggestion in his five-year-old daughter's head, he wanted her to defend her opinion.

"How do you know he loved her?"

Kit Carson & his wife, Grass Singing

Hebe puffed up her cheeks and fiddled with the hem of her dress while she searched the air for an answer. Kutty waited with his arms crossed self-righteously and pretended impatience by tapping his foot.

"She makes good soup," she offered meekly.

He burst out laughing, "Good soup? I see. Well, good soup is important."

"She is Indian. He is White."

Kuttiomp and Wénise exchanged a look of surprise.

"He is a man. She is a girl. Two people," her father pointed out.

Were it not for kindergarten last year, she could have seen that. On the eve of the first day, her little arms and legs buzzed in excited anticipation. It wouldn't let her eat more than two bites of oatmeal. Bursting with alacrity she skipped through the autumn leaves beside her mother who must have asked her ten times to "calm down." The winds of change blew the feather she had secreted in her hair. The yard was full of children, Whites, apart from several Negroes in a clique by the wall.

"Where are all the Indians?"

"They might be there; sometimes it isn't easy to see who is what, silly as that sounds since we are all humans, all God's children." In the next breath, she reminded her to only use English words. "Indian words are special for Wénise's house, or the powwow," and she removed the feathers from Hebe's hair. "No one else has a feather. You want to be like everyone else, don't you?" Hebe shook her head, but her mother insisted, "Yes, you do. That's how you make friends."

At day's end, Gaye-Lee met Hebe with a smile, "There she is, the school girl. What did you learn today?"

Dryly, she replied, "Our teacher is Miss Smith. I have a hook for my coat. I have my own desk...."

At dinner, Kutty asked about the first day with great interest.

"The teacher is Miss Smith...We sat on the floor...I'm the dark one in my class."

"Kah mutate wunnetu," Kutty complimented his daughter.

"You are beautiful too, Daddy."

He tried to lure more from her, but she shrugged and went in her room to draw.

Kutty and Gaye-Lee discussed whether her plummet from enthusiastic to blasé was cause for concern. Gaye-Lee concluded it was not; it was her reaction to being "surrounded by strangers in an unfamiliar place."

"Maybe. Or she realized school is society's tools to fill a man so full of their values and beliefs and ideas, he has no chance to be a free thinking individual, you..."

Gaye-Lee sputtered charmingly infectious gasps and titters.

"Piffle Kutty. You spent eight years on your doctorate!"

"Guilty as charged," he grinned "Let's see how she does."

By October Hebe was still in the throes of ennui, but she was up and ready every day which her parents interpreted as a good sign. On the intercom, the principal announced, "Because Halloween is on a Tuesday, you may wear your costumes to school." On October 31st, clowns, princesses, cowboys and a lot of Indians filled the drab halls with festive colors. Miss Smith asked for volunteers to "show us how your character behaves." A ghost was first. He waved his arms and let out a "whoo-oo-oo-oo." The clown unintentionally made them all laugh when he tripped over a chair and fell down. Cinderella was a blonde and the Fairy Princess a red head dressed almost identically in pink tulle dresses and wearing dime-store tiaras. They stood up together and shuffled nervously by their chairs and did nothing. The fairy held up her magic wand.

"Poof. You got your wish."

Miss Smith initiated applause, so they could sit back down. Peter, a dog, was next, but he didn't wait to be called. To the amusement of the class, he charged right at Hebe, a cat, and startled her out of her seat. Round and round they went. Hebe stopped, and they exchanged "Hiss!!" and "Bow wow!!" several times, and then she whispered to him. She curled up on the floor. He leaped, panted and pawed as if he wanted to continue playing and placed his arms on the floor which raised his behind high in the air. He wiggled it as a dog does his tail eliciting spasmodic ha ha ha's followed by "Aww's," when he lay on the floor in peace beside the cat.

The two cowboys began firing shots at the two Indians replete with feathers in primary colors and toy weapons.

"Stick 'em up," Johnny demanded pointing his plastic pistol at Robbie, the Indians.

Robbie pulled out his rubber knife and pretended to stab him.

"No. No. No Robbie. You have to scalp him!!"

With merry enthusiasm, the teacher took up his rubber weapon in hand, straddled Johnny, pulled his head up by his hair and pretended to slice at his head quite vigorously.

"Ow!" he protested to a raucous chorus of laughs, blechs and icks. "You're hurting me."

"Indians were nasty fighters."

"Indians are stinky," the fairy princess added loudly holding her nose.

"And stupid," the second cowboy added. "Ugh. Me eat now."

Hebe's face reddened as she tried to suppress feelings that gnashed her teeth.

"No! You're stupid! We were fighting for our land."

"And you lost you stinky Indian."

"Your grandfather steals," was all she could come up with in reply to the cowboy's insult.

The dismissal bell rang, and the children lined up to file out. In the courtyard, Hebe saw several classmates being collected by their older brothers and sisters, and they pointed at her. The Fairy Princesses sister glared at her, so Hebe rushed to the gate where she saw her mother.

"Here kitty kitty," Gaye-Lee sang out sweetly.

Hebe meowed and licked at her paws, nothing more.

In the weeks that came, Hebe was on tenterhooks. Miss Smith and two children brought comic books bearing pictures of Indians scalping and brutalizing Whites. In one, an Indian, who reminded her of Skinny Iroquois, was about to bash a child onto the ground next to his dead mother, and "bash" became their "word of the day," and Miss Smith taped it on the wall under "Our Vocabulary." The list was comprised of those the children had heard on the radio, at home or that came up during the class. Miss Smith wrote them all down except "son-of-a-bitch" and "bastard" which elicited a startled, "Oh!" and she paused.

"Don't you know?" the child asked, "Son-of-a-bitch," he repeated. "My mother says it to my father."

"I have heard *of* it, but that is a grown-up word, and..."

"Bastard," the boy yelled and giggled.

"*Both* are grown-up words."

At some point during their brief hours together, they recited the list. Deliberately, cinnamon and influenza defied proper pronunciation by all except Hebe. Then Miss Smith stood in front of the list and gave each a chance to spell American, drawer, ghost, behave, ballet, hamster. By design or by accident, Hebe always ended up with "scalp." Every now and again, the Fairy Princess, pointed to the word and then to Hebe, but Hebe was unfazed. She had withdrawn into herself. Beaming, she showed her mother the enveloped with her first pupil's report because Gaye-Lee laid it on the table so she and Kutty could open it together after dinner. She stood eagerly awaiting praise while they read it.

"Taking turns; Learning the rules; Practicing good manners and the grade is N. I. What is that?" her mother asked.

Kutty read the definition, "N.I. means Needs Improvement."

His face went blank. Hebe was genuinely dumbstruck. She made all the projects. She never talked, and then she remembered.

"On Halloween is all!" burst out of her mouth, and she blubbered, "Miss Smith told everyone 'Indians scalp and we are cabbages," she bawled.

"Cabbages?" her mother echoed.

"Savages. Indians are savages," Kutty clarified.

Unrestrained crying prevented Hebe from answering any questions. They lavished consolation on her until they had brought her back to herself and put her to bed. Gaye-Lee and Kutty talked. They felt responsible for her suffering because they had not prepared her for such circumstances. They had fallen in love and gotten married, and the only person to put up a stink was her mother; she didn't attend the wedding. Their marriage was only legal in a dozen states, so they couldn't travel everywhere in the U. S. When they were searching for an apartment, Kutty had to step into the background. Renters were eager to have tenants such as Gaye-lee and her husband, a research scientist in Aeronautical engineering at M.I.T., but they suddenly had family members who needed the apartment when they saw Kutty's dark face. They ended up renting from her parents, and being separated during the ten days she spent in the hospital when she had Hebe. Disparaging looks were shot at them from every direction when he escorted her in. An orderly came up and took her suitcase from Kutty and suggested, "Your chauffeur should get your husband," and guided her down the hall. Fear that the staff might do something underhanded to harm the baby or her forced the fabrication of a story that her husband was traveling for his job. Recently protests for civil rights appeared regularly in the news; discrimination had not entered their personal sphere—until now. The moon crested in the sky while they discussed the foolishness of their oversight. No recourse came to mind. To be fair, Gaye-Lee wanted to hear Miss Smith's reasons for the marks and was hopeful at least one would be, "my mistake. A teacher doesn't assess a student based on an isolated incident."

In the morning, she accompanied Hebe to school, to her class where the first thing that caught her eye was the Indian chopping into a man's head with "scalp" written on it and then the others which Hebe had not mentioned. Miss Smith was arranging her desk. Every few movements, she paused and admired the diamond ring on her left hand.

"It appears congratulations are in order, Miss Smith. Have you set a date?" Gaye-Lee asked civil as ever.

"Mrs. Holmes, I assume. This is unexpected," she gazed at her ring again. "Yes, a June wedding in Connecticut. We bought a house there. My fiancé vice-president of his father's manufacturing company, Menil Mills," she vaunted.

Gaye-Lee raised the possibility that she may have inadvertently mismarked Hebe's card.

"Me? An error?" Miss Smith responded haughtily. "No. Children like Hebe are not expected to perform well."

"Children *like* Hebe?" Gaye-Lee echoed. "Five-year-olds performing? I assume you mean the Pledge of Allegiance or...Hebe reported everyone in a circle and shook a jar of cream to make butter?"

Miss Smith's cordial demeanor faded and she snipped, "to perform is to behave" and brought up Halloween. Her version of events involved Hebe running helter-skelter chasing Peter and frightening him, so he "didn't want to play anymore."

You daughter raised her voice—to me, the teacher! This is how we are treated by the ill-mannered," she lowered her eyes to Hebe, "coloreds and mixes with innately deficient intellectual abilities."

Gaye-lee fumed but kept smiling, "I see. I know an American Indian man with advanced degrees in aeronautical engineering from MIT, a research scientist. Doctor Holmes, Hebe's father, probably the reason she is the only child in your class who can spell, deliberately."

Hebe rattled it off as if she was at a spelling B, "Deliberately, d-e-l-i-b-e-r-a-t-e-l-y, deliberately."

She slipped her hand in her mother's as the bell rang, and the pupils filed in. One of them let out a whoop, but stopped when he saw her mother. At the door, Hebe turned to the teacher and stuck out her tongue.

"Don't make it worse," Gaye-Lee muttered under her breath.

At the park, they fed the squirrels. Gaye-Lee saved her breath for Kutty at the dining room table. She wanted him to decide what to do.

"Kindergarten is not required--if we send her to Smith's class, she will be there but not be there."

"Like Wénise!? Hebe asked concerned.

"What on earth is she talking about?" Gaye-Lee asked.

He explained while Hebe revisited the moment in her mind. Her father had brought Wénise a photograph of herself, but it made her cringe.

"That's you in school, right?"

"I am not there," Wénise insisted quietly.

"Oh. He thought that was you."

She stopped sweeping.

"My name is Wompi Mieúck Askeete, Bright Meadow, not Elizabeth. So, I am there but not there Kuttiomp, cowáutam?"

On the ride home, Hebe tried to find Wénise in the photograph. All the boys and many girls had short hair; they could not be Wénise. The women in her family prided themselves on their luxurious hair, and Wénise's was legendary. It hung to the middle of her skirt, and she had heard, "All boys liked it." Hebe asked her father to point out Wénise. Her jaw dropped when she saw she had cropped hair.

"She is there. Why did she say, 'there but not there?'?"

Kutty wracked his brain for a way to simplify the saying.

"When she was a child, the government forced Indian children to go to schools far from home. They could not be Indian there. The rules were: short hair, that uniform, Christianity and English and only English! Anyone who broke the rules, didn't get dinner, got a beating…or…"

"The Cháuquaquock did that?"

"That's right," he chuckled at the old Wampanoag word for Whites.

"You see that girl in the photograph? Is that Wénise?"

"No. Not really. The Cháuquaquock were mean to my Wénise!" she gasped, "If they try that again, I will take the rifle and shoot them."

"Don't worry Nuttah. They won't. Times are changing."

At the dining room table, with Gaye-Lee, Kutty gave Hebe his decision. She would start school next year with a new teacher.

Hebe placed her small hands on his face and shook her head.

"Nosh, times are not changing."

The Great Bird, Wuchowsen

III

Thunder & Guns Peskhómmin! Boom!

Massachusetts 1951-1954

Between the Strawberry and Buck moons, there was a gathering at the Palace, the one spot large enough to accommodate their entire Wolf clan and the Holmes extended family that spanned time and included many nations. Since the Sachem, Carries-a-Club had gone to dwell in the Southwest with Kawantenuit and the ancestors two years ago, the oldest person in attendance was the powwáw, Sokanuum Nootau, Rains Fire, and there were at least two newborns. All tolled, they were mostly Wampanoag and Passamaquoddy but the gentle nets of marriage and brotherhood had caught Nipmuc, Chocktaw, Ojibway, Iroquois, Chumash, Mikmac and Seminole and several spouses who were from the Caribbean, one from Korea, and one White woman, Hebe's mother Gaye-Lee. Pale and honey-blonde with green-eyes, she shined effulgently in a simple cotton dress among the bevy of dark beauties in colorful regalia adorned with bird feathers, bone, antler and fur. Hebe imagined the guests surrounded completely by eagle, turkey, deer, wolf or rabbit spirits to see antlers they had shed or tails, feathers and skins that had been taken. She was sure Mosquand, the Bear Spirit, was there because medicine man, Sokanuum Nootau, Rains Fire, regalia sometimes included the skin of a full-grown bear. He was so big and tall, that skin didn't drag on the ground, not even a quarter of an inch.

At powwows and private gatherings, many men wore breech-cloths, which they made themselves and swore by for comfort. "Sedwa'gowa'ne, of the Onondaga Nation was "the seventh son of a seventh son" and an activist who wore them all the time. His sinewy body earned him the nickname Skinny Iroquois. He was a hyperactive man with hollow cheeks, highly visible on any street in yellow sunglasses and his regalia, which included his breech cloth. Proudly, he accepted tickets across the country for indecent exposure, which he added to the pile he had accumulated for disorderly conduct, speeding and inciting a riot. He used them as props when he spouted his rousing revolutionary rhetoric, which was all the time. The historical perspectives and insight on national American Indian activities were informative and entertaining despite their racist overtones, but his inflammatory, profanity laced, delivery offended the ladies. Those with jobs and responsibilities, needed to take care of their families, were not able to protest in the name of fishing rights or collect signatures to bring broken treaties to court. They did so vicariously through Skinny. He was so popular that a conversation with one person easily became one with three or a speech to fifty. Wénise had seen it happen but preferred it didn't at her family events. Already, he had Adchanan-He-Hunts, in his twenties and Púck and Momonchu, twelve and fourteen around him. Though Púck was the youngest, she knew him best so she had asked him to help keep an eye on Nuttah. Quite pleasantly but loudly, she shouted a reminder to him.

"Skinny! This is a gathering, not a rally."

"Of course, Wénise. Talking about my breech cloth is all."

She rolled her eyes and waved an admonishing finger at him."

"...but Adchanan, you got a breech cloth, you gotta' wear it like Púck here. It's all interconnected man."

"Skinny you are one of the craziest...What's connected? You mean my breech cloth?"

"See these?" he shook his wad of tickets, "these treaties; they're broken. And we don't have our land now richer rich with centuries of our bones. The Whites..."

Púck was gesturing toward Hebe with his eyes.

"What? Nuttah?"

Skinny Iroquois picked her up by her waist; her arms and legs dangled, and he held her face to face with Púck and Momonchu who smiled at her.

"Look at those eyes. Look at that hair, and the feather! A beautiful Indian girl if ever I saw one. She needs to know. All children need to know, so they can carry the message into the future," he declared and set her down.

Slightly intimidated, Hebe scooched close to Púck's leg, and he laid a reassuring hand on her shoulder. The males were antsy and tempted to leave, but they were curious as to how Skinny was going to link European conquest to breech cloths. Besides, there really wasn't any escape. Experience had taught them until Skinny had chugged along the circuitous tracks back to the point he started out to make, he would keep talking, and he did.

"It's all bologna. The Whites and their feet man stomped onto our land and into our houses, and they stomped us down but not out. Our fire is too big, too bright. They can't. You know why? See this?" He pulled a large iridescent slab from around his neck. "When I was over-seas, I thought I was dead man. Bullet hit me right here, and this abalone didn't even break. That's our spirit, the abalone. They are going to get fucking tired of stomping on us before we give up," he took an-other breath to continue.

Adchanan interrupted, "I thought this was about a breech cloth."

"Stay with me," he insisted. "I know I am obsessed, pissed off. What can I say Adchanan? When I talk to American Whites about this," he shook his head," they say, 'That was a long time ago,' like time excuses their lies and crimes. 'The people were trying to help you?" How in the God damn Hell is cutting a man's nose off or slaughtering his wife and feeding her to your dogs helping? All the while, they are putting more weight on their feet. You want to be cool with us? Show some respect. They got a law up in Maine says you gotta carry a shotgun to church in case American Indians show up, and more of the same in Boston. Indi-ans are not supposed to be in the city without musketeers escorting them."

"Skinny, they are not going to enforce those laws."

"Sure. And these treaties," he waved his tickets," are not broken.

"Skinny, Marisol is waiting. Stay focused. Breech cloth bla bla bla..?"

"They tried to kill us all. That didn't work. They moved us out of their sight, don't want to be reminded, they didn't really win. That didn't work. They tried to make us invisible, dress like them...Shit!"

Hebe gasped and covered her mouth as if she was the one who had sworn.

Skinny dropped down on his haunches, "Sorry Nuttah. Don't repeat that okay?"

When he stood up, Wénise was there

"But I am still here. *We* are still here," Skinny continued and slapped Adchanan on the shoulder, "that is what my breech cloth says man," he concluded and smiled at Wénise. Then he jiggled his loins and whooped, "Feels good. Keeps a breeze in my..." seeing Hebe he chose his words carefully, "fruit tree, gives it space, and I need a lot of space."

The boys laughed. Hebe picked up Púck's breech cloth flap and peeked.

"Hey Nuttah!" he protested with an embarrassed smile.

"I saw your bahooky, but no fruit," she sputtered childishly into her palm.

"No," he stammered. He meant, uh..."

Wénise took her by the hand and eyed the rest suspiciously.

"She will know in time. No a rally Skinny, not here," she warned, and he nodded.

He and the men passed her on the way to the food tables, and she heard him boast, "I got so many tickets I can make a bonfire man," and she realized she would have to watch him.

Púck and Momonchu emulated Skinny, which their elders allowed because his far flung stories encouraged them to read more, but there were limits. Mr. Josephs insisted Púck wear trousers when he went into town.

"I am not walking down the street with you with your rear hanging out."

"Hanging? Grampa, my butt looks good. The girls will faint in the street if they see it."

His tawny bottom was visibly firm and shapely, but Hebe had never fainted upon seeing it or anyone else's, and at the gathering, there butts everywhere. Dressed in their traditional best with Mother Earth beneath their moccasins, they formed an enormous circle two and three deep around the fire. Then as they and their ancestors had for hundreds of thousands of moons, they smudged and stood silently.

Sokanuum Nootau offered tobacco to the four directions and prayed, "Nuppeantam Kiehtanit, nummag ne wuttamauog. Ohke, nummag ne wuttamauog. Okummus nepauzshad, nummag ne wuttamauog. Wutt∞tchìkkìnneasin nippawus, nummag ne wuttamauog. Taubot ne-anawayean. Nummag ne wuttamauog adt yau ut nashik ohke: wompanniyeu, sowanniyeu, pahtatunniyeu nannummiyeu. A'ho."

After, the drums, po-po-wutt-á-hig… po-po-wutt-á-hig… po-po-wutt-á-hig filled the air. Couples crossed arms and two-stepped and solo fancy dancers in whispering feathers and tintinabulating cones competed. The women prepared food and cooked with an eye on Wénise whose dishes always tasted best. They had asked for recipes, but she didn't use them. Deftly, her fingers lifted ingredients from unmarked containers and sprinkled or tossed them in without measuring. The men were on the east side of the Palace butchering a deer and digging a fire pit, except for Kutty. Wénise had special chores for him.

"Go up to the gutter and clear whatever is blocking it, tighten the water pump handle and check out the Winchester's trigger; it sticks," Wénise complained.

Hebe trailed him everywhere, and then sat on her heels to watch what he did to the rifle.

"See that? Ahque," he warned. "It's a hair trigger."

Wénise brought them lemonade.

Nuttah held up her hand, "Ahque. It's a hair trigger."

"Taúbot neanawáyean. I will be careful."

She gave Hebe the jar of Machemóqut, the mosquito repellant she had made, and the family swarmed around. Marisol was being "eaten alive." Whiffing the salve, she yelped at its pungency, but when she observed the bugs avoiding Hebe, she held her nose and stuck out her arm.

"Okay, do me."

When Hebe finished, Marisol read the hand written label aloud, "Mach-e-mó-qut? What is this, Nuttah?"

"Cohosh. The bugs hate it."

"If they can smell, I know why." She wrinkled her nose and snapped her fingers, "Mach-e-mó-qut, that word means cohosh?"

"No, it doesn't."

"What does it mean?"

"Machemóqut, it stinks."

"It stinks!?" she let out a long witch-like cackle.

All afternoon, Hebe heard her offering repellant and asking recipients to guess the meaning of Machemoqut. When Marisol sashayed her question to the men, the women's melodic tenor on home remedies tensed into low clucking caution and criticism of her as they followed her with their eyes. Under a canopy of breasts and hands and bellies, Hebe heard. "Watch out for that one." "Must a made those pants from salami skin." Another replied, "They do belong in a butcher shop window. Are you sure her husband is called He-Hunts and not sucker for cheap lunch meat?" They covered their mouths and their bodies shook as they contained themselves. "You know that marriage isn't going to last. It never does when you marry out of your race," was followed by "That's right. Stick with your own or else you..."

One of the women discreetly tipped her head toward Gaye-Lee and cut the woman off. Empathy welled up in Hebe's young heart. She put her arms around her mother.

"I love you."

"Hebe, why don't you go and play."

After what she had just heard and seen, Hebe preferred to stay with her.

"I love you too," Gaye-Lee replied beneath the talk that had shifted to succotash. "Don't you want to be with the children?"

"They went home with Nini."

"Not Nini's children. Right there, girls are playing jacks. They are a little older, but they won't mind. See?" she asked pointing to several American Indian girls.

"Not now, thank you."

She had approached those girls earlier. The tallest glanced fleetingly at her and asked who her parents were. Proudly, she picked out Kutty and Gaye-Lee. Smirks darted through the girls' lips, and then the tallest curtly gave the excuse of the game having already begun to refuse her. Assuming, she could join in when they began again, she perched on a nearby rock. A girl with thick cascading, black hair and nut brown skin showed up a few minutes later and asked to join in. They scooched aside and made room for her without asking any questions. When Hebe walked away, their collective snicker confirmed their rejection and brought tears to her eyes.

"There she is," a woman remarked directing the women's' collective attention at Marisol rubbing salve on He-Hunts who had put on his breech cloth. She was very pretty, and Hebe liked her big laugh. Why the women made unkind comments was a mystery to Hebe.

While the women were gossiping and exchanging tidbits, the men were discussing their manly interests. It was easy to guess what they were by their location, the cars, the stone wall, the pump and the cornfield. Eventually, they returned to the food that would be ready later.

Gaye-Lee no longer minded if Hebe stayed. She had been to enough gatherings to know the women didn't have much to say when the men came around. It was difficult to be heard above the men's bluster on the wide variety of American Indian concerns, and the women wanted to hear what they were saying. This time, there were future fantasies based on past reality never having happened which invariably began with "if the invaders hadn't come, we would..." and ended with, "but they did." Days remembered on reservations were pitched in high tones with elevated chins while those in Indian schools were spit out with downcast eyes. The relatively temperate discussion on why so many American Indians joined the United States military efforts in the wars led to a heated debate on whether or not they should have, and then someone brought up the new Termination Act. Their collective attention was on the powwáw, Sokanuum Nootau, who had puffed on his pipe, laid it down and waited quietly to tell a story to those who wished to hear.

"One day an old wolf was out hunting, and he ran into a buck he had crossed paths with from time to time for many moons. That buck used to give good chase, never on a day the wolf was hungry enough to catch him. Now the deer's antlers had grown big, and he was thing. He would be tough for sure, so though he stood still and would be easy prey, the wolf did not give chase. They sat by a stream and talked as old friends. The buck noted he was thin because men had moved closer and closer and limited what he had to eat. "Their dogs always bark at me." The younger deer were fast; he had grown slow. The wolf liked the buck. He did not want to find him dead and bring the pack to eat him. "Too bad you are not a wolf. The strongest is alone when he goes out to search for food. He returns to us. We are seldom lonely or too lean." The buck loved his kind, but he didn't have too many days left in him. He confessed, being a wolf sounded interesting. The wolf presented him with several berries which he claimed, once eaten, would change the buck into a bushy carnivore living close to the ground. He would be able to run with the pack and travel far and fast for food. He warned him to think long and hard because "the spell only works one way, one time." When the change was complete, the buck was to howl. The wolf would howl back, so he could find his new family. The big buck spent two more days searching for food, wandering. On the third day, he ate the berries. His antlers fell to the ground. He took a step. His hoof was a paw covered in fur. The trees were much taller. His body writhed and he panted. At last night fell.

'Ow-Ow-Owoooo!' he howled.

The promised reply came. The buck, now a wolf, joined the pack, and he wasn't lonely anymore. On the first day, the pack surrounded a bear cub in a trap and devoured him. His belly was full. He didn't remember being a buck, but he felt different from the other wolves. One afternoon they were out, and the lead wolf gave the call to let them know he found a good meal, and the pack sprinted behind. When the buck-wolf arrived, his companions were noisily ravaging a deer. He didn't know why, but he got sick. He could not eat it. The longing to be himself, who he no longer remembered, ached more than loneliness. After many moons with no food, he was dying. No way to keep up. The pack left. Alone, he sank beside a berry bush and prepared to go in peace. The day grew cool. The sunlight played in the leaves and dappled a doe's back while she sipped water from a brook. She had a nice plump, rump and would make a fine feast for a wolf, but he was not moved by his stomach. He was moved by his heart. He wanted to be near her, feel her sweet nose on his velvet antlers. He approached. She did not run away. She gave him a coy shoulder. He pranced and thumped his feet to make her look at him, and at last, she raised her eyes. They dark as lakes in the night, lighted with the sun's reflection.

Their beauty drew him nearer. He looked in. Reflected in the middle of their light, he saw a great buck..."

The Buck-Wolf

Sokanuum Nootau returned to his seat and his pipe while the men the men nodded and exchanged comments. Skinny Iroquois took advantage of the large crowd assembled to hear the medicine man and, with cat-like agility, pounced into the center. He checked over each shoulder as if he was about to tell a dirty joke, and then intrigued the men with his steely gaze and hushed rapid fire spiel.

"Taúbot neanawáyean, Sokanuum Nootau, as always, you have spoken poetically and wisely. To any who do not know me, I am Sedwa'gowa'ne, seventh son of a seventh son, but you can call me Skinny Iroquois. I want to take a moment of your time to enlighten you. I know you are all smart, but you are all busy. Here's what's going on. Congress is ending tribes," he informed them; rumbling erupted. "That's right. The resolution says it is the policy of congress to end our status as wards of the United States. Stupid me, I thought since they took out land and gave to they owed us for stealing our country," he stood on a chair. "This is more crap they hand us in the name of a gift, as helping, religion, treaties, liquor, reservations, education in their schools, citizenship...not me," he raised his Haudenosaunee passport."

"Yeah. We should all have those. You did the right thing Skinny. Spread it around," a man called out."

"Talk to your tribal leaders. So the Whites gave us the reservations in the middle of nowhere and forced us on the Trail of Tears and along the Bosque Redondo, and now..."

The audience that had been lulled into philosophical ponderings by Rains Fire was fired up; their movements sent puffs of dust into the air. "They gave the land to Indians, so the only way they can get it back is to say we are not Indians."

"Can they do that?"

"They are doing it. Indians in New York, California, Texas and at least a half a dozen tribes do not exist anymore. The last gift is a bus ticket to nowhere, some grunt job. You take it, and by this law, you can not go back. You are one of them. This is..."

Peskhómmin! Boom! Flapping and cawing shook every leaf on the trees and darkened the sky with birds. The women screamed. The men jumped. When the hubbub settled, Wénise was there, shotgun in hand.

"Skinny! We all want to wake up tomorrow five hundred years ago. Nothing you say is going to make that happen. We came together to-day to enjoy each other's company and this beautiful day the Creator has given us. Cowâutam?"

"Nux, Nowaútam Nnowaúntum Wénise," he replied and bent his head in deference.

The men and women reunited by the food where they hurriedly packed up the leftovers and changed their clothes. Leaving too late was dangerous. There was not one street light on the back roads.

Hebe begged her parents to let her stay. Before she had finished asking her mother had given a flat, "No," which her father, right next to her, heard, but Hebe waited. Smiling softly, he waved her on her way, and she headed for the woods. She and Wénise often took that path to the pump or the neighbor or to collect herbs, and her voice was part of her. She heard her as if she was there. "Stay in sight," and "This is a good spot," or once in a while, "There is your Mishquáishim." The bushy, red fox frequented a spot in the tall meadow grass for sunning or flailing his legs in the air to scratch his back on the ground. If he happened along when they ate lunch outside, Hebe threw him a remnant hunk of duck or fish. The weak strength of her child's arm usually landed it three feet in front of her, too close for his comfort, and he waited for them to leave, not last time,

"Hub, hub hub," Wénise ordered.

Instead of coming, she stood in wide-eyed amazement. Mish-quáishim walked right up to the food, devoured it and lay at her feet awaiting more. It was the first of a half-dozen times, and he stayed long enough for her to talk with him. She spoke to him with her voice, and just like the neighbor's cat, Wanderer, the fox spoke to her with his mind. The very first day she returned the following summer, she told Wénise she wanted to see him. Her great-grandmother knelt down and gave her the chance to "stay behind," something she had never done before.

Stay behind. By myself? Why? She asked herself.

The answer was Twenty-Men's rifle.

"Mishquáishim!?" she asked in a trembling panic.

"He is very sick."

"Make him better. Call Sokanuum Nootau," she pleaded. "I will take him soup."

"Soup will not help Nuttah. He has an evil sickness. Any animal, any person can get it. There is no cure."

"Let him die in the woods like the other animals," she whined.

Eye to eye, Wénise asked, "You know I wouldn't shoot your little, red fox if I didn't have too?"

Hebe shook her head. Temperate as ever, Wénise loaded her rifle. Hebe went with her. They passed through the woods and across the meadow where Hebe glanced at the spot where they always saw him. Wénise tucked herself against the bark of a tree and blew into her fist duplicating the chilling, high-pitched cry of a wounded animal. The hair on Hebe's neck stood up. After a while, she repeated the cry, and Hebe's spirit leaped but fell. She saw Mishquáishim, not dotting in energetic grace from tree to tree, but wending in a clumsy stagger. His coat was dull and mangy, and he was emitting a low guttural noise. A cry welled up in Hebe's throat, and she threw her hands over her mouth. Mishquáishim dragged closer and bared his teeth at nothing. Wénise repeated the cry, and he spun around quickly as if he thought it came from behind him. He crouched against the earth. When Wénise repeated the cry again, he jumped high off the ground, and for the last time. Peskhómmin! Boom! thundered the gun and caused everything to go in slow motion. Hebe watched the single bullet cut the air and hit the target, Mishquáishim's furry heart. He hung suspended in mid leap. His eyes rolled back. His legs dangled as freely as they had when he scratched his back on the lawn. Motion speeded up an instant before his body hit the ground. Hebe hid behind Wénise when she watched for movement. There was none; she inched closer.

"Nnowaúntum Mishquáishim."

Salty riverlets ran down Hebe's cheeks.

"Me too. Mishquáishim, Nnowaúntum. I am sorry too," she told him, and asked "Wénise will Twenty-Men will take care of him?"

"I don't see why not. He was a young fox, a good fox. Kiehtan will let him in."

Though she had seen Mishquáishim shot dead, she was sure he was in the woods on her way back to the house the night of the gathering. She took two steps in his direction, and the foreboding "Ooh-ooh, ooh-ooh," of an owl stopped her. A spirit might have shape-shifted into Mishquáishim to lure her into a trap. She offered a quick prayer for her fox before hurrying to the Palace.

"Fireflies? Hello Fireflies? Stay on. I can't see. Please?"

There was no reply. They had flitted away as fireflies do. Not being able to see more than a foot in front of her heightened her fear, but she heard Wohwohkau trotting near and panting.

He will lead me home. "Good boy Wohwohkau. You are so smart. Take me home boy." He did. As soon as she saw Wénise and her rifle silhouetted on the path, she was relieved. "I am here."

The house lantern illuminated her four-legged companion. It was not Wohwohkau, but the fox Wénise had killed. He spoke.

- 38 -

"This way."

"Wénise You didn't kill him!" she announced excitedly.

"Oh yes, I did, but maybe you saw the fox's spirit."

She gave her a handful of strawberries.

"Wuttáhimneash for a fox?"

"I gave them to you, but if a Mishquáishim likes them too."

Mishquáishim

"Mishquáishim?"Hebe whispered from the edge of the woods, but he didn't come. She popped a berry in her mouth, dropped the rest to the ground for him and waited again for a moment, but he didn't return. Halfway to the house, she felt his presence in the air and rushed back. He was not there, but neither were the berries.

"I'm glad we didn't kill you dead Mishquáishim."

"What is taking so long?" Wénise asked from the path.

"He trusted me, and then he ate the berries."

"So young and you have a fox spirit? How special. He will come if he senses you are afraid, like tonight. And if there is real danger, he will let you know."

"How?"

"You have to wait and see."

Hebe walked more freely because she knew Mishquáishim would give her a heads up if she were in danger. Nothing frightened her, and she had almost forgotten about the spirit, but then, on the last day of August, the day of wild rain came. The unusually chilly morning encouraged her to linger in the warmth of her bed while she and Anùm planned their day. Mishquáishim let her know he was there by leaning on her leg. She sat up to see what could be the matter. Except for the spectacularly dense, grey clouds covering the sun, nothing appeared out of place, and it was quiet, very quiet, too quiet. Peskhómmin! Boom! An explosion shook the house so hard her bed rattled and adrenalin shot through her body.

"Nìtchwhaw!" "Mother!" she called and wrapped the covers tightly around her.

Peskhómmin! Thunder beat forcefully on the skin of the sky and reverberated though the house, and suddenly waterfalls of rain gushed from the clouds. In her almost seven years of life, she had never seen such rain. It wasn't drops; it was sheets of grey-white water unfolding from the sky, billowing, flapping and tattering in the violent ululations of the wind. In her bare feet, she dashed to see. Mishquáishim whimpered. The mammoth bird Wuchowson circled the trees. Wénise told her the greatest winds came from him flapping his wings. His powerful eyes were focused on a spot under the tree, and she hoped it was not Wanderer, the downstairs cat. Lightning zigzagged electric blue veins through the grey.

"Mother!"

Wuchowsen bowed their sky-high oak as easily as a sapling and dragged the drenched greenery of branches over the fences while rain pummeled the world. Gusts from Wuchowson wings rocked a round, yellow taxi creeping toward the curb.

Nìtchwhaw is in the taxi. She is in the taxi.

Transfixed to the cool wooden floor planks; she leaned forward to see if she was right. Electric blue and yellow lightning tore the sky straight across the horizon. Sirens unwound wails of emergency in the distance. The driver struggled against Wuchowson's might just to open his door. He buried his head in the bend of his elbow, shoved his cap under his arm and trudged to the passenger side. The slippery leaves underfoot threw him off balance, and his arms flew out to keep him upright. His hat scudded over the river forming in the street.

"There she is!" she blurted out.

Mishquáishim growled audibly, and Hebe wanted to move, but fascination with nature's pernicious performance had shifted to fear for her mother. Hebe shuffled in a panicked circle, and then pressed her nose against the glass. Before Gaye-Lee lifted her pregnant body from the back seat, she kissed the pink-gold cross around her neck. Art, the sandy-haired downstairs neighbor, darted out to help with a large black umbrella. Wuchowson did not like it. He huffed the flimsy cloth inside out and puffed it into a somersault in the direction of the driver's hat. Hebe held Mishquáishim tightly and knocked so vigorously, she drew the adults' rain-drenched gazes to her. Art slipped and almost fell. Gaye-lee's eyes grew wide in horror at the sight of her daughter alone in the window, and her lips formed words which Hebe could not hear but by their shapes, she guessed them to be "Get away from the window." Obedience failed in the face of her anxiety over whether her mother would make it into the house; she stayed. With Art and the driver on either side of her, they formed a lumbering twelve-limbed beast. Though it looked frightened too, Hebe wanted to run to it, to be enfolded in its protective end arms.

The city's warning siren wailed and lightning crazed the dark and reminded her of Bert, the Civil Defense turtle's message: "Now, tell me right out loud. What are you supposed to do when you see the flash?" "Duck and cover," a chorus of children's' voices replied.

Along with Anùm and her favorite party dress, Hebe crawled under the desk. Mishquáishim huddled beside her. Peskhómmin! Thunder cracked and the dreaded atomic explosion mushroomed into the heavens.

Mary

IV

What's wrong with Nitchwhaw?

A little chickadee sang. ""Ktsee-gee-gil-lassis—Ktsee-gee-gil-lassis. Ktsee-gee-gil-lassis." Hebe held her fist closed tightly around a coin she had caught in a dream. This time it was a silver dollar. Usually she could recall where she had been in her sleep but not today. The heavy Zenith television, recently purchased and placed in a prominent spot in the living room, was at the foot of her bed. Either it was very early or the electricity had just come back on because the only broadcast was the test pattern. Evidence of her mother's vigil hung from the rocking chair, a half-knitted baby blanket; a. novel and an empty glass stinking sweetly of stout. Her temples throbbed, and her head was too heavy to lift, so she waited for her mother to come back and take care of her; she always did. Mother was a magically recurring image in her life that concretized reality and imparted a sense of security in her. She tried to remember the last time she had seen her, but her brain was not working.

"Ktsee-gee-gil-lassis." rather than try to sit up, she stretched her neck. Sprawled from one end of her room to the other was the largest branch from the oak tree. The chickadee popped up between the leaves. "Ktsee-gee-gil-lassis." She pulled the curtain back for the bird that fluttered its wings in the breeze and flew into the day. Moving very slowly, she slid down to check for additional disoriented or perhaps wounded birds. There, in a puddle under the branch she discovered a note. It read, "Hebe, Wait for Daddy. Love Mother." Her footsteps, unusually heavy from the pregnancy vibrated the planks. Hebe thought the extra weight might be the reason for her change. Over the last few months, she lashed out at Hebe with venomous words and smarting slaps. She hustled back under her sheets. Gaye-Lee came in and shook the fancy dress Hebe had taken with her when she hid under the desk. It was rumpled and wet.

"Why would a little girl mop up the floor with her dress?" she asked.

"I didn't mop..." Hebe began.

"If the cleaners can't restore it, we will have to throw it away."

Hebe gasped at the idea.

"I am just teasing you."

Hebe was dubious because not that long ago, she had spilled milk on Anùm, and he disappeared for an entire day. She found him in the trash that night and cried and cried. Gaye-Lee refused to let her take him out because he was covered with milk, "souring by the minute." When Kutty learned what she had done, he retrieved the stuffed dog. Just as quickly, her mother snatched him away and dunked him in the kitchen sink. Hebe screamed. For a moment, her father was flabbergasted.

"I have a lot of words for you my darling, but I never thought cruel would be one."

When she explained about the milk, he maintained, she should not have thrown the toy out. Buy he did acquiesce somewhat and defended her mother's actions to Hebe by saying, "she doesn't always explain what she is doing or say what she feels." Hebe observed that to be true. Gaye- Lee did not ask if she wanted juice. She brought it in and held it there until she took it.

Hebe assumed her father had gone to his office already. She perked up when she heard him cough. Into the laundry room, she shadowed her mother where, bare-chested, he scrubbed a shirt on the washboard. Her mother's eyes traced the well-toned muscles of his long, lean, body and his poetically rugged face that had held many a woman captive. Wherever the family went, ballet class, the tennis, court, a restaurant or a party, there were lady admirers. Discreetly and boldly, they fondled their buttons, and if she was nearby, they invariably asked, "Is that your daddy?" and when she answered, "Yes," they looked over each shoulder, and then asked, "Is your mommy here?" When being in a family way made it difficult for her mother to carry the groceries, Kutty drove her to the store. Each time they turned down a new row, the squeak of wobbly wheels and the clip-clop of high heels followed them. Halfway down aisle three, Hebe saw as many women intermittently checking the shelves and her father who was discussing dinner with her mother. They took a step toward the produce, and the women, now numbering five moved in that direction. When Gaye-Lee stopped, so did Kutty, and so did the women. Hebe giggled.

"What is so funny?" Gaye-Lee asked

"Daddy is the Pied Piper."

The Pied Piper

Her mother's repellant vibes hurried the cackle of coquettes in reverse except one. She brazenly strolled toward them and paused to offer Kutty a smoldering smile which he appreciated but did not dare return.

- 45 -

Gaye-Lee approached the woman's cart containing only her pocket-book.

"How lovely," she remarked and removed it. "I saw one just like this in—aisle seven."

"Aisle seven?" the woman echoed quizzically.

"Yes," Gaye-Lee replied and deftly tossed the bag over the top shelf of canned goods.

It sailed into the meat department. "Hey. The hides are coming back for the cows," they heard the butcher say.

What's wrong with Nìtchwhaw?" Hebe asked Kutty softly in ear.

"One day you will understand," he told her and smiled at his wife's bold expression of jealousy and possessiveness.

As calmly as if nothing had happened, Gaye-Lee returned to her list. "I prefer fresh to frozen vegetables, don't you?"

Kutty bent his head in agreement, and as a family, they ambled to the produce.

***

Looking as piqued as she had that day in the supermarket, Gaye-Lee asked Kutty what he was doing in the laundry room.

"Washing my shirt."

"But you have two dozen boxes from the ..."

"I want this one."

He turned around and saw Hebe. He let the washboard fall into the stream of water and it sent a spray everywhere. Her mother stepped back. He picked Hebe up, and she babbled a story that ended with the words, "...silver coin from the dream." She stuck it up in front of his face. He winked at his Gaye-Lee who knew he had placed it there.

"Did you bring that back from dreamland?" he asked in a voice full of wonder.

Gaye tried to snatch the coin, but Kutty pulled her hand away and shared a laugh with his little girl over being, "faster than mother."

"I don't know why you fill her head with all that nonsense."

"What nonsense?"

"You put it there!"

"No Mother. I brought it back from dreamland."

"Why is it so difficult for you to play along? Just because your mother packed you off to that boarding school and treated you like a stranger, doesn't mean you have to treat your children the same way."

"Daddy, what's wrong with Nìtchwhaw?"

"Tatta Nuttah.

Kutty dismissed Gaye-Lee with a kiss on the cheek. In the hall, he shook out his shirt, gave it one last snap, smoothed out the wrinkles, and then slid his arms into it.

"Wénise embroidered my name on."

He pointed to the word *Osh*, in dark blue on the pocket.

"That says father, not Kutty."

"Same thing," he smiled.

Putting on a wet shirt was one more of Kutty's quirks, "One simply does not do," her mother declared. Hebe tried to remember them: red wine with fish; cold spaghetti on the back porch for breakfast; tennis shoes with his slacks, and dancing paúskesu. Hebe laughed to herself when she thought of him dancing naked because she was sure he was not. All the men wore their breach cloths and if they danced enthusias-tically, an onlooker might get an eye full, but they were not "naked" as she heard one of their maids whisper to a friend on the phone.

"Take good care of Nuttah," who he embraced wearing the wet shirt.

"Kutty, what will the neighbors think?"

"How could I possibly know that?"

"You are no stranger to protocol. They think we don't have a laundry maid."

"At the moment we don't. All we have is love."

Pleased with the smile his words brought, he kissed her and left.

Gaye-Lee hung out into the nacreous light of September's second morning. She toyed nervously with the cross dangling from her neck. Kutty stopped to light a cigarette.

"Bye Nosh. Good luck with your meeting."

He threw his arm up and waved; she waved back, and then he waved again at Gaye-Lee. She did not wave back. He continued down the street and disappeared around the corner. She threw the ashtray that shattered into a fountain of crystal globules.

"He is stark raving mad Hebe!" She yelled and slapped Hebe who knew reacting escalated matters.

What's wrong with Nitchwhaw? she thought.

To her surprise, she knelt down and gave her a cool embrace.

"What would you like to have for breakfast more than anything else in the whole world?"

"Pancakes," was her stock response and as if she expected it, Gaye-Lee pulled out a pitcher of batter she had already prepared. After eating and washing the dishes, they made fudge. Beneath the sweet, chocolate fog, the day passed in a series of images: her mother unfurling the newspaper featuring the hurricane; her mother opening a bottle of stout; Tinker Bell fluttering around in bold coloring-book outlines; her mother hanging her stuffed dog on the clothes line by his ears; a monstrous red and black truck with an arm that reached into her bedroom and removed the branch; her mother opening a bottle of stout; tongues of bleached clothes snaking through the ringer; a river of knitting flowing over her mother's stomach; fillet tips on the cutting board; the miraculous sight of pink roses still on the vines behind the house which they placed in a vase; her mother opening a bottle of stout; Howdy Doody's smiling freckled face on the television and her mother pounding veal steaks with a mallet.

At six o'clock, Kutty's brass key clicked the lock and opened the apartment. Hastily Gaye-lee rinsed her stout glass and put the bottles under the sink before she tied on her apron. Hebe ran into the pantry to play a game of hide and seek. The wait was sweetened by cooling fudge and shortened by counting the mason jars of green beans, and then she heard the voices on the other side of the door. Her every sinew tingled with anticipation. Nothing happened.

"Where is the toilet?" she heard a man and then footsteps in the hall.

Gaye-Lee's hushed tone did not conceal her vexation about Kutty not giving her any notice, especially when she had no help which was often the case because she fired them regularly. The last one had Kutty's silver lighter in her apron pocket, and she failed to convince Gaye-Lee that her intentions were only to polish it. The presence of this unexpected guest heated her mother's choler as the others had, friends and the odd new acquaintance Kutty brought home. There had been an opera singer, a magician, a navy officer and the accordion player with his instrument who neither she nor the neighbors will soon forget. The most sparks flew with the appearance of a slim green-eyed Cuban club singer over whom Kutty was "watching" while her brother, his friend, took care of some business downtown.

"Kutty she's got every man in Cambridge watching over her, she doesn't need your particular attention. Get rid of her."

And he did, along with himself, for a couple of days. When he came back, she though there were going to be fireworks. There weren't. Her father had brought her a gift and he talked and talked and talked. He was master at damping fires which Hebe thought the Dutchman's presence had ignited.

"If I arrived in Holland and the institute did not have my office ready, and I had no local cash, and my host family was not home..."

"Oh my goodness. Is that what happened? Does he..."

She stopped and offered a cheerful, hostess smile to the Dutchman who stepped in. Kutty put on the air of a showman.

"Allow me to introduce my esteemed colleague at the Massachusetts Institute of Technology, Doctor Hans van Rensselaer who has, only hours ago arrived from the Netherlands, a genius..."

"Please Doctor Holmes," Hans protested modestly

"Doctor, this is my wife, Lady Gaye-Lee Livingston, daughter of the sixth Earl of Linlithgow.

There's that funny name again the sixth Earl of Linlithgow. Nosh is really trying to be fancy, Hebe thought in her hideaway.

She pressed her face to the keyhole, but their stance only afforded a partial view.

"Lady Gaye. Enchanté," Hans clicked his heels.

He bowed and kissed the back of her mother's hand infusing a coquettish lilt in her response.

"Merci liebe, Herr Doctor Van..."

What are they doing? Hebe asked herself and stifled a giggle.

"Hans please," he insisted.

Kutty had piled all the china and silverware for the meal onto the tablecloth, pulled the corners together and slung the noisy bundle over his shoulder. Gaye-Lee and Hans gawked in wide-eyed curiosity. Kutty explained.

"Don't you want to eat outside?" he asked and toted the bag out to the porch overlooking the yard.

Hebe spirited from the pantry and skirred to the bathroom to hide. It was totally dark which scared her, so she groped for the light switch with as much stealth as she could muster. Her fingers almost knocked over the orange juice glass she had forgotten there in the morning. When she heard footsteps approaching in the hall, she flattened herself against the wall and held her breath. When her father stuck his head in, she planned to roar like a lion and wave her arms. Ants of excitement crawled under her skin as footsteps approached in the hall, but then they stopped.

Maybe it is the guest.

Impatience and curiosity peeled her from the wall. One beastly roar was joined by a second and she screamed at the top of her lungs. Kutty turned on the light and she saw Hans and him. Kutty hugged her.

"Nuttah!"

"Kuttah," she replied.

"We fooled you."

Hans smiled at her.

"This is my daughter, Hebe. This is my new friend, Hans."

"Toneska,"

"Toneska," he repeated.

"He speaks Wampanoag," she squealed.

"Is that what you speak? "Hebe, the Greek goddess of youth, right?"

"Yes, she was named after the goddess. Gaye-Lee was traveling in England, and she saw a statue by Canova at…some estate in England."

Peeking over Kutty's shoulder, Hebe eyed Hans from top to bottom. He was lanky with pale blonde hair hanging to the bottom of his chin and dressed almost identically to her father, in a white shirt with a pocketful of pens and khaki slacks. He carried a briefcase and a camera hung around his neck which he used on Gaye-Lee. Click! Flash!

"Pregnant women are so beautiful, the epitome of woman, a mother. I will call this The American Lady.:

He took the bread basket from Kutty. Gaye-Lee pursed her lips in disapproval.

"A prayer first."

"Ah yes. Wampanoag praying Indians?"

"Not in my family. Our people had no idea what those ministers were preaching about."

"How did ministers translate the bible," he searched his mind for words, "like Philistines—firmament—unyielding or creepeth…seems an insurmountable task."

Her mother chimed in, "That is true. The psalms are full of idioms such as "tongue struts through the earth' and…"

"'Remove the foreskin of your heart,'" Kutty added.

They all laughed, and so did Hebe, though she had no idea what was funny.

"The literacy rate was only around thirty percent among the general population in the 17th century Hans.

"So the well-educated missionaries could have told them anything.

Hans read, "Their throat is an open grave,'" means lying, right?"

"It does. With so many Biblical words on the tip of your tongue, perhaps you have a prayer?"

"Bless us, O Lord, and these, Thy gifts which we are about to receive from Thy bounty through Christ, our Lord, Amen."

"Amen," Hebe echoed.

"Perhaps you can tell me what you two get up to in that Aeroelastic Laboratory at M.I.T.? After all this time, I haven't a clue what my husband does," she complained.

"Maybe because after so much time with his experiments,"

"Experiments?"

"Yes, how else will he find methods to analyze the nonlinear aerodynamics of slender configurations with vortex separation?"

"Oh my goodness. He never told me that."

By the sound of her voice, Hebe knew her mother was still annoyed that, in front of a guest, her father refused to say grace. The tension between them was palpable over the porcelain salt and pepper shakers, a Dutch couple in traditional costumes. The ceramic pair was usually puckered up to one another on a tiny bench. Recently used, they sat apart on its ends. Hebe thought she could bring her parents together by placing the seasonings in their usual romantic positions. They remained tense.

Napoleonically Hans inserted one hand in his shirt and leaned back.

Hebe ferreted in her stew for a vegetable. Hans' nudged her.

"What big eyes you have. And so dark. Isn't it difficult to see out of such dark eyes?"

She squinted at him baffled by his remark.

"Come on we'll get them to talk again he whispered. "Kutty, what's this quiet? What about the jazz?"

He had broken the spell of disagreement. Kutty jumped up and darted indoors. An instant later, under his zeal, the Victrola's metal wheels squeaked across the polished parquet and crashed onto the weathered, oak, porch boards.

"What a great old music machine."

"Isn't it? It belonged to my father in law. I always admired it, and he left it to me. Wait 'till you hear the sound."

He placed the bulbous forearm on the thick disc, and they bobbed their shoulders to the beat and shot off "Yeah Man," in appreciation of the musicians' execution. Kutty snapped his fingers as loudly as casta-nets.

"He snaps good. See, a tunuppasog," Hebe told Hans and showed him her father's palm near his thumb.

"A turtle," Hans noted.

"A snapping turtle," Kutty corrected. "When I was a kid, I picked up a cast iron pot and got a bad burn, shaped kind of like a turtle, a tunup-pasog."

Gaye-Lee and Kutty moved to a wicker settee by the wall where they unwittingly sat in the same pose as the Dutch salt and pepper shaker lovers. She put her feet up and nestled against her husband while rapt in his explanation of the music. Hans took their picture. Hebe contem-plated Hans billowing cigarette smoke and deduced him to be a happy man because his lips turned up at the ends. Hebe felt as peacefully as she did when she and Wénise went out in the boat and drifted on the lake. Her mother had served almond liqueur which neither man fin-ished. She took a sip. Hans his raised his eyebrows up and down. Playfully, they both stuck out their tongues.

"You will be a real heartbreaker."

He snapped a photo. The flash went off and immortalized her with a sparkling milk mustache which she wiped away with her napkin.

"Watch."

He balanced a lit cigarette on the table edge. With a sharp bang on the table with his palm, he sent the cigarette flying into the air and caught it with his mouth. Taking an unlit cigarette, she tried, but failed. The cigarette rolled off the table, off the porch and into the darkness. Kutty and Gaye-Lee were engaged in a tender tête-à-tête.

"How old are your?" she asked.

He answered by flashing all of his fingers twice and then those on one hand.

"How many is that?"

She puffed up her cheeks as she did when she was thinking, and answered, "A lot!"

He laughed and challenged her to blow out a match, and she did quite easily. Playfully she held one up for him at arm's length, but he succeeded.

"Wauwunnégachick, very good."

"You remind me of my sister Marika in Amsterdam."

"Shhh, no bad words," she advised behind her hand.

"It's okay. Amsterdam is a city in the Netherlands?" Do you want a little brother or a little sister? "

"A brother. Do you have one?"

"Just the sister and Lucky, my dog. He got lost in the storm."

"Oh no. Yours too? Mine is down there."

"Let's see if he wants to come up."

He whistled so loudly, the downstairs neighbor came out.

"Gaye-Lee? Is everything all right?"

Kutty swelled up his chest, swaggered to the railing and replied, "Just fine."

The diners leaned over the railing. Art backed away from the lower patio. The shadows cast horns on his head, and his eyes reflected orange. Last summer he was a frequent visitor to their apartment during the day, and he accompanied her and her mother to the Cape. Kutty never missed an opportunity to don his hand made regalia, socialize with his own and dance. There was no convincing her mother to go, and Art offered himself as a chauffeur, "to see Gaye-Lee safely to her mother's house." On that drive, Hebe noticed he didn't smell. His absence of odor and his mysterious appearances made her suspicious of him.

"I thought you went to California."

"I came back."

Kutty dropped his arms possessively around his wife.

"Shall we invite your friend up for a drink," Hans proposed.

"He helped Mama from the cab yesterday."

"Why did you whistle?" Gay-Lee asked her clearly miffed.

"To call the dog," Hans declared and laid a comforting hand on Hebe's shoulder,

"Art will you get my dog from the clothes line, please?"

A smile wormed its way through Art's thin lips. Slowly, he crushed his cigarette jewel in a silver pocket ashtray and strode to the clothesline. His movements were stiff and military-like. A few rungs up the rose arbor-ladder, he handed Anùm to them. After a light drizzle of thanks and parting words, they filed inside. Gaye-Lee reminded Hebe of bedtime and her prayers.

"How is 'If I die before I wake a prayer? Can you imagine saying that?" he asked Hans who did not answer. "How can a person say that and sleep?"

Hebe stood waiting for further instruction.

"Go to bed!" Gaye-Lee ordered sternly.

"Cowammáunsh"

"Stop that! You know I don't understand."

"She said, 'I love you,'" Kutty whispered.

"I love you too Hebe," she called after Hebe and reverted to religion discussion with Kutty. "Everyone believes in something."

"I believe in plenty; the sun, the wind—and I believe in love."

He reached for her hand which she put in her apron pocket.

Hebe snuck back in, tugged on Hans' sleeve and she gestured for him to come with her. Neither of her parents heard him excuse himself. Briefcase in hand he followed her to her room. The sound of glass breaking caused him to jump. Hebe patted his shoulder and spoke the words she had heard many times before.

"It's okay. Sometimes grown-ups get angry."

The horse on her phantasmagoria galloped beneath puffy clouds around the walls, and she left to change and brush her teeth. Hans opened his briefcase and examined a few documents in a folder. The framed photograph of Canova's *Hebe* caught his eye. Next to it, were several small baskets and a man in a leather fringe jacket carrying a rifle and standing by a horse. "Kit & Apache," was written in cursive on the back; the "i" was dotted with a heart and the names "Nuttah and "Wénise" were in the baskets. He leafed through her notebook of drawings and childish sentences, but Hebe whisked it from his hands and gave him a sour look.

"What does Nuttah mean?"

"My heart, in Wénise's language. Maybe you will meet her one day, but you will never meet Kit or Grass Singing."

"Why is that?"

"Nup-u-pan-eek, I mean, they died. They are dead."

"Right."

He chuckled at himself for not having figured that out. As soon as he got up, she pointed to the hall.

"Remember? The bathroom is that way."

The open briefcase invited a peek at the contents, typed pages with words rubber stamped across the top. UNITED STATES AIR FORCE, TOP SECRET, CLASSIFIED and a diagram. Curiosity pulled her fingers to them, but her upbringing held it in place. Hans bluffed in. Hurriedly he slammed the case shut and stuck her hands behind her back.

"I didn't touch it."

She changed the subject by showing him *The Rabbit Story an Algonquian Tale.*

"Bunny butts…Bahooky," she giggled and pointed to his.

He grinned at her childish way, but while she dug through her pile of slim, oversized volumes, anxiety churned Hans' insides over whether she had seen the documents. They contained top secret information about the work for which he and Kutty had been recruited for their expertise as aeronautical engineers. It was so secret that the stationary had no letterhead, address or telephone numbers, and the men they had met only used code names, Black Ace, Thunder, Chances. They had a way of showing up wherever he was and whisking him away as they had Hans at the airport yesterday afternoon when he arrived in the

United States. Exhaustion fogged the meeting he guessed to be a barracks which went on until 2:00 a.m. "Vigilance and excessive suspicion *are* justified," the half dozen men had each repeated several times. In the afternoon, they gave him his luggage and delivered him to MIT, to Kutty. "Vigilance and excessive suspicion *are* justified," he muttered out loud and worried about what she had seen in his briefcase and who she might tell. He glanced at her weighing her two final choices, "The Man Who Married the Moon," or "The Rabbit Story," and was reminded that she was six or seven. A gnat of paranoia bit him again because she read incredibly fluidly with dramatic flair. Moving closer to her on the pretense of "seeing the pictures," it was clear she was reciting most of it by heart, and he relaxed. He complimented her, and she offered to read another one next time. She lit her sage. The tendrils of smoke snaked into the air, and she washed it over her body with he feather, and he did the same.

"Nuppeantam..."

Hans placed his palms together, but she separated them.

"Hold them up," she ordered. "Nuppeantam."

The burning sage smoke layered the air, and he coughed.

"Oh I am so sorry." She pat his back. "The workmen put wood over the window because Wuchowsen blew out the glass. Next time Mr. Hans, we can make cocoa. Okay?"

"Sure. Maybe when I..."

Hebe had talked herself to sleep. He pulled the cover over up under her chin. Kutty walked in and waved wildly at the smoke.

"How much sage did she burn?"

"It smells sweet. These baskets her grandmother made are incredible."

"Thanks. Actually, she is my grandmother, her great-grandmother, Wompi Mieúck Askeete, but as a joke we say Wénise. It means old broken down woman, but she is more able than any of us."

"Yes, it's funny how some people grow old and some age. Does she live on a reservation?"

"Not anymore. We were on the Passamaquoddy up in Maine with Twenty-Men and..."

"Why so many?"

"Only one. That's my grandfather's name," he clarified.

"I was impressed. Hebe recited a prayer in your language.

"She gets that from Wénise."

Kutty kissed her cheek and beamed with pride. Then he leaned his ear toward the hall to determine Gaye-Lee's whereabouts. His thumbs up signaled all was clear, and Hans opened his briefcase. In the lingering haze of smoke, the two reviewed the documents and spoke with so little breath that only fragments of sentences and solitary words reached Hebe.

"...liaison with the Shoshone."

"...French...Russian too?"

"... special projects... "

"Air Force facility west of the Mississippi"

"... Q-clearance."

"Area...51... U-2...."

"Lake...Dreamland... Dreamland... Dreamland..."

Gaye-Lee's chair dragged on the kitchen floor and yanked the men's heads up simultaneously. "Kutty" she beckoned mellifluously. Hans hastily stuffed his papers back in the case, and they tip-toed out to meet her leaving the phantasmagoria's illuminated horses to run into the night.

The Rowboat

V

Cow-e-tom-pá-tim-min

Hebe's young life proceeded along its simple route. Breakfast was at 7:00, lunch at 12:00, dinner at 6:00 and bedtime at 9:00 during the week. The familiarity of faces and predictability of activities provided her with a sense of security, even the brash, blue jay screaming "Jay—Jay—Jay," who awakened her. She had complained to Wénise about him for being a "big-mouth bad boy," but she defended him. "That is his way, and we live in his world. We don't go to friends' houses and tell them how to talk, right? I know he is pushy and greedy and noisy, but he calls to warn birds when hungry hawks are near." Ever since, Hebe was happy to hear, "Jay—Jay—Jay." Puffy cumulus clouds hung in the blue, and she waited for Osh, mother, master of ceremonies, to start the new day, but she did not come. Aromas she was used to usual aromas of bacon, coffee and after-shave were missing.

"Where is the weatherman on the radio?" she asked Anùm. "Is that bird talking to us?"

The jay's shrieking grew louder and louder as she walked down the hall to the kitchen. Grandma Livy delicately shaped silhouette included a generous, nest-like hat made larger by its flowers.

"Oma? Grüß Got."

Out of habit, she rushed to hug her grandmother though she knew she preferred not to touch children who she found "sticky from who knows what." She patted her gently on the back.

"Your parents have gone to get your new brother or sister. Isn't that nice?" Stirring the boiling oats on the stove, she remarked, "Nicht das Beste aber essbar," and asked, "What time does the maid arrive?"

To Hebe, Grandma Livy seemed nicer when she spoke German, so she whenever she could, she used those words she knew.

"Keine Zeit."

"Mary, Fiona, Cecelia, Patricia, all were good. What fault did your mother find this time?"

"She moved her bahooky too much when she cleaned," Hebe giggled and got down on all fours and showed her, "Like this."

"A demonstration is not necessary, Hebe," she served oatmeal.

When she saw it, she suggested, "We could make toast too."

Her grandmother agreed and examined herself in the reflection of a large spoon.

"Ihre Hut ist schoen."

"Danke Hebe. It is beautiful...and new. If you have a sister, her name will be Annalisa."

"I want a brother. He can beat people up."

"If you would be quiet, no one would need to beat anyone up."

Hebe's face flushed at the thought of school where she was uncomfortable. Her father's genes had given her skin a tone that looked like a tan and differentiated her from the all-White students. The first question they asked was not "What is your name?" but "Are you Italian?" or "Are you from Spain?" When she answered or they found out, they made fun of American Indians. When she spoke up, the result was teasing and shunning which is why Oma Livingston was of the opinion that treatment was her "own fault," that had she "kept quiet no one would have known." The experience instilled in her a fondness for animals and a distrust of non-family members.

Last summer on Cape Cod, she finally had a different experience which began on the day her mother and grandmother were went to a function in far too many clothes to be comfortable on a hot summer day. Seeing Art was a big surprise, he usually didn't arrive until later in the season. Gaye-lee went in his car and her grandmother in her own with her chauffeur. He waved to Hebe and addressed her, as he often did, as "Miss Hiawatha," which annoyed her. "Minnehaha is the girl," she must have corrected a hundred times, but as a Harvard graduate, she was sure he knew that, so he was not her favorite person. He was always so clean, so pressed, and odorless.

How can a person not smell? Everything smells; garbage, flowers, newspapers, ponds, everything, why doesn't he?

The staff was there, but they were all busy, including Kathleen, Oma's favorite maid, who was lousy at keeping an eye on her as she was told. Hebe wiled away the hours as she pleased. Aimlessly walking around was a favorite pastime. Her first stop was Barney's the weathered wooden shop at the fork in the dirt road where she bought a handful of wax bottles drinks. No bigger than her pinky, they held but a few drops of liquid to quench her thirst without resulting in the need to pee. The pond was a long, long walk away, but its stunning prettiness rewarded her. Hot and exhausted she arrived, checked around for Pukwudgies and prepared a spot to enjoy nature. She smudged the area and offered a prayer.

"Nuppeantam. Kiehtanit, Ohke, Okummus Nepauzshad, Wuttootch ìkkìnneasin nippawus, nummag ne wuttamauog. Taúbot neanawá yean."

Afterwards she reclined on the soft, dry ground under an Oak and scanned the sumptuous summer vista of grass and reeds around the water. It was difficult to keep her eyes open, but above the breeze blowing, frogs' ribbiting and the birds chirping, she heard a girl's voice.

"Hey! Hello there."

The white sun blurred her view.

"Over here!"

A girl waved from a rowboat in the pond. She was wearing a white dress and a straw hat which was clearly too large for her. It spun in whichever direction she moved her head. Hebe waved.

"What are you doing?" the girl asked.

"I am sitting."

"Me too—Do you want to sit together?"

Hebe beckoned her to shore. Her fine features and fair complexion reminded Hebe of a painting she had seen in the museum. The girl identified herself as Anne Atkinson. She was going into the third grade in the fall.

"I'm Hebe Holmes," she replied and pointed to the gables through the trees, "That's my grandmother's."

"Mrs. Livingston? We know her."

A clump of reeds trembled and a tiny light grey darted out.

"A raccoon," Anne squealed and jumped back.

"A Pukwudgie," Hebe whispered, "Watch out."

"A what?"

"Pukwudgie!"

The diminutive hand shot out again, ignited a fire from nothing, slapped it out and vanished back into the blades.

"See. Let's get out of here," Hebe urged excitedly.

From the rowboat, Anne glanced nervously at the spot where the fire was.

"Don't look! Just ignore them Anne."

They pushed off and Anne asked about the Pukwudgies. Hebe shared what she had learned from Wénise.

"They are elves."

"In fairy tales elves are helpful."

"Not Pukwudgies. They were devils. Start fires. Steal food and can kill you."

"Kill!? They are so small."

"Doesn't matter. They killed giants."

"Really?! Our people knew a family on Noepe...Martha's Vineyard. They had five boys. The mother and father were Squant and Maushop. He smoked a pipe, and they were such big, gigantic giants, they ate whole whales like French fries. But Maushop was our friend. He shared the meat. If we needed a tree, he picked it like a flower, the whole thing. And you can see the big rocks he put in the water to make a bridge to the mainland. But those evil little stupid Pukwudgies killed his sons. Five!" she emphasized holding up as many fingers!"

"How utterly awful," Anne gasped.

"Maushop was very sad—and very mad! He grabbed them like toys, and he threw them with all his muscles. They smashed to the ground miles and miles away from Noepe, in the mountains, here, there, all over Anne. They might be at your grandmother's house."

"I will be careful. I can't believe they didn't die?"

"Some did. You saw them! The meanness protected them."

"Is the giant dead? What happened to him and his wife?"

"Their hearts were broken. He took her away, but he visits. We know he is there when we see his pipe smoke over the water."

Anne assumed she meant fog or mist, but she believed the tale because she had seen that tiny hand in the grasses on shore snap its fingers and start a fire.

Pukwudgies

"That is a good story Hebe, but...well, I met your grandmother, Mrs. Livingston, and she doesn't look American Indian."

"No she isn't." She tittered at the idea of Oma sitting on the ground outside shucking corn, "My father is."

"Oh you're half. Me too and…Whoa!"

The wind blew off, her hat and initiated their long, wending chase after it. Once they were close enough, Anne stretched out with the oar dipping the boat deeply to one side, but she succeeded. Frivolously, she stuck the dripping hat on her head with a good bit of victorious vim and toppled into the pond. She ordered Hebe to "Go on the other side," and she did. Anne dress skirt was souses and tangled, so she couldn't free a leg to slip over the edge. Pressing as she was caused the rowboat list to the point of capsizing. Hebe saw Anne's leg, and the next thing she knew, they were both in the water.

"Pukwudgies," and laughter came out of their mouths..

They decided to swim along side the boat to the shore which was not very far. Hebe ducked under the water to see what had stuck her.

"Anne, look!" she exclaimed, "I am standing on the bottom."

The water was only as high as her shoulder. On the shore, they delighted over their escapade and laid their dresses on the bushes to dry and plucked the pickerel weed from each other's hair.

"What are your halves?" Hebe asked.

"My father's family comes from the "Scottish Highlands "forever," my grandmother says. My mother is French and…" she added in a mock upper class accent, "of the House of Bourbon."

"What is wrong with that?"

"Nothing. One is Presbyterian and one Catholic."

"There was a Mohawk girl—Tekakwitha. She became a Catholic. Didn't want to get married. Didn't work on Sunday. The women thought she was lazy, not religious. She went to live with the Missionaries.

"She could have gone to my school, Institut de l'Assomption Lübeck—in Paris. Almost all Catholic. The girls asked. I told the truth, Presbyterian."

"You did?! "Weren't they mean?"

"They still are." Anne sighed. "It's hard to be in the middle, isn't it?"

"Yes! I had better go. My mother is going to kill me," Hebe worried aloud and cut her eyes in the direction of Grandmother Livingston's.

I'm having a birthday party."

"Happy birthday."

"The invitations have already been sent, but I will ask my mother to call Mrs. Livingston to invite you if you want to..."

"Yes, please. I would."

"Me too. Hebe, teach me a word in your language?"

"Okay. She grinned mischievously, "Moose."

Confused, Anne emphasized, "Your language."

Hebe giggled out, "Yes, moose, and there are more."

"That's funny! Wait until I tell my mother I speak Indian."

Anne wanted more, and Hebe challenged her to repeat the greeting, "Toneska," which she did with ease, and "Cowetompátimmin." The effort raised a tensed eyebrow, so Hebe broke it into syllables, "Cow-e-tom-pá-tim-min."

"Cow-e-tom-pá-tim-min."

"Very good."

Hebe threw her arms around Anne.

"What does it mean?"

"We are friends."

"Perfect," Anne repeated, "Cow-e-tom-pá-tim-min."

Hebe felt as if she had a tummy full of sunshine, and she beamed at Anne while she shoved the boat off. They sang row, row your boat until they grew bored with it and then they just drifted silently in each other's company. Checking the shadows for the time, she knew it was early afternoon, and she rushed to beat Gaye-Lee back to the house. She did not. Her disheveled appearance and the abalone shell tattled to where she had been and what she had been doing.

"The pond!" Gaye-Lee snatched her by her hair.

"Ow. Ow. Ow," she cried holding her hair close to her head, so her mother could not yank it from her scalp.

"Ow. Ow. Ow," she repeated and sucked air in through her teeth to deal with the pain.

Oma Livy ordered Gaye-lee to "release her" and Hebe to "Take your bahooky up to the tub."

Before complying, she mentioned she had been invited to a party, but her mother answered, "No," before she had finished.

"The Atkinson's are lovely Gaye-Lee. A party is a good opportunity for Hebe to meet children from good families, so when things work out with Arthur..." she stopped when she and Gaye-Lee saw Hebe was still there.

"Go upstairs!" they ordered in unison.

Hebe scrambled off excitedly.

Oh goodie. Livy's letting me go. I am going to a party.

"Had you chosen a husband like Arthur in the first place..."

"How many times are we going to have this conversation? I had suitors like Arthur, better by your measure."

"Yes. Cynthia Barth recently wrote, and her son, who attended Oxford, is still..."

"Mutti! For God's sake, Kutty is brilliant and well-connected. We went to a dinner for three of his mentors; they are all Nobel Laureates. That is pretty civilized."

"I was only letting you know the Barth boy is still available.

"However, I am not."

"Your poor father..."

Her mother's mention of him incensed Gaye-Lee, and her retort burned with spite.

"Let Papa rest in peace. I never told you, but…Those nights you went to bed and assumed he stayed with you because you did not find 'jazz with jumping Jigaboos entertaining?' As soon as you were asleep, he joined Kutty and me in the South End. He was particularly fond of High-Hat and Wally's. He was quite a good dancer and that singer..."

"Don't be absurd. Malcolm ..."

"And by the way, the Barth boy is still a bachelor because he is a fairy Mutti."

Hilde Livingston was in the habit of walking away when she considered a conversation over, and she did.

"Hebe is not going to that party," Gaye-Lee shouted after her pouring a drink. "I refuse to let you control her life too."

Opening the faucets all the way let the water create the powerful white noise that silenced the adults bickering. And it whipped the half bottle of bubble bath in the tub to create a foam as thick as homemade meringue. With it, she created a beehive hairdo and a beard. When she heard her Oma coming, she ducked modestly under the bubbles. Hebe wasn't certain she had heard correctly. It sounded like, "Tomorrow we will shop for a dress and a gift to take to Anne Atkinson's party." By the time she had cleared the foam from her head, Oma was gone, but the next day proved the statement correct.

Gaye-Lee was furious her mother accepted the invitation she had refused and refused to talk to her or Hebe. Shopping with Oma, Hebe discovered, meant choosing from a prearranged selection, and she was prepared for the worst. At the boutique, a yellow dress was among the choices, and she picked it immediately. For Anne's gift at the jewelry store, she pointed to the silver pen. Oma complimented her.

"Yes. Good, much better than that corn doll you were twisting together."

Hebe tucked it in her patent leather pocketbook where Oma would not see it. During the short ride, Hebe fretted over who would be there and what kind of reception awaited her. The first thing she noticed through the window was the girls' dresses and how similar they were to the one she had been allowed to choose. She thanked her grandmother again who smiled, exited and exchanged pleasantries with Anne's mother. Anxiety overwhelmed Hebe, and she could feel herself leaving her body but was held in place when she heard, "Do—not—run, Anne." When she opened her pocketbook to get her white gloves, the corn husk doll popped out. The grandeur of Anne's house caused her to second guess its value as a gift.

"Toneska!" Anne greeted her bouncing into the car and throwing her arms around Hebe, "Did you make this for me?!" she asked delighted at the sight of the doll and dragged Hebe out to her mother and friends, "Maman! Regarde."

"C'est charmant Anne," she told her, and offered her compliments to Oma Livy, "What a lovely gift. Those from the heart that we make ourselves are the best, aren't they?"

She led her inside.

"This is my little American Indian friend Hebe, isn't she cute?"

The ebullient girls pulled Hebe into their celebratory circle where she sang and danced and ate Anne's birthday cake. After the other friends had gone, she and Anne sat in the colorfully fragrant rose garden, talked of dreams and watched the sunset. She had already added their friendship to the list of reasons she loved summer.

"The look in Pia's eyes froze her."

VI

Disappointments

By the time first grade came around, Anne and Hebe's postcards had already traveled back and forth half a dozen times between Paris and Cambridge with the words "Bonjour!" and "Toneska!" which Hebe wrote in block letters. The friendship bolstered her belief in people, and when September and school days arrived again, she refused her mother's offer to escort her onto the blacktop and marched ahead alone. She looked back; her mother was gone. A patch of blue, globe thistle by the fence caught her eye and she crouched down to examine it more closely. Mishquáishim's fur brushed her leg, so she took a deep breath, *Okay. I'm ready for it.* A remark whacked her in the head.

"Is this the injun?"

On the ground beside her, was a pair of hard, brown Mary Jane shoes. They belonged to Clio's older sister, Pia. Her hair flamed around her face and popped auburn embers into her blue eyes. She spoke in an outdoor voice as big as the Western skies under which her family once lived. Hebe's kindergarten classmate Mary had warned her about Pia who she labeled called "a mean cowgirl." She had tried to frighten Mary her into joining her posse of younger girls who she bullied into being bad and concluded, "I am afraid of her." Hebe took her time looking at the flower before she got up. The top of her head reached under Pia's chin.

"Injun," Pia repeated and poked Hebe in the chest knocking her off balance.

"I am a person!"

"A prairie nigger person." To her minions, she boasted, "We use 'em for target practice where I come from. She brought her puffy, white cheeks in front of Hebe, "Say, I'm a prairie nigger.

69

Pia's voice attracted other children. Hebe's could feel her heart beating as she never had before. There was no way she was going to repeat anything, and the girl had been too much of a show off to back down. She flipped one of her braids forward, and it scratched Hebe's forehead.

"I am a person," she repeated.

"You say what I told you to say. Prairie nig-ger..."

"I am tan," Hebe shot back," hoping her trembling was invisible.

"You don't," Pia barked and gestured for her girls to grab her.

As the older girls, intent on hurting her came closer, fear pulsed black and red haze in front of her eyes. Her mouth went as dry as ashes and filled with the taste of sick. They easily wrestled her to the ground where she kicked and scratched and screamed and wriggled every way she could to no avail. Pia pulled up Hebe's skirt and pulled down her underwear, and all gasped. Pia's minions let go of Hebe as if her arms and legs were hot.

"It *is* a tan," a girl exclaimed covering Hebe. "You were wrong Pia."

"Was not. Prairie niggers come in all colors....Bok-bok bok," she clucked at Hebe who was dusting herself off.

Fighting or the possibility thereof had never been discussed in her house, and she did not like it. Alone, she ambled in the direction of the flowers by the fence where she had begun the school day to begin again. Pia yelled out.

"Where ya going, chicken?"

Her voice was so brash, Hebe was sure Pia's relatives in Montana must have heard her, and it alarmed the frail home economics teacher. She rang the brass bell with intense purpose to summon teachers and alert pupils to the rough behavior, so they might stay out of harm's way. Instead, they lunged excitedly toward the fight. Hebe didn't see the sky or the tree tops, just the juveniles crushing together egging her and Pia on to engage in the rare display of girls' playground pugilism. Pia clucked again and slammed both her hands on Hebe's back. The assault made her dizzy. She spun on the heel of one shoe but did not utter a word. Animal instinct overrode etiquette and she butted her head into Pia's throat, and she punched Hebe in head. She doubled over. When Pia bent down to make fun of Hebe, her braids dangled loosely. Hebe yanked them as hard as she could and Pia yelped and chased her around the circle of onlookers. When Pia slipped on a leaf and landed on her back, Hebe straddled her chest which gave her the upper hand.

"Get off me prairie nigger!"

"Assótu! Machemóqussu!" Hebe snapped.

Poised to return the bonk on the head she had received, she froze and looked in Pia's eyes. All at once, it was a plea for help and a mixture of pain and fear and anger exactly like the one she had seen in Mr. Joseph's dog, Wohwohkau after a vicious stranger had stuck him with a dart. He limped to the darkest corner of the yard and whimpered in pain, but he growled off anyone who tried to help.

"Go ahead and hit me," Pia urged. "When I get up, I'll kill you."

Hebe got up.

"Come on."

Pia spit at her hand. The burly gym and math teachers hauled them to the principal's office. After a length of time that allowed them to calm down, he informed them that their parents were going to be "so disappointed in them, especially you Pia. You are much older," but he added he was going to give them a chance, "one chance," he emphasized to prove they could do better. Pia was sent to her class with a note, and he walked little Hebe to the nurse to have her "knee bandaged." From there she was not sent to class but dismissed because they only had a half day. Her mother must not have known; she was not at the gate. A cloud of despondency floated around Hebe while she dragged herself home, knocked on her own door and rang the bell like a visitor. When no one answered, tears streamed over her cheeks, and she sat on the ground under a tree.

"I wish Wénise was here," she confessed to the oak.

An acorn fell at her foot.

"Wénise?" she asked casting a glance at the canopy of branches.

Another acorn fell and another and another which inspired her to gather them. As Wénise had taught her, she selected the acorns with their "hats on" and inspected their cool shells for worms. Stuffing her book bag vanquished the morning's drama.

"Hebe?" Gaye-Lee asked from the porch in front of Art's door.

"Hello. There was a half a day," was her downcast reply.

The bandage on her daughter's knee dropped her down to look at it. "What in the world…"

"That's because I am a prairie nigger…" she announced matter-of-factly.

"What?!" Gaye-Lee gasped.

She rummaged through her lifetime of proverbs and aphorisms to relieve the slur's barbs, to console Hebe and herself; none seemed appropriate. Slumped in a chair, Hebe wept over her position in the world.

"You didn't tell me? I am a half-breed."

"Because you are no such thing. You are the opposite. You are double. You are double because you are two, all of me and all of Daddy."

"Tears trembled on her light brown eyes lashes.

"Double?" Hebe asked.

"Double," Gaye-Lee repeated firmly.

When she saw the acorns in her school bag, she suggested making acorn cakes with Hebe though they were not her favorite. That night when Kutty tucked Hebe into bed, he asked her to tell him the story.

"Her barrette cut my head. Look."

"A barrette did that? What did she want you to say?"

"A bad word," and whispered it to him, "prayer nigger," and then out loud added, "That is not nice at all."

He didn't want to get off topic with a discussion about how to pronounce prayer and prairie, so he agreed with her.

"Five girls nosh."

"She didn't fight you herself?"

"No. They showed my bahooky to everyone. When they let me go I was like Kit Carson's best fighter."

He laughed, "Good. Very good, a warrior like Weetamoo."

"Yes. She fell and I jumped on her," she demonstrated on Anùm. She wanted me to hit her, but I did not want to hit any one."

"No one does."

He wanted to share his philosophy about the tragedy of being human and how it means learning to dodge the ubiquitous dust of ignorance that has been blowing around the universe since the non-existent beginning of time which he knew she was too young to understand. There was nothing he could say, so he held her closely. Standing up to the bully, four years her senior, discouraged the children from taunting her, but Pia had the advantage of being older, bigger and familiar which she used to discourage her posse and their friends from socializing with Hebe. At recess, they skipped rope and played hopscotch or just linked arms. After two occasions of being shunned when she tried to join in, she sat reading on her own. When Hebe visited Wénise, she wanted to hear the whole story while she set a kettle of water on the stove. Wénise sprinkled herbs for tea from a little pouch into cups.

"Did you know Mother Earth had two sons? Twin boys. Glooskap was good, and Malsumsis was bad, truly evil. He knew about the plants that heal and the plants that are useful. Did he grow those? No. He grew hogweed, nightshade and hemlock to..."

"The bad ones."

"Yes. He was a mean person Nuttah. He had snakes and a bear and a cougar and he only fed them a little-little, kept them hungry, make them vicious. But his brother, Glooskap? Oh, he was the opposite. Everyone loved him. He was kind and trusting, too trusting. He made a mistake and told Malsumsis a big secret."

"That's not a mistake. He has to trust his brother, cuz..."

She stopped because Wénise was shaking her head and warned her to be careful.

"Nunnukqussenát Nuttah. Relationships give no character information. After Glooskap confided to Malsumsis that the feather of an owl could kill him. What did Malsumsis do?" Hebe shrugged.

"He put the owl feather in the bow and shot Glooskap. Whoosh!"

"His own brother?!"

"His own brother," she confirmed.

"Wénise, I don't like this story. It is too sad."

"Wait Nuttah...Glooskap had so much good in him, he was stronger than death. And he came back to life, but he did not want Malsumsis to kill him every day."

"What happened?"

"He watched him very carefully and one day at the river, Malsumsis was jumping around the fern plants. Glooskap remembered Malsumsis told him they would kill him."

"Ahque, you say."

"Yes, beware. And Glooskap was careful. Quick, he yanked out the fern and whipped it, roots first, on Malsumis' chest. He died right there. But he had so much bad in him..."

"Like those Pukwudgies, he was stronger than death."

"And he came back to life but not as a man. He shape-shifted into a black wolf. Now? He can only come out at night."

Thoughtfulness wrapped Wénise and Nuttah in quiet, and they sipped their tea.

Halloween that year Mary Beth invited, "the whole class" to her house. When the day came, parents' cars waited by the high black iron gates and the students piled in. Safely in her parents' car, Pia ordered the girl riding with them to "Close the door quick. Don't let the stinky, half-breed come." Hebe watched the driver who she assumed to be Pia's father laugh. The cars roared away. Alone in the grey, aftermath of

74

their noisy, rainbow-costumed departure, she decided she didn't want to go anyway.

In November, the teacher brought in a print, the First Thanksgiving. Bobby made fun of the American Indians because they were sitting on a blanket on the ground.

"Me Tonto," grunted Bobby, before making ape-like sounds, "I eat with hands. Ugh."

The class roared; the teacher banged the desk with a ruler. When they settled a bit, she acknowledged Hebe's raised hand.

"It is Nickómmo and..." her courage faded.

"Hebe's got the heebie -jeebies," Bobby declared.

Waves of laughs rolled through the children again which brought the ruler down. Her apprehension morphed into anger.

"The pilgrim lady is handing out cornbread..." she looked nervously around at the quiet class. "Everyone eats corn bread that way. The people are thanking us. We showed them how to grow corn and..."

"No they didn't!"

"Yes. Bobby, Hebe is correct," the teacher countered and gestured for him close his mouth, "Is that all Hebe?"

"It's Nickómmo," she mumbled and sat down full of satisfaction.

She had stopped them for once. At Christmas, there was no present for her at school; even though, they had all written their names on pieces of paper and put them into a hat. She had put the gift she bought for Suzy under the class tree. When they were all handed out, she took the eraser and went to the girls' room where she passed enough time for all the gifts to have been opened. Valentines Day, she did the same. All the children had covered shoeboxes to collect their Valentines. There was only one in her box. The image was an Indian with a tomahawk. The words read 'Me go on warpath till get um Valentine." There was no signature. The students laughed when she opened it. On the way home, she ran into her mother who was unexpectedly coming to pick her up at school. Hebe tried to rush her past the trash where her pink Valentine's box was half crushed inside. Her name was written on the side in large letters sprinkled with red glitter. Gaye picked it up.

"Is this where you put it after you worked so hard?" she searched her up and down, "Where are your Valentines?"

Hebe dug at the snow with the toes of her shoes and brushed the powder from her coat to prolong pulling the top off the box. Gaye-Lee helped her.

"Oh you did get a Valentine," she said and never imagining Hebe had thrown it away, struggled to retrieve it.

February bit at their faces as Gaye-lee opened the envelope. A generic child-like figure in a stereotypical costume of a feather in a headband carried a hatchet. He ran in front of a heart which read, "Me Go On 'War Path Til Get Um Valentine." Inside, "To Injun Girl" was printed in crooked little letters; it was unsigned. Gaye-Lee let out an "Hmpf," and pursed her lips.

"I am mistaken. This is not addressed to you. It must have fallen into the trash."

Tears that had collected in Hebe's eyelashes dropped onto Gayle-lee's glove when she took her hand.

Crash! The pot top falling in the sink called her back to the present. Oma had returned.

"How long are you going to keep company your Müsli?

"Did Mother get the baby yet?"

"Soon. Very soon.'"

Art appeared at the back screen door, and tipped his hat.

"Good afternoon Mrs. Livingston.

Propriety dictated his gait, his choice in clothing and even the length of his laugh. He was correct to the point of boredom but his presence delighted her grandmother.

"Oh, Mr. Higgins!"

She unlatched it, and he marched in with a bunch of flowers and a roll of very large white papers which he spread out on the table before sitting in her father's chair.

"Look Hilde. All glass. The entire wall. It faces the beach."

"How extraordinary. Higgins shall be added to McKim, Bullfinch, Cabot..."

Art's face reddened with the high compliment, and he shuffled his feet.

"Where are my manners? Good morning, Miss Hiawatha."

She greeted him without looking up from her cereal. He lit a cigarette, and then flashed a big smile. The phone beckoned Grandmother Livingston, and she went in the other room to answer it. Hebe looked at Art's elegant hand resting near the crystal ashtray. She studied his ring, and read to herself. Harvard VERITAS. It was very pretty, but she didn't tell him.

"My father sits there."

"Oh really?" he asked coolly.

Oma Livingston stormed into the room positively beaming.

"It's a boy! We have a boy!"

Hebe jumped up, "A brother?! I have a brother? Let's hurry."

"Not you dear. The hospital does not allow children. We are going to trust you to behave until your father arrives.

"Isn't he going to the hospital?"

Instead of an answer Oma Willie advised, "Don't open the door. Don't plug anything in. Don't turn anything on. Don't cook. Don't hang out the window like a fool. Just sit quietly and read to Anùm."

The back door closed. Her grandmother's face appeared in the small, round porthole window while she adjusted her flower-adorned hat. Then she was gone. Hebe was alone. She let out a little scream of frustration and began a minor rebellion. She turned on the radio and the television, pulled the Hoover from the closet and vacuumed the floor. She pulled off her socks and threw them in the air. Amid the dizzying din, the phone rang and she jumped as if someone had walked in on her. She undid all the things she wasn't supposed to be doing, put her socks back on, and finally answered. The caller had hung up. On the balcony, in her spot hidden from the street by the trees she noticed the world lying at anchor in mid-afternoon's port. Not one car passed. Not one person's footsteps sounded on the sidewalk. Not a leaf flitted on the end of a twig. Nothing moved. The challenge she set for herself was to catch the first thing that budged. The rag man and his horse-drawn cart clopping by distracted her and she stamped her foot. Everything was in motion again. Eventually, balcony sitting became prosaic, and she went in. The picture album of her parents' wedding helped to pass the time. She studied the guests for recognizable faces. Wénise's sun-reddened complexion shined between the two fat hair buns she had wound on either side of her head. With her glass bead earrings sparkling and a touch of lipstick, she was a real beauty, not a grandma. The image inspired Hebe to change into a one of her mother's cocktail dresses. To the strains of the Strauss, she donned a puffing tulle and chiffon dress and waltzed Anùm.

"Just a minute," she called in response to loud knocking.

Halfway to the door she ran into Hans holding a beagle.

"This is Lucky. Kutty asked us to look in on you."

They took off on his motor scooter to the ice cream shop and the Franklin Park Zoo. Lucky barked at everything. Hans joined her in tumbling down the grass and swinging high on the swings, but the best was zooming up and down the hills.

"Hold tight."

Her cheeks were hot from the sun and her skin itched from the grass. She was exhausted to the point of tranquility from the unexpected afternoon of fun. In the kitchen, they made a salad together, and they planned to read later. Her face ached from smiling.

"Cowetompátimmin," she told Hans.

"Yes, Cowetompátimmin?"

✳✳✳

What did a boy named Jude look like? Hebe knew what a Joe, or a Dennis, or a Phillip looked like. She had never even heard of a Jude until now. He was a wiggly, pale pink bundle of joy in green knitting behind the bars of the clean white crib. His hands with their teensy weensy fingernails were not even a fourth the size of her own. He had a small, inchoate face with navy blue eyes that her parents told her didn't see well yet. The one thing she noticed was that he smiled all the time, everyone noticed. Kutty gave him an Algonquin middle name, Ahanu, he laughs.

His arrival brought about change in the house. It took on the essence of diapers, sour milk and baby powder. Old mahogany furniture was moved out to make room for new, white furniture stenciled with balls and bears and airplanes was moved in. A wardrobe and a desk were crowded into Hebe's room. The wardrobe blocked the light from shining on her face in the morning, so she tried to move it. No luck. The only solution was to place her pillows at the foot of the bed and sleep upside down. She came home from school to find a bunch of daffodils on the desk. A note card dangled from them which read, "to Hebe Jeebie" and when the maid came in, she asked her to read the curly, cursive script.

"Dear Hebe and Anùm How are you? I have been busy with a new project. But we will see you soon. Enjoy the cocoa. Love Hans and Lucky."

"Thank you Kathleen."

She skipped down the hall to show her father, but he was arguing with her mother.

"So Gaye-Lee, your mother wins."

"No. No one wins."

"Mesalliance. That's the word she used for us?"

"You don't understand, I..."

Hebe opened the door, very carefully.

"Go to your room!"

Her father pulled her into his arms, "Don't yell at her."

From the way her mother scanned her, she felt she hated her.

"If I had married a local the tribe, I wouldn't have to tolerate your mother and those people looking down their noses... But I fell in love with you."

"And I with you, but..."

"How can there be a 'but?' She's getting to you, isn't she? Tell her butt out."

"She's my mother."

"I'm going to get ice cream. What flavor do you want Nuttah?"

"Everything's okay," he told her. "Peach ice-cream. I will bring it back, okay?"

Somehow, she nodded her head through the thick suspicion of doubt that he would not, and he did not. At dinner, the three generations of women ate in silence. There were eleven and a half lima beans on her plate, and she knew it was not a good night to leave them. Fortunately when Jude cried, her mother ran to him and her mother ran after her, and she was able to divide them between their plates. She smudged her room, prayed they would not find out and tried to stay awake in case her father returned with the ice-cream.

In the morning, she stumbled into the kitchen, opened the freezer and stood on tip-toe to see inside. The frost-covered testimony of her father's faith and love, a quart of peach ice cream, was there. With the cold cardboard container, she marched down to show her mother and get permission to have it for breakfast. She barged into the bedroom.

"Nosh! Thank..."

Art Higgins was stretched out on the bedspread on her father's side of the bed with his arm coiled around her mother. They were goo-gooing at Jude. They stopped. Hebe backed out and pulled the door closed before they had a chance to say anything.

"Hebe," her mother called out sweetly, "Hebe, answer me."

"I got ice-cream for breakfast," she announced.

After waiting two seconds for an objection, she concluded she could have it, served herself and sat trying to understand what was going on.

I hope Art is not going to baby sit me.

He did not. Oma did. Wherever she went, Hebe went and always on foot. Hebe collapsed into Bonwit's millenary department where they had big comfortable chairs. The sales girl brought out the selection she had waiting and then her grandmother tried on hats. Three were sent to the house, and then they trekked to a bookshop downtown. The walk drained so much of her energy that she did not have enough left to spar with the Sandman. The Harvest moon rose in the sky and. dwarfed

80

the leafy silhouettes. Suddenly stars exploded in her mind, and then the sun's fingers danced on her eyelids, and she realized, she had fallen asleep. There had been more changes in the night. Packing barrels and cardboard boxes were everywhere. Large men in work clothes were wrapping dishes, rolling up the oriental rugs and lowering the piano from the balcony to the front lawn. A workman rubbed her bushy head and greeted her cheerfully.

'Good morning sleepy head.".

"Who are you?"

Her mother looked unusually beautiful, Jude was in her arms and she was in Art's. When he saw Hebe, he dropped his arm.

Where are they taking everything?

"Good morning Hebe."

"Good morning," she echoed.

"We are going on a little trip," her mother answered.

"With all the furniture?"

The world and all that was familiar to her had somersaulted around in the long blinking of her two eyes. Queasiness groused in her tummy. The floor swayed and she swooned. Time sped up to the blur of a pinwheel.

"Go down and get in the car," Gaye told her.

Art's black Cadillac was idling by the back steps. Colorful as a lifesaver wrapper they fluttered down the back steps. Gaye wore a bright red, well-tailored suit with a small belt accenting her waist and carried Jude bundled in blue; Hebe wore a green plaid dress. She kept glancing back at the porch, at her house, her home. Suddenly she bolted around to the front to see the front window from which she watched the world.

'Hey, Hiawatha, we're waiting for you," Art called out.

As slowly as a trickle of molasses, she stepped to the idling vehicle.

"Get in the car, and I mean this instant," her mother ordered impatiently.

She didn't budge.

"Come on Hiawatha. We're going to get pancakes. Your little dog would like that, wouldn't he?"

When he reached to touch her forearm, she moved away from him and got into the car. From behind the barrier of the front seat, she watched his lips kiss her mother's cheek.

"Hiawatha is a boy," she advised Art for the thousandth time and rolled the window down.

"Leave it closed," Gaye-Lee ordered...

She rolled it down anyway, stuck her head out and witnessed life, as she knew it, pass away in a blear of elm leaves and houses. Maybe they were not going far but around the corner. She didn't know. She didn't ask. She just sat there in the back unheard and unseen. Both adults kept consulting their watches, so she surmised they had a schedule.

Art stopped in Cambridge. Her mother wanted a photo of him at Harvard, his Alma Mater on Massachusetts Avenue. Hebe watched from the back seat as he asked a passerby to take it. Propriety pulled his hand out of his pocket and flicked his cigarette to the ground before all the muscles in his face flexed into one of cool condescension. The passerby discreetly rolled his eyes, quickly snapped the photograph and escaped further obligation by claiming he was in a hurry. A pair of Vespa scooters putted into the square carrying her father and Hans, the force capable of stopping the seemingly incongruous course of events. Clearly, they were looking for her. She Jack-in-the-boxed out of the car and dashed across the street.

"Nosh!"

"Come back," her mother called from the window.

In her father's familiar arms, tears washed her confusion down her face. Her liquid, black eyes brimmed with adoration. When Art strode toward him, he set her on the sidewalk next to Hans and waited. An autumn zephyr rustled the dry ivy on the curving wall. Harvard Square held its history-dewed, breath, and the venerable, brick buildings verily bristled as the two dominant males flared their nostrils, swelled their chests, and they hung their arms battle-ready at their sides. Hebe counted twelve cobblestones between the men's' shoes as they exchanged words she could not hear. In her mind, they would finish, and her father would sit her on his scooter, and they would get ice-cream. Instead, he walked her to Art's car and opened the door for her.

"Can you wait here please," he asked.

Art was at the wheel. The window was rolled up. Her father talked to her mother in the front seat. He steadied himself by placing his palm on the window for support. She reached up and touched the tunuppa-sog and studied his hand which was an important part of her life. It brought the blankets under her chin before she fell asleep; offered her gifts; danced over the piano keys to accompany the family in songs; fought with tweezers and glue to operate on her little crystal horse when he lost his tail in a fall; tossed her mother's finest chiffon shawl in the air to explain the ways of wind currents; held the shiny new silver dollar she brought back from dreams; it did so many things. A partial handprint remained when he moved it. Her mother hung her head over her lap averting Kutty's eyes. Hebe tried the handle but the car was moving forward.

"Stop the car Mr. Higgins?" she pleaded in a high, frenzied pitch.

"Nuttah," Kutty called to her and waved.

She spun around in the seat and knocked off Art's hat and used it to cover his eyes

"Let go!" he shouted.

"Oh Dear Lord,'" Gaye-Lee exclaimed.

Art pried her loose and flung her into the corner, and then reached up and ran his fingers through his hair. Her mother's hand slapped her bare calves. Hebe felt a weight on her chest; she couldn't take a breath. All she saw was red and black.

"Hebe?"

Her mother repeated, but she and her voice faded to grey and then black. When Hebe opened her eyes, she cuddled her stuffed dog, snuggled into her bed and listened for the birds announcing the end of the bad dream and the beginning of a new day. When she unstuck her leg from the car seat, it was evident she was not in her room but Art's car.

"Everything is all right Hebe. One day, you will understand,"

She didn't want to understand. She wanted things to be the way they were.

Hotel del Coronado, Coronado, California

VII

California Revelations

Del Mar, California, Autumn: 1954

Art and Gaye moved the hands of their watches back three hours to California time. The dazzling brilliance of the fine, white gem of San Diego burned off yesterday's grey dawning in Boston, but the airplane ride's nausea lingered in Hebe's stomach which ached from filling a half a dozen air sickness bags. The Ionian summer lifted her spirits, but she wanted to be miserable, for her mother's benefit to make her suffer for having yanked her away from her father and her life. In the coast's eternal sunny season, Hebe found a cheerful squint into the warm rays more natural than a scowl in any direction. She kept close watch for her mother's glance, so she could pout and frown and look miserable. The glare from the sun on the windshield was blinding, so Art pulled over to buy sunglasses. The rented car, like his, was a Cadillac which announced the promise of a generous tip to the gas station attendant tanning his face. He hopped to his duties, removed his red cap dusted his clothes and smiled. Hebe noticed every person, in every doorway, under every tree and in every car was wearing sunglasses. Art had to use his hand to block out the sun before he went into the dark shop next to the station. Gaye –Lee turned. Hebe slumped and dropped her head in a posture of dismay which her mother ignored. Outside in front of the windshield, Art modeled several pairs of sunglasses until her mother nodded and pointed to "those."

"Doesn't she look spiffy?" he asked when Gaye-Lee put hers on. Art produced another pair with tortoise shell rims. He handed a pair to Hebe.

"For you Hiawatha,"

"Jeepers. Thanks."

She liked them so much she overlooked his misuse of Hiawatha, placed them on the bridge of her small nose and gave Anùm a genuine Cheshire cat grin of satisfaction.

"Now I am spiffy too? Thank you Art."

Unaware that Hebe had a clear view between the seats, Art stroked the entire length of her mother's leg.

"Here we are, California."

He nuzzled his face in her mother's neck.

Hebe cleared her throat to remind them she was there, but the moment deafened them to her. Shyly, Gaye-Lee raised her lips for him to kiss. From Hebe's perspective, his profile moved in slow motion toward her mother. Her father, Wénise, The Palace, Mr. Josephs, Púck, the tree in front of her bedroom window, all she had understood as life poured into a tub, and as soon as Art's lips pressed against her mother's they swirled around and around as if the plug had been pulled and washed down the drain, kitonekqué. Suddenly, the adult sunglasses which had teetered on her nose moments ago pinched; she placed them on Anùm. Without one observation about the peculiar scene of swaying palms and pastel houses into which they had moved, Art and her mother cooed a dreamy melody of embellished with mmm's and mm-hmm's. Her mother pointed.

"There is a quaint place."

The Poppy Chaparral Motel covered vines of electric orange flowers.

"I know. That must be why I booked us in there," Art told her.

He registered and returned to escort them inside, except Hebe who dawdled and then struggled with the heavy car door. As soon as she entered the lobby, Mishquáishim brushed against her calf. She surveyed the area which was cool and dark and empty, other than a grey-haired, grey-skinned, old desk clerk. She headed in the direction of her mother's skirt hem which flagged around the corner, and he snapped his newspaper and stared at her.

"Get out of here!" he blared and held up the small framed sign adorned with poppies.

She checked behind her to see whom he was addressing. There was no one. She held onto Mishquáishim's fur, raised her chin and headed toward the corner. He jumped up so quickly, the chair legs yelped on the tiles. Anger puffed all the lines out of his face.

"You dirty little spic."

Spic? she asked herself and read the sign out loud, "Welcome to California..."

"Is something funny?" he asked through his teeth and bounded over the counter.

Mishquáishim pushed her to run. She wanted to, but fear stuck her feet to the floor and tightened her throat, but a scream rushed out of her in a pitch and volume that panicked her mother and sped her back to the lobby with Art and the baby. Gaye's eyes traveled from Hebe to the clerk and then to the sign.

"Oh?" she declared, and turned to Art for words."...

"Don't bother," Art advised and led her out.

Hebe remained squinting at the sign, trying to read it. The man let out a big, "Boo!" and shook in amusement when Hebe fled to the street.

He doesn't like any one!

The thought frayed her nerves and flooded tears onto her blouse from behind her sunglasses.

"So much for quaint," Gaye-Lee noted.

"What is a spic?" Hebe asked.

"A stupid word."

"Sorry." Hebe blurted out.

"Whatever for?"

"We can't stay because of me," she answered and broke down.

Gaye put on a smile, "You saved us from a place with bad people. We want to be with nice people, right Art?"

"Indeed it is. Indeed it is, and I know a place full of them."

That was the Hotel Del Coronado. She had heard Art speaking about the hotel that was supposed to be so great. He drummed cheerfully on the steering wheel all the way there. The staff's graciousness dispelled the racist incident, and though, The Del, as it was known, was grand, its separate villas had the desired charm of an inn. Art and Gaye settled in with a nap, and the sitter, Joan a local teen, dropped by to invite Hebe for an unofficial tour of the hotel and a ferry ride to San Diego.

Joan had the kindly manner of a girl from a loving family which made her easy to be around. Every time Hebe looked up at her, she smiled. Out front, she produced a drawing from *The Wizard of Oz.*

"The man who wrote this story, um," she scanned the page for his name, "Frank Baum. He stayed here for months and months. He made the Land of Oz look similar. He really liked it."

"But he didn't like Indians. He wanted to kill us all," came out of Hebe's mouth.

She had heard Skinny Iroquois say almost the exact same words to her father to turn him against the film which he called "clever."

"What did you say?" Joan asked making a face because she was sure she heard but not correctly.

"Thank you. So I can say I stay at Oz."

"Aww, aren't you the cutest."

Joan also told her there was at least one ghost there and told Hebe a brief story about its resident ghost, Kate Morgan. Whenever she paused,

Hebe acknowledged her with an "uh huh," but she was not paying attention. She was preoccupied with figuring out why she felt so small in San Diego. Joan showed her the "exact spot," on the ocean's edge where Kate had been seen many times over the last sixty years.

Hebe raised her eyes to the ravishing Pacific. A shiny layer of sea spread over the flat breadth of sand and mirrored the sky full of clouds. They hopped from one to the other and pretended to fly among them. It was fun, but not as cooling as she wished.

Joan suggested they go to a stand of trees, but the palms' narrow trunks only provided long stripes of shade. Hebe had bigger shade in mind, the kind offered by a sprawling elm whose numerous branches created a veritable room of cool darkness where she could stretch out. The next stop on their agenda was the ferry; Joan promised the ride to be "fresh and breezy," and she took Hebe's hand. On the way to the boat, she became aware of the amount of space in California, not just between the pastel buildings but over head. Within minutes of the ferry had crossed the bay to the San Diego where she expected the skyline to be high and jagged with urban buildings; it was not. Beneath the tall palms of Horton Plaza, Joan pointed out the Grand Hotel and told her, "a famous gunslinger, Wyatt Earp lived there for a long, long time." The tour had begun, and to Hebe's great relief, Joan used the trolley and the bus from which she saw buildings of historical importance, Balboa Park, the zoo, and the Mission and on and on. Joan had attracted the attention of at least two of the many sailors on the bus. When they passed the Grant Hotel again, Hebe asked if Kit Carson had also been there. Joan was dubious. At the bungalow, she offered to "sit Hebe or the baby or both anytime," which they were going to "consider once they were settled."

The sun burst through the wall, a window from floor to ceiling facing the beach. Rays danced on the rafters high above the polished terra cotta floors and the openings on the catwalk leading to more rooms. The giant, green palms unfurled their fronds over the entryway and the living room near the kitchen. The sum of light and height and originality of Art's palatial design held them in awe. He grinned with pride.

"It's almost fifty to the apex," he pointed out. "Two thousand, five hundred square feet. Is that enough room for you?"

"Quite," she answered and ran her hand over the couch.

"That's for presentation. We will buy our own of course."

Shielding her eyes from the sun invading every corner, she re-marked, "It is beautiful, but..." she swept her hand across the wall which was all window, "We need a curtain."

With considerable head-scratching as to why anyone would want to cover such a spectacular view, the burly, bronze California workmen installed a lined, cream-colored curtain. Immediately it proved itself incapable of inhibiting the sun's intrusion. Three days later, with the same grumbling of incomprehension, the workmen replaced it with one in burgundy which filled the room with soft rose; Gaye-Lee was pleased.

Life in Del Mar hung another curtain, one which divided Hebe from the family. Hebe first noticed it at meals. Art had to commute a long distance to his office, so he had breakfast early and dinner very late. Because two of Jude's feedings coincided with Art's, Gaye ate with him which left Hebe to eat alone. Art's colleagues and their new friends came for cocktails. There were no family gatherings or other children. No trips were planned to Grandma Livy's or Wénise's, and she never heard her name any more, only Gaye and Art. It was: "Art won't like that's "Art wants it this way's "I'll have to ask Art," "Art this," or "Art that," Hebe was tired of it. The school bus dropped her off, and she car-ried on with her child's life, but no one took notice of her or checked to see if she was there. One day, she pressed her face up against sliding doors leading to the patio and look at them, Art and Gay holding Jude. Art was as pressed and sharp and Gaye coiffed and radiant as ever. They went out to the Country Club or to the Douglas Hotel to enjoy jazz, places "children are not allowed." They lived like two palms grow-ing side by side, branching out in different directions, so Gaye-Lee had little reason to scold or hit her.

She was not completely alone, for Mukker the jaunty, setter who lived up the hill in the big pink house the beach came to her window and barked invitations to come out and play. Together they would head off to the ocean where she amused herself with his game. It was always the same, to terrorize the waves. Woofing fiercely until they receded; he romped triumphantly as if he, and not the sun, the moon and gravity had power over them. As soon as the inevitable next wave splashed his furry red rump, he charged again, and again to the point of exhaustion. Then, he thumped his whole body onto the sand next to her and panted.

"Cowetompátimmin," she told him patting his head.

"Woof-woof," he replied.

Even though she knew the weather was cool and getting cooler in Boston, she longed to be there. New England's wondrous spring and summer lasted all year in Del Mar, but the sun did not burn as blindingly beautiful without her annual visit to the Palace and Wénise, rides with her father, extended family gatherings, the powwows, the animals and her Kiehtan house in the woods. Margarita, the Mexican cook and housekeeper, made up for the loss of humanity as best as one person could. She was shorter and rounder than the maids any of the parade of maids who had worked for them in Boston, and her hair was as black as a raven. Several Saturdays after the family had arrived, Gaye-Lee let out a shrill scream. Art and Hebe rushed down to the kitchen and saw Margarita in the kitchen rocking Jude who was quite peaceful. In broken English, accompanied by deliberate, experienced hand gestures, she asked Gaye-Lee what she would like to have for meals that week, showed her where she was to write the information in the future and placed the baby in his pen. Gaye-lee assumed she was from the staffing agency, so she began an informal interview. Margarita's English was too minimal to respond to Gaye's numerous inquiries with anything other than a smile. Her body burst into a vigorous, cleaning routine involving rags, brushes and assorted cleansers. Art made one of his bragged-about phone calls which promised to "find out anything about anyone," and learned Margarita had worked for the former owners who promised she could resume for the new occupants, if they didn't object. She was unaware that Art and Gaye-Lee had not been consulted.

"This might work out very well Gaye-Lee. The son is a mechanic, her sister a seamstress, another relative handles the grounds, and obviously, no one could clean this place alone. She has a team of family members on staff."

Oblivious to his inquiry, she was down on the terrazzo floor scouring in the very same position for which Gaye-Lee had fired a plump shapely, German woman. Margarita was neither built nor dressed for tempting the opposite sex. Impressed by Margarita's zeal and with no one else up for consideration, Art and Gaye began discussing whether to keep her.

Margarita washed her hands before she approached them.

"Scuse me señor. Martini?"

"Martini?" he glanced at Gaye, "How about this for help?" he asked and nodded. "If it's good, no trial period is necessary. She stays."

Gaye laughed. The Martinis were excellent, "The best I have ever tasted," Art remarked. Gaye agreed, and Margarita' and her family were hired.

That particular evening, the family dined on the terrace in the sticky, ocean breeze, and they were served by Margarita. Several times, she explained what they were eating, but one knew exactly what it was. When she spoke, she began with a clear triplet of understandable words in English followed by a hundred in Spanish, then smiled and clasped her hands together.

"Is good?"

It was an exotic meal but "A winner," Art deduced. It complimented the wine Art had selected. They drank a toast, Hebe included. Her mother was as rosy as her red satin cocktail dress, and with high spirits, she flung her arms around her daughter.

"We're going to be so happy."

They were, though each had a complaint. Gaye-Lee wanted a maid that looked like a maid, so she presented Margarita with a black uniform with a little white collar and apron. In it, Margarita didn't resemble the maid she had in mind. Her plump form required a dress large enough to accommodate her girth, but she didn't have the height to take it up giving her the appearance of a large pillow with white lace trim, sandaled feet and a rebozo which her mother referred to as "that shawl." Margarita had at least two lengths of cotton fabric woven in various combinations one more red, gold and the other shades of blue, not just to wear but to help her. From what Hebe could tell red and gold was for chores, tied around her as a sling, it held groceries at the store, dishes in the kitchen or bulbs in the garden where left loose, its fringe whisked insects away or folded, it provided her a place to kneel The blues, usually tucked in her bag, could also be folded as a place for her head on the couch when she rested, or tossed over Jude to ward off a chill. It was part of her, and now it was part of the uniform. She also insisted on wearing her black felt hat which came down to her ears just above the long plaits of hair on either side of her head.

"No hat please," Gaye-Lee insisted and removed it.

"Si, sombrero," Margarita countered with a merry chuckle as if Gaye-Lee was teasing her.

After going back and for a dozen times, Margarita playfully placed the hat on Gaye-Lee's head, and along with Hebe giggled, she giggled. Defeated, her mother placed it in on Margarita.

"Gracias señora."

With a big smile, she shuffled into the kitchen. Somehow, that exchanged resulted in a compromise because the black uniform and hat did not show up in the house again.

"She just doesn't look like a maid," Gaye groused to Art.

"Why does that matter? Anyone who works twelve hours a day and makes a killer martini should be allowed to wear whatever." Hews dissatisfied with the "pompous, Nouveau-riche sons of theater chain owners out here who only seem interested in who has what," but Hebe had no idea what that meant.

Her own complaint was that she did not want to be where she was not wanted; but that was minimized by Jude's incredible baby cuteness. He unwittingly exercised his eye muscles and tried to focus on an object. His tongue darted gleefully in and out of his mouth and sent saliva down his chin and cheeks. Whenever he saw her, he squeezed, wriggled his whole body and threw his feet out stamping at the air. Suddenly strange objects appeared and stopped him; he squealed in relieved delight when he discovered they were his toes. Hebe hurried home to spend time with him after school, once she was enrolled.

The first week had come and gone after Art shared "a bit of interesting information," he had heard at the club.

"I don't know how it came up but the Indian kids are segregated in the schools out here. Supposedly there is an IQ placement test, but it might be rigged against them because they all end up in the dim wits classes."

"Dim wits class?

"That is not the official title. They mark their transcripts with retarded. What about overseas?"

"From what I recall, I would need Kutty's consent as well. We are still legally…" she shot a glance over her shoulder at Hebe.

The evening before their visit to the All Saints Academy, they had dinner on the patio Hebe's favorite place to eat. Margarita took Jude, and Art left. Gaye-Lee announced that she had to have "a very important discussion with her, very grown-up," but she didn't say anything, not one word. She poured another drink.

"Do you mean today?" Hebe asked.

Gay-lee nodded. "You father and his people are human beings, Hebe, really fantastic. I never want you to think anything else…"

"I miss Nosh," she interrupted and pouted.

"I know but…but…" shame caused her to falter. "Remember Miss Smith and the problems you had? One way not to have any problems is to keep your father a secret. You can not, you must not tell anyone you are a Wampanoag, or any kind of American Indian…"

"But I am. I am Nosh and Wénise, not just you" she sniffled.

Gaye-Lee was crying too.

"I wish I was not born," Hebe bawled and wandered off.

Art held Gaye-Lee back and consoled her.

Featherless and in Mary Jane's, Hebe still stood out like an almond on a vanilla-frosted cake among the assortment of fair-haired students. The fear of letting her racial identity slip had rendered her reticent. No one bothered or befriended her. In the hall with a pass to the lavatory, she heard two older girls talking about her in pleated and poodle skirts at their lockers.

"See? They are accepting Jews," Poodle skirt told her.

"Impossible. My mother will transfer me. She must be a Chicana?"

"Don't be stupid. They couldn't afford it. We better find out."

With inept discretion, they bumped into her, blocked her path when she tried to go around them and feigned niceness.

Expressionless, she listened while Pleats led the inquest.

"You're that new little girl in Miss Langley's class, aren't you?"

They interpreted her silence as a yes.

"So where are you from?"

"Boston."

Right in front of her face, as if she couldn't see them, the girls exchanged baffled expressions over her unpredicted reply.

"We live near La Jolla. Where do you live?"

"Del Mar."

Poodle skirt elbowed pleats, "What does your father do?"

"He is an aeronautical engineer. Excuse me," she informed them and tried to pass.

They blocked her and asked in unison, "Habla the espagnol?"

"What?" Hebe asked and wrinkled her nose.

They let her pass.

Pleats shouted after her, "Who brings you to school."

"The maid," Hebe shot back. She remembered seeing them last week, the day she almost didn't go to school. Overcome with melancholy, she sat with her head hanging down fighting back tears. Margarita pulled the car over and took her in her arms. She cried aloud but kept apologizing.

"Tears are meant to fall. We don't hold back our laughter. Why should we hold back tears?" she asked.

Hebe pulled away and stared at her bewildered.

"Margarita? You speak good English."

"I studied English in school, and I have lived here a long time. I don't say much when I am working. Too many words complicate life," "Entiende?"

Hebe shook her head back and forth.

"People are more comfortable if they think I do not understand all."

Hebe told her all about how she missed Wénise and her father, the only ones who understood her language. Margarita sympathized and assured her that over time, she would "miss them less."

"I will never forget them less."

"And they miss you Hebita, and they are waiting to get the letter from you."

"What letter?"

"The one you write about the new things in your life, the things you see that they can not. People leave their friends and family everyday. We always have a lot to talk about when we see them again, but you can write and tell a little bit."

The Del Mar school was only a few years old, so it was clean and bright and new, not dingy, old and like the one back east. When the windows were open, a palm leaf insisted on popping in by her seat. She was accepted at school and she made a friend at home, Margarita's daughter. She was skinny with budding bra-free breasts beneath her soft shell sweater. She was casually draining all the empty wine and champagne bottles into two separate glasses and stealing glances over her shoulder at Margarita snoring softly on the couch. Hebe startled her when she came in dripping wet through the door from the pool. Their eyes met. The girl smiled. Hebe brushed past her and pulled a bottle of wine from the wine rack in the lower cabinet and plunked it down.

"You are not going to drink that, are you?"

"Are you Hebe? My mother talks like you are a baby."

"But you see I am not."

She poured two glasses.

"I'm Rosalita.'"

When she took the glass, Hebe noticed one of her arms was considerably smaller and shorter than the other one.

"I was born this way. God made me different," she asked seriously, held out her arm, looked at it and smiled, quite pleased.

Just then, Margarita sat up sleepily from her siesta. Hebe grabbed Rosalita and breezed out to the striped umbrella Hebe had planted on the beach earlier.

Little by little, they drank the whole bottle. A fit of the giggles overcame them. They stifled them to let an old man to walk by, but as soon as he passed, they busted up even louder than before. Once they had their wits about the, they zigzagged down to a piece of driftwood on the beach where Hebe buried the empty bottle with several others. Rosalita stared in disbelief.

"You are crazy."

"Maybe sometimes"

Impulsively, the two charged off in an inebriated pre-adolescent gust of exhilarated prancing down the stretch of beach and into the clear blue water temporarily oblivious to Rosalita being fully dressed.

They laughed at the oversight when they came out. She peeled off the dress to dry on the sand.

"You dummy."

Rosalita chased after her. She yanked the string on her bikini and the top came off. They rolled around in the warm, gritty sand where Rosalita playfully pinned the breathless and giggle Hebe down and lay gently on top of her.

"I'm not a dummy."

She kissed her cheek, glanced down at her own barely visible breasts and then at Hebe's.

"Hey. We're bosom buddies."

They stood up and rubbed their nipples together, in a wiggling, inebriated dance and then walked arm in arm back to the water to wash the sand away. In the water, beneath the naked blue sky, bees buzzed in Hebe's head. The world pulsed yellow, and white from behind the fading veil of wine and Rosalita reached for her hand. Hebe was filled with joy.

Unfortunately, Rosalita went to a different school. The next day, she missed her during math, her worst subject. A hangover added to the torture of pounding her way through the pop quiz. Completely absorbed, she didn't hear the teacher call on her. The class laughed. When the teacher saw tear-streamed face, she excused her to the nurse. She had to use her hands to find her way to the door. A haze in front of her eyes veiled reality all the way to the nurse's office.

Art came to pick her up. He had an angry tense expression which she knew she had put there. He hated to be interrupted at work. She sat close to the passenger side door. He reached over with a caring pat on her leg and assured her that they would be home soon without changing his expression. Without another word, they drove home. Gaye was shouting incoherently inside the house.

"What's wrong with Nìtchwhaw?"

"Go up to your room."

These simple instructions were not as easy to follow as they sounded. The intense light of day pouring in the open curtain spotlighted the kitchen counter piled high with the many wine bottles she had taken over the past couple of years. Even from a distance, Hebe recognized the yellow labels. The line of questioning Gaye pursued assumed Margarita was a thief, and she wanted to know how many bottles she had taken. She tapped a pencil on a pad where she was calculating the amounts. Margarita shook her head.

"No se nada," she kept saying.

Exasperated Gaye slapped the housekeeper with her palm. When Hebe saw her beautiful Margarita, singer of songs, maker of cookies, mother of her bosom buddy being both falsely accused and slapped, she charged to her defense. She pummeled her mother who pushed her to the floor.

"That will do," Art stated more loudly than Hebe had ever heard him speak and he reached to help her up.

"I drank the wine," she confessed in a shout, "not Margarita. She is telling the truth. She doesn't know."

"Was you Hebe?" Margarita asked with wide eyes.

Art suggested the housekeeper take the afternoon off, and she left/ Gaye spun around, grabbed Hebe by her hair and slapped her.

"Drinking wine. You're only seven..."

"I am almost nine," she shot back to her mother who did not seem to be in her body.

In her place was a monster with the blazing green eyes. Hebe felt blood dripping from her nose and mouth and screamed, but Art spoke to her mother.

"Gaye-Lee? Gaye-Lee!" Art called as if she was far away and he was desperate for her to come back.

Hebe saw her mother's spirit waft into her eyes and focus on her daughter's bleeding face.

"I'm sorry," she offered more to the room than to Hebe.

"Please try to control yourself," Art told her softly and closed the curtain."

He and her mother disappeared into the house and Hebe slunk up the stairs where she sat. When she didn't respond to the dinner bell, her mother brought a tray to her and left the silver tray on the vanity. Hebe ignored her until she left, then lit a candle, and noticed an envelope by her plate. Thinking it a note from Gaye, she left it. The gossamer, voile curtain lured her to the window where she saw her mother and Art dancing on the terrace below. She wished she could dive from the window, an invisible bird into their togetherness, not to break them apart, but to dip into the love between them and catch just a few drops on her downy wings.

She snatched the letter off tray. It was from Brookline, Massachusetts, number 219 Warren Street, an address she had never before seen. It held a photograph of a motley group which included her father and Hans and a couple of letters.

They wrote!

They missed her; they signed "love," and in between, her father offered an explanation for his past and future silence. "I have to travel so much and far. India may be next."

Thanksgiving vacation had begun, so she rode her bicycle into the travel agency in town. The agent, entertained by her small client's inquiry about passage to India, provided the information and recommended her parents call to book the trip. There were all together too many numbers in the cost of such a trip for Hebe to go now. She went to the soda fountain at the drug store and asked the clerk to double check her calculations. He confirmed the disheartening reality that if she saved every cent of her $2.00 a week allowance, she would not have enough for years.

The only passage available to any land her father visited was at the library. The city was in the process of building a new one, and the temporary location was the Casa del Prado, an elaborate historical building in Balboa Park all the way downtown. She was not supposed to go by herself, but books peopled with curious characters and interesting words had a draw so powerful she was willing to risk the, as yet unknown, consequences and take the bus or pedal to them. No one was likely to see her except Art who was in the habit of giving clients mini-architecture tours. She had avoided him a couple of times. He preoccupied with his speech and with no expectation of her being downtown, had yet to spot her. That changed one day when she arrived and walked her bike on the sidewalk to look in store windows. Not quite ten feet away, she saw him yammering about Horton Plaza, and she hid in plain sight and waited for them to go. Art had brood shoulders and was a good six feet although he appeared taller in a hat, and dressed in his sharp, distinctly conservative New England style, he solicited subtle signals of eager and immediate availability from the opposite sex. In the brief span of time she had been watching, he returned a nod and a wink, and after the group went their separate ways, a woman in the group remained with him. Her curvy-arched eyebrows matched her jet black hair. The brim of her hat brushed his jacket, and he flicked it playfully and saw Hebe from the corner of his eye.

"Hiawatha."

He removed the woman's fingers from his Jacket and beckoned her over. "This is Gaye-Lee's daughter, Hebe. This is Miss Gonzales—one of my firm's clients."

Art, do you have my lighter?" she asked casually and put her hand in his pocket.

He lit her cigarette.

"Did your mother change her mind about you coming into town by yourself, Hebe?"

While he waited for the answer he already knew, Miss Gonzales slid into the car.

"Be back for dinner and mums the word."

A client? She was awfully close and they drove off awfully fast. And what was with mums *the word.' Hmmm. Is he telling me he won't tell mother if I don't get back in time for dinner? How about I get back when I want to, and I don't mention Miss Eyebrows?!*

She was not sure what, if anything, Art was doing. She didn't want to waste time thinking about it. The librarian helped her compile books on India. Crushing crowds of women swaddled in brightly colored saris and sandaled men in turbans pulling rickshaws. Huge bony cows adorned with orange flowers paused among the traffic on dusty, un-paved roads and jungles full of elephants and Bengal tigers.

Tigers! Nosh! Ahque! Please be careful.

Eventually, she wrote it in a letter. With no address for her father, she sent it in care of Hans, and she wrote to him too.

VIII

A Prayer & an Answer

The sun sprinkled air was charged with negative tension borne of the ardent verbal duals in which her mother and Art engaged. Tiresome, mindless topics sprouted with the frequency of dandelions, and weeds that they were, they reproduced. Dogged conviction, usually fueled by mixed-drinks and a flair for the dramatic, raised their voices, flailed their arms and walked them out of and immediately back into the arena where they refilled their cocktails and their egos and resumed railing. Occasionally Hebe tuned in. Gaye-Lee declared fog an enemy of her hair and expressed a desire to move to Arizona where it never rolled in. Art disagreed, especially with the word "never," and then veered into a completely unrelated discussion by insisting "Arthur Miller was trying to get attention by courting that bimbo, Marilyn Monroe."

"She is not a bimbo," Gaye-Lee defended.

"What in the world do they have to talk about?"

"Interesting conversation is most likely not the first thing that pops into a man's mind when he meets Marilyn Monroe."

"So you admit it; she is a bimbo."

"I admit no such thing."

Back and forth her mother and Art went. Then there was the great grey-lavender debate which began when Art fished for a compliment on his "new grey suit" which Gaye-lee identified as "lavender." Considering her suggestion that we would wear a girlish color an affront to his masculinity, he grabbed her by the wrist and dragged her to the lamp to prove his point, and when that failed, outside to the sunlight.

"Exactly. Lavender.

They continued when he returned home with a swatch of fabric he had collected from the tailor.

"Without the lining, it is indisputably grey."

She dropped it on the lavender couch, and though to Hebe it blended right in, Art stood by his gray perception.

All those words, all that energy. Why? she asked herself but wished her father had argued with her mother because she seemed to like it. *Otherwise, why do it every day? Is that why she left? I don't care. They don't care about me.*

That was how their oversight in acknowledging her and including her made her feel, yet Hans and her father, though absent, loved her. The correspondence, which came more frequently from Hans, and the black and white photographs were here proof; she had four so far. Her father dancing in his breech cloth at a gathering at Wénise's by Hans and Kutty, looking quite collegiate, sat side by side; each had his arm around the other's shoulder in their tidy lab at MIT. In another, they sat beneath a cloud of cigarette smoke surrounded by their motley troop of

Beat friends in a nameless East Coast café. They smiled at her. Hans held up a book to show the title, *When We are Here Together*, her father held a cloth napkin with the marker-scrawled word, "Cowàmmaunsh," I love you. She hung it above the wooden chest in which she kept their sheaf of tender missives. She imagined being there with them. Gaye-Lee scoffed every time she saw it.

"If you stay out of Hebe's room, you won't see Kutty...I mean it. You know, 'out of sight out of mind?'"

As soon as Hebe laid her eyes on the black sweater her father had sent her for Christmas, she knew her mother was not going to approve., and she didn't, not the color and not the way it clung to her well-developed body, the very reasons Hebe liked it. Most of all it came from her father. The faint scent of Agua Lavanda told her, he must have wrapped it himself. The blender, a gift from Art to Gaye-Lee and himself crushed concoctions they were sampling them; it had become their new hobby. Hebe stood on the catwalk and admired the Christmas tree which reached up to her floor. Art was at the bottom sorting tinsel and humming a Christmas tune when he caught sight of her descending the stairs in her black sweater. He gave a small wolf whistle. The blender stopped. Hebe modeled oblivious to the salaciousness with which he devoured her curves. Guilt snapped his head to Gaye-Lee. She was glaring at him.

"I told her father she was too young for a black sweater.

"It's from her father. What's the harm?" Art asked and ran his eyes over every inch of the sweater again.

Hebe was trying to comprehend why her father had called and she did not get to speak with him. The sweater had triggered a tiff, so she went to the entertainment room downstairs to keep company with her darling little Jude. She felt good in the presence of his effervescent, disarmingly adorable toddlerhood. Vivaldi's intense and edgy piece *Summer* sawed through the floor signaling to Hebe that the tiff had escalated to an argument which music usually did little to veil. The tension dropped Jude's head on his chest and he wept. She consoled him and lured him outside by challenging him to catch her. The cool sea air washed the cobwebs of discontent away. On the shore in the moonlight, he gazed at her while she sent up a prayer.

Nuppeantam Kiehtanit, please find a way for me to get away from here...even for a little while, she prayed in her head and then out loud. "I pray. Great Spirit," she began.

Jude's small voice lost the "S" but managed to echo, "'pirit" and squealed.

"You said it! You are so smart Ahanu. Say, Okummus Nepauzshad?

"Kummu'."

pointed at the sky. Disbelief opened her mouth at the sight of an ageless woman suspended in mid-journey from the sea to the moon. The waterfalls of her hair poured over buckskin dress and she looked right at them.

"Ahanu? Do you see Grandmother Moon?"

"Kummu'" he repeated.

They watched her rise until she vanished.

Before the sun had risen, Hebe curled up at her window and checked for Okummas Nepauzshad, but all she saw were workers on the pathways. Three had mistakenly opened her door in search for a bathroom, and she redirected them down the hall. The extravagant preparations the winter wonderland Christmas party Gaye-Lee and Art were hosting were a perfect tumult, and they were not around. The longest car she had ever seen in fire engine red brought Margarita. A dusky young man with sunglasses resting more on his high cheekbones than on the bridge of his nose sat behind the wheel His crisp, white shirt, unbuttoned nearly to his belt, was tucked in at his narrow belted waist. His muscles bulged under his short rolled up sleeves. She ran down to open the door for them. When he came near the sensation of a hot, baked potato steamed inside of her. The distinct aroma of Aqua Lavanda and bubble gum filled the air as Margarita showered her with kisses. She stepped back and radiated with pride.

"Hebe this is my son, Tony, back from Mexico."

Beaming with pride, she pinched his cheek as if he were a baby. "And," she pointed to the car and tittered, "his coche, the Cadillac de... no sé...Tony."

"Cadillac Series 62 Coupe De Ville and—I borrowed it."

Tony lifted his dark glasses and set his naturally seductive sights on Hebe.

"Mucho gusto."

"Hi," she almost whispered, held her chin up and swished girlishly under his arm.

Above the din of workmen dragging in bare winter trees, Margarita gushed over the Christmas tree, and then panicked because she needed to go back to the store.

Tony volunteered, and he took Hebe with him. She was a little nervous because it was the first time she had ridden in a car with a stranger, so she dawdled outside and measured the car from end to end with her pocketbook.

"Come on. Get in."

Tony revved the engine and the wheels spun a cloud of grey smoke behind them before the car zoomed into a broad, blurry stripe of red on Sunrise Highway marking the direction out of Del Mar. It was the first of innumerable rides because since his return, Margarita forgot "esto" or "aquello" almost every day.

One afternoon, she was expecting them to arrive with Rosalita. Not doing so created a *rat-a-tat-tat* quarrel in Spanish. Between the words and gestures, she understood that he had driven away without Rosalita because she was not ready to go when she was supposed to be. Too respectful to walk away from his mother, he listened to her soft harping on and on and on but stopped it by slamming his hand on the counter.

"Okay. Bien, I will go back. No ella le dará la lata…I will take Hebe."

Pleased, Margarita pinched his cheek.

"You have to bring her back here mijo

"Sí ¡Por supuesto! In the car, he warned Hebe, "Don't say nothing."

Squinting at the horizon, she felt as if a shawl was dragging over her body. It was Tony. He popped the glove compartment and invited her to choose a pair of sunglasses from his spares.

"Graci…"

She covered her mouth because his bluster had frightened her. His heart melted.

"What does a nice doggie do if you tie him on a short leash?"

"He barks."

"That's me," he confessed and barked, "Wow wow. Say anything you want."

"¡Vamos"

The streets and houses were much closer in Logan Heights.

"There they are!" she shouted excitedly.

"Who?"

"The colored people."

"Ha! True. What do want them for?"

"To know I am in real world, the one that includes everyone."

"The Negroes are mostly in Sherman Heights, not here." He darted his eyes from one place to another, "There's some Chinese over there for you, and the Filipinos are over on Market Street. The rest is the best," he concluded and hit his chest," Chicanos baby, and we are all down here on the flat of the hill."

"Not all," she reminded him pointing to herself.

"Oh, yeah, now they got a little Indian girl up in Del Mar. That makes two. You and old Nigger Nate. Ha Ha Ha!"

The slur slapped out her response, "Do not say that!"

"No! I don't mean it in a bad way."

"There is no good way. You are stupid."

"Haven't you seen the sign on Palomar Mountain, on the road, Nigger Nate Grade? He was an old guy. I mean more than one hundred! He was the only one not White up there. He was the uh...uh...uh... deception that makes the rule or whatever that saying is."

"But now there is me, and my brother Jude, Ahanu."

"Dios! Three? Like an invasion," he laughed and cranked the radio.

"R-r-r-r, Ja! Ja! Sing with me baby. Bam-ba-bamba. Bam-ba-bamba. Bam-ba-bamba..."

"Bam-ba-bamba. Bam-ba-bamba. Bam-ba-bamba..." she sang.

In Del Mar, a neighbor would have called the police, but their noise was absorbed into Logan Heights. The rapid, rolling Spanish language pulsed into the air at a hundred and fifty beats a minute. The Garcia's porch functioned as a second living room complete with a coffee table, lamps and a painting on the stucco wall. Rosalita, two young cousins, Chico and Pepe and Tony's pals always seemed to be there. Hebe saw a different side of Rosalita because as the only girl in the casa, and a petite one at that, she had to be bossy to get the boys to help her, and if they didn't she was not above hollering one inch away from their noses. All the household chores, shopping and meals fell on her slim shoulders. Hebe enjoyed helping. One afternoon they finished early and she talked Rosalita into gathering acorns in the yard. They sat together as she and Wénise used to and began the process of peeling, oven-drying and hand grinding the meats into meal. Rosalita kept asking her what she was making.

"It's delicious. Wénise, my great grandmother taught me."

"Sure is a lot of work."

"Patience is one of the most important ingredients in anything according to Wénise. You'll see."

Tony and the cousins peeked in and insisted they were "not going to eat that stuff."

"Good. More for us," Hebe quipped.

Rosalita rolled her eyes. By evening, the drying, leaching, grinding and mixing process was complete, and they made fritters. When she sat the golden circles next to the frijoles and tomatoes on the plate, a sense of pride welled up in her.

"Only special people enjoy these," she told the young Garcias. "But if you don't like them, I will take them."

Rosalita, who had sampled the fritters in the kitchen, loved them, and snatched one up immediately.

"I already know, I am special people," she blurted.

The cousins also bit into the cakes right away and made yummy sounds. Tony inserted a bear-size hunk in his mouth and neatly placed several more on a dish for his friends yammering outside by their cars. Sated, the cousins took off. Hebe told Rosalita more about Wénise and the New England woods while they washed the dishes. Tony barged in.

"¿Dónde están las cosas?"

"You ate some and took the rest to your amigos."

He turned on the high heel of his black Spanish boot and left in a staccato of footsteps. Nearly every single time Tony drove her to the Garcia house, he demanded "the cosas" which were very labor intensive.

"It would be easier if they were bigger."

"Mucho más grande Hebita."

She and Rosalita made a point of gathering acorns and squirreling them away in a closet. When time permitted and "the spirit moved" them, they carried out the initial steps of peeling, grinding, and leaching in order to have the flour ready. They did not wish the preparation of food for Tony to interfere with their more important pastimes of sewing, daydreaming about dates with boys, experimenting with hair-styles or doing their nails, though Hebe was only allowed to wear clear polish. Rosalita had a crush on a junior at the high school, "a white boy," she added who she was "praying" would take her to the dance.

"What dance?" Hebe asked wincing in pain as Rosalita plucked her eyebrows.

"A little pain for a lot of boys," she told her.

"I don't need a boy this much."

"You are a baby. Wait until you have a boyfriend. You will change your mind."

With a finishing touch of mascara, she rotated Hebe toward the mirror. In her place was an older girl, a prettier girl.

"And don't sit like that all floppy sloppy like that Hebita," she complained and showed her how to sit, pose and hold a boy's hand. hand when he lit her cigarette.

Though Hebe didn't smoke, she followed Rosalita's instructions to the letter because she was older and, based on the photo album, more experience. In every shot, a boy had his arm around her shoulder or her waist, or he was leaning into the frame to be near her. She must have known something, though she had mentioned "cousin," quite a few times. The album was a thick as her bible, and, in addition to Rosalita's admirer's, it held the entire population of Garcia's, the paternal grand-parents in Northern California; the "crazy uncle," the spinster aunt, ten more married aunts and uncles and cousins by the dozens. A loose photo of a bride and her bridesmaid caught her eye because they were incredibly young, children, maybe eight or ten. She put it down and tried to make sense of it, and picked it back up. The heebie jeebies ran through her which made her scream which startled Rosalita. She slapped her playfully.

"Don't do that! You scared me.".

"She looks like a bride but she is a flower girl, right?"

"Idiota! You are not Catholica, but...every body in todo el mundo knows that is a picture of the confirmation in the church."

Rosalita beat her with the flimsy photo.

"Then where are they? What happened to them?"

The answer was a wide-eyed question, "Are you one of those crazies who just knows things?" She bounced down and extended her open palm, "Tell me when I am gonna get married."

Hebe waved her off. Rosalita changed the subject by pulling her communion dress out.

"Mira! My auntie made it. Come on, try," she urged and helped Hebe into the dress backwards to make room for her breasts.

"You're gonna get all the boys with these boobies,. Rosalita swelled up her chest and posed. "That's how you show them without showing them."

"How do you know?"

Rosalita grabbed her by the wrist and they blew into a room across the hall. It was dark; the windows were closed. The intense energy redolent with a blend of musky perspiration, cigarette smoke, bubble gum and cologne indicated they were in Tony's room. Rosalita turned the skeleton key in the lock. From under the bed, she slid a stack of girlie magazines and a bottle. Hebe watched her suck down a healthy gulp before she extended it to her. The clear liquid lit her throat on fire and stole her breath. Rosalita squeaked at her inexperience and patted her gently on the back when she coughed.

"I forgot you was a gringa."

"I am not a gringa."

"Why are you so touchy?"

"I am only half a gringa."

Rosalita slapped herself on the forehead, "What are you talking about? Gringa means you are foreigner."

"Then I am really not a gringa!."

"In Logan Heights you are."

Rosalita opened one of Tony's drawers. The saucy, half-clad women were clearly the models for Rosalita's poses. The Mescal burned Hebe's inhibitions away, and she studied them.

"¡Muy cachondo," Rosalita sang out holding up a pair of red, silk women's panties.

"Why does Tony have those?"

"Probably going to give them to his girlfriend."

"Why does he buy them underwear?"

"No. No. No, calzones." She flapped Hebe's skirt up and burst out laughing. "Ja ja, ja! White cotton. You are such a little girl."

To see herself in the mirror on the dresser, Rosalita stood on the bed.

"I want to try."

Hebe took another drink before they mimicked, with great difficulty, the women's positions. Eventually, they tumbled into an untidy heap of limbs momentarily embracing before tumbling into the fabric puffs. Already on the border of drunkenness, they didn't hear the key clink on the floor. Angry that the girls had trespassed but amused by their condition, Tony leaned his tall form cockily in the frame with his male friends and cousins crushed up behind him.

"1 didn't invite you in here," he enunciated with his usual machismo and waved the boys away.

Rosalita made it across the hall, but Tony grabbed Hebe. He closed the door.

"I didn't' mean to scare you, Mamasita."

With the deliberateness of a rancher inspecting a heifer he ran his eyes over her body which was spilling over the too-small Communion dress she had on backwards. He grabbed her upper arm, sniffed the nape of her neck and squinted at her mascara and lipstick. In a seductive voice, he wanted to know who she was.

"Are you the girl I brung here?"

"You see I am."

"No I don't. I see a lot of make up."

Their eyelashes almost touched. He let go of her arm, but magnetism held them in place. He sucked air through his teeth and broke away.

"Niña. Niña. Niña! Wash your face. I can't take you home like that."

Hebe watched the sun split into two in Tony's sunglass lenses. He tugged on her skirt and she scooted over on the seat next to him. She could hear him chewing his gum. They drove onto a small road to a stucco mansion atop a hill and waited for the gate to open. He kissed her lightly on the lips and slid his hand along the length of her ribs. She pulled away.

"That is not polite."

The unfamiliar rejection stunned him. "You don't you want to kiss me? Me!?"

She took his gum out of her mouth and threw it on the ground. "Disgusting."

A woman appeared in the brightly lit entranceway and, standing at the gate, supervised Tony taking a large box from the trunk and carrying it in the house. Hebe peeked in the rear view mirror to see if she knew who she was. Her dramatically arched eyebrows were all she saw and all she needed to see to identify Mrs. Gonzales. On his way back to the car, she tugged his sleeve to bring her closer and unwittingly jut her pelvis forward. Neither touched the other, though hey were almost eyelash to eyelash. The stealth with which they hung there reminded her of two hungry wild cats at the zoo who had been mistakenly thrown but one piece of meat. Mrs. Gonzales moved. Tony remained perfectly immobile. She tucked money in his pocket, but he still didn't budge which bothered her. He grabbed her flank in the crook of his arm with such suddenness that she whimpered in surprise and he took Hebe's breath away. Just as quickly, he snatched himself back and got in the car. Mrs. Gonzalez dotted woozily across the lawn.

"That's my stepfather's client."

"Gita? With her husband's money, she can be a lot of people's client," Then with some hesitation, he added, "She lets me use this car whenever I want."

"How many cars does she have?"

He backed up to the driveway where two more cars gleaming luxuriously.

"A Rolls-Royce Silver Cloud and a Lincoln Continental Mark II, like Elvis Presley has. The V-8 engine..."

"Which one is the same as Elvis Presley?"

"I just told you," he snapped sharply.

"Barking again? I don't like you any more."

"Sorry. Sorry. I forgot you don't know nothing. The brown one is the Rolls Royce; the black one is the Elvis car."

Except for his gum chewing, the ride home was quiet. When they arrived, he took it out and placed his lips to hers while he nudged at the edge of her cotton underwear with his knuckle. She felt light-headed, but she didn't respond; she didn't know how. He leaned back to interpret her behavior. His ego had dismissed the possibility that she was not attracted to him, so he asked her age.

"Almost eleven," she bragged.

"No mames!" He emitted a grunt and let his head drop. It hit the horn, and the beep snapped him upright, "Hay carbon," he winced and adjusted the rear view mirror.

"So you don't like me anymore."

"Tony likes all pretty girls." He traced her breasts with his finger, "But I have seventeen. I am a man."

"Seventeen? That is a teenager! A man is twenty-nine, like my friend Hans."

Jealousy beat wildly in his possessive Mexican heart.

"Who do you know who is twenty-nine?" He stared at a photo she presented from her plastic pocketbook. "That's a mujer. Look at all that hair. Who else is in there?" He grabbed her bag. "This is your father," he announced nodding in approval and held the picture beside her face. "You look like him. Who is this?"

"His name is Kit," she told him amused by his ignorance and grabbed her photographs out of his hand. "You are a rude teenage boy."

"Sorry. Come on!" he pleaded. "We will go to a party. But, don't say your age," he advised and kissed her.

She didn't remember getting out of the car or her feet touching the ground. Her mother's potential slap-happy reaction settled in her shoes and made them two heavy weights which slammed the ground into her feet. Prepared to face her wrath for having been gone all day, she walked in. She didn't say anything, not one word, not then and not the next day. Silence was the punishment. Art claimed not to notice anything.

When Margarita arrived, she mentioned the situation to her.

"Are you sure *she* is not talking to you?" she asked with a wink and a smile. "Maybe *you* are not talking to her."

Hebe shrugged. For three days, her mother meted out a punishment of silence and ghosted past her, but Hebe pretended not to see her. She had letters from Anne and Hans. In his last letter he wrote, "If I was a magician, I would put all the people I love together in one place. I live with several good friends in a big house. It's great, so when you come, call us. Everyone wants to meet you." He had printed the number of miles, 2,582, between the city of San Diego on one coast and Boston on the other. He was much farther than Tony, a mere twenty miles over the border in Mexico and scheduled to return on Friday. Anticipating him to keep his promise to take her somewhere, she occupied herself sewing an off the shoulder dress. He had gone to Mexico, and she missed him and the warm, loving familial fold of the Garcia household and the girl she became when she was there, 'Hebita", a pretty, powdered Latina. By Friday morning, her mother was speaking to her again, and Tony showed up. "Be ready when I come to pick you up," was his way of asking her out. Stars exploded out of her eyes as she refrained from jumping up and down. As soon as he was gone, she called Rosalita who bubbled over with excitement of Hebe dating her brother and she leaped into the future.

"Mi cuñada."

"Sister-in-law?! Rosa, it is one night, not a marriage proposal."

"You never know. Don't forget how I showed you to do the make up. Exactly like that. I seen the girls he likes."

Hebe pinned her hair up, laid her cosmetics on the vanity and practiced applying mascara and eyeliner. The door swung open. In staggered the monster who, once thoroughly soused, seeped out of her mother. With her hair coiffed and made up, Gaye-Lee did not recognize Hebe, and she cut her eyes to Margarita.

"Who is this? What the Hell is she doing in my house?"

"It's your daughter, Hebe," Margarita explained.

Though only ten and a half, Hebe was 5' 6", and Gaye had to look up to scrutinize her face.

"Are you going to a costume party? Just who the Hell are you supposed to be?" she asked.

"She was just playing like my Rosalita when..."

"Oh shut up. What do you know? Call Kutty in here" she demanded.

"You mean Señor Art..."

"Who? No. I mean my husband Kutty! How in the God damn Hell do you work for someone and not know this name?" she asked standing in one place while her body wobbled around unsteadily in an elliptical path She regained her composure and smiled with half her mouth, "I'm sorry Patricia...Forgive me."

Patricia?! She was the girl who worked in the house in Cambridge a couple of years ago.

"I'm sorry," Gaye-Lee repeated to Margarita and tried to pat her arm but ended up running her fingers down her torso before she spoke excruciatingly slowly, "I want you to get my love, her father, Ahanu's father. Bring him in here. He can talk to her, maybe in Wamp-a-no-ag. Vamp-a-no-ag," she slurred playfully. "That is how my mutti pronounces it, with V, but it's Wamp-a-no-ag, isn't it? Wamp-a-no-ag. Wamp-a-no-ag. Wamp-a-no-ag," she repeated as she executed a sloppy, little powwow dance.

When she righted herself, he mouth and facial muscles indicated she was laughing but there was no sound. Hebe was absolutely stupefied, and she could see by Margarita's expression, she was not certain what to do.

"It's okay Hebe," she muttered under her breath, "I thin', your madre, she is borracho, but really really really."

"Shhh. No talking during the Grand Entry. Kutty," she sang out sweetly, and goose bumps covered Hebe.

It was the exact tone with which she had called her father when they lived in Cambridge, and had not heard since they left. Gaye-Lee's eyes fell on Margarita.

"Why are you still here? You were supposed to fetch him," she reminded her testily. "Must I do everything myself?" she asked loudly and made the mistake of moving too quickly in her intoxicated condition.

She stumbled onto the bed. A pin from Hebe's dress stuck her and she hissed and raged and violently ripped the fabric.

"My dress!" she cried and lunged at her to grab it..

Ever so quietly but forcefully Margarita pleaded in Hebe's ear.

"No! You can make another. Please..." Margarita pleaded.

As soon as her mother made eye contact with her, she stopped. Hebe could see her struggling to place her face.

"Get out of here," she shrieked, recoiled from her, threw down the dress and picked up the scissors.

'Margarita made the sign of the cross and cried out with an urgency that left no room for interpretation. 'Run muchacha! Run away!" "Run!"

Hebe blew down the stairs and out to the beach where the brisk, winter wind whipped down her updo. Mukker trotted down the sand carrying a stick which he dropped at her feet. Quaking inside and out, she tried to convince herself what had just happened had not just happened. Mukker barked instructions at her, thinking she had forgotten their game, but she sat down. He left the stick, and thumped down next to her, a gesture whose sweetness almost tempted her. She explained that she "just didn't feel like playing today." Good friend that he was, he stayed, and they watch the ocean roll. She sobbed and then cried out loud. Mukker whimpered, and then sat upright and released an elongated howl which made her laugh. After a while, she threw the stick for him. Hebe was certain her mother would be resurrected by evening for the plans she had made with Art, so she played with Mukker until his owner whistled for him.

"Hello Hebe," she chirped and scrooped down the stairs in a cherry red taffeta cocktail dress as if she was oblivious to the earlier and twirled around for Art whipping up "two for the road." From her window, Hebe watched the water rippling in the swimming pool below. She knew Art was in the doorframe because she heard his lighter snap shut.

'Your mother and I think you might get along better in Boston with Hilde, your Grandmother Livingston."

What about Tony?

"There you will have the ability to cultivate friendships that are more…in keeping with your family's social status, and the schools are better."

Dumbfounded by his proposal, she brooded over her future and shuddered envisioning herself marching interminably though the streets behind Grandma Livy like a little dog, *a tired little dog*. Other than twice a year, on Christmas and her birthday, she had had no contact with her.

Now I am supposed to live with her! What do I tell Rosalita? Because my mother calls Tony a bad influence, so we can not be friends!

Rosalita sent her a letter in which she apologized for "what I did. What is it? Tony is mad because I made the acorn cakes, and they were not good like yours."

How stupid. We live so close, and we have to write.

The idea of another long, afternoon in isolation was unbearable. As soon as sleep carried the family away, she snuck into Art's office and walked around his wallet on the desk a dozen times before she picked it up and copied the numbers for the cab company and the expense account he used for everything. She arranged to be picked up at the intersection of North Rios and Lomas Santa Fe Drive which was a five minute walk from the school and dropped at the Broadway Pier. In the morning, she mentioned "an after school thing," to extend her hours away from the house. She was antsy waiting in plain sight at the intersection. A car slowed down, and "Get outta here, you spic!" was chucked from the window with a rotten orange, and she worried that the cab might not stop, but it did. At the pier stood in line for a ticket until the cab was out of sight, and then took the bus to Horton Plaza. Sneaking around was exhausting, so she sat on a bench by the fountain and contemplated hurrying home.

To what? My room? It's too early for Rosalita to be home. I'll go to Balboa Park.

A throng of men in uniforms and street clothes were boarding a lumpy, monochrome blue Air Force bus. The officers at the rear were reading documents on a clipboard. A gust of wind whipped them into the air where they whirled around and then wended to the ground and Horton fountain. Bystanders happily joined the officers in retrieving them, and the activity converted the men's previously serious conversation into amused banter. One paper smacked Hebe in the head. CONFIDENTIAL was stamped in large, red, uppercase letters and United States Air Force in black lending importance to what was a strange cryptic map. The bus was pulling out.

"Wait!" she cried running behind it. "Sirs! Excuse me!"

The blasting diesel engine muted her plea, but she caught up to the bus when it stalled and banged on the side. It lunged and jostled the men off their feet; hats, shirt sleeves and hands pressed against the window. There was the distinctive tunuppasog.

"Nosh? Nosh!"

Intuition told her that little snapping tunuppasog scar was not a figment of wishful thinking but her father's hand. Its image spurred her to the library. While conducting a careful search of dozens of books for the places on the map, words from the deep recesses of her mind, bubbled to the surface: Dreamland, Air Force facility, Q-clearance, and

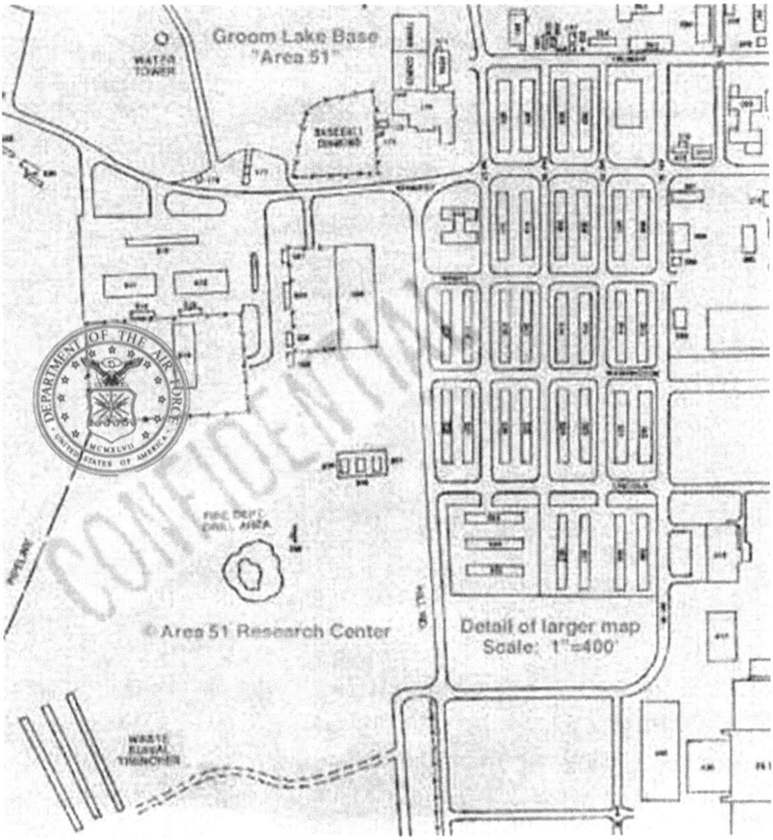

The Map

Area 51, but she didn't know why. Surrounded by the chaos of open books, she was a perfect picture of confusion; the librarian offered help.

"I have to find an address to return an Air Force document."

"Official stationary has the address on top. Otherwise," she tapped on a page, "write to headquarters in Washington D. C."

Air Force Chief of Staff General Thomas White
1670 Air Force Pentagon, Washington, DC

Hello Mr. General Thomas White,
My name is Hebe Holmes. I live on Sandy
Lane in Del Mar, California. My father's name
is Kuttiomp Holmes. He is a smart air scientist.
We lived in Cambridge. Is he on your air base
Groom Lake "Area 51?" Confidential.
I found your map in Horton Square.
There is no address. Where may I return it?

Merry Christmas Sir.
From, Miss Hebe Holmes
on December 13, 1957

To keep the map from falling into the wrong hands, she did not include it with her letter to the Chief of Staff. Unsure as to whether she should be so bold, she hesitated in front of the mailbox. The lid squeaked open. A man, who assumed she could not reach, politely took it from her, mailed it with his and then tipped his hat and left. Done. It was sent. Wuttootchìkkìnneasin Nippawus burned off nagging speculations about the palm and the map and her fidgets over being caught playing hooky.

What's the point of playing hooky if I don't have fun?

Her favorite bench was in the park was in the dense, cool shade where she viewed passersby as actors as she used to on her balcony in

Cambridge. A fantastically coiffed blonde in black sunglasses and a scarf was already there, and they exchanged a smile. A frisky puppy assumed they wanted to meet him and fawn over his cuteness and charged toward them, dragging an old Negro man in the process. He wore a Panama hat and big-waist pants held up with suspenders. He stuck his rear end in the space between them and lowered it to the bench with the aid of his cane. Satisfied with his accomplishment, he grinned and lit a half-smoked cigar he had pulled from his rumpled jacket pocket, and he began to talk.

"He's a gift for my great-grandson—a surprise—I'm keeping him at my place. Only have him one mo' day."

The threesome's shared love of dogs drew them into conversation, and then he gave his eye-witness account of Balboa Park's highlights over time.

"Didn't used to be much here, the animals; it was just a park. Took ten years to build the California Pacific Exposition; it was all about Spain. The conquistadors and kings were on the Prado. You could meet them. And there was a model Panama Canal, not a train set size. You could walk in it. President Roosevelt and his wife came. They were as close to me as that tree.—The next one was 1935, that's a little clearer in my mind. It was about progress or the economy," he shook his head, "but the country was in a depression. "That building and that one," he singled them out with his cane, "I watched them go up. And…," mischief glinted in his eyes, and he puffed on his cigar, "they made a garden. Hasn't been so much doin's about a garden since Adam and Eve," he grinned, "cuz girls was in there, and they were naked!"

"Naked? the woman exclaimed.

"As the day they was born," he confirmed and savored his carefully preserved vision. "Don't get the wrong idea. The girls weren't sellin' nothin'. No one went in there with 'em. A high fence went the whole way round, but with holes, not no stingy, good-for-nothin' holes for your eye. They was a good size. Your whole face would fit. I know. I paid my money and I saw those girls—couple or three times I went without my wife," he confessed with a smile so big, Hebe could see almost all of his teeth.

The puppy had chased two squirrels up nearby trees, pawed at their laps and the bench repeatedly and barked himself out and curled up by the bench.

"What's a garden have to do with the economy?" Hebe asked.

"I don't know. But the newspaper reported the biggest heap of money made was from charging change for a peek at girlie goodies," he grinned.

"Like burlesque?" the blonde asked.

"That's right. Oldest game in town."

"You sure know a lot mister. Mind if I ask you something?"

"Mind? How could I mind? Old people just keep on living so young people will ask us questions. The problem is they usually don't. Ask."

"Did you ever hear of a place, Groom Lake or..."

"Matter of fact, I have. A old Shoshone friend of mine, brings me some herbs from over that way. He mentioned the U. S. government got trailers big as buildings and guards every which way. But Honey, that's hundreds of miles away. Why?"

"Just a name blowing in the wind."

The woman took a photo of the sleeping puppy, and the old man asked to take one of them. They helped him to his feet. The puppy sat up in anticipation of leaving.

"I hate to leave gorgeous girls like you, but I have things to do."

In parting, he touched his fingers to his hat brim and toddled heavily away.

Hebe and the blonde agreed he was "a nice old man." Out of "curiosity," the woman asked if she had runaway.

"It is the middle of a school day. "

"Not really. I am going to visit my friends in Logan Heights."

"I could use the company if you want a lift.

On the way, Hebe talked about Wénise and her father. She showed her his picture.

"Oh he is a fine man...perfect...tall, dark and handsome, as they say."

"And brilliant people say. He is a special aero something engineer," I was certain I saw him on a bus today."

"Doesn't he live back east?"

"I think so. I'm not sure."

"Oh gee, that's too bad."

"No it isn't. He is doing top-secret work, for government."

"He must appreciate your understanding his absence. Scientists and politicians work around the clock."

"They do?"

"Sure. They don't have much time for us, the ones they love, but they need us." Marilyn pulled over. "It was nice to meet you."

"You too,"

Hebe smiled and just sat there. While waiting for her to get out, the woman chatted about her dog, Los Angeles and a man she met, but the tender forsaken air of her passenger touched her heart.

"You know what I found out?" Hebe shook her head. "I found out time is an invisible soldier. He slays people's patience, their days, and their lives. People always try to catch him, to slow him down or stop him, but they can't. Time is a terrible thing.

"Not always. It kills bad memories."

"You're right, but you know what?"

Hebe gazed at her mesmerized.

"Time has one big enemy."

"Who?"

"Not who, what? Loneliness. Loneliness can beat time. It eats time and grows big and fat. Loneliness eats light and common sense, and if you are not careful?—Loneliness will eat you too," she cautioned. It goes after, rich, poor, fat, skinny, even dogs."

"Dogs!"

Marilyn nodded, and they sat in contemplative silence.

"Did you read that in a book?"

"No. Why?"

"It is a really smart thing for a woman as pretty as you to say."

"Gee thank you." I hope it doesn't find a sweet kid like you. Here." She handed her a card, "But if it does, promise you will call me."

"Thank you. I promise," she glanced at the card, "Marilyn

IX

"*No la Chava!*"

The perpetual confetti of vivacious sound welcomed her to the Garcia's neighborhood. December was a little cooler, but they still conducted life outside. Weeks ago, Christmas dawned in the colorful decorations heightening the festive and religious atmosphere. An elaborate crèche sprawled under a makeshift manger on every lawn complete with the Three Wise Men, angels, cattle sheep and often a devil or a mermaid which she had never seen anywhere else. The boys waved from down the block and called, "Rosalita! Hebita, she is coming!" and ran excitedly toward her in welcome. Tony lifted his head from under the hood of his car, strode to the middle of the sidewalk and stood with his arms spread wide beckoning her to run to him which she did. Rosalita slapped her shoulders.

"Why you didn't call me or write me? Nothing?"

Hebe yammered about the threat of being sent back east, and Rosalita had news about her "dream boy," who had turned into a nightmare when he became a reality and tried to grope her.

"¡Cállate," she warned Tony before a word came out of his mouth and turned to Hebe, "He's gonna say, 'That's what you get for going with gringos. He hates them."

"But you called me a gringa…."

"Rosa you don't know. Hebe ain't a gringa. Hebe is a Meztisa."

"I am?"

"Yes, half Indian, but that's okay." He called to everyone, "Vamanos! Sunday drive."

They loaded themselves into Tony's red bullet, and he shot them down the streets in pursuit of recreation along the roads which eventually led them across the border to decoration festooned Tijuana. Green and red stars cut from aluminum twinkled from their strands overhead. Open markets brimmed with woven blankets, straw hats and leather pocketbooks hanging over burlap bags of rice, baskets of corn meal, beans and vegetables. Merchants with their handicrafts in their hands rushed to the flashy, new, red car carefully cruising along the crowded way in search of a place to park. Young men shouted out in approval or ran their work-calloused hands over the vehicle inching along among people and an occasional donkey. The boys grew impatient, so Tony pulled over and they climbed over the sides to go visit a favorite uncle. Rosalita was going to visit friends and Hebe if she wanted to join her.

"She doesn't want to meet anybody," Tony snapped and draped his arm around Hebe.

"Me neither. I will stay with you," Rosalita teased.

He searched through Rosalita's purse slung over her short arm and took three tubes of lipstick which he held in front of Hebe. Rosalita gestured for her to take one.

"Now! Lárgate!" The force of his command moved Rosalita back "Etllamé a mamá," he reminded her.

Tony bought hair combs from a woman in the street, unbraided Hebe's hair, swept it up and put in the combs. Her eyes twinkled with appreciation. Then he ordered her to take off her socks and "put on some of that red lipstick," to age herself a little. Arm in arm with his girl-lady, he strutted though the streets like a lord. She was elated. Being near him, she had the sensation that she had eaten sunshine. Women threw him smiles and he ignored them. Hebe snapped several shots with her camera. She had her fingers crossed when Tony took a photo of her in an over-sized, black velvet sombrero.

"Viva Mexico!" she cried and threw her hands up.

The merchant was perturbed when they didn't buy it. To appease him, Tony bought a jangling pair of colorful earrings.

'That's for you Hebita. You give me a kick the way you get so excited about things, little things."

"Maybe this is the best day of my whole long life."

"Of course, it is. You are with me."

At a stall in the city, The first stop they made was the Cathedral of Our Lady of Guadalupe. Uncharacteristically, Tony humbled himself and bowed his head in prayer. He pulled the edge of her dress, so she would kneel which she did not.

"Aren't you going to pray?"

Tony crossed himself in the aisle His mighty machismo reinstated his head to its chin-up position about a half a block from the church. She had been hungry for a different view and Tijuana was a smorgasbord of dishes, the smallest of which was a Chihuahua in a miniature Mexican sombrero. The Mexican hat dance was elaborate and not at all like the one learned in school. Tony paused in front of a poster for a bullfight. The image of the bull stabbed all the way through with long sharp sticks upset her, and she tugged on Tony.

"You don't have to see it. I am not in the mood for that today."

They stopped to have a cool drink and Tony invited the Mariachi band to their table. Hebe grinned from ear to ear.

This is the craziest Christmas ever.

Unable to hear over the music, she sat contentedly, drank in the scene and amused herself with Tony's rapturous table manners. Margarita was proud of him and called him a gourmand. Last year after Christmas dinner when he had gone, Gaye-Lee summed up as "a pig." Grunting was, in fact, part of his vocalized appreciation of holiday fare or any. When he was served chicken, he admired its appearance, hung his head over it, inhaled its aroma and separated a leg or thigh. He waggled it in front of his face as if teasing himself and then licked the juicy meat and sauce. Invariably, it ran down his chin bringing out his unusually long tongue to retrieve any escaped drops. Not a shred of the meat remained on the bone which he sucked. The display fascinated and excited Hebe. She didn't know exactly why only that his sniffing, lapping and pawing awakened a fantasy in her for being a chicken part. She watched him in the Mexican cantina and waited for him to run his muscular napkin over his face. When he did, she burst out laughing.

"Your tongue is so big," she remarked.

His chest puffed up in acceptance of the great compliment.

"Gracias mi amor. And then ordered, "Coca Cola et un ron y Coca Cola."

The jukebox numbers were punched to a popular tune. The whole room let out a cry of approval. Tony escorted Hebe to the floor under the attentive gaze of the young wolves around the perimeter.

"Abuzados he cabrones," he warned.

Oblivious as to why he might be keeping an eye on them, she followed. One stepped out and discreetly knocked her purse off her shoulder and then replaced it too caringly for Tony's comfort. When he saw his fingers touch her skin he seethed.

"Esta es mi vieja, vamos entendiendos putos?" he asked quite close to his face.

He twirled her around and caught her on his arm.

One beat later, Hebe and Tony were in the eye of the lights strobing on the human carousel of figures. To slow songs, they ground up and down and round and round but to the fast ones, they undulated their bodies like ribbon candy in the making. The physical sensations filled her with lightheartedness. Perspiring, but exhilarated and filled with adoring trust let, she fell freely into Tony's arms and eagerly accepted his dance-floor exploration of her body. She could have lingered in the secure comfort the embrace gave her forever, but he gently whirled her and playfully slapped at the edge of her skirt. He never lost contact; their fingers touched the whole time and she felt connected to him. When her eyes burned from the smoke, she was glad; it meant this was not a dream. Two songs later, Tony led her outside to could cool off. Only the silver wrapper of his gum crumpling in his hand and their ardent inhalations interrupted the momentary silence of their spot. Tony leaned against a post; Hebe leaned against his torso. Together, they let out a sigh of contentment. He rested his chin on her head and focused on the distant shadows beneath the trees.

"Hey! Hey! "Ya valios madre."

The volume of Tony's voice escalated as he became aware his car was not where he knew he had parked it. He sprinted down the road shouting at the top of his lungs, "Ya valses madre."

Hebe followed him to a clearing under the trees. Mishquáishim growled by her side, and she buried her fingers in his fur while Tony threw his arms up and stomped the ground with both feet.

"Que pedo con el coche?" he hollered. "Hijos de puta!"

The car was gone. Nervously she moved toward the lighted street. From there, she saw several flashlights shining in the shadows and the three policemen who carried them. She didn't understand what they were saying. Tony put his hands in the air and one of them shined the light right in his face; his eyes were wide with fear.

What do I do?

Mishquáishim nudged the back of her knees with his nose. The last time she ignored him, she got knocked out by a tree. She took off running but stopped because she had no idea where she was going.

In a few hours, it will be light. I'll find that Guadalupe church.

A harsh Spanish command whipped her, and she ran.

"Perate. Hebita!" Tony yelled.

She could not stop. A split second later, Tony pleaded.

"No! Don't!' No la chava! No la chava!'"

Not the girl? That's me. I am the girl, she told herself but continued running until she heard Peskhómmin! Blam!"

Having fired a warning, the officer trained his gun on her.

"¿Por qué no te voy a detener?" he asked her.

Her knees were knocking together.

"¿Conoces a este cabrón?"

Conoces a este cabrón. She was unable to process Spanish, and she wanted to let that be known, but when she opened her mouth, English didn't come out either. The officer pulled out his handcuffs, but her large, dark, liquid eyes brimming with innocence disarmed him.

¿Lo conoces?" he asked but she stared blankly, so he pointed to Tony. "Ese hombre. Lo conoces?"

"Margarita's son," she replied softly tipping her head.

Handcuffing her small, thin wrists was impossible, so he tied them with hemp rope and escorted her and Tony into the back seat. Tony spoke to the police, and she heard, "Americana."

"They think I stole the car—and you!" he whispered. "You told them I didn't, right? Right?!" Tears rolling over her cheekbones stemmed his questions and he assured her, "Everything's going to be okay."

"No. No it is not. It is never going to be okay, Tony."

Befote he could reply Gaye-Lee had opened the police car door and dragged Hebe out with such force that her earring fell off. With her hands bound, she unable to pick it up and unable to fight back which made Gaye-Lee stop.

"Why is she tied up?" she asked and called Art's attention to the rope.

"My good man, she has committed no crime. Tony is the one who kidnapped…"

'Kidnapped?!"

The border officer raised his pistol to strike Tony. Hebe charged and head butt him in the stomach. Art yanked her back and Gaye-Lee slapped her but Hebe didn't feel a thing. Art untied her and tossed the rope on the ground. She ran to Tony who had managed to unlock one cuff. He caught her in his arms, and in front of her mother and Art and Grandmother Moon, he kissed her long and passionately. No one interfered. With his love on her lips, she held her chin up and walked to Gaye-Lee and Art but stopped when she heard him sing out, "Mi amor'!" The impulse to run back pulsed in her veins until a brown Rolls Royce beckoned her attention. It pulled in by the red convertible, and the ribbon-candy silhouette of Gita Gonzalez emerged. Casting her eyes

around the scene, she met Art's gaze, and they acknowledged each other in a barely perceptible glance before he directed the oblivious Gaye-Lee toward their car. Tony's voice slashed the hot, dusty night.

"Hebita! Te amo!"

He raised his uncuffed hands over his head and sprang up and down like a winning prizefighter. Silently, she waved and then trailed behind her parents, despondent and suddenly exhausted. Gravel hit the underside of the Cadillac as it crunched to the road to the United States.

I am glad Gita got Tony out. Who else could he call? *But I wonder... How did they find us?*

***

Other than Jude, no one in the house spoke to Hebe until Christmas Eve.

Art appeared at her door and punctuated his words by knocking his ring on the door frame.

"Good news. You're going to Boston on Monday'. We'll have Hector bring the suitcases so you can pack."

Hector? So they replaced Tony with that old man. It's not right to make him work on such a big day for him. "Tomorrow is Christmas Art. Señor Hector is probable at Mass. Christmas I can get them myself."

"Sure kiddo."

He and gave her a box from Margarita. There was mascara and lipstick from Rosalita; the earring she had dropped at the border and a golden necklace from Tony and a crocheted shawl from Margarita. When she flung it over her shoulders, a manila envelope fell out. It read, in Margarita's hand, "Hebita, I found your mail."

I knew you were keeping these from me Mother!

Inside were letters and holiday cards from Anne in France and Kutty from the unknown. He explained he might be "invisible for a while longer," that his research required him to be "incommunicado," and after a message to Jude, he signed, "Cowammáunsh," I love you. "Cowammáunsh," she said aloud. The last letter she opened was on official Air Force stationary. It was a response to the inquiry she had sent ten days ago, but it did not include any actual answers. Not one sentence gave a clue about where her father was at all, and it completely denied the existence of "Area 51."

Maybe the map is part of a game the military is playing. I don't know

It was the first thing she packed.

No la Chava!

Office of the Secretary

DEPARTMENT OF THE AIR FORCE
WASHINGTON DC 20330-1000

Miss Hebe Holmes
Sandy Lane
Del Mar, California 92014

Dear Miss Holmes,

This responds to your letter to the Secretary of the Air Force regarding "Area 51."

Neither the Air Force nor the Department of Defense owns or operates any location known as "Area 51." There are a variety of activities, some of which are classified throughout what is often called the Air Force's Nellie Range Complex. There is an operating location near Groom Dry Lake. Specific activities and operations conducted on the Nellis Range, both past and present, remain classified and cannot be discussed publicly.

We hope this information is helpful.

Sincerely,

J.A. RAMES, Major, USAF
Chief, White House Inquiry Branch
Office of Legislative Liaison

WRIGHT BROTHERS FLYING
FIRST SUCCESSFUL PLANE

MODERN AIR FORCE BOMBER
AND FIGHTER PLANE

WASHINGTON
DEC.
17
9:00 A.M.
1957
D. C.

50th Anniversary of
U.S. AIR FORCE
FIRST DAY OF ISSUE

Miss Hebe Holmes
Sandy Lane
Del Mar, California 92014

- 131 -

Angelic little Jude's effervescent excitement over Santa Claus having arrived saved Christmas from being another tense day on Sandy Lane. His glee was positively infectious and Gaye-lee and Art laughed in spite of themselves as he squealed and stamped after each gift he opened. Art examined the cufflinks she gave him, one a protractor, the other part of a ruler with sincere appreciation.

"Thanks Hiawatha."

"Sure," she replied in acceptance of his fossilized error. Gaye-Lee had not opened her gifts, a book and the framed image of the Virgin that Tony had given her. Gaye-Lee had not opened hers.

Unable to fight back the sadness any longer, she went for a walk and dissolved into tears on the sand. Mukker pawed at her sympathetically. He laid his big square head on her leg until his owners called him.

"Bye Mukker!"

The next day, she was filling the two brown suitcases; Jude tottered in to tell her, "I love you."

She held him for a long time.

Art came to announce that he and Gaye-Lee had brought Chinese food home for dinner, "and your mother is in a state. Best to leave her alone."

That night, Hebe crawled into her sheets emotionally spent.

She wished she could hold onto the hands of her clock in order to provide her mother more time to get dressed. The clock ticked and ticked and ticked, but Gaye-lee didn't come. Hebe departed hopeful to the last moment that her mother would come and hold her, even if it was a grim, half-hearted embrace. Gaye-Lee didn't appear. Hebe left and pretended to look at the clouds while she stole a glimpse at the window. Wuttootchìkkìnneasin Nippawus drew her attention to the glint of the pink-gold tone frame of the Virgin of Guadalupe. Just as she was about to get in the car, she heard Margarita's hurried shuffle.

"Hebita!" she cried and enfolded her in her arms, "I miss you already mija"

"Me too Margarita."

Margarita & Hebe

Mount Vernon Street, Boston

X

Sóchepo, Back East

Mount Vernon Street, Boston
Monday, December 30, 1957

In the waiting area she read magazines passengers had forgotten or deliberately abandoned, and the raw, damp, cold seeped into her bones. Kathleen pierced repeating, "You-hoo," and waved across the waiting area. According to her, the snowstorm had stranded her on Cape Cod. Snowflakes as large as down fluffed around them at the cabstand. Fortunately, Kathleen brought a coat; she tugged on the sleeves, which only reached her wrist bones and tried to close it.

"Such tremendous diddies. At your age, I didn't even wear a brassiere."

"Sometimes my classmates make fun of me."

"In a couple of years, the girls will envy you and the boys will love you for them. Come to me first if you need anything, but you won't be telling Mrs. Livingston I smoke—Okay? Okay?"

"Naw. I was thinking about California."

"California," she echoed in a dreamy sigh, "I'd like to be going there myself someday. It looks so beautiful in the photographs."

The cab sloshed its way through the historic Beacon Hill streets while Hebe gave enervated answers to Kathleen's questions about living "in an always sunny place." Unwittingly, Hebe elevated herself in Kathleen's eyes by tattling Gaye's preference for her over Margarita.

135

"I was trained; a lot of people isn't. Your father reminded me of that just last summer. He always ..."

My father?' Was he here?'

"Sure. Last summer, he come up to the house," she lowered her voice and covered her mouth with her hand to keep her conversation private, "some lawyers and your grandmother met about the divorce. But your father was having none of that. What a romantic. Imagine him thumbing his nose at fifteen thousand dollars. I seen the check with my own two eyes when I was cleaning up the table. "

"Fifteen thousand dollars!"

"Laughed right in your Mrs. Livingston's face, he did. 'Gaye-Lee still loves me. I can feel her here,' pointed right to his heart. He left. Just like that. Oh, what I wouldn't do for the love of a man like that."

The driver checked her in the rearview mirror as house on Mount Vernon Street. He toted all her suitcases up the snow-dusted stairs to the first floor. He caught Kathleen admiring him when he scraped his shoes off.

"I can carry you in if you like."

Kathleen blushed and tittered while she squeezed into the small space he left for her to open the door. Inside, he placed the bags down with a thud, and pushed up his jacket sleeves flaunting his strong forearms.

"Anything else?"

Before Kathleen could answer, he made the first move flirtatiously offering her a cigarette, which he lit while she gazed playfully into his eyes. Their dalliance rendered her invisible, and she deliberately ignored them. The high chandelier's cut crystal droplets refracted tiny broken rainbows on the fancy, black, fireplace fender; the richly carved window frames; the lined velvet curtains pooling on the floor; the leather books, and the Steinway grand occupied the spot it had been assigned by her grandmother decades ago when she emigrated from Europe. The heavy valances and soft, silk oriental rugs on the floors smothered her footsteps. The solemn oil portraits' lips painted shut for all eternity, added to the overall resounding quietness of the house.

I am already suffocating.

Exhausted from her travels, she took the rickety, wooden elevator to the top, the fifth floor and stepped into the hall. A whispering tintinnabulation beckoned her from behind a door partially ajar. Curiosity cooled the room almost unbearably hot area and gave her the strength to investigate. Chandeliers dangled from iron hooks old crates and one gloomy trunk addressed to her grandfather. Resting in its bed of straw were ribbon-candy thin goblets trimmed in silver, blood red fruit dishes and a photo album. The incredible heat formed perspiration beads on her brow and rushed her through, though a painting of Oma Livingston and a friend in Viennese costumes fascinated her. On the back "Brunhilde & Gretel" was written.

So that's why they call her Hilde.

Abandoned though the things were, she was sure Oma would notice if the album was not right where she left it. She always talked about pictures but never alcohol, and she had never seen her take a drink. So she left the photos and too the bottle of dark cognac. Sitting in the hot room dried her throat, which burned when she swallowed. Amid a flurry of sneezes, she left promising herself an exploration as soon as possible. The claustrophobic size of her dim room reminded her of a ship's third-class cabin, so she decided to sit in the back garden after she called California. Perched on the edge of the bed, downstairs seemed miles away. She swigged her cognac, which not only soothed her parched throat but also the anxiety of suddenly separating from her life in California. Rivulets of sweat pooled on her body, soaked her hair, and left her weightless. Floating in the dense black nothingness that exists on moonless nights high above the woods, she was strangely unafraid, and checked to see if she should be by calling for Mishquáishim. When he didn't reply, she concluded it was a dream.

A white, hot summer sun rose in a split-second, but then it incinerated in the sky. In the intense, dying embers, she saw dozens of children in metal cylinders with their troubled faces protruding from the ends. From such a great distance, it was difficult to tell what the containers were.

"Not a dream, a nightmare. Someone is putting in trashcans and throwing us away. Roasting dishes? No one eats children, do they?"

A canister tumbled end over end over end at her altitude and it passed so closely she her own head sticking out?—

Spaceship beds! That's what they are, alien spaceship beds.

"This is real!" she bellowed. "Nosh, anúnema! Wénise Help! Aliens have taken me. Help!"

Fast as a spinning top, the canister whirled into total blackness. When she opened her eyes again, Doctor Ives was beside her.

"Welcome back. Take her out of there," he ordered. "Anyone who can scream like that should not be in an iron lung."

"Iron lung?" she asked his reflection in the mirror. "Is Oma Livy here?"

"No, but her girl came to take you home."

Home, she repeated over and over until millions of needles of bright sunlight thawed the white hospital room into her old Boston balcony. Somewhere her father was whistling as he used to when he walked in the street below the big yellow windows of the old house. The increas-

138

ing volume led her to believe he was approaching and poured comfort into her soul.

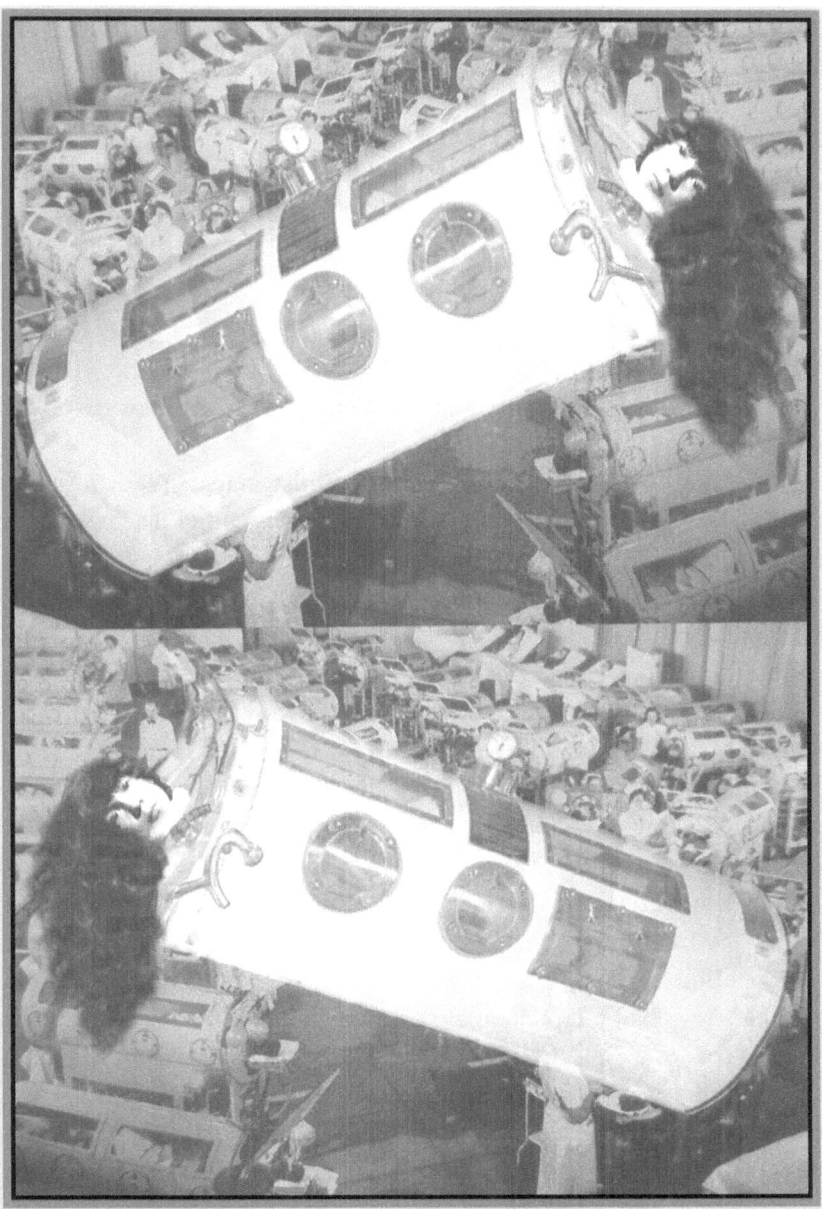

She awakened at Oma Livingston's to the sound of her alarm clock. Nearby on the table was a letter from January 17, 1958 with "Belated Happy New Year!" written across the top and to her relief, little else. Usually everything was put away, out of Grandmother Livingston's eyes; along with her nose, were in everything she did. Oma would require her to ask permission to sneeze if she could. Requesting it was difficult and seemingly pointless because, until the last weeks in California, she had grown used to being independent, and because Oma Livy rarely granted it. She was eager to see Wénise. Grandmother Livingston planned to "have her for tea."

That will never happen.

Oma flat out forbade any visit to Hans.

"That is simply out of the question."

Hebe wanted to know why and mentioned that she took care of herself in California.

"Your mother has told me about your misbehavior. You disgraced her. The time she has wasted over you...' she stopped mid-sentence and shook her head from side to side.

Hebe knew better than to ask again. Though a full two inches taller than her grandmother, she felt as of she was five-years-old. She stared at a pattern of flowers on the carpet until her grandmother turned and walked regally back to the era from whence she came and closed the door. In her room, Hebe sipped her Cognac and jotted notes about what she would write to her mother, the illness, the maid's rumor of her father's ever-bright love for her, and a promise to be different. She sat front of the mirror. The pretty, young confident girl once reflected Rosalita's mirror was now a misfit. She couldn't write a single word. All she had to look forward to was shopping. To her surprise, her grandmother allowed her to go alone; although, she could not select what she liked. Livy had telephoned ahead with the list. All were set aside for Hebe to try on, plaid skirts; coordinated blazers in grey, navy and plaid; woolen tights and brassieres. The saleswomen had her age, not her size, so she expected a child. Nothing fit from that department. The feel of the new clothes, the fineness their quality and her conservative appearance pleased her. At last, her grandmother would be pleased. The saleswomen oohed and aahed over her figure. One complimented her by telling her she "could be a model," and they all agreed.

In California, the Del Mar school went from kindergarten to twelfth grade, but the Boston school only went to sixth grade, which made her one of the tallest, and nature had provided her with a generous bosom. The first day, the pupils shushed one another when she walked in because they mistook her for a teacher. This time it was not color that separated her from the others but size. They left her alone and she had the joy of strolling through the park everyday. During the winter, nature dusted the dark branches in white, but the day after Valentines, she almost buried them in snow.

Thank you sóchepo.

Blizzard conditions resulted in school being cancelled, but did not prevent her from bundling up and going outside. Listening to the innumerable, snowflakes crackling on the hibernating world, she realized how much she had missed it, even the stinging cold. At night, the ice and snow sparkled in the bridge lights. She took a picture to remember in case she had to leave again and to share with the Gracias who had never seen snow.

Winter Snow in the Public Garden

Rosalita's letters kept her informed about their lives out west in pages and pages filled with minutia. Tony only sent a phrase or two with a leaf, a half a stick of gum, pictures of himself and recently a cocktail napkin. As usual, Oma Livy soft-shoed unnoticed into the room. She stared at the curtains on the floor by the window.

"You should have told me the curtains had fallen. I will . . ."

"I took them down. Other than the big curtain in the living room, we didn't have any in California. They shut out too much light. "

"No curtains! I don't know what on earth is wrong with Gaye -Lee. The curtains will be rehung, and you will have to clear this wall Hebe. The wardrobe will be moved here for your summer clothes which…"

"Summer?! I thought I was just here for the school year!"

Grandmother Livingston's response was to leave. Somehow, without Hebe having notice, she had placed a small jar on the nightstand.

"Guaranteed to fade unsightly dark skin," she read and then threw it against the wall and shouted, "Thanks Grandma."

The room closed in on her. Livy would not let her leave without an invitation or a purpose to a definite destination. Her purloined Cognac and book of American Indian myths offered escape, companionship and glad memories of Wénise and nature on the weekends. On school days, she rushed out the door. One Friday in a secluded corner of the yard, there was another mature-looking girl, a pale, round blonde who was smoking.

"Hi. I am Bozena,"

She had a heavy Eastern European accent. Hebe introduced herself and warned her about being kicked out for smoking. From her response, Hebe understood she was "hoping that to happen."

"I have a husband. I am too busy for school. They send truant officer," she complained rolling her eyes.

Hebe asked why she came if she was married.

"School doesn't know. Marriage license not translated, but soon. I don't want to be here and I don't want to go to jail neither."

"Jail! Naw. They just send the truant officer. And he has to find you."

"Really?" Bozena's face lit up. "Are you sure?"

Hebe nodded.

"This is good information. You look like Italian people. You Italian?"

"I'm not. I am…" she paused and decided she could avoid race if she said, "I am a Californian."

"California. Mmmm. Must be nice. Make sexy with legs on shoulders warm sand on my back."

"Do what?"

Bozena flinched and flicked her cigarette away. Her eyes were fixed behind Hebe on Miss Young, the bony, old teacher who spent the entire recess wobbling in her too-large shoes and chain- smoking.

"Cigarettes!'?'" she rasped and exhaled a cloud. "Follow me."

Punishment for smoking was being lashed with the rattan.

The boys were whipped on their open palms in front of the class and the girls on their legs in the coat closet. That thin, wet bamboo smarted like Hell, but any time Hebe had been hit, she refused to display any reaction at all which annoyed the teacher. Miss Young clopped across the black-top yard in her too-big, square heel shoes assuming the girls had been sufficiently conditioned to obey which they did but only as far as the steps. Bozena yanked Hebe's hair and cut her eyes to the street. She bolted away ithout waiting to see if Hebe was coming. She did.

"Girls! Girls!" Miss Young called and clapped her hands.

"Go Tetones!" shouted several boys in unison.

The remarks were lost to excitement buzzing in their ears and their shoes swift pattering. They ran until they got to the park. Bozena had several pairs of heels in her bag. She offered a pair to Hebe, and they put them on amid a flurry of pink magnolia blossoms.

"Okay, but don't you have a closet?"

"Sure. School will not let me wear high heels. Girls should wear them always for look sexy."

"I don't think I can walk in these."

Bozena showed her, and Hebe tried and fell but she got it.

"You are a fun friend."

Bozena slipped her arm into Hebe's. It was the first time anyone had touched her with affection since she arrived in Boston. Nestling closer to Bozena's big, soft body, she listened to her tale. She had almost finished school in Poland but quit when she married.

"There I am woman, wife. Here I am a child. They test me. Now? Grammar school."

Hebe had never heard of anyone getting married so young, but Bozena insisted it was not "so young," and it was "not problem if husband is twenty-one like my Bolek," she sighed.

From what Hebe could father, Bozena's ambition was to keep him healthy, so he could make as much money as possible in order to buy her everything her heart desired, which was not much. Pots and pans and a new nightgown "for sexy," she blushed. He worked in a meat-packing factory and at The Steam Room, her uncle's strip club.

"We are here," she announced and waved her hand at one of the girlie posters. "This is terrible picture of Bonny. Her behind is better, more bigger and she has handles more handles than me.

"Handles?"

"Yes, for man to hold."

"Tony never did that."

"Then he doesn't know how to make good sexy."

"What? He is a very good kisser."

Bozena cocked her head quizzically before she asked, "How old are you?"

"Almost eleven."

"Okay. Now I'm understand."

From her bag, Hebe presented the photos of Tony and Hans who she identified as "sort of an uncle." While Bozena lingered over the photo, Hebe explained their pen-pal relationship, which came about, due to her controlling Oma Livingston.

"I don't trust this one," Bozena said dismissing Tony. "Better marry 'sort of uncle.' He is no blood relative, so your children will not have feet like duck. And he goes to M.I.T.? Good. M.I.T. means money in the future."

"No," she laughed, "It means Massachusetts Institute..."

"I'm know, Hebe. Listen to Bozena. Go with him. I will visit in big house he will buy for you."

Bozena strutted confidently into the cavernous black mouth of the club belching smoke to the bump and grind music. Hebe hesitated but followed her.

"He's out back. Honey," a girl from off stage called out to Bozena.

She rushed off so quickly, Hebe lost sight of her. She stood in eerie neon lit space. Mysterious goop pulled the soles of her shoes when she took a step. The male silhouettes slumped against the back wall, their heads bent over drinks. Those at tables by the stage in front shifted around and sipped their drinks until the stripper had removed every-thing but pasties on her upward tilting breasts and underwear that Hebe deduced to be half a lace handkerchief tied with skinny ribbons. A long tassel dangled from each of the three pasties. Many patrons froze, completely spellbound, in anticipation of her next move. Cigarettes burned between fingers. Glasses were poised at their lips. The dancer dropped her panty tassel onto a man's shoulder in a well-tailored suit.

"Could you help me get it off, Honey?" she asked in a baby voice.

Nervous chuckles undulated through the space, and he blushed and held up his hands. With the men's good-natured ridiculing and the stripper's coaxing, he reached for it, and they cheered. He tugged the tassel, and she thrust her pelvis forward with practiced theatricality.

"Oh harder," she cooed, and he tugged again.

"Harder!" the men shouted.

He put his drink down, placed both hands on the chord and tugged mightily. The tassel came off and they released all their tension in a cheer as boisterous as if he had hit a home run, but she had not exposed herself. She had had a second smaller lace panty beneath it for which the men applauded. She minced seductively across the stage and shook her bottom; the lights went down. The man in the suit stood up and offered his hand to help her from the stage. She sat in his lap and mussed his hair. And then spotted Hebe.

"You got a great set of jugs doll. You here to audition?"

Anonymous hands lifted Hebe onto the stage. The spotlight came on and thawed the crowd into a white haze, but she could feel their lecherous eyes, hear their wolf calls and clapping. The ceiling fan came into view. It was miles away. Her knees knocked as vigorously as they had in Mexico when she saw the policeman's gun, and an anticipatory silence fell over the crowd. All eyes were on her. A stray magnolia blossom from the park floated from her hair. She was completely dumbstruck. An old man lumbered under his flabby girth, and puffed up the stairs.

"Come on. Shake it up girlie. Look at this. We got ourselves a Gypsy Rose Lee," he told the audience, "Don't be scared. Like this." He demonstrated by throwing his head back and shimmying his meaty shoulders.

A man's voice boomed so loudly it shook the tables.

"Quit sweating on my stage Herb, and get ridda that girl!"

No one moved. He whisked her onto the floor.

"What the Hell is the matter with youse putting her up there?" He leaned down and asked paternally, "Which one of these dirty bums did put you up there?"

Shaking visibly, she fidgeted with her hair and replied unintentionally softly, "Well sir...I don't know, but one of them looked like Santa... the light..."

The Art Show

"Santa!" he exclaimed and ignited a blaze of laughs with his. "Santa is on the naughty list," he announced.

"I have to go now. Where is Bozena?"

"Oh are you Bozena's classmate, Hebe.

She smiled hearing her name, and he threw a dishtowel over his shoulder and yelled, "What did you do to my niece's school friend? You bunch of dirty dogs," and bent back down to her, "Indian girl? You do look like an Indian."

He let out a war cry, "Woot woot!"

"Tank, you act like a stupid." Bozena declared.

"That ain't stupid, is it Hebe?"

Fear rippled in her cheeks; she shook her head.

"Aw come on Hebe. Don't be afraid of Tank. He is big pussy cat."

"Keep your little school friends out o' here Bozena. You're gonna cost me my license."

"No problem," she kissed his cheek. "We go to my place."

Bozena's three bedroom apartment was crowded with relatives noisily busy with their well-oiled routine cleaning, arguing, smoking, talking and laughing while preparing a hearty dinner, "obia." Hebe fit easily in the familial fold. The stout aunt nonchalantly handed her flatware and napkins to set the table. In the warm food-scented air, she carried out her newly assigned responsibility as if it were her daily duty. She felt as comfortable and welcome as she did at the Garcias. The women in the house served dinner on a table, expanded with three leaves, stretching it from one end of the room to the other. Obiad turned out to be a beet soup, and there were steaming dishes of kotlets, cabbage and mashed potatoes smothered in a rich, Polish sauce. Grins and friendly pats on the arm or strokes on her head toppled the language barrier throughout the night. There were not enough chairs, so the aunt, who buzzed around the table catering to the meal's' trivial needs, scooted Hebe over and sat with her. She draped her heavy, dough-colored arm over her shoulder and cuddled closely much to everyone's amusement. And, at one point, when the cheerful conversation escalated into a heated discussion, Bozena translated.

"They talk about two years before anti-government riots in Poznan and," she paused to listen, "what might be happen when Gomulka is not freed."

"Who is Gomulka?" Hebe asked.

"Important leader. Will tell you later."

Even though Hebe didn't know a word of Polish, she followed much of the conversation. It was a skill she had developed sitting among the Garcias when only spoke Spanish but it was exhausting to keep up. Her mind wandered.

If I can go here, I should be able to go and visit Wénise. She might have to call my grandmother. I could try to find Hans.

Hebe had stayed away from Tony and Rosalita because she knew they would send her to Boston as punishment. She doubted Oma Livy would send her back to California, for disobeying, so she relaxed.

"Na drzowiel!" she toasted and drank with the others.

The quietest man at the table was quite old and frail. He lowered his lids when he threw his shot back and kept them closed until he had tasted every drop, and then he hobbled out. Pleasant whispers breezed around the table and Bozena translated.

"They say, they hope Uncle Premestaw will play violin."

Play the violin? It took him five minutes to get out of his chair, and five more to walk to the door.

Uncle Premestaw

He was an elder though, and Hebe was prepared to clap politely no matter how badly he played. Raising his instrument under his chin rejuvenated him. Gleaming-eyed, he skimmed his bow across the strings with incredible agility, grace and speed. He dipped slightly toward the floor, stretched toward the ceiling and emptied the sweet, warm contents of his tune into her soul. It spilled over and sent tears down her face. He stopped and she clapped; Bozena stayed her hands.

"He is not finished."

When he was, they sprang to their feet applauding and calling "Bravo!" as did passersby in the street below. With the chairs and table were pushed aside, Uncle Premestaw inspired them to dance the Polka. Dosey doeing among the gladdened faces liberated Hebe's glee. She enjoyed a fleeting fantasy about returning to Beacon Hill and finding Oma Livy worried and happy to see her. She was neither; she was not even there. A note for Kathleen rested on the kitchen table with instruction, the hotel telephone number, return date and her itinerary in New York. She was at the Waldorf-Astoria for "personal matters," and after Kathleen completed a list of duties, she could do "as she wished."

She does have a heart. She gave Kathleen time off, but what about me? Oma completely forgotten about me or she would have told her to sit with me or that someone was coming.

Upon rereading the note, the date for her return jumped out at her. It was ten days from now. The phone rang, and she hovered over the receiver before answering.

Hebe had fun imitating Kathleen's lilting Irish accent.

"Livingston residence."

"This is Miss Kennedy," announced her school principal.

Hebe felt as if Mrs. Kennedy had just walked in, and she wanted to hide. She hoped the principal would hang up, but she just kept repeating, "Hello? Hello?"

"Yes, Marm."

"May I speak with Mrs. Livingston?"

"I am sorry, Mrs. Livingston has gone away. This is the housekeeper."

"Oh, I see. Do you know if she took her granddaughter along?"

"Yes. Is there a message?"

"No, that will not be necessary. Thank you."

"Do I have an Irish accent," she asked and winced not having any idea what compelled her.

"Yes, but I understand you perfectly."

"That's very kind. Thank you."

As soon as she heard Mrs. Kennedy hang up, she replaced the receiver in the cradle. Nervous laughter rolled out of her in waves until her ribs ached.

"I'm free! I am not trapped here like you,'" she told each European ancestor's oil-painted face. "I am free!"

"Many a night I saw the Pleiades, rising thro' the mellow shade, Glitter like a swarm of fireflies tangled in a silver braid." (–Alfred, Lord Tennyson – 1837 *Locksley Hall*)

X

The Celestial Seven

April 30, 1958

The bowing gnarled limbs of ancient trees and shrubs prevented the entrance to Warren Street from being visible from the street. The cab, which had jostled along the cobblestone cow paths of Beacon Hill, rolled smoothly along the tree-line streets of Brookline Hills, and the ride went on and on and on.

Perhaps finding Hans is not such a good idea today.

There were so many trees between the houses and they were very far apart. Then she saw the street sign, Warren.

"There it is," shot out of her mouth.

"Looks like the end of the world."

"I hope the beginning of one."

"Me too Miss."

Warren Street was neither an end nor a beginning. It was a destination all its own, a precious New England treasure tucked away in a rustling tissue of lavish greenery. It was the land of the privileged, Yankee gentry. The homes vaunted no elaborate, rococo heraldry, no vulgar, Vegas glitz, no conspicuously trimmed gables. Any fancy adornment would have been superfluous to the mansions set on the green hills back from the road. Regally, they stood in the proud silent, simplicity of understated elegance. They were built by the refined, unpretentious progeny of old money and filled with possessions inherited, objects d' arts so exquisite and priceless they didn't have to shine to attract the eye or flaunt worth. Nothing was superior to their familial connection, to their provenance. Hebe squinted for people as they cruised up to the gigantic Southern Colonial house.

"Gosh, that house looks bigger than my school! Maybe there's another Warren Street," she suggested shifting in the back seat.

In his rearview mirror, the driver watched her counting her dollars into her lap. He turned off the meter and steered the car under the late winter canopy of branches by the Brookline Reservoir.

'What number was it again?"

"219, " Hebe answered.

"This is it, 219."

"Are you sure?"

"You go up and speak into that box on the gate. I'm going to wait to see if your friends are there. If they are, I'm gonna wait till you get in."

Hans' name had not been in the telephone book or near the box on the gate that read, *The Birches.* She announced herself on the intercom as "Miss Hebe Nuttah Holmes" but only asked for Mr. Han'" because she didn't know how to pronounce his surname, Van Rensselaer. The gate popped open.

"Thank you."

She waved to the driver.

He beeped and she waved. A large cloud moved away from the sun and let it spotlight the remnants of snow on the sleeping lawn lapping down one hill and up the slope of another.

What have I done?

A peacock shrieked from behind a tree hastening her step. The bird fanned its tail into a dark rainbow of iridescent feathers and squawked again. She couldn't believe something so beautiful could make such an awful noise. In her pumps, black cashmere sweater and a drop of make-up, she was certain she appeared well beyond her ten and a half years as she wished to show Hans how grown up she had become.

"Welcome."

"Thank you."

"You may wait here."

Ever so gently, he took her pink coat and left her in the hallway.

Two women and several curious cherubim peered down at her from the ceiling trompe l'oeil. A larger than life statue of Hebe filled the corner. And in the room across the hall, a group of people scrutinized a painting. Before she could investigate, Lucky's loud baying and the clickety-click clicking his toenails brought him down the stairs. The sight of him crashed through any airs of maturity she had hoped to exude. She got down on her hands and knees to kiss him and picked him up until he wriggled free and barked at Hans.

"Nuttah! Let me look at you. There's the sweater. It looks swell."

She placed her hands on her small waist. The gesture drew his eyes to her full, firm breasts for a moment and he shook his head.

"Come on and see out house, *The Birches.*"

Hebe asked about her father and expressed her concern because she had not heard from him, "but there was a man on a bus in San Diego, a military bus. He had a tunuppasog on his hand. Maybe it was nosh."

"It's possible. I think he is at Groom Lake, a place ..."

Hans placed his index finger over his lips and bent down to tell her she needed to wait until they were in private.

"Eyes and ears are everywhere in a house with a large staff," he whispered in her hair.

Anxious to hear what he knew about her father, she missed much of his description of the rooms, some of which had name plaques. Based on a whiff of Agua Lavanda, she guessed *The* Jazz *Quarter* to be where her father, Kutty stayed.

"Is he working on Air Force special projects? What about Dreamland? See it is stamped 'Groom Lake Area 51.' The letter didn't make any sense to me," she declared and held the papers out to Hans.

Suppressing his surprise at how much she had learned about something that was supposed to be secret and her boldness in writing to headquarters in Washington D. C., he inspected the documents. He paced and wanted to know when Kutty had last contacted her and what he had written, "exactly."

"He was going to be invisible and incommunicado for a while longer."

From atop a dresser where he had perched, Hans saw Hebe as she was when he first met her and then in Harvard Square being driven away from her father. Kutty's anguish over her leaving and his own to help had moved Hans deeply. Now, she stood before him, the same girl sent away by the mother who took her. He asked her to join him on the roomy sofa.

"Once Kutty told me you guys, Indians, have a lot of names."

"We do."

"And one of them is a special name that only you and your god know; you never tell anyone---ever.

"Kiehtan? That's right."

"The job your father has right now has the same rule. Only he and the company who hired him can know anything about him and what he is doing."

"But what if aliens from space take him away?"

The seriousness of her expression stifled his urge to burst out laughing.

"My friend Noni, from Havana, is convinced there are flying saucers and space aliens, and he has a hundred newspaper articles to prove himself right. As an aeronautical engineer with a doctorate in science, I will believe it when I see the evidence.

"No aliens?" she asked while he shook his head. She flung her arms around him. "Thank you, Hans. I am so glad to see you."

"Me too. Come on. There is more to see."

They left *The Jazz Quarter*, and Hans continued the tour to a statuary patio, a garden, a skeet range, and lastly, the pool. It stretched from the lawn to the living room inside. Hans stripped down to his briefs, stepped in and waited for her. Unabashed, Hebe did the same and shivered in her panties and training bra Lucky barked along side, as they swam into the living room where the group she had seen earlier was talking about the painting. They stopped to applaud the pair who stood dripping wet in the living room. A maid gave her a towel and a robe. Hebe recognized their faces from a photo Kutty had sent so long ago. They welcome her as if she was a long-lost and expected niece.

"This is Countess Clair de Lune de la Mar de Maupassant."

"Just Rem is fine."

Hypnotized by her uniquely violet eyes, she followed her graceful move to the sofa. Rem, Hebe later learned from Hans was short for Mrs. Remington, her beloved childhood nanny. Her elegance in motion was a remnant from years of serious ballet an accident had tragically reduced to a pastime. That afternoon she ran across the expanse of polished wooden floor, fluttered her arms as if they were wings and vaulted into Hans' arms. Her body melted down his torso to the floor.

"I'm getting too old for this."

"When I sssee you, I hear mumumumusic,' 'Floyd stammered.

Those were the first words Hebe had heard him speak all day. His fingers were always running up and down the keys of his saxophone whether he had it in his hands or not. Hebe guessed he let his hair hang in his face because; even though, he was handsome, at times, the whites of his eyes were visible all around his irises, like a madman. Holly swept the hair from his face from time to time. Oil paint mottled her slim fingers. Though petite, her footsteps and laugh were thunderous.

Noni was Holly's classmate from the Artists' School where he studied dance and acting. His thin shirt and slacks delineated the hills and valleys of his well-toned muscles. With the swaggering crotch- forward gait of a confident womanizer, he walked over to her and threw his arms out to the sides.

'"To be, or not to be a dancer," then let out a dramatic sigh, "when everyone knows I am such a good actor. Noni, at your service." He bowed at the waist.

Nell sized Hebe up as she did all the girls she perceived as competition.

"You are a child."

"Yes, the tallest one in my class."

The clique exchanged ideas in the white parlor, lunched at the tables in the arboretum, and played croquet on the lawn before retiring for afternoon naps. There were fresh flowers in all the rooms, including hers. Rem's lady's maid entered and her dark-face unearthed visions of Tony and the Garcia's, and she felt guilty for not having thought about them. Lucky barked at the door. Nell and Holly shooed him away. Early in the evening, the girls showed up, and dressed her up as if she was a doll. They wrapped her in a flouncy, yellow, cotton dress and with a wide yellow sash around her waist tied her into their coterie.

In the magical flickering of dozens of candles on the dinner table, Noni offered a toast.

"Oh like a ball," Nell gushed.

"Yes, like a Ball," Floyd confirmed and rolled his eyes and Rem disapproved.

"That is unkind Floyd. Every young lady should wish to be invited King Baudouin of the Belgians royal court ball. And it is high time he had one."

"And Hans app-pp-proves?" Floyd quipped.

"He is sitting right there. Ask him."

Noni tapped on the side of his glass to remind them he was waiting to make his toast. They all raised their glasses.

"If music be the food of love, play on. Give me excess of it, that surfeiting, the appetite may sicken, and so die."

Rem complimented him with, "Perfection."

"Contessa you honor me too much."

Hebe, overcome with awe, sat quietly. Via Holly, Nell had gotten wind of Floyd's remark and childishly tossed her dinner roll at his head but missed. Hebe peeked under the table to see it was on the floor, near one of Rem's feet. The other rested shoeless on Hans' chair between his legs while ran his forefinger over the top of its arch. Hebe popped back up and into the conversation.

"Abstract Expressionism is all about expressing subjective emotion. How can we say, with any credibility, that De Kooning is better than Pollock or vice versa?" he asked.

The image of the misplaced foot was momentarily diminished by the conversation.

'Last year, I bought one of each. I paid $300 for the De Kooning and $75.00 for the Pollock, so perhaps..."

Floyd interrupted Rem.

"Re-re-re-educe all to mmmoney. Ssso American."

"As a British-born French citizen, I agree."

"'Though she be but little, she is fierce," Noni said of Rem.

"Abstract expressionism is to art world what jazz is to music, an American phenomenon. We do come up with one or two good things," Holly announced.

Upon hearing the word jazz, Floyd fingered his invisible instrument.

"DeKooning is clearly the better..."

"Said the Dutchman," Holly shot at Hans.

"No. Not just because he's Dutch. I don't want to argue. I do want to note that Hebe makes seven of us." To fill their blank faces he added, "Last night we discussed the Buddhist concept that some souls move in cycles of life and death together, as a group, and we wished we were seven rather than six, so we could be a group of seven celestial bright stars like the Pleiades. And now, with Hebe, we are seven."

"If we are going to be souls in a cycle together we still cannot be the Pleiades."

"Why not?" Nell asked.

"Our macho friend Noni does not want to be affiliated with a group of girls. As you all now the Pleiades from Greece are seven sisters..."

"No," Hebe disagreed, and they all turned to her. "They are boys to the Plains Indians."

"Los Indios to the rescue. Cuéntanos!"

"Do tell Hebe," Rem urged...

"Okay. A long time ago, there were seven boys who spent all their time playing gatayu'sti. That's an old Cherokee game. Maybe you have seen pictures of it. A boy rolls a stone wheel along the ground and the other players throw sticks to hit it. Not regular sticks, long ones, as tall as Hans. So even though the mothers asked them to do chores, they wouldn't. They just wanted to play gatayu'sti, eat and sleep. The mothers needed their help, and they came up with a solution. When the seven boys were napping stones, they took the stones and boiled them like corn which they served to the boys. They complained and the mothers explained, 'Stones are what you get from playing gatayu'sti. Corn is what you get from the cornfield.' Their sons misinterpreted the mothers' message to mean they didn't want them and decided to leave. They went to the back field and danced the Feather dance—round and round they went and prayed to the spirits to help them. So the mothers went to find them and discovered them dancing. At first, they ignored the boys, but then one of the mothers cried out, "Look!" The boys' were rising into the air. Every time they went around, they rose higher. Their mothers ran to catch them, but the boys were already as high as the roof, except one. Do you know what she did?"

"What?" Floyd asked with genuine interest.

"She used the gatayu'sti pole and knocked him down."

"What about the other six?" Nell asked.

"Wait. That boy didn't land on the ground. He hit it so hard, he went into the earth, and it closed over him. The other six wound up in the sky and became the Pleiades. Until this day, the Cherokee call it Ani'tsutsa, The Boys."

"That was very good...",

"Merci Nell."

"But Hebe, the Pleiades is seven stars and if one is in the ground..." Hans paused for her to continue.

"Yes, well the whole village was sad, especially that boys mama. She wept over that spot in the ground for so long, she soaked the ground. One day, she and the other boys' mothers were there, and in that spot, she watched her son rise up from a sprout to a pine which, to the

Cherokee, has the same bright light as the stars. The boy grew and grew until he reached his friends in the sky. And then there were seven Hans."

"I love tales that explain things," Nell declared.

"So we have the Cherokee boys and the Greek sisters. "What if we are the Celestial Seven?"

"Hebe. Have you been abroad?"

A bright blush flowed up into her cheeks, partly out of shyness and partly because other than the trip to Mexico, she had not gone far.

Being asked questions and participating in discussions with The Celestial Seven was fun. She promised herself she would read everything she could, so she could be more involved. Part of her new routine helped her achieve that goal. After school, the girls had Shale, the driver pick her up from school en route to their acting and history classes, and she sat in with one of the other. By Thursday, several of the grammar school classmate, who had snubbed her, were impressed by the chauffeur driven car, her new clothes and asked her about her family. Two had invited her to come home with them, but she had no idea how their families would react. Except for Bozena, she ignored them.

When the weekend arrived, the Celestial Seven slid into silk coats, cocktail dresses, and furs and drove in a caravan of three cars to the Hi-Hat in the South End. Hans closed the divider between the driver's area and the back and rolled a fat cigarette. It reminded Hebe of burning moss when it was lit. Each one took a puff and then Nell offered it to her, but disapproval tensed Rem's face and she knocked Nell's hand away. Hans toked mightily and incinerated the end down to the paper end, popped that in his mouth and magician-like threw his hands out to the sides. Hebe was seized by an attack of the giggles unparalleled in her entire lifetime; her jaws and stomach already ached.

"I am so sorry."

At The Hi-Hat, they would have to step out of the car into the throng of patrons, and Rem was not about to make her entrance with a girl who was involuntarily high and unable to control herself. On the pretense of stretching their legs before "a long evening of sitting," she had Shale stop around the corner. Hebe repeated her apology and Rem dismissed it with, "that happens sometimes." She shot flaming daggers of disapproval at Hans and Nell who left. She stayed with Hebe, and tried to help bring her down by suggesting a "deep breaths of fresh air. It is always like a chimney in there." Hebe was fine by the time Noni and his recent lady friend drove up followed by Floyd and Holly. In the restaurant downstairs, the maître d greeted them warmly. Floyd was not among them; he had responded to jazz calling out to him from the stage upstairs. A parade of dapper men and couples stopped by; Rem extended an invitation to one or two. Hebe could not keep up with the conversation as it revolved around their recent travels to places she had never been, art and finally, Marlon Brando, an actor. Cybil, a ravishing blonde hissed in outrage that Marlon had won an Oscar for *On the Waterfront* which she "did not "care for at all," and harshly criticized the actor before huffing sensuously off with her escort in tow.

"See that Rem. Anger can make even such a beauty a monster," Noni remarked.

"You must forgive Cybil. All those years ago when *Streetcar Named Desire* was at the Wilbur, the playwright, Tennessee Williams, Tenn as he preferred, had an après party at the Ritz. And it seems Mr. Brando did not return Cybil's interests which she…well flaunted."

"A knock-out like that doesn't have to flaunt? I would…"

"Exactly Noni. Most men would, but not Mr. Brando. His preference for sordid seduction is expressly exotic."

A waiter carrying a telephone on a tray was walking and repeating, "Mrs. Maupassant?" until Rem heard him, and he brought the phone to the table.

Floyd was calling to let them know he had been asked to play." Up they went to the quasi-lit venue, dense with strata of cigarette smoke, glowing in the candle light. Their table at the front was so close to the stage, Hans could sit his drink and the ashtray on it to make more space.

"Thank you for coming, "Floyd announced without stammering.

On stage, he shape-shifted from a skittish, indoor, New England feline to a cool, jazz cat. He puffed on his cigarette and rocked back and forth. When he tossed his hair off his face, he had a never-before-seen smile as big as a highway. The din simmered down, and his words streamed smoothly out of his mouth. After he introduced each member of the quartet, everyone clapped. He directed the spotlight to The Celestial Seven's table and Hebe.

"This one is for my little sis, Hebe everybody," he announced.

The spotlight found her while the crowd applauded. Rem whispered for her to stand up.

Hello."

She waved and slunk, embarrassed and thrilled into her chair.

The musicians were not quite set yet. Floyd wet his reed and played two notes.

"*Somewhere Over the Rainbow!*" Hebe blurted out excitedly

"Whatever my little city Indian wants, and you cats better groove along or Hebe will get out her gun and," he snapped his finger to jog his memory. "What did you do to the rabbits? Dust what?"

Hebe was amazed that Floyd recalled the words. She didn't think he was listening when she told him about Wénise shooting at the rabbits. The spotlight returned.

"Dust their tails."

"Dust your tails!" he repeated into the microphone.

The patrons yukked boozily, and then they relaxed into shadows amid the red hues. For a split second, the universe held its breath. The pianist began. The drummer and the bassist swept and plucked a rhythm that put locomotive wheels on the club. Floyd tapped his foot and exhaled a cloud of smoke before he blew into his sax. Every now and again, "Yeah man," or "Go live!" shot out of the crowd. Her focus remained on Floyd who lurched wildly fingering his sax, vibrating her heart and she liked it. Bent back with his eyes closed, he pushed out the same two notes with which he began and Peskhómmin! Boom! Applause filled the air. He had masterfully lured them into the music with the familiar melody but furtively veered over the edges of unfamiliar improvisation where he allowed their souls to loiter in comfort in space, and then delivered them back to the club. Hebe marveled at his ability to play with her mind. Once she told him, "I feel like you are taking me into the woods that I know like the back of my hand. But when we go in, it's a strange and beautiful place, and it's different every time!" She raised a random cocktail from the table, downed it and jumped back on to the merry-music-go-round evening.

In the bright mid-morning light, she had to squint to see. She smiled and put on her sunglasses.

Those were not virgin drinks.

Attempts to piece together the evening exacerbated her headache, so she gave up and carefully slid back into bed.

* * *

Hebe strolled into school with Rem who had asked to see "this school of yours." Hebe's jaw dropped. Grandmother Livingston stepped out of the principal's office. There were no words of greeting, no smile, no formality.

"Where have you been?" she asked clearly annoyed. "I was going to call the gendarmes."

"Lady Livingston?"

Hebe's eyes grew wider.

Lady? Lady Livingston? Does Rem know her?

"Countess de Maupassant?" Grandmother Livy softened her tone considerably. "Did you deliver my granddaughter? Allow me to apologize for any trouble she may have caused."

"Miss Holmes was invited to my home in Brookline Hills, The Birches where she has been for almost a fortnight. Certainly you knew that or you would have reported her missing."

"Yes, certainly. Run along to class," Oma Livingston told Hebe.

Before entering the room, Hebe observed the two women. Each was a road leading into the unforeseeable future, and she didn't know which would be open to her at the end of the day. For the next six hours, time ticked by painstakingly slowly. On the sidewalk, she scanned left and right without spotting either woman. Hans and Nell arrived on his scooter and uplifted her spirits, but then they dashed them by telling her Rem and Lady Livingston were stuck in traffic.

They've been together all this time?! What awful things did Oma say? I will never be allowed at the Birches again.

"Oh, they took a detour to pick up some of your things."

The car pulled up. Her iridescent abalone shell rested on Rem's fur coat in the back seat; she explained that it was too fragile to pack in the suitcase. As the car glided toward Brookline, they sat in the calm quiet of two formal acquaintances. Curiosity as to what was going on unsettled her. She reflected on the places to which she had been in her young life, how incredibly different they were and tried to imagine the future, how many more places, how many more people there could be if she could go with Rem. The stars aligned and her wish was granted. With a quick, cool embrace, her grandmother stepped into her own awaiting car and disappeared. Rem beckoned her into hers.

"Lady Livingston" as Rem called her, had a death in her family and was sailing for Europe. She was obliged to take Hebe who was in her charge, but she did not have a passport. It would take weeks to get one. From the bar in the back seat, Rem poured a drink before she continued to regale Hebe with the interconnectedness of Austrian history and her grandmother's life.

"Archduke Ferdinand's assassination led to a declaration of war on Serbia which led to The Great War which led to her family's reluctant move away from much-loved Vienna to British Colonial Hong Kong."

Hebe's head was spinning as she tried to make sense of the sentence.

"Your Oma had hoped to return to her music-rich Vienna, a wondrous place, but she met Lord Livingston, your grandfather and fell in love. Did you know your grandfather was an Earl?"

"Malcolm."

"What?" Rem asked.

"Grandfather's name was not Earl. It was Malcolm," she corrected, enunciating clearly.

Rem chuckled at Hebe's naïveté, *which* she found charming.

"Yes, of course, my young American dear. I shall explain another time. The point is your grandmother was prepared to go home, back to her dream. Your grandfather decided to move to America, the Wild West to a lady like your grandmother. There are no upper and lower classes, no titles."

"Just skin color."

"So you can imagine her surprise when your mother arrived home with an American Indian," Rem commented with a wry smile. "I wish I had been there."

"So do I."

"Your poor Oma is in quite a state. Kathleen is packing..."

"Kathleen!? She takes her maid and not her granddaughter?! "

"You have no passport, and however could she function without a maid? I couldn't. The choices you have are to return to California, stay here with one of the aunts and uncles, the Holmes, and of course you are welcome at The Birches."

"What about with Wénise?"

"You have often mentioned her, so I did ask your Oma, but Wénise lives too far."

And she did. Moving in with Wénise sisters and brothers would not be the end of the world, but not having seen them for so long would mean a lengthy period of adjustment full of prying questions. California was familiar. The Garcia's and Jude, who she missed the most, would be glad to see her, but she could not guess what Art and her mother's reaction would be. Rem's smile tugged at her heart; she would truly miss her and her family, the Celestial Seven.

The Birches

XI

Intrigue Under the Flower Moon

The full, white, Moon that May rolled into the sky shined brightly through the open curtains. Hebe had noticed when she was a small girl in Cambridge and in La Jolla, it often brought with it high drama broken into multiple scenes. She put it out of her mind and consulted her daily planner. Her hours were full. When she was not at school or with tutors in French, photography and math, she supported the Celestial Seven's artistic efforts. Most recently, she had gone to Rem's dance rehearsal at the conservatory; Noni's performance at The Sanders Theatre; Hans' photographs at a private gallery; Holly's paintings at the Museum School; Floyd's music at a coffee house in Cambridge and Nell's perpetual training for her desired ladyship everyday at home. How many times had she gone up and down the marble staircase, chin up with a book on her head so she could perfect a confidant and elegant entrance? Willing disciple to all, Hebe learned from them on a daily basis as they practiced in front of her or offered to teach her. Flattered by her intense interest, they answered her never-ending questions and guided her young hands. Photography was the easiest; the sax the most difficult, not just because it was almost impossible to produce even the slightest sound but because Floyd was so unpredictable and explosive to be around.

The only things that interrupted his playing were drinks and pills. Hebe thought they lined his pockets because anytime he dipped in his hand, it came out with one. Once she saw him mindlessly pick up a pill from the table and swallow it. Holly appeared with a glass of juice because apparently the medication was hers.

"No!" she cried out in frustration.

"Was that yours? Ssss-sss-sorry," he stammered.

"Yes. They don't work if I don't take them Floyd. Unless you want to have a baby!

She rushed out. In the afternoon, Hebe asked Rem if they were going to have a baby shower for Holly.

"Oh. You heard about the birth control pill?"

"I am confused. Are they going to have a baby?"

"Not if he only took one pill, but who knows how many Floyd has taken? That is what Holly meant."

Hebe saw his room in her mind. Empty prescription bottles without labels and liquor bottles with labels stood and leaned among the phonograph album covers strewn over the bed and floor, it was impossible not to step on them, but she felt comfortable there. Amid the reek of booze and smoke and jazz, the loud music cleared her head. Floyd let her know she was welcome with a nod of his head and gestured to a soft chair. He almost never spoke in his room, but when he did it was on random topics, happenings at a club, a book store San Francisco or "a little back street, on the Left Bank in Paris," he had been everywhere. Mostly he talked about the jazz players on the album covers. The Hawk and Cannonball, both saxophonists, were two of his favorites. A string of their notes could spring Floyd to his feet, and cause him to shout "Yeah!" and bop his head with a force that fanned his hair over his eyes. Near to the speaker, he listened intently and then joined in. The waves of music tossed and turned his body and Hebe's too. Sometimes on his soft silk carpet, it motivated her to dance. One day he was setting a new reed.

"You like the mu-mu-muusic so mu-mu-much," he stammered, "here, see how it feels."

She shook her head, placed her hand on his cheek and asked, "Why don't you stammer on all the words?"

"I used to. And I am glad because ssstammering is why I took up the sax. Hard to-to-to talk with this in your mouth. Here. Try, for me."

She shook her head, "I told you, I can't."

"If you can breathe, you can blow."

He waited so long, she took the horn, and blew, but the only thing that came out was air, no actual notes.

"That was good for a first time, especially for a chick."

"Okay. Let me try again."

He gently poked her in the stomach and suggested, "Here. Get air from here."

Emulating what she had seen him do, she closed her eyes and blew a long note. She didn't want to stop, but she had to. She gasped for air.

"How do you play a whole song?"

"Practice. And then after a while, you get used to it."

He blew so hard, the squirrels that lived in the tree by the window came out. No one else heard. Rem had wisely installed on the top floor of The Birches, essentially a soundproof space. Except for playing "gigs," socializing downstairs, which she Rem insisted he do if he was to live there, and hanging with Holly, he rarely went anywhere. When Holly showed up, Hebe followed her intuition and left them alone together.

Nell invited her to help select her wardrobe, a task that reminded her of her times with Rosalita, but it was not as much fun. She took herself quite seriously because she was intent on having the space marked occupation in her passport read, "Lady" as Rem's did. From far across the sea in Belgium, her mother, Countessa Godelieve, filled her schedule with charities, teas, all sorts of events where she might meet suitable bachelors. Hans didn't seem to mind, in fact, he encouraged her to go. They both knew he would never pass muster with her mother. Nell wished he would try harder to prove himself and be more of a boyfriend until she learned her mother attempting to orchestrate a rendezvous between her and the Shah of Iran. She squealed with delight. The newspapers had been buzzing with rumors that he might have to divorce his wife Saroya because she could not have children. He needed a blood heir. Hebe remembered Saroya because Rosalita had gone on and on about a mink cape she had worn somewhere.

Rosalita is a realist, she decided *and Nell...Maybe Nell is insane and, selfish. It is sad, really sad that the he has to leave his love, but Nell is excited that this will give her a chance to be with him.*

Why marrying a man with a title was so important to Nell eluded Hebe completely. Rosalita was only a year or two younger than Nell was, and she was quite clear on her goal, a guy, guapo, who treated her nicely, had a job and a car. To attract him she swayed her hips as much as possible, kept her make-up fresh and her hair coiffed. Styling it was a challenged because her left arm was shorter than her right, so she had to tilt in awkward positions that made her laugh at herself. She always did, not Nell. She behaved as though she already had an invitation to meet the king, and she practiced her royal curtsey and stiff gait.

"Tell me if my hips are wiggling,"

"No. You are as straight as the wall."

"What about this dress?"

Hebe had run out of compliments and wanted her to go downstairs to Rem's mirrored dance studio, so she could see herself from every angle. This led to the first scene of the full flower moon drama.

✳✳✳

Oddly, the door, which was never closed, was closed and locked. Hebe dropped down on her knee and saw two nudes through the key-hole. A muscular back and butt came in and out of view. Two dainty pink silk ballet slippers slid onto it before it disappeared and there was a loud roar. Nell dropped down next to Hebe.

"I know who that is. It's Hans!?" she blared.

His Charles Atlas physique rose next to Rem wearing only a lamp-shade on her head.

"I can't see Nell, but I think Rem is practicing."

"With the door locked?"

Nell shoved Hebe aside, saw for herself gasped and pounded on the door with both hands.

"Hans! Hans! Ouvre la port. Ouvre moi!" she cried out.

Following a muffled conversation, he flung it open, and saw Hebe. He covered his nakedness with his hand and bent down with a smile directed at the keyhole to distract Nell from catching sight of Rem scurrying out the other exit.

"Why are you shrieking?" he asked calmly with a big smile, "Rem and I were..."

"Je ne suis pas aveugle. J'ai vu. J'ai vu. Salaud!" she yelled two inches from his nose with tears steaming down her cheeks. "You will be sorry when the Shah makes me his empress. We will chop off your stupid head!"

She stomped childishly away.

The very next morning, the news came that the tryst with the Shah would be impossible. To Hebe's unbelieving eyes, Nell sought comfort from Hans' lap.

✳✳✳

The second scene starred Noni. Out of the blue, he suffered an onset of paralysis that affected half his face. Unable to enunciate clearly, his understudy was called. He was getting rave reviews. The doctor called it, Bell's palsy, was "usually temporary," but the word "usually," gnawed at Noni and compelled him to try to speak which was futile. Desperation darkened his eyes while his efforts to enunciate ended in drool.

✳✳✳

Rem's was the third; it influenced the whole house. It began with the arrival of a tall, gentleman with two steamer trunks and a wall of luggage.

"Everyone, this is Philipe. Philipe, everyone," she announced, pulled him into the house and her quarters. Atmospherics ensued. Rem booked endless international phone calls, and it rang quite often. No one knew anything about him. The two discussed and bickered, and occasionally, exchanged a fleeting kiss on the lips. No amount of observation or eavesdropping revealed whether they were friends or lovers, but Noni was certain "it's about sex." Hans guessed "money, Nell love and Floyd "drugs" which set Holly off.

Recently, she had become irritated with him lately.

"Drugs. Everything is only drugs to you!" Holly barked at him.

In response, Floyd put a pill in his mouth and swallowed it down with his whiskey that made Holly wince and seethe.

"You didn't give us your guess on the Philipe enigma."

"I don't care what their story is. I don't care about anything but my paintings. I have to get out of here, work on these pieces for the new gallery in P-Town this summer."

"So you are leaving me."

"No Floyd. I am not leaving you. I am going to my studio," she cooed at him as he clung to her sleeve.

The disharmony unsettled Hebe and she ghosted off on into the next scene. Usually busyness kept realities' harms at bay, but now, she could not stop thinking about them. Little Jude smiled at her from his picture frame next to Kutty, Wénise, the Garcia's and Gaye-Lee. The blues infiltrated her soul, and the room quintupled in size.

Oh, what spirit is here? Time to smudge

Hunting for a match, she came across a men's magazine in one of the drawers. Leafing through it triggered the memory of drinking Tony's Tequila with Rosalita, and she really missed them. She turned the page, and the abundantly built brunette centerfold unfolded. Her perfectly arched eyebrows were unmistakably Art's client in San Diego, Mrs. Gonzales.

So that's why you are so popular. You are a whore.

She drew a mustache on her, and smudged her space. The smoke cleansed her spirit and lifted her cares to the edges of the universe. She gave thanks for the people in her life, one of whom was Bozena.

Her sixteenth birthday arrived, and it was on a school day. Still Rem gave Hebe the chance to take her friend to the Tea Court in the Copley Plaza. Rem also bought her a pair of high-heels, so she and Bozena would be dressed similarly. The birthday girl showed up giggling and glowing in a new pale pink dress. She mentioned her husband's promotion as one of his gifts to her because it meant he didn't have to work, "at uncle's girlie bar no more." Bozena always brimmed with contagious joy. It was one of the reasons Hebe "really, really liked her." When she told her she was American Indian and not Italian as Bozena had guessed, she didn't question her or make any negative comments; she never did. She was particularly ebullient on her birthday. The other place she liked was the courtyard at the library. As planned, they gathered an armful of book and sat there reading. Hebe surprised her by producing a gift from a plain brown shopping bag. Bozena squealed so much, Hebe was almost as excited to give the gift, as she was to receive it. Giddily she clapped and admired the fancy wrapping paper. Upon opening it, she gasped and turned bright red.

"I love. I love. I love---Bolek will love."

Bozena lifted the lavender peignoir set from the box, whirled around and kissed Hebe again. She was eager to go home to show Bolek and begged Hebe to come with her, but she didn't relish meeting a roomful of strangers and offered the excuse that she was "expected, and could not," and accompanied a dancing Bozena to the subway. It was such a glorious summer day, Hebe decided to walk home. Forty-five minutes later, she stopped to say a prayer for a cat crossing the busy street. A black car blew by and then backed up slowly. The Birches' driver Shale opened the door and released Rem's voice.

"Hebe where have you been? We searched all over."

Philipe bowed to Hebe's hand, which he kissed. Rem called Henry from the car to make the necessary arrangements at her Pierre Hotel apartment.

"Yes. Hebe will be with us in New York."

"I will? New York?" she asked excitedly.

"Philipe and I have business there, and of course we want to see your Texan who conquered Russia."

"van Cliburn?" she confirmed raising Philipe's eyebrows.

"Alors, a fan. Do you have his record?"

"Floyd does. I like the different concerti, and I love the cover. He is so cute."

"Yes, that he does," he agreed and gave Rem.

At the station, Hebe counted the cities she wanted to see along the way, but the train rocked her into a siesta. Outside of Pennsylvania Station, skyscrapers clawed through the grey air at the sky. Millions of heavy feet and cars crushed the streets and sidewalks into Mother Earth. *What have they done to her?* Her answer came in the shape of Central Park visible through her window at the Pierre Hotel, and she smiled at the trees. Evidence of Rem's minions awaited in the hotel closet where they had placed everything she could have needed. A storm of confetti buried the crush of humanity lining Broadway's streets and hanging from its windows to see van Cliburn.

The Texan Who Conquered Russia
Van Cliburn Receives Hero's Welcome in New York

Starstruck, Hebe jumped up and down uncontrollably, gushing, "It's him. It's really him!"

Philipe and Rem had politely but firmly elbowed their way to the front of the crowd. She saw van Cliburn a few feet away. The excitement rushed her toward the car and through the security. They grabbed her, but the pianist signaled for them to let her go. The little girl in her best dress bobbing up and down excitedly amused him. When they made direct eye contact, she greeted him.

"Hello. I'm Hebe from Boston!"

His winning smile stopped her in her tracks. Rem recalled the experience of being infatuated with a famous person; she could not remember whom.

"Hebe, breathe!" she advised when she returned and asked Philipe, "What are we to do with her?"

"Nothing. The little girl is having excellent taste in men."

CARNEGIE HALL PROGRAM — SEASON 1957-1958

Monday Evening, May 19th, 1958 at 8:30 o'clock

COLUMBIA ARTISTS MANAGEMENT, INC.

Presents

VAN CLIBURN

and

THE SYMPHONY OF THE AIR

Guest Conductor:

KIRIL P. KONDRASHIN

(U.S.S.R.)

in a program featuring the Piano Concertos played by all finalists in the Tchaikovsky International Violin and Piano Competition—1958, at Moscow, U.S.S.R.

Luncheon

given in the honor of

Harvey Lavan r. van Cliburn Jr

Winner of the first quadrennial

International Tchaikowsky Piano Competition in Moscow

by

The Honorable Robert F Wagner

Mayor of the City of New York

Menu

Aperitif

CONSOMMÉ VIVEUR
TINY CORN STICKS

———

*Beaulieu Vineyard
Georges de Latour
Cabernet*

ROCK CORNISH HEN
PILAFF OF RICE
NEW STRINGBEANS SAUTÉ

———

COMPOTE OF PEACHES

PETITS FOURS   MACAROONS

———

DEMI TASSE

Waldorf Astoria   Wednesday May 20, 1958

"Hebe, we are going to be at a luncheon, so no squealing."

"I'm okay now. I don't know what happened to me yesterday. I was crazy."

As composed as a princess she sat, but when Philipe brought van Cliburn to the table, she blushed brightly.

"The girl from San Diego," the pianist recalled with that smile.

"Yes. Your music is um... I really like it....it's terrific. I can feel it in my bones."

"What a great compliment. Thank you."

His agent whisked him away, and there was no opportunity to speak with him further at the luncheon. Hebe was glad because she didn't know what else she could say.

Next on the schedule was the Waltz Evening at the Sheraton East, for which she was much too young. She frowned but was secretly re-lieved that the thirty-six hour whirlwind was losing its strength. With her last energy, she called her friends, first Nell who was not at home, then Bozena who was happy to hear from her and then Rosalita. They embarked on a gabfest and ended with more girlish screeches when Rosalita shared that she loved "John my 'gorgeous gringo." It was still early in San Diego; Jude would still be up, so she placed another long distance call. The telephone rang and rang and rang and stopped. Someone picked up the receiver; she heard loud music.

Finally Gaye-Lee answered, "Hello?"

The sound of her mother's voice sent tingles through her limbs and lifted her soul. She missed her.

"Mother?"

"What? Who is this? This is the Higgins residence.

Mrs. Higgins? What happened to Mrs. Holmes?

"Hi. "It's me, Hebe."

"Stevie? Stevie Who?"

"Hebe!"

"Who is it?"

"He-Be," she repeated slowly.

Art's voice came across the wire, "Steve, you son of a gun. . .

Hebe hadn't uttered a single word, but Art yelled.

"We will call you when we get back from Acapulco."

Clank, clunk and silence. The operator asked Hebe if she wanted to get the connection back.

"No wrong number. I have to find the right one."

Showering cleansed the negative call from her mind, but as soon as her head was on the pillow, it retuned. A piece of her was certain she would get a postcard from Mexico and another wished it truly had been the wrong number. Feigned sleep was her way of tricking herself into actual sleep, so she squeezed her eyes closed.

Rem's perfunctory evening silhouette wished her "Goodnight," through the open door dividing their rooms. Their voices were low, but she heard them talking.

"Father will never fire Britt, Philipe. She has been his nurse for a long time...and she is excellent."

"That stupid spy should be excellent for what he is paying her. For her silence, she wants one of my Eakin paintings."

"The nude of him carrying the woman?"

"Bien sûr que non Remy. The two men wrestling."

"Wait. After father had you committed you observation, Dr. Pierre wrote a report, 'pas homosexual," right? 'Not homosexual.'"

"Observation?! A cord from the wall to my brain!"

"I remember. It was horrible. We could not get your hair flat on your head for a week."

Philipe laughed while he was crying.

"I was carrying Bridgette Bardot and Catherine Deneuve's pictures in my wallet to present Depierre when he brought up attraction. Mais de Pierre was beau. I almost could not stand up to leave. Comprends."

«Philipe! »

"I confess. Alain Delois was in the photo with Catherine, but it didn't matter Rem. That doctor does what he does because he is the same as we are. I think he loved me."

«Non! Scandaleux! »

"Yes. You know, he has a birthmark like a bird?"

"Such good friends and still ordered shock treatments?"

"For the records. The worst result was I might forget a few days. It was horrible! Until today, the smell in those hospitals..."

"Jen e comprends pas Philipe. After all that, what could Britt know?"

"About de Pierre and me. We are together. She must have seen us."

"Did she tell father? Is that why he has the marriage clause in the will?" He shook his head, "Alors, this is so easy Philipe. Father cares about the family reputation, not who you sleep with. No one will believe Britt unless..."

"No. No photos."

"Men in your club always have a veritable harem of female admirers. Desirée, right? She is beautiful beyond description. You could…"

"I could get through the wedding, but …" he shivered from head to toe, "the wedding night, pas possible Rem."

"Some men rather enjoy women."

"And some do not. Why should I have to give my virtue to receive my inheritance?"

"You have given your virtue for considerably less Philipe, and I don't think father's will stipulates bed sheets be presented as proof of consummation. A marriage license will do, perhaps a photo…"

"Anyone can buy those. He wants the announcement in the paper, the lineage. …I must find someone and soon… le plus tôt possible."

"Stay calm. He has a bit of time left in him."

"I hope you are right. If he goes, and I have no wife… I am a pauper."

Hebe sneezed and took Philpe's breath away.

« Mon Dieu! Do you think she heard?'».

"She is asleep."

« Mais elle éternua! »

"People sneeze in their sleep. And even if she heard every word, so what?"

"You like her because she is a like you were Rem."

"Sweeter than I ever was."

She shut the door. Philipe opened it on the next day for their final breakfast together in New York.

"Bonjour, bonjour."

Finding her friendly as always, he dismissed his paranoia that she had overheard the conversation and posed a new threat to his secret. He hugged her warmly.

« Tu vas me manquer Hebe. »

« Moi aussi. I will miss you Philipe. »

« Rem m'a demandé de voir si tu es prêt. Oh sorry. Anglais. »

« Le français est bien Philipe. Je comprends."

Paranoia arose again as to whether she overheard the conversation last night, but he smiled.

"Fantastique, but I must practice my English."

"I will be ready in an hour."

She prayed Rem would call for the car. Over the past week, they had walked almost non-stop, up the Empire State Building, through the Metropolitan Museum, around Central Park, in the United Nations, countless stores along the streets and back to the hotel after Italian, Greek and French dinners. Her legs ached. As soon as she was up and dressed, she was eager to see what there was to see, even on foot. She had no idea when she would be in New York again. As wished, a car was behind Philipe's stacks of Louis Vuitton luggage adorned with labels from innumerable trips to faraway places. In no time, they were at Pier 86 and aboard the ship. The premier class deck was light and spacious with rooms just for writing, cocktails, observation and of course dancing and dining. Philipe's multi-room suite mirrored the one in the hotel except the ship's had a small balcony, but he wished them adieu from the crowded deck. The horn sounded, the band played, *Anchors Away*, and passengers threw colored confetti and streamers from all decks connecting one last time to friends and loved ones on the pier.

"Bon Voyage!" Hebe and Rem called and blew kisses.

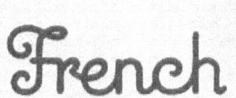

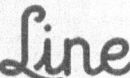

Provincetown

XII

Bicycles & Boundaries

"The Heavenly Town"

Oh, a heavenly town is Provincetown
Whose streets go winding up and down.
The air is crisp with briny smells,
The time is told by chime of bells,
The painters sketch each little nook,
In colors like a children's book.
Yellow shutters, windows pink,
Purple shingles, trees of ink.
Front street, Back street.
Narrow winding lanes.
Many colored fishing boats,
Sails and nets and seines.
East end. West end. High sandy dunes.
Wonderful by moonlight
Or in shining noons.

Reciting what memory allowed of the Provincetown poem, Hebe and Nell rode their rented bikes along the seashore road toward the ancient dunes interminably shaped and changed by the winds of the world blowing in from the cool, grey Atlantic. In unison, they began to hum the same song, *The Blue Danube* and gushed, "I love that!" Nell bowed to Hebe, and they danced so gracelessly they fell on the grainy beach in a guffaw of limbs. After guessing the shapes of the clouds puffing past, Nell volunteered the story of how her affair with Hans began. Hebe folded her arms behind her head and listened.

"We were in Kenyan with my mother, my boyfriend, Olivier," she stuck out her tongue, "and Arnaud, his father, there for Countessa Godelieve."

"Who?"

"My mother. My father died when I was six. There was no end to her suitors. Anyway, Olivier and I walked into the bar, and my eyes met Hans', so blue and sparkly. Of course, he couldn't take his eyes off me, though he was there with someone else, a local black girl, supposedly from a good family, but still..." she sniggered.

"Still what?"

"She was still a black girl. I don't think you understand. Alors, on Safari the next day, he didn't try to hide his attraction to me at all!! That night, quite by chance, we were outside together. It was so magical. We walked under the moon. It cast its spell. No one was around. And soon we made love with the lions roaring. It was so exciting."

"Lions? Weren't you afraid they would pick up your scent?"

"No. We could hear them, but they were eight kilometers away, and the princess had gotten closer in... "

"Another princess story?" Hebe giggled and Nell clammed up. "Just tell me."

"This is a real princess, the princes Elizabeth ..."

"Who?"

"Why don't American people read the newspaper?"

"We do Nell, but in 1952, I couldn't read the newspaper."

"Why?

"It was not in our picture books in kindergarten."

"I keep forgetting you are a baby; you act older. Princess Elizabeth was with Prince Philip—so dreamy—on their honeymoon at the

Stanley Hotel. When they left for the next one, the Treetop Hotel, she forgot her chapeau.

"A hotel in a tree?!"

"Yes."

"My Kiehtan tree could be a hotel."

Nell ignored her and kept on talking.

"The wild animals come right to you, but you are safe."

"Wow, I want to go!"

"It is still there. Alors, Princess Elizabeth was there with Prince Phillip for their honeymoon. During the night, her father, King George VI died, and he was not old. Can you imagine? On her honeymoon! The Kenyans say it was because of the hat."

"Like a superstition?"

«Exactement. »

Nell leaped up and ran with abandon to Hans awaiting her with outstretched arms. With his chin was on her head, he ogled the undulating body of a girl passing by, and Hebe suspected Hans didn't love Nell half as much as she loved him. The intoxicating scent of the salt air infused with spray roses overcame her. The brilliant New England summer seascape unleashed the ghosts of her ancestors who paddle their boats and dug for clams, and then they vanished.

The Celestial Seven had split the living arrangements between Rem's house in the quiet environs of Pilgrim Lake just outside Provincetown and a cottage a few blocks from its bustling center. Holly's easel became one of the many that made P-Town the artists' haven that it was, and Floyd's sax blended in with the music scene. Noni needed "as much sky as possible to search for UFO's," and "watch the girls," Rem added. For the Fête de la mar they had raised a tent on the beach. Noni referred to it as "headquarters," and it resembled them with his copious documents on UFO's neatly heaped in stacks on two card tables.

"You don't believe UFO's are real, do you Noni?

"CIA, Air Force. Go to a museum. You will see the saucer in eighteenth century religious paintings and old newspapers, 1865 for example. What about this? It's from a Brigadier general."

He pushed a document at her.

"I am not an expert."

"You don't have to be. Let me know if you see any suspicious lights in the sky, ones that move too fast or that don't move at all."

"Sure Noni.

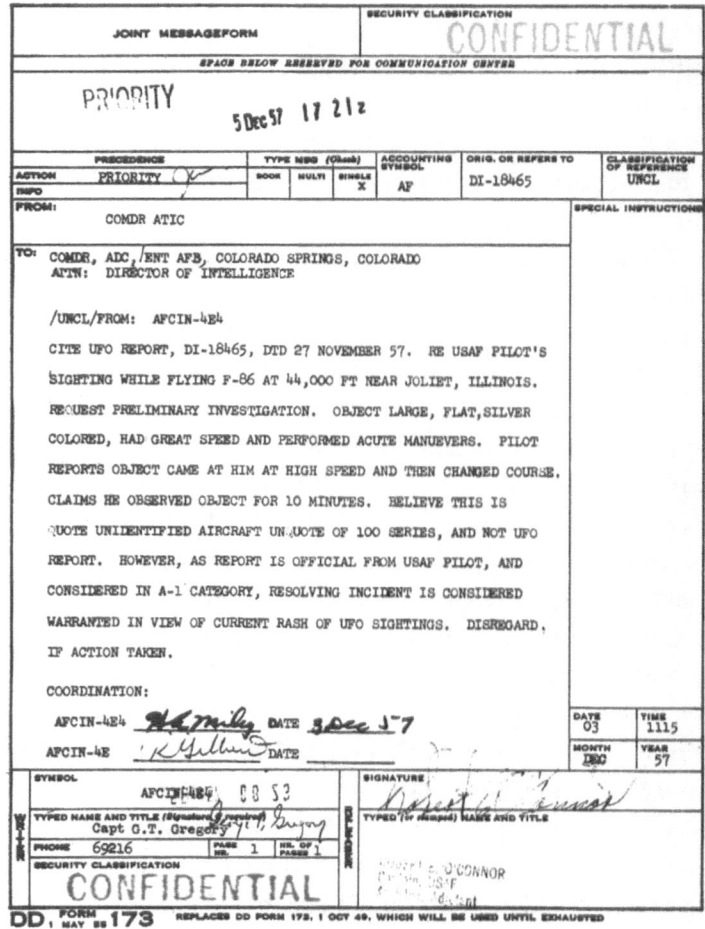

Word of the party had spread though town and lured spirited vacationers and artists to the beach. A short middle-aged, black man in dungarees and a beret threw himself in the sand and played is bongos. Catching the rhythm in her hips, a shapely brunette flung her shoes and arms over her head and performed an interpretive dance. The music coaxed Floyd out of his niche and sound out of his sax, and the musicians conversed in glances and notes amid dune-top rhythms that energized the revelers. They flung their arms wildly in the air and gyrated their hips.

During the musicians break, Noni took center stage and recited a poem in Spanish, though it was unlikely that anyone else spoke it. Noni's performance hypnotized them, in particular a petite girl with tumbling locks of hair. When he finished, he slithered beside her but she showed no further interest.

"Better luck next time."

Hebe had unwittingly wounding his male ego.

"Luck?! What are you…? I don't need luck."

"That's not what it looked like Noni."

"Because you did not see our eyes talking. Hers was begging, 'Take me. Take me right here in the moonlight, and mine, mine asked 'What moon? All I see is a delicious woman with stars in her eyes. But I can't do nothing. I have to focus, get my UFO evidence." A light moving in the sky pulled his attention upward. "A plane at this hour?" he noted suspiciously. "Hebe, May I borrow your camera—please? Please? Please? Please?"

That made it impossible for her to refuse, and she handed it to him. Noni paced back and forth on the edge of the sea. Closer to the tent newcomers arrived. Hebe didn't feel much like partying, so she went off on her own where she saw newcomers join the gathering and the bonfire burn brighter and brighter and then dim as they trickled away. From her dark edge of the gathering, sadness seeped into her marrow. Home beckoned her, not The Birches, Pilgrim Lake, the Beacon Hill house or the one in Del Mar but the one she had yet to find, the one where people eagerly awaited her. Never having left the non-existent place, she had little chance of returning. A"psst" from Rem saved her from drifting further out on the sea of melancholy she often sailed on sleepless nights.

"Come inside. We decided we might as well stay all night and see the sunrise. Besides Nell and I need you."

"Que sueñes con—los Angelos!" she called to Noni.

His teeth gleamed in the moonlight when he shot up his arm and replied, "Y tú también mi amor."

"Here it is Hebe," Hans and I went back to Pilgrim Lake, and found the postcard from the Hotel."

"You didn't have to go all that way for a postcard."

"I didn't. Hans and I…um…"

Rem saved her from confessing they had gone back for a brief romp.

"We needed blankets to stay on the beach," and taking the card from Nell added, "I didn't know you had been to Kenya."

"That's where she met Hans," Hebe chimed in.

"A mighty tree to hold a whole hotel. I forgot, what kind is it?

"Fig," Hebe and Nell answered in unison.

They planned the next day that Hebe was in favor of beginning at dawn but Nell and Rem after brunch. Vapors of sleep had been swirling around the tent for some time, and they soon succumbed and were quiet. Noni swaggered in to his sleeping bag in the corner and sighed in defeat, for there had been no UFO's. Holly and Floyd managed to navigate a river of drinks back to the tent and pour themselves sloppily onto their blankets. Rem caught Hebe's eye and pointed to the little beagle Lucky. He had chased gulls and retrieved sticks from the ocean all day and was, at last, curled up next to Hans. He lay on his back without any covers. His skin was steaming and his lips turned up in a smile.

"We were cold, so we asked him to sleep next to us" Rem whispered, "but he complained *he* was too hot. Can you believe it?"

Before she could answer, Rem had closed her eyes and fallen asleep, but she could not. *Sleep,* she repeated to herself over and over and over, but it was not working. The tent flap opened and a slim blonde in the nude woman slipped in, spotted Hans in the lamplight and straddled him. She swept her long hair across his face and kissed him until he groaned and kissed her back. Hebe grabbed her blanket and scrambled outside.

I hope Nell doesn't wake up. She loves him, or she thinks she does. How could Hans do that with a stranger? They made love in front of lions! Men are stupid! But Hans is not. As soon as he sees it is not Nell, he will kick that woman out. She is the stupid one! Yeah. She is, not Hans.

At dawn, smoke from Maushop's pipe rose from the water. Apparitions of her ancestors dug for clams and fished until they vaporized in the sunrise. Hebe collected paint pots and shells and wrote post cards to Jude and the Garcias. On tiptoe, she peeked in and smiled to see the blonde woman had gone, but not one of the Celestial Seven had awakened. She would begin her day alone. Her plan was to get coffee in the town at the Mayfair and buy stamps. Once she was on her way, she could not break the exhilaration of whizzing past the weathered cottages. She pedaled on and arrived at Pilgrim Lake where she had a hot shower and coffee.

6:30 am. *They are probably all still sleeping. There is no one on the road. I wanna see how far I can ride in an hour.*

She launched herself down the road, pumped, coasted, pumped, and coasted until she didn't think she could push one more time.

8:09 *How many miles have I gone?*

Her thighs smarted, but a soda vending machine inspired her and she made it to a restaurant and she hobbled inside to use the restroom and buy s fountain drink. Sipping her root beer, she kicked herself for not writing down the telephone number of the Pilgrim Lake house. The friendly woman behind the counter remarked about how quickly she had drunk her root beer and refilled her glass.

"I rode all the way from P-Town," she told her.

"By yourself?" she asked.

"Yes, but I am going to go back right, so..."

"It will take longer to return. It must be a good twenty-three miles, all told that's more than forty miles. You wanna call someone? I would."

Hebe began to question the wisdom of her trip. She accepted the waitress' offer to use the phone, but no one answered at Pilgrim Lake.

"Lemme have the number. I'll try later. I'm not saying you can't do it. I'm saying you will be tuckered out. Write it here," she demanded kindly and slapped a napkin in front of her.

Hebe complied and chatted with her, so she could postpone leaving until after she needed the restroom again. She stepped out into the shining day ready to go, but her bicycle was gone. A boxy, green pick up truck rolled up to her, and she saw the bike in the back. The burly driver leaned over to the passenger window; he had on a grey cap and shirt, like a meter man.

"Hi. I'm Tom. Ya have a flat."

"I do?"

"Get in. I'll drive ya back to the beach, Hans 'n them in P-Town."

As she put her hand on the truck door, she felt Mishquáishim.

"Thanks Mister."

"Tom."

Mishquáishim growled. *It's okay. He knows the Celestial Seven.*

The truck jerked ahead before she closed the door and headed in the opposite direction of Provincetown. The waitress bolted into the parking lot waving her arms. A sharp tension chirred in the air with blasting radio. Hebe stayed close to the door and hung on tightly.

"There's a spot up here I can hang a U-ee," Tom informed her.

If there was a spot, he missed it. The urge to be out of that truck, out of that seat and out of that moment, grabbed her chest and shortened her breathing. Mishquáishim shoved her into the passenger door. Tom asked if she liked rock and roll. She shook her head.

"Jazz, I like jazz. Where is the turn?"

"Right up here on the left."

She searched the landscape whizzing by the open window. Nervous energy bounced her leg up and down. Tom reached over and laid his big, rough palm on her long, slim thigh. Involuntarily she recoiled, and then instinctively smiled to hide her fear.

"Be careful. I drank a gallon back there," she warned. When we pass by the store again, stop so I can use the restroom, please."

"Sure thing."

He lit a cigar and zoomed right by the turn off, and a strange numb sensation came over her. As soon as she saw the sign for the filling station, she yelled.

"There!" She pointed," "There's a place. I gotta go."

"Damn it! Now I gotta go."

Scanning the road for a gas station, he massaged his way up her thigh. Her nerves up like porcupine quills.

The image of spunky Princess Pauline dueling over flowers lunged into her mind and released a blast of courage.

"I'm used to it," she announced bravely.

Mishquáishim growled so loudly, she was tempted to open the door and throw herself onto the road to cause a scene, but there weren't enough cars to attract attention. *I'll have a chance at the gas station.* She did. He bolted out as if he had forgotten she was there but suddenly glanced over his shoulder. From deep within, she hauled out a happy face and added a deceptive trusting singsong to her voice.

"Meet you right back here Okay?"

For appearances, jumped up and down as if battling the urge to pee. The second she saw the gas station door close, she climbed onto the truck bed, threw her bicycle to the ground, got on and peddled for her life down the road. She dismounted and hustled her bike into the woods behind the thick screen of summer leaves. Soon, the sound of the road grew faint, and she paused. Her body shook from head to toe, and she breathed deeply to calm down. She rode for a while, and then stopped.

I am near Wénise's! *There is the big branch where the raccoon sits. That is my Kiehtan tree? There is the stone to pound corn!*

Soon, she was on the path she knew well. A plume of smoke swirling up from a distant roof let her know she was right, but an eerie quiet rippled in the air, and Mishquáishim had returned. She left her bicycle and as furtively as a shadow hurried toe-heel in the direction of the cabin, but all was not well. Wénise, with her shotgun in her hand, stood in the yard as motionless as a hunter with her eyes trained on her prey dead ahead. Before Hebe could see what or who, Wénise, still facing forward, spoke to her in Wôpanâak to let her know she saw her.

"Nuttah, Kunnúnnous,"

"You speak English?" the man asked.

Hebe didn't have to see who it was; she recognized Tom's voice from the pick up truck. He lumbered his grey clad, barrel body toward Wénise.

"Yes, I speak English. You are trespassing."

 He apologize and with feigned concern told her that he and his daughter, "the little scamp," had been playing hide 'n seek, and "I have to find her." Wénise neither responded nor budged. He mopped his brow.

"Sure is hot. You got anything to drink?"

"You are trespassing Mister," she repeated sternly and raised the shotgun to waist level.

"Sorry to have bothered you ma'am."

He tipped his hat walked up to his car. Wénise checked up the hill to be sure he was gone and beckoned Hebe to come down. Anger tightened the muscles in Wénise's face when she heard how her great granddaughter had come to be an unexpected visitor.

"Did he put his hands on you?" she asked, and when Hebe hesitated, she added, "If he comes back, I will string him from that tree and slice all his skin off with a dull clam shell."

Wénise handed Hebe the shotgun.

"Are we going to shoot him?"

"Do you remember how to use this?"

"Nux Wénise. One hand here, the other one here." She cracked the breach, loaded the cartridge and held it as properly as an experienced hunter.

"Go ahead."

Hebe showed her the chunk of wood in the distance she was going to shoot. Tschuk—Tschuk, Blam! She almost hit it. Pride stretched across Wénise's face. She set up another target and then another.

"Remember, in 1873 Winchester had no safety," she warned, "Line it up. Take your time."

The third shot was a bull's eye. Wénise nodded in approval. While they cleaned the weapons, Hebe explained to Wénise that the Celestial Seven were not responsible for her encounter with the man. She had gone off on her own.

"You learned a good lesson," Wénise told her.

Hebe asked her if she could borrow the shotgun to shoot skeet at The Birches. Wénise did not answer right away; she never did. When they were finished, Wénise leaned the loaded Winchester against the cabin in the shade, and took her shotgun and a pail to get water.

"Mr. Josephs should be home about now. Run over. Tell him I want to see him. When you come back, fill these two pails at the pump and bring them to the house. We need plenty of water. The powwow is here tonight."

"Cowammáunsh Wénise."

"Me too Nuttah. I love you too."

Mr. Josephs was, like Wénise, a reticent, elder who lived more outside on his land than in his house; although, his was considerably larger than The Palace; everyone's was. No matter how hard he was laboring on a project, he always lifted his dark, face mapped with life and smiled when he heard her coming which, to her amazement, he could do whether she was wearing her hard sole city shoes or moccasins. He worked while Mr. Josephs supervised, sometimes puffing his long pipe.

Púck was there summers to help out, but when his chores were done, he went on adventures in the woods. He allowed her to tag along mostly because he was not as good at hiding from her as she was at tracking. The adventures were not always pleasant.

"Ribbit. Ribbit," croaked a helpless tinogkukquas whose green camouflaged him from Púck but not her.

"Where is he?"

"There."

To her absolute horror, Púck speared the cute, green creature through the middle, and he flailed his long limbs as he was dying.

"Ah ha ha!" Púck laughed and wiggled him under her nose.

The macabre sight spirited her back to The Palace. Mr. Josephs and Wénise asked her to explain why she was alone, breathless and in tears which she did including Púck's, "Ah ha ha!" The elders shook their heads and called him what he was "Nunkon-omp," a young boy who is not a man, but Mr. Josephs did not like the idea of killing for killing's sake.

The families, including the other neighbor, Nini and her children gathered to welcome the dawn with a prayer. Afterwards Mr. Josephs chucked Púck in the arm.

"Tell them what you had for dinner last night.

Púck stabbed at the ground with his toe and out of his mouth came, "Ribbit. Ribbit."

When they were alone, she told him she was sorry for tattling on him, but he confessed that he should not have killed the tinogkukquas for no reason. That was long ago. He was not a Nunkon-omp any more. All the muscles in his lean torso bragged visibly when he raised the ax. He split the log. Mr. Josephs waved.

"I heard Wénise shooting. She dusting tails over there?"

193

"Nuttah! What's buzzin' cuzzin?" Púck asked and leaped over the pile of logs, hugged her warmly and stood back to check her out. "What a dolly you are."

"Why did you cut your hair? Skinny Iroquois says..."

"Don't cut your hair. I know." He lowered his eyes and ran his hand over his buzz cut, "Yeah but Skinny doesn't have to work or live..."

"You are lucky."

"Oh yeah? Why's that Nuttah?"

"You have a nice face."

He flashed his teeth, glowed from the compliment, and then jut his chin at a fat, black car with a red roof.

"Yours?" she guessed.

"Yup. A Bel Air Chevy with a..."

"Púck!" his grandfather called, "You can't go nowhere till you finish with this wood.

Hebe walked him back to the pile.

"Mister Josephs, Wénise wants to see you, sir."

"Better get my hat," he acknowledged and went into the house

"I'll take you for a spin later," Púck promised and raised his eyebrows flirtatiously.

Prancing up to Wénise's, she felt a crackle in the air that stopped her in her tracks. Water rippled in the pails on the path. The Winchester still leaned against The Palace wall.

Wénise would never leave that there this long.

At the top of the slope leading from the road to the Palace, she saw Tom's boxy, green truck, and she had no doubt that Wénise was in danger. At the cabin window, she spied her great grand mother tied to a chair while Tom rummaged through cabinets and drawers.

"Come on old lady. Where is it?" he asked glaring down impatiently and slammed the wall with his palm.

"Does your mother know where you are?"

"Shut up about my mother," he snapped, hurled a vase on the floor and slapped her face.

The whack his palm made when it struck traveled through her and the wall and punched Hebe in the heart.

Kiehtan anúnema nukquenauwèhhik anúnema. *I really need help, but the Josephs' house is too far. Nini has no gun...no phone.*

The Winchester was the only answer. She slid the barrel over the window ledge into the cabin. .

"Don't you have anything worth anything old woman?" he asked.

"Plenty. All that land and those trees..."

He backhanded hard enough she toppled to the floor, shoved her rib with his boot and aimed a handgun at her. Perspiration beaded on Hebe's forehead and she lined him up in the cross hairs.

"Get up!" he commanded. "You gotta have some money around here. Just tell me where, so I can get going."

Hebe took a deep breath. Peskhómmin! Boom! Wohwohkau barked. Mr. Josephs, who was on his way, began to run. Tom lay on the ground gasping, clutching his chest. Wénise took the gun from Tom. Unexpectedly, the irrepressible need to be somewhere else overcame Hebe, and she bolted into the woods.

Mr. Josephs entered and saw the man bleeding on the floor and the gun in Wénise's hand.

"Did you..." each asked the other.

"I didn't shoot him, and you didn't shoot him so..."

Wénise shrugged and told him, "The shot came from there, the window."

Outside, the police and four of the Celestial Seven whom the waitress at the diner had contacted met them. When they heard, "There was a young girl here, said she was going back to P-Town, but she got in a green truck that sped off awful fast," they went to find her. One of the officers introduced the other.

"I'm Rouse. This is Swain. We're looking for a girl..."

"Yes, Nuttah, my great grandchild, almost eleven. You might go in there and ask that man if he is still alive."

"Alive? Swain, go see who's inside, would you?"

Babble of concern erupted over where she might be and whether she was all right.

"She was at my place a while ago, probably went by Nini's."

Swain emerged with Tom whose side was soaked in blood.

"He's hurt pretty bad. Says he don't know who shot him.

Rouse nodded approvingly.

195

"No one knows," Wénise volunteered.

Swain led Tom, wincing and staggering in pain, up the hill. Wohwohkau continued barking incessantly, and Mr. Josephs excused himself. Two gunshots rang out.

"Swain?!—Jimmy?!" Rouse called out.

No reply, no sound, nothing for a moment, and then the truck engine started.

"Jimmy"

"He got me Rouse. And the gun."

Rouse slunk among the shrubs by the road to get a better view. Tom appeared, aimed the handgun at them and fired. Blam! They all hit the ground. He jumped into the truck. Blam! He fired at Swain. Blam! He fired back. Rouse jumped in front of the truck. Blam! Tom fired at him. Blam! Rouse returned fire, and Tom's head fell on the horn; it blared for a long time. Sirens unwound closer and closer, louder and louder. An ambulance, a fire truck and two police vehicles jammed the narrow country road for a couple of hours during the investigation and clean up. The officers panted and perspired. Wénise sent Noni and Hans for pails of well water Nell ladled out.

"That's the best water I ever had," Officer Swain told her.

Wénise smiled with pride. Hans told him, they would try to identify the man who shot the now dead suspect. The officer didn't think it was necessary unless they wanted to thank him.

"If it wasn't for whoever, this lady here would be the deceased."

He promised to 'keep an eye out' for her great grand daughter and the caravan of officials drove out of sight. Mr. Josephs returned with a veritable nation of American Indians who came through the trees. The sun glistened silver on rifle barrels, glass beads and small metal cones on the women's' colorful dresses. All their arms were full of fruit and boxes of food as they surround the Celestial Seven quartet.

"I feel like I a pioneer," Rem joked nervously to Hans.

"The important difference is we were invited."

"Where is Hebe?" Noni asked.

"I think I know," Wénise replied confidently while she was placing rocks in the clearing for a fire.

Hans and Noni were recruited by the men to set up for Powwow. They opened up a deep pit where they built a fire and covered it with a seasoned, six-foot grill. Rem and Nell relaxed in a pair of folding chairs until Wénise dropped a basket of string beans and an open newspaper in front of them. She snapped off the ends of one, tossed them on the paper.

"That's how you do it," Wénise told them dumping a mound of beans in each of their laps.

Nini and her little girls ducked through the low archway in the trees. Wénise waited expecting to see Hebe. When she did not come, she padded onto the soft dirt path leading to the ancient elm.

It had survived several lightning strikes and a tornado. The bolts left scars running the length of its enormous trunk, but the powerful winds almost felled her. She used the swirling air to fill her branches with a plea for help to Maushop, the giant. To help herself, she dug her roots in as deep as she could and she wept when she heard the sound of the trunk cracking loud as thunder. Suddenly a hand appeared. Maushop had come. He bolstered the elm with another and placed a big boulder for them both.

One afternoon when Mister Josephs, Wénise and Hebe were there together, Hebe went into the huge hollow tree trunk.

"Mr. Josephs. Wénise! Watch Kiehtan make more people."

She clomped robot-like out of the elm.

Wénise laughed, "Yes. What a beautiful little girl."

"What is she doing?" Mr. Josephs asked Wénise.

"I told her Kiehtan made people out of trees and..."

"She took 'out of' trees literal. Kids. Why is she walking so stiffly?"

"I don't know. Something she saw on the television."

"Television. That will ruin her mind."

Hebe was enchanted by the elm which, though struck and fallen, was full of life. The bark housed bugs, the trunk squirrels and its branches high above the rock, an owl and birds.

"It's a magic tree, a magic Kiehtan tree," she declared on that day and often returned to it.

Wénise knew that she had built a cozy fort inside, so that is where she went.

She called out, "Kiehtan, you have any people in there today?"

Hebe emerged immediately and started talking a mile a minute.

"I was going to Nini's but I didn't want to leave you. I didn't know if I was supposed to tell Nini what happened. I don't even know what happened when I shot that man."

"Oh. It was you. You shot him."

"Did I kill him?"

"No. You did not, but he is kitonekqué"

Maushop, the Giant

"Kitonekqué?---Gone forever?" She tipped her head.

"Yes. He shot at the police."

"I'm so sorry."

Hebe burst into tears.

"You saved me. The policeman said you did."

"They know I shot him?"

"No. They know someone did."

"I am so glad."

"Not as glad as I am child. I decided you may take the shotgun for skeet—and you may choose among the collection for a rifle as a memento of Twenty-Men.

"Taúbot neanawáyean."

"You are welcome but…" Wénise waggled her finger and warned, "Any report of misuse, and I will take them..."

"No. Never. Never! Taúbot neanawáyean! Taúbot neanawá-yean"

"You are welcome."

The sounds of the drummers practicing drown out the frogs and birds on their way back to the cabin. Before joining in the festivities, they sent up a prayer.

Wénise prayed in English, "O Spirit, you are the only One. Watch over us."

"Kiehtanitoompasuk naunt manit wadchanish," Hebe enunciated slowly but clearly and correctly.

Wénise glowed with pride as she heard her language, once forbidden for her to speak, flow from the mouth of her great grand daughter. She repeated it in Wampanoag with her, "Kiehtanitoompasuk naunt manit wadchanish..." When they had finished, Nuttah, reclined on the bed and sank into the cradling fragrance of Twenty-Men's buckskin rifle case rising from the wooden floorboards and Wénise's rose water hair oil on the pillow. A warm sense of belonging radiated her from her heart to her fingertips. The smoke spiraled her spirit to the outer edges of the galaxy.

Wénise & Twenty-Men á Paris.

XIII

Wénise

Ktsee-gee-gil-lassis - Ktsee-gee-gil-lassis sang the Chickadee. Swaddled in the familiarity of powwow drums, cries and chants, Hebe had snuggled on Wénise's bed and fallen into a deep, dreamless sleep. From the snippets of conversation wafting though the window, she knew the girls had stayed over. And Nell was the reason a kettle was on the stove in the middle of the summer.

"It is impossible to wash in cold water," she whined at the washbasin outside.

The girls greeted her with soft applause.

"Our young heroine has awakened," Rem announced.

"Guess who?"

A pair of hands covered her eyes. Detecting the painter's linseed oil, she knew who it was.

"Holly!' When did you come?"

"Now! Floyd and I felt ditched until we heard you were scouring the Cape for Hebe. Is she all right?"

"Très bien. Tout va bien."

Nell whined impatiently for hot water, "C'est mon eau chaude encore?"

"But I want to hear," Holly insisted taking the water to Nell. "We girls are all alone, you know? Hans and Noni dragged Floyd off with a couple of American Indian guys."

"Probably that Mr. Josephs. Nice of him to take the men off our hands for a while."

The girls read the undersides of Wénise's belongings as if they were in a shop. Now and again, Rem read the maker's mark.

"Minton?! Positively princely. If yesterday's fool burglar had any taste, he could have taken any one of these and made a fortune. "How did your great grandmother come by these?"

"People gave them to her or she bought them in Europe," Hebe explained.

She pulled an ancient photo album off the top of the cedar wardrobe and opened it to the first photograph, Wénise in a gown at a fancy party. Rem and Nell were dazzled, but they didn't have a chance to examine it closely because Wénise returned and they were embarrassed. Hebe immediately retrieved the album and handed it to her with an apologetic glance.

"I don't mind. Rem and her friends may enjoy it."

Rem had won her heart the previous night with her concern for Hebe. Tears of relief had rolled down her cheeks when, after the tenth time she asked, Wénise took her to Hebe asleep on her bed. She asked if the Celestial Seven or at least she could stay, "so Hebe will not feel abandoned." She shared the circumstances of Hebe coming to live at the Birches.

"Her grandmother Wilkinson can be a challenge for a little girl, or..."

"Or anyone," Wénise concluded. "Thank you for taking her in and offering her so many opportunities."

"We all enjoy her. This vase is quite rare. May I ask where...?

"My mansion ladies always give me..."

"Mansion ladies?" Rem asked.

"Like Grandma Livy," Hebe explained, "in those places by the sea. They all love Wénise because she works magic with nature. Even the deadest of dead flowers come to life to see her."

"Taúbot neanawáyean, Nuttah."

"You should be proud," Nell told her scanning Wénise's lush land.

"Kuttabotumish. My ladies say that too, but Kiehtan created nature, gave it as a gift."

"And you maintain it."

"Each and every person who has a drink of water should. They do not understand that they are here for the earth. It is not here for them. Some of the ladies want their gardens to grow with no brown leaves. To me, those brown leaves have as much beauty as the buds. They want all the flowers to be one color, to bloom at certain times. Impossible really. Nature is her own mistress, but I try to help. They give me those things. Once, long ago, I got an ocean voyage."

Hebe knew those words were the first line of a story she always told and invited the others to sit and listen with a pat on the bed.

"When we first got married, we lived in the caretaker's house on the Ochre estate. Twenty-Men shoed their horses and built cabinets, whatever they needed, and I took care of the flowers and trees. She liked my succotash; they both did. At times, they came to sit and talk with us. It was a two-way street, and they invited us to dinners in the main house," she chuckled. "Twenty-Men didn't like to get dressed to eat, but he was a handsome one without all that stuff, my Twenty-Men.

Releasing the breath that carried his name blackened her hair and faded the navy circles around her irises to a deep, youthful brown.

"Yes. The ocean voyage was a little scary, all that water. We stopped in England first, and then we went to Italy. Twenty-Men and me were sure the ship had sailed in a circle because we met so many American Indians; we were in every country. And Negroes too, some from Africa! An American Negro Mr. Du Bois won awards for his exhibit about how intelligent and accomplished his people were in the United States, made all that talk about dark people being inferior as shameful and ridiculous. He had photographs American Negroes in fine clothes."

She paused, though the girls didn't know why. Dark memories of discrimination and Indian school life seeped into her mind.

"Where did you stay?" Rem asked bringing a smile to Wénise's face.

"Place Vendôme in a hotel with the indoor plumbing, and electricity. It was too bright for Twenty-Men and me. We would go for long walks at night. I liked his stories and he liked to see Keesuch sparkling in my eyes," she giggled girlishly.

Venice, Italy

One night Twenty-Men led his young love to a grove of trees beyond the streetlamps where he could see Keesuch, the Heavens in her eyes. Along the way, he told her about a man he had met in the lobby the previous day, L'homme de Bombay. He was a gaunt brown man from India dressed in his native garb that resembled a long nightshirt and white pants. Discreetly he invited hotel guests he had carefully selected to join him in the bar. There he offered them his «première guide de Paris» services. Twenty-Men overheard the hotel reception inform a curious hotel guest, «Après trente et une ans, L'homme de Bombay? Fin. » Twenty-Men was intrigued. *Thirty-one years? Finished?* What did it mean? He introduced himself to L'homme de Bombay called Vyas. He scrutinized Twenty-Men closely and glowed with pleasure.

"You are a Redman, correct? A pleasure to meet you."

Over cognac, Vyas spun his yarn. Decades earlier in 1869, he had become a victim of mischance that separated him from the Indian Noble whom he served and his entourage. The day they all left France to return to Bombay, Vyas went to a jewelry shop to buy a souvenir for his wife. He wanted to examine a particular jewel but the front of the store was shaded, so the shopkeeper directed him down a corridor to back window bursting with sun. A commotion lured him back to the front where he discovered the jeweler lying in a pool of blood on the floor. He tore off a strip of his garb and tied it around one of the gushing wounds.

« Voleur. » whispered the shopkeeper and gestured toward the street.

Vyas ran out and shouted the French word, almost the only one he knew.

« Voleur ! Voleur ! »

He returned to the jeweler who gestured clearly for Vyas to stash the remaining jewels in a pouch secreted between the floor and the counter. He did. A group of the shop's neighbors hurried to the jeweler's defense. Not having seen who called, "Thief," they surmised the bloodied, Indian Vyas to be the culprit and attacked him. He declared his innocence, but the jeweler could not confirm it because he was unconscious. In short order he was arrested, tried and imprisoned. The Nobleman returned to India without him. Months later, the jeweler recovered and sought him out to express his gratitude. To his horror, Vyas was ailing in prison. He procured his release and, at his home, he and his wife nursed him back to health. When he was well, the shopkeeper rewarded him with the jewel.

"Another man from your land brought this for me to sell. He called it, 'the light of India.' I never did and he never returned."

"I can not take it, not if it belongs to someone else."

"It belongs to me and I insist. Had you not been there monsieur, I would not be alive. If he ever returns, I will settle the account with him. Please take it."

He did. Little by little, Vyas learned French and the history of Paris well enough to earn a living by giving tours. The man from the East was a fascinating novelty to tourists, and L'homme de Bombay, as he came to be called, did well. He couriered support to his family and had almost earned his passage home.

"Then war with the Germans,"

His eyes glazed over remembering those had days, but he stayed on in France because "running back with empty pockets was running back to servitude. With a few more tours, I could begin my trek home."

"You have been here two decades! What is there for you now?"

Vyas hung his head, "Nothing anymore. I received word—my wife died a year ago."

Twenty-Men threw his arms around him in a mighty embrace. Vyas wiped away a tear.

"Cry. It washes out the pain. Just remember to stop because it changes nothing. The past is passed. Go forward. Undiscovered beauty might be in your future."

Vyas glimpsed into the reception area and rubbed his hands together.

"C'est vrai. I could wait a hundred years for her."

Twenty-Men turned to see Wénise, grinned from ear to ea.

"That is for me to do. She is my wife."

"You are lucky."

"I am. And you, Vyas are a good storyteller. Good luck going forward."

They shook hands. Vyas ran after him and handed him a velvet box.

Twenty-Men knew it held the precious jewel.

"There is a receipt inside. No danger reliving my misfortune."

Twenty-Men reached in his pocket.

"Redman, I can not charge you. It was a gift to me. Let my brilliant light of India shall go around the world," he declared and hugged Twenty-Men.

"I didn't think it was right to take it," he told Wénise in the shadow of the Parisian grove of trees.

Wénise's voice dropped when she told the girls, "My heart fell a little because—of course, I was expecting him to present it to me."

"He didn't?!" the girls asked.

"Oh, I didn't need it. I already had the voyage, the Exposition and Twenty-Men. We stayed out for a long time. We are used to the outdoors, not harsh electric bulbs. He left ours off, so when we returned, we had a window full of starlight and the 'light of India.' I wore it to a fancy dinner in Paris."

The men returned carrying baskets of blueberries except, Noni. He brought up the rear openly flirting with Nini.

"I swear he could meet a woman on a desert island," Rem remarked. The Celestial Seven offered to do whatever they could to restore her grounds to their pre-Powwow glory and help with the chores. She had a list, straightening the stonewall along her property; repairing a hole in the roof, sharpening tools, splitting wood and filling the water barrel.

That night at the Pilgrim Lake house, the impromptu party by the sea, the hunt for Hebe, the Powwow and the day of chores up at Wénise's sent them straight into the doldrums of vacation fatigue.

Wénise & Twenty-Men, Dinner in Paris

XIV

Everyone Goes Away

The Celestial Seven had ebbed on Cape Cod's shores and flowed back to the Birches for the remainder of the summer. In September, they all left for separate horizons. Nell was the first to leave. She had a maternally arranged triste with Vittorio, an Italian Marquis on an island in the Aegean. When she was packing, Holly popped in to say good-bye and mentioned she was next because she had to shut herself off to complete her portfolio for the art school.

"What? And leave Floyd? Remember what happened before?"

"He's fine, Nell. May I ask you something?"

"Sure."

"If you love Hans so much, why are you running all over the world chasing men to..."

Offended, Nell bat her big eyes and tempered her volume to say, " I—do—not—chase--men."

Hans and Noni got lost behind the house in order to conduct "serious field observations resulting in" at least five scientific words Hebe had never heard before. She had tagged along when they showed Rem the network of metal that reached up into the sky and had bright circus red and taxicab yellow blades.

"Oh a windmill. Why didn't you say that?"

"Isn't it incredible?" he asked Rem.

"As Hebe said, it's a windmill."

Hans flicked on a switch. Gears ground slowly, and then the stable was dimly illuminated. Waiting for Rem's response, he chewed the inside of his mouth, shoved his hands in his pockets and paced. Rem was not particularly impressed but liked the idea of being a benefactor to his special science project, so she consented to it. After that, the sight was off limits except to fellow researchers from the university.

Holly and Floyd were gone from view. She was voluntarily stuck in the web of music and dependency he had spun throughout his rooms upstairs. Rem left for an annual party in Tangiers. Why Rem would go so far for an event she described as "a lavish affair attended by anyone who is anyone anywhere with painfully predictable entertainment," until she mentioned to someone on the phone, "Yes, my love will be there." Many suitors called for Rem. She kept them waiting eagerly for unfashionably long periods and eventually, with no sense of hurry at all, nonchalantly descended the stairs. Smiling politely, she gave an assessing gaze, which shook a few gentlemen's confidence, and then, as if to say, "You have passed," she presented her gloved hand. Bob never had to wait longer than fifteen minutes before Rem's stunning entrance. She glided mellifluously down and extended her ardent hand on the last step.

Hebe was the only one of the Celestial Seven who had been formally introduced to Bob or seen him for more than a few minutes. They all wanted to know more about the man who had done the seemingly impossible and impressed their fabulously desirable but famously selective Rem. Holly mentioned knowing "of him," but true to her Boston Brahmin ethos, offered nothing more. In an unexpected and patently bourgeois move, Nell engaged her mother, "revered in certain circles," for her background ferreting skills. "Sans a nom de famille," she doubted she would have success, and she did not. Floyd spotted Bob at the gallery opening where Holly had her last premiere, and when she was occupied, he made discreet inquiries. The sum total of his report to the Celestial Seven was "That's Bob," and it concretized suspicions that the gentleman was probably of the Yankee caste, though his style was his own. No stiff square-shouldered jackets for him; he dressed casually in slacks and sweaters and often carried a tennis racket. Hebe had spent the most time with him, and they all wanted to know "what is he like?"

"Bob is really smart. He went to Harvard University! Well and, he is charming…He has been all over the world, speaks a few languages and …Oh, he likes to laugh, but not too loudly. That's all I know."

"What do they do together?" Nell asked.

"I don't know. They are not public about being boyfriend and girlfriend. They act like sunflowers when the sun is in the middle."

"Sunflowers?

On the tarmac, Floyd saw that Hebe had spoken literally. A few feet apart, Bob greeted Rem and stood shoulder to shoulder with her waiting to board. Their mutual attraction overcame propriety and drew their faces together.

"Your sunflower analogy rings true Hebe. Genuine attraction is palpable in many ways, isn't it?"

Hebe couldn't hear him over her heart beating already missing her friends. Rem rushed to Hebe dropped to one knee and held her so tightly, Hebe got a mouthful of perfumed mink.

"I know what you are thinking," she began. "But we are not leaving you. For one reason or another, everyone goes away, and then they come back."

Her words warmed Hebe's heart but didn't prevent her from sobbing all the way back to the Birches. Seeking consolation from her friends was futile as they were away, Bozena with her husband and Anne Atkinson was busy with her social calendar. Holly and Floyd were there but cached in his room to enjoy each other before she too left. Hebe cast her lines to distant California, including the librarian to let her know why she had not returned her books. Rosalita's response was four, single-spaced, double-sided, handwritten pages; the first half was devoted to the meticulous details of what she and her boyfriend said and did. As a heading for the next paragraph, she wrote "Tony. I guess you already read this from him. Quickly, she opened Tony's letter. Half a piece of chewing gum was included with a sentence about life in the military. He closed with "I miss you too much." The back was blank. She read Rosalita's. "Tony married a gringa, ja ja ja, cuz she got pregnant. Now, I am Tia Rosalita." The words strung Hebe's emotions into a cat's cradle comprehension and disappointment of his missing her "too much" yet marrying "a gringa." Rosalita was also busy making acorn cakes. She sold at a few local stores. When she replied, she wished her luck and hoped to "taste them myself soon."

News of Tony's nuptials had temporarily soused her burning desire to write. She turned to a few of the staff for companionship. Rem's "Wizard of Oz," Henry, was the estate's most stoic resident, and he proved rather quickly that being "friendly" with her was inappropriate. He never initiated or engaged in conversation; he only answered questions he was asked. The groundskeeper Ichi was much freer and shared a bit of his knowledge about plants and trees and flowers that rivaled Wénise's. The most loquaciousness was Stable Master, Mr. Thomas who spoke with a lilting Scottish brogue. Of course, his subject was usually the horses whom he knew better than his children. At a glance he saw which had an upset tummy, was hungry or in a bad mood. They whinnied in adoration when Mr. Thomas came into view whether or not his pockets were full of apples and acorns.

The day Holly departed, Thaddeus Oberland Sheridan III, Tossie, arrived by her invitation to help move art supplies to her new studio. Floyd had asked Hebe up to listen to records, but his eyes frequently wandered to the yard beyond the window.

"Did you see his new car Floyd?"

"Yes, Thaddeus has come into his inheritance," he remarked dryly, smacked the shutter closed and gulped down a few pills with a swig of vodka.

"I'll be back in a bit."

In the shade by the stable, she worked on a cornhusk doll and talked to Mr. Thomas. Tossie galloped across the lawn on Jupiter, the largest horse at The Birches. Ichi shuffled out of the greenhouse and collected the clumps of grass dug up by the hooves. Because his position did not allow reprimanding guest, he muttered to no one in particular.

"Horses not good for grass. We put pea gravel on path. They should ride horses on the path."

Everyone Goes Away

Tossie peered down the bridge of his generous nose and without as much as a "Hello," demanded to be told Holly's whereabouts. She trotted up.

"That's right. On the gravel," Ichi the grass back into the ground, and then he glanced at his watch, "Time for the *Lone Ranger*."

"Tossie, this is Hebe Holmes, Rem's charge."

'His tight jaw bit out a, "Yes. Hebe? Sounds… Jewish…"

"Greek, the Greek goddess of youth," Hebe clarified.

"That should have been your first guess," Holly smirked demurely.

She patted her Chestnut Bay filly, surveyed the horizon and bolted off with Tossie on her tail. Hebe had not seen Floyd come down, but she heard him holler from the greenhouse.

"Bugger off."

The troubled emotion in his voice drew her inside. He paced between the plants and ran his hand repeatedly through his hair.

"You saw them fawning all over each other."

"I think they are just friends."

"Once they used to be more."

"And then she chose you, right?"

"Now he is rich as Croesus."

"Holly doesn't exactly need money."

"New topic Hebe!" Floyd snapped.

"I know she loves you."

"Love is not always enough."

His silk smoking jacket billowed into a cape as he stomped off. Shielded by the living room curtains Hebe bore witness to Holly leaving that night questioned her love for Floyd. Tossie gave her bottom a healthy goose and shot a wry glance up at Floyd in his window. In the Daimler, she surreptitiously planted a smooch on Tossie's lips, and then squeezed through the narrow leather sunroof to blow him a kiss.

"I'll submit my portfolio soon and be back," she promised merrily.

Floyd's vibrant blue irises grayed with her words, and he skulked into isolating listlessness. Hebe had checked on him, and no matter how dark his mood. Empty booze bottles were stacked and cracked and broken in the boxes inside and outside his door. Music that used to permanently rain down from his quarters now only came once in a while from the record player, never from his saxophone.

Every night, Rem checked in. All went well, for three days but by the fourth, The Birches old boards creaked loudly missing the full weight of occupants.

Even the house can't sleep.

Wine helped. After a couple of glasses, she carried a photograph of Ahanu to the window.

That's where the horses live. You would like Lightning. See that dark lump on the blanket? That's Lucky, the Beagle. He is sleeping. This is Monsieur Rothschild; he doesn't have much to say."

The gossamer curtains drew in the rich scent of night- blooming jasmine making her breathe more deeply. When she smudged her room and prayed, she heard Ahanu's little voice say, "'pirit,' as he had on the beach before she left California. He was sitting in the chair play-ing with one of his trucks. It dropped to the floor, and he climbed down. Stretching on the floor beside him, she heard his little voice singing the song she had sung to him countless times. "We are the stars which sing; We sing with our light; We are the birds of fire; We fly over the sky," and she put his picture away to ease the pain it brought to her heart.

"Ooh-ooh, ooh-ooh. Ooh-ooh, ooh-ooh," hooted an owl outside.

"Are you trying to tell me something," she asked and scanned the dark grounds beyond her window.

Except for Hans' windmill squeaking by his tent ablaze with mid-night oil, all was calm. She was anxious for him to develop her film from P-Town, but he did not receive visitors when he was working at that hour, so she left the film in the crate in front of his photo lab. Back in her room, she tipped her head and drained the very last drop from her second wine bottle. Oddly, the more she drained it the heavier it weighed in her hand. By the time it thudded and clinked on the floor, Rothschild had taken her into a consciousness beyond troubles. For that reason, she stowed him in her Kit Carson thermos and packed him in with the lunch for her car tour the following afternoon.

She handed Shale her itinerary with Mount Vernon Street as the first stop. In the attic trunk was the postcard she had seen her first day there. On the front, her Livingston grandparents were featured in splendid 19th century attire at a horse show. Their images sent an unexpected ping to her heart for her grandfather. He shined as brightly as Wut-tootchìkkìnneasin Nippawus whenever he had seen her, even in the hospital when he was sick. She knew the nurses found him special too because she heard them declare, "Always has a kind word…'bahooky.' That word for "butt" made everyone laugh. In the image, Grandma Livy leaned against a railing behind him; an enormous hat framed her face. She was a pretty and pleasant lady, not the sourpuss she had become.

Lord & Lady Malcolm Livingston, International Horse Show, circa 1900

Maybe her spirit died when he did, and she is lonely without him.

She tucked the picture in her pocket, and out of habit she to smooth the bed. No matter how tightly she tugged, a stubborn lump remained, and pulling off the covers, she discovered Anùm.

"I didn't forget you," she lied to her stuffed dog and heaped him close to her bosom.

There was nothing else there she wanted. Her former home, in Cambridge was next. Shale opened the car door and she stood staring at the great French doors. Her five-year-old-ghost waved, and she waved back.

"Shale!"

"Yes, Miss Hebe Jeebie."

"Shale that's me...that's me when I was little, when I was happy."

There was no one he could see.

"I see Miss Hebe Jeebie.:

Apparitions of her parents appeared on the back porch with their arms around one another. Hans was there, many moments of her young life. Continuing to the school, she tripped over the step she had to use the railing to climb which heightened her awareness of how much she had grown. A car engine gunned her back to the present.

"Hoh Nuttah!"

A black and red Chevy screeched up beside her. Púck stuck his nut brown face out the window prickled her skin so pleasantly from head to toe, and she walked to him with her hips involuntarily sashaying from side to side.

"I'll give you a ride. Hop in."

"I can't," she answered sweetly and instinctively ran her fingertips across his muscular forearm.

"Okay, next time."

Púck shared a long, deep kiss with his passenger out of view.

Hebe averted her eyes.

"Maybe next time we're on the Cape"

Grinning electric with lusty adolescent hormones, he replied, "Cool Nuttah or are you only using Hebe now?"

"Nuttah to you."

"Hebe?" Púck's girl asked over his wheels spinning a patch of rubber onto the ground.

Pia? Hebe asked herself. *No. It can't be, that's doesn't make any sense. There are lots of girls with red hair.*

She contemplated her small life from atop her bed at the Birches where she had stretched out with Anùm for a nap. No sooner had she closed her eyes than Noni rapped and burst in without awaiting invitation.

"Noni! I did not say you could come in."

He apologized and feigned calm dignity just long enough to ask, "How are you today?" and then rapidly gave her reply, "Fine?"

"Yes, but I miss Rem."

"Me too."

Oozing mirth, he gave the reason for his intrusion.

"UFO proof because of you. I have UFO proof because of you!"

"Me!?"

He laid a photograph on the bed

"Is that a UFO!" she gasped and then squinted suspiciously. "Wait a minute. You and Hans are playing a trick on me. How did you…That is a hat or a coin or…"

"That is a photo from your camera—your film," he kissed her cheeks.

"But *you* borrowed my camera in P-Town, remember?"

"Hebe if I saw a flying saucer, I would have yelled."

She was convinced it had been manipulated.

"I left the camera on the table, and there were a lot of people at the beach party that night. Anyone could have taken it Noni."

"Maybe me," he quipped cockily and reveled forth into the hall.

His fervor's remnants had chased away the sandman, so she forgot about a nap, ordered afternoon tea and took her guns outside to clean them.

Lucky knew from experience that when a person sat at the table, food was possible, and he sidled closer. The assorted savories smelled scrumptious. Gazing at Hebe with charmingly pitiable eyes usually weakened her resolve not to break the, "no treats" rule. Failing with that approach, he resorted to whimpering or pawing at her leg. Nothing. He pretended to give up by nestling into the grass but soon realized he had unintentionally dozed off. The screen door banged and roused him, and the maid with the shiny tray of dishes was fast on her way. He barked to remind Hebe he was still there and interested in morsels, no matter how small, and she placed a few savories on a plate for him. Within seconds, he had wolfed them down, licked his lips and collapsed into luxuriant indolence.

Hebe set about cleaning her old weapons. Rem had offered her "a newer model," but Hebe declined with, "Wénise gave me these. This was her rifle and this one belonged to Twenty-Men. They tell stories."

When one had to be sent away for repairs, she was left with the 1873 Winchester that she could not use for skeet. She accepted Rem's offer.

"Which one would you like?"

One, and only one, captured her eye; it was "so pretty," she could hardly believe it was a gun and hesitated to touch it. Rem was pleased.

"Someone finally adores my Barella. Take it!"

"I can borrow this one Are you sure?"

"It's perfect for you. It doesn't even weigh three kilos. 16 gauge."

It came with its own case and the cleaning tools she laid on the garden table. Ichi joined her with a bushel basket a third full with bright red paper cranes. Obsessively, he folded more and tossed them in.

"Ten out of twelve."

"Cranes?"

"Clay pigeons. I saw you shooting. You are very good."

"My great grandmother taught me."

"Not great grandfather?"

"No he died. She never found another."

Ichi patted his plump chest.

"True love? That is very rare—usually impossible to replace."

Staring at a crane on the table and in the fresh spring air, he shared the love he and his wife had. She was the daughter of a French professor living in Japan in the 1930's. Ichi, at that time, was a self-described non-romantic who would not date non-Japanese because he did not find them attractive and believed in racial purity along with the rest of Japan.

"There is only place for Japanese people in Japan. To marry non-Japanese creates many problems. More for child—Konketsuj, we call them."

"Konketsuji? Does that mean half-breed dog?"

"Maybe like that, but no dog. In university, I studied botany. Our class made life drawings in the gardens enclosed in glass. I finished my leaf portfolio, and I wanted to draw a flower. None I liked bloomed that week, next week, next. I gave up and drew bark. One day, between the trees—there it was," he paused, to cup his palms around the vivid memory, "royal purple orchid. I walked to the spot. Nothing there. Then it went by the window. I hurried out. Her father held the flower in a pot and invited me. 'You may come to my house and draw.' I met her there."

"Who?"

"Lulu, my wife."

"The French girl? What about racial..."

He shook his head back and forth, "Loves destroys stupid thinking like that." Melancholy mist coated his eyeglasses and he continued making paper birds. Five cranes later, he was again himself. "An old riddle for a young girl. A man sleeps and dreams he is a butterfly. That butterfly sleeps and dreams he is the man. He wake ups up. Is he the man who dreams he is the butterfly, or the butterfly who dreams he is the man?"

"What did he eat for breakfast?" she asked seriously.

Ichi's flesh jiggled in amusement.

✳✳✳

The empty mail tray in the hall made her feel rejected. Why didn't her mother write? She did not understand and longed for it to be two days later when Rem and Nell would return. For companionship, she read in the library. Noni stepped in.

"No more flying saucers? "

"I need a break."

She rang for ice, cola and limes. Noni usually added sugar to all his drinks and she was sure he had added some to the colas; he didn't, but out of habit, he had poured rum into both glasses by habit. From the innumerable volumes, they selected poems and read them aloud. After the second drink, her eyes ran over his shapely thighs filling out his trouser legs and then proceeded up to his full mouth and thick black hair.

Anne is right, he could be 'a movie star, like Ricky Ricardo,' and what did Bozena say?—'Wide shoulders for making good sexy.' Rosalita used the same words for him that she uses for cake, "Que Rico!" I guess he is cute.

Noni tossed a magazine onto the table, and the thud brought her back to the library. He named the girl on the cover and three more.

"I dated all. I am a hunter."

"Are you sure? Maybe you are the hunted."

Too buzzed for philosophical musings, he jumped to the carpet, put on a record and pulled Hebe out of her chair to Merengue. Soon the rum's spirit, the music's rhythm and her torso's innocently erotic sway overwhelmed him and closed his eyes. He was no longer with the little girl, Hebe but a former shapely, paramour undulating desirously in his arms. Holding her tightly, he indulged in her breasts pressing on his stomach, but when he moved his leg between hers and rotated his hips, she became uncomfortable drew back and repositioned herself.

"Noni, I don't like this dance!"

"Let yourself go!"

He planted a wet kiss on her clavicle.

She cuffed him in the head and pushed him away. He mistook the gestures he had experienced from older girls as coyness, and grinning excitedly, he grabbed by the wrists and danced her backwards into the wall.

"Noni, Stop! Ya párale!"

And then she screamed. The needle scratched through the music, and it ended. Hans boomed by the side of the record player.

"Zeg! Noni?" he boomed, "What the fuck?! Let her go!"

Snatched from his lascivious trance, Noni jerked his head away from her neck and his hands from her body. The walls and furnishings moved phantasmagorically around the walls, and she shook her head. Recovering from the abrupt interruption, Noni breathed heavily.

"Don't tell me nothing Hans. You think you bed the lady of the manor and you are in charge?"

"My friendship with Rem is not your concern."

"Who I dance with is not yours."

"Excuse me."

Hebe pressed her lips together and hurried out with her savories clinging to her esophagus.

"It is when you choose an eleven-year-old, our Hebe."

"Eleven! Que? Dios!"

Noni's "Dios," was the last word she heard over her involuntary retching as she tapped up the stairs to throw up in the bathroom.

How did this happen? Rem is probably going to send me away. What have I done?

The floor slanted under her, and she struggled to stay on her feet until she reached her bed. She grabbed Anùm, and let her body sink into the mattress. It flattened into a carpet, lifted from the bed and moved around from corner to corner and from the ceiling to the floor.

Okay. This is a dream, a stupid drunken dream. It has to be.

All at once, the carpet soared through the open window at an incredible speed that whipped her hair straight back and panicked her, but Mishquáishim's absence indicated she was all right. She held on tightly. The carpet listed to the starboard side; she was flying over the map that had blown into her possession in San Diego. As the carpet descended, the buildings and trees became real. Men on the runway flashed red lights and the carpet zoomed up and down. Two flocks of birds, one black and one white, soared above them and dove at her, and she buried her head under her folded arms in duck'n'cover fashion.

The mantle clock chimed three. Her eyelids scratched down over her eyeballs, and she was happy to see she was at the table in her room where she kept the water pitcher. A note card was standing by it. She drank a glass and read. "Cara Hebita, Lociento," written in blue ink and "Noni is an idiot," written in black as was, "See you tomorrow, Hans & Noni." The card lifted her spirits but did nothing for her headache. A shower helped. As was often the case, she heard music coming from the jazz suite upstairs. There was blues from two old colored men who had crashed there the week before and boisterous but beautiful singing from a big busty opera singer before that. Today it was popowuttáhig, powwow drums. She saw them on hills of the Birches. More than a hundred Native Americans lined up for the Grand Entry and stood as hushed as a field of corn. Deer tails, porcupine quills, hawk, eagle and turkey feathers provided the finishing touches to their regalia and honored the animals who gave them. The jingle dancers' smallest movement tinkled and chinkled the metal cones they had so painstakingly sewn on. Shawl dancers spread their great fabric wings and adjusted their fringes. The drum began. CHO mah bah ah, CHO mah bah ah. The beat seemed to be coming from the musicians' quarters on the next floor. It sounded like American Indian musicians playing live. Or was it in her head? She couldn't tell.

Maybe Floyd. Poor guy. Why doesn't Holly call him?"

Putting on her robe, Mishquáishim brushed against her leg and she stopped. The syllables of the drum were spoken by a low, ghoulish voice, "CHO mah bah ah." She had heard it before but she could not remember where. Something was wrong; she just knew it. The feeling grew so strong that she tucked her shotgun under her arm and went to investigate. The Jazz suite was completely empty except for the echoing, "Cho mah bah ah, Cho mah bah ah." Goosebumps covered her arms as she tiptoed up to Floyd's floor. She followed the gun barrel into his dark quarters reeking of musk, stale cigarette butts and animal guts. She saw the cute, green frog Púck had speared wiggling terrified and helpless and Mishquáishim's furry bleeding heart when he hung suspended in mid leap before he dropped to his death.

"Floyd? Floyd, are you in here?"

Her ankle cracked on the edge of the dresser. When she reached down to rub it, her hair swept across the back of Floyd's head buried in the carpet.

"Floyd. Floyd? Oh my God Floyd! What happened?"

Clicking on the lamp illuminated her answer. Muscles and ligaments spilled out of his forearms from his elbows to his wrists. Blood pooled under them. Instinct took over, and she tore the pillowcases into bandages.

"What have you done Floyd? What have you done?!" she asked softly.

His eyes opened. His breath barely carried his words, "Cho mah bah ah," and then as if his neck had broken, his head fell onto his chest.

"Cho mah bah ah," she repeated faster and faster and to her surprise they came out as "Abamacho."

Abamacho! The Devil?

"What?! Floyd open your eyes! Floyd. Help!" she screamed at the top of her lungs.

Silence. There was no time to try to find who was at the Birches and where they were, so she aimed at the stand of trees outside and fired the shotgun, Blam! Floyd tapped her leg, and she leaned her ear next to his face.

"Holly?"

He moved his head from side to side.

"I will call her and have her…"

With all the strength he could muster, he continued shaking his head.

"No. Please. Don't tell Holly."

The possibility of his request being the last he would every make, encouraged her to agree and to promise. As soon as she did, his head flopped onto his chest and his body onto her lap.

He is not dead. He cannot be.

Placing her cheek up to his nostrils, proved her right, but hardly any air was coming out. She decided to solicit help from Kiehtan. Uncertain as to whether he responded to prayers for Whites, and thinking Floyd might be a Christian, she recited the prayer she remembered in English and in Wampanoag to cover both bases.

"Our Father which art in Heaven—Nooshun kesukqut Hallowed be thy Name—Wunneetupantamunach koowesuonk. Thy Kingdom come,

—Peyaumooutch kukkeitassootamooonk. Thy will be done in Earth, as it is in Heaven—Toh anantaman ne naj okheit, neane kesukqut...." Something, something bread? Oh no! What is next? Hold on Floyd. Oh ...deliver us from evil—webe pohquohwussinnan wutch matchitut; For thine is the Kingdom--Newutche keitassootamooonk, kutahtauun, the Power, the Glory, for ever—nuhkesuonk, sohsúmóonk michéme kah-mich éme. A'ho. Er... ah Amen."

Floyd's chest rise and fall with a big breath.

"Kuttabotumish. Kuttabotumish," and turned toward a crucifix on the wall, "And thank you too."

Henry, Mr. Thomas, Ichi and Shale stormed in with the upstairs staff on their heels. Hans and Noni pushed in. His eyes went right to Floyd and he crossed himself.

"¡Santo Dios!"

Henry clapped his hands and disbanded the staff which curiosity had crushed into the doorway.

"How nice that you have nothing to do at dawn," and glanced at his pocket watch, "in but two hours," he announced scattering the servants.

Hans blankly held the phone prepared to dial and stammered, "Henry, should I call the police...an ambulance or..."

"Excuse me sir," Henry answered and gently hung up. "We can manage on our own."

Mr. Thomas and Ichi brought a cot from the *Jazz Quarter* to move Floyd into the service elevator to the garage. The only vehicle that could accommodate him lying flat was Mr. Thomas' new Edsel station wagon. When they slid him in, his arm dangled lifelessly off the sides. Hebe burst into tears.

"Hebe. He will be okay. I saw worse than this in the war. I think it is shock," Ichi assured as Mr. Thomas and Shale drove slowly down the rear driveway.

In the gloomy, grey half-light, Noni's silhouette that included Floyd's saxophone sprinted after the Edsel. It stopped for him and then they were gone.

Is that the last time I will see Floyd?

The experience draped a funereal atmosphere over morning at the Birches and dispatched the Celestial Seven to separate hideaways to recover, except Hebe. As if totally unaware that anything had happened, she put on her boots for a visit to Lightning. Mr. Thomas had told her, "He really likes you," and supplied her with a kit of brushes and mane combs which he showed her how to use. The activity satisfied her immensely because Lightning sighed in appreciation just as Wénise did when she rubbed her feet at day's end. When his mane and tail were fluffed and his coat shined brightly, she held up a large mirror for him, an act that Mr. Thomas said was "silly."

According to him, "the structure of the horse's eyeball reflects a huge shape, not your love's labor." He was probably right because he always was when it came to horses, but he had not considered the horse's manito, his spirit's eyes. Those were the ones through which Lightning saw how beautifully she had groomed him. She was positive because he pulled his lips back over his big teeth into a smile.

On her way to the stables, reality shot a barrage of arrows through her denial and knocked her into a state of shock. Floyd's mangled white muscles spurted fountains of blood and drowned her brain in the red seas of horror. The lawn rose up to her knees, and she steadied herself by clutching the refreshing dew-coated blades she shook uncontrollably from a paroxysm of weeping.

Hans ran from his tent and carried her to the library where she buried herself in the corner of the couch. Noni was already there sprawled out on a chair with a drink.

"Where are the girls, Noni?"

"Tangiers and Greece, remember?"

"Yeah, then we have to keep an eye on Hebe."

"It's my fault, you know?"

"You? How? Floyd had completely shut himself off, up there day and night and night and day after Holly left. It wasn't you. It was us. We should have invited him," Noni lamented." We should have done something."

"Yet nothing would have worked. Floyd was headed down that path. The aesthetic individual engages in inner battles to escape reality,' isn't that what Kierkegaard wrote?"

"Killing yourself is not Hans. Our boy Floyd would not have done this man. Oh!" he exclaimed pulling his hair. "Oh my God Hans—They got him."

"Who?"

The aliens. They abducted him and..."

"Noni, Stop!" Hans bellowed. "Floyd wasn't abducted..."

"No arguing. Not now please," Hebe interjected. "Should we call the hospital Hans?"

"He is in intensive care."

"Can we visit?"

"Not yet Hebe. Rem feels Holly should know."

"I promised Floyd I wouldn't tell her," Hebe whined.

"I doubt Floyd will remember. And *you* are not telling. Rem is," Hans clarified.

"Yes, when all of us are together. Don't worry, Hebe. He can't be mad; you saved his life.

"Yes, that's right. Well done Hebe."

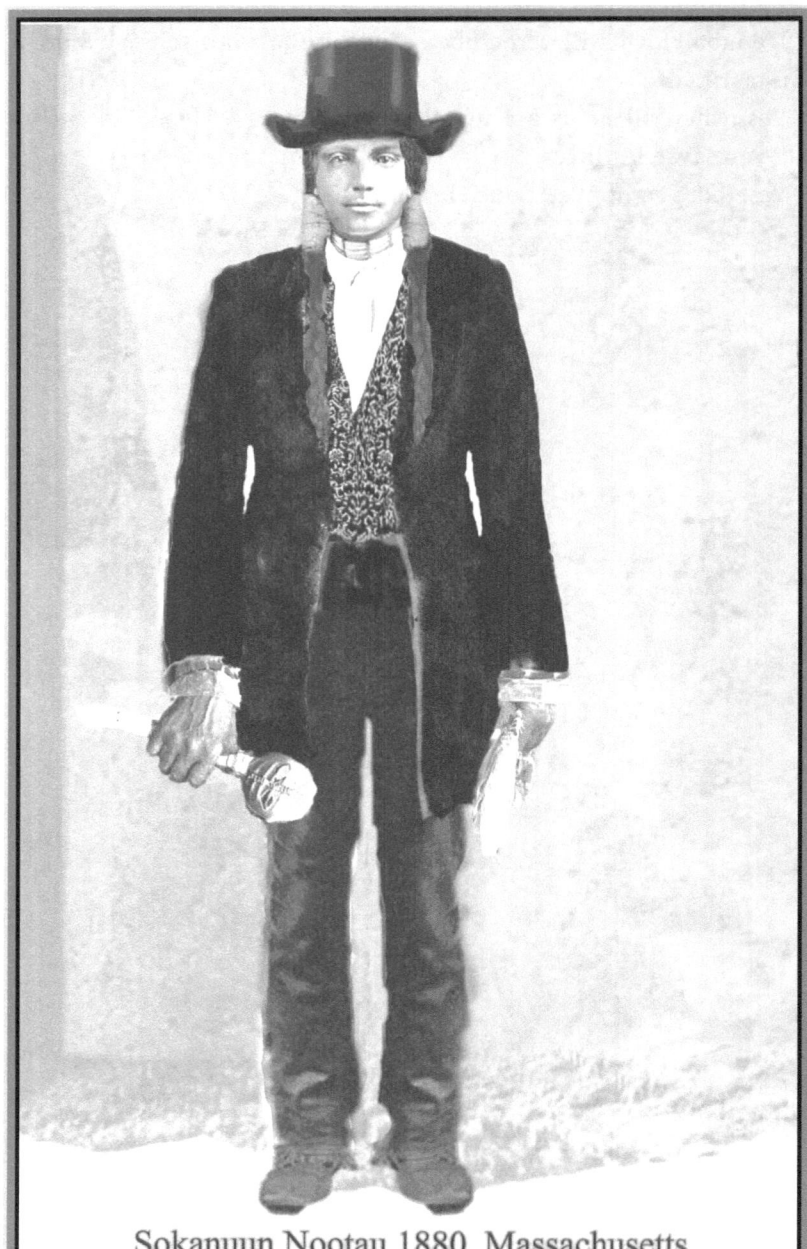

Sokanuun Nootau 1880, Massachusetts

XV

The Powwáw,
Sokanuum Nootau – Rains Fire

On Saturday, The Celestial Seven had an intimate soirée to celebrate their reunion and welcome Philipe who had returned with Rem. With all the adoration of a pet anticipating its long-away owner's arrival, Holly focused on the entrance for Floyd. Nell enthusiastically recapped her sojourn to the Aegean in tremendous detail and shared in tedious detail Vitori's every flirtatious gesture and compliment, mostly for Hans' benefit. Seemingly preoccupied, he surveyed the ceiling and smoked. Rem preferred not to talk about "Barbara's party in Tangiers," but to show them, once the film footage had yet to be processed. With an almost imperceptible head bow, she nodded to Henry to commence the dinner service. When Holly saw him press the buzzer to the kitchen, she became distressed.

"I had a feeling Floyd was going to be late. I had such a strange dream about him, a little while ago. Aren't dreams funny? They are so real sometimes. Let's wait for him, shall we?" Her eyes flitted from one blank face to another. "What? What is going on? Tell me!"

Rem explained Floyd's absence without the words, "tried to kill himself," or "slashed his wrists," or even "hospital." She signaled Henry who stemmed the dinner service.

"Cheri, Floyd is not coming to dinner…"

Love, grief and fear pooled in her eyes, whitened her pallor and shoved her from her chair in a breathy panic.

"I will go up and talk..."

Rem shook her head, "He is not there."

"No? Then where?"

"He was wrestling with the black dog when..."

The words felled Holly, but Hans sprang forward and caught her before she reached the floor. Rem swept her hand toward the door.

"The couch in the library is comfortable."

The three left and she returned alone.

"Holly will return presently."

Their doings and plans became the topic. Hans slid into his seat and discussed how well his project was progressing and Noni added, "It is incredible. If I did not see it with my own eyes, I would not believe it."

The men rose from their seats as Holly walked in with a faint smile, and finally the dinner service began. In the interlude before dessert, Hebe offered to tell a story about the Wild West, and they were all ears.

"Oh, this is about Kit Carson."

"It is Hans."

"How could you possibly have known that?" Rem asked

"When Hebe was a very little girl," she had a picture of him and his horse on her night stand."

"Did she tell you that?" Noni asked.

"No. He was there. He is "sort of an uncle, right?"

She kissed his cheek, blushing deeply; Hans pat her arm sweetly.

"Kit Carson. He lived a hundred years ago. He did a lot but we are going to come into his life when he was a trapper. He was a teenager and only as tall as Noni..."

"Awww, only 167 centimeters?" Hans noted.

"169, Noni corrected, "and small packages have big surprises."

"And Noni, like you, Kit spoke Spanish, of course English, and a few Indian languages too. Because he was out in the woods and plains among the Indians and animals. He was familiar with their tracks. He could predict the weather, and he was strong."

Hans stood up and flexed his considerable muscles.

"Not beautiful muscles. Aggressive muscles."

"Aggressive muscles?" Hans asked.

"I guess. He killed a mountain lion with his bare hands, but he didn't like to fistfight or anything. He lived out west where nature is so..."

"Majestic," Hans interjected.

"Voluptuously textured," added Holly.

"Peaceful," Philipe sighed.

"Lonely," Noni threw out drawing glares. "What? There's no girls?"

"There were, the good-time girls in town and Indian girls in the wilderness. The problem was if a trapper found an Indian girl, he was stuck out there forever."

"Why is that?" Nell asked.

"A lot of reasons. The Europeans considered themselves better than Indians, more civilized, and they had a different religion and didn't believe in different races marrying.… Besides, most Indian women didn't speak English, so it would being in town would be scary. The frontiersmen who did marry Indian women were called squaw men. Kit Carson vowed never to be one, a Squaw man."

"Never say never," Noni reminded everyone.

"That's right. The Mountain Men Rendezvous was a big camping party where they trade, fish and shoot, drink, meet girls..."

Noni rubbed his hands together excitedly, "Girls. Yes. Now we're getting somewhere."

"The men tell stories and fill up on whiskey on one side, and the squaws prepare food on the other. One time, Joseph, was there. He was a big, Canadian with a reputation as a lout and a masher..."

"Ah ha, the mujeriego," Noni giggled, "Like me."

"Coureur de jupons," Rem translated quickly for Nell.

"Yes, but the Rendezvous had rules. One was 'leave the women alone or leave the Rendezvous,' which meant none of the good cooking. But at one get together in Wyoming, Joseph had caught sight of 'la plus belle fille,' he had ever seen. She was so pretty, he was willing to break the rule and risk losing his supper. 'Règles. Règles. Ne me parles pas de règles! Je vais là-bas,' he told the trappers. They didn't try to stop him; he was such a rowdy bully, a few egged him on hoping he would get himself kicked out. When he strode across the field, the men singled out the girl, an Arapaho, and agreed she was 'real pretty,' and 'must have just come of age,' because they didn't remember ever seeing her before. Kit knew no good came from 'Rendezvous' booze and broods,' so he steered clear. Joseph went to the women's area which incited a huge commotion…"

"And got kicked out?" Philipe asked.

"Not completely, just back to the men. They tried to joke off his rejection, but he threw himself down in a sulk and drank. Later on, the music started, and it was time for the soup dance. Each girl set her pot of soup out in a row. The men and women make two lines on either side. They dance toward the pots, but the girl gets to choose the man she wants to taste her soup first. Joseph grinned and danced his best right near the girl he liked, but she ignored him and danced toward a different man. Joseph bashed him in the head… knocked him down."

"Quelle brute!" Holly declared.

"Yes. The girl ran like the wind, and he ran after her. Bets were made on 'the squaw or the fool,' but Kit didn't put any money in. He got a big dish of food from one of the elders and went off by himself. They say he really liked to watch the stars and listen to the woods. The camp was tuned out except for cheers and a loud clear voice. "Ah Ha! Back alone. A trapper ain't no match for a squaw!" Kit, pleased she got away, surrendered to sleep. Small twigs snapping opened his eyes, and he saw a girl on horseback. The vision of her sitting sweetly on the steed with stars sprinkling all around took his breath away. Their eyes met…"

"He had good dreams that night," Noni interjected.

"Probably, but the next day, Kit saw Joseph chasing a girl. One of the Arapaho braves caught her and walked her back to the big Canadian. It was her, his starlight girl. She broke free and ran crying right up to Kit. In sign language, she asked for help…"

Hebe made the gesture and the others imitated it.

"One of the mountain men who spoke Arapaho let Kit know, he could not help her because their customs say the Canadian won her beating the other guy. The brave was her brother. Kit went over the brother to her father. He asked the father to marry her! The father didn't want trouble with his son over his daughter. He proposed…"

"A duel!" Rem declared.

"Yes! On horses! Big old Joseph was sure he could beat Kit. In front of everyone, they charged at each other on horses, and then they fired at the same time. Joseph's hand was badly wounded."

"And your Kit Carson?" Holly asked.

"He got grazed in the head, but he got the girl. He married her. WaaNibe—Grass Singing.

"Grass Singing," Nell sighed. How romantic."

"Yes very, but I have always been curious," Rem began, "how do American Indians keep the soup hot?"

"I don't know about all peoples, but my great-grandmother, Wénise dropped in a hot stone from the fire."

The dramatic opening of their dinner was vaporized by cordials, wine and the story. Nell asked Holly about her romance.

"So where did your gentleman go, Thaddeus Oberland Sheridan III. He was quite...you know."

The Celestial Seven held their breath to see if Holly had had enough wine and collected herself enough to handle the inquiry she had.

"Ha ha. I would have to be a polo pony for anything to have happened."

He had galloped off to Newport after their first weekend. Rem assuaged Holly's upset and recruited her to the cause of redecorating Floyd's room.

"You and Philipe. A change is always good and we need to clear the negative energy from the space."

"That is a really good idea," Hebe agreed.

The Celestial Seven listened intently to the revelation of how a spooky, telepathic transmission of the word, "Abamacho" had alerted Hebe. Rem's eyelashes fluttered, and she placed the back of her hand on her forehead.

"Non! Quelle horreur est-il cette fois?" she asked and immediately stared at Noni.

"No. I don't want to get the priest?"

"We have to do something, a spirit is here," she whispered. "It sounds like possession. When I was a child in Tananarive—in Madagascar, a friend of my mothers had a similar experience, spoke in an unfamiliar tongue.

"But Possessed? Are you sure?" Nell asked.

"Possessed! I tell you the woman's head spun like a... a...un hibou, and..."

"Hibou? An owl?! That's biologically impossible," Hans interjected.

"Say what you want; we saw it. . ." Philipe assured them. "Floyd did not create the evil. It was attracted to him because he was vulnerable."

"Maybe it is an alien who…"

Rem curtly dismissed Noni's theory.

"Spirits Noni, spirits are not aliens Noni. We need someone who deals with spirits to protect all of us. An exorcism is not an execution; it is only an eviction. The spirit's survival instinct sets in and it enters a new body, any one."

To see Rem, who was usually imperturbable, unnerved by the circumstances concerned Hans so much he was able to put his scientific skepticism aside and tried to persuade Noni to call a priest for her peace of mind. He flat out refused, and they bickered boisterously.

"Excuse me," Hebe repeated several times before anyone heard. "I know a powwáw…"

"A medicine man! Bring him. Right away, please Hebe."

"Rem, I have to see if he is avail…"

"Double his fee. Triple it. Whatever he wants."

When the soirée wound down, Rem, Philipe and Hebe were off to the Plaza. Upon seeing the shotgun, Rem stopped Hebe.

"Cheri, why don't you bring the little stuffed dog, Anùm, for protection?"

"He can't make any noise. Spirits hate noise."

"Remy let her bring it," Philipe urged.

They lapsed into a French conversation, so Hebe called Púck on the car phone to ask him to contact Sokanuum Noootau. He was reluctant to drive all the way to the Cape.

"I'll have to sit and listen to old people talk, wait for Wénise to write a note to Sokanuum Nootau, drive it to him. Drive…Why don't they get telephones or cars or bicycles?

"Stop trying to impress your White girlfriend. She…"

"Look who's talking. You little city Indian."

"I would rather be a city Indian who respects our kehchisog than a nunkon-omp without good sense."

The words for elders brought Púck to his Native sensibilities. Sheepishly, he acquiesced.

The shotgun under her arm drew curious glances when they walked into the hotel, but no one spoke. While the suites were readied, Philipe went to the bar and Rem took Hebe the Palm Court "to discuss a serious matter" she assumed would be her encounter with Noni, or Floyd. Even the simple mention of his name spotlighted his slashed arms. She was half-right.

"I heard Noni was giving you—dance lessons," Rem began.

"Don't be mad at him. That was not his fault."

"Did you invite him to put his hands on you?"

"No."

"Did he ask if you wanted him to?" Hebe did not respond. "Then it was his fault. He is older. He took advantage. He is a nice man, and he will not do that again—but men will. If you do not want them to touch you, you must say that, loudly in simple terms such as, 'no' or 'stop'. If they continue, the etiquette is clear."

"It is?

"Yes. You are allowed to scream, punch, bite…"

"Bite?"

"Yes. Men who revert to their animal urges don't understand words.. And on an unrelated topic, in Paris, I met with Lady Livingston.

"Wow. You and Oma Livy in Paris."

"Indeed. She has extended her stay. We have formalized my guardianship of you with your mother's permission. She felt your staying where you are would be more convenient, so…"

Hebe interpreted that as Gaye-Lee rejecting which sent tears trickling over Hebe's cheeks. Rem repeated, "More convenient, that's all."

Hebe wanted to know why Rem agreed to take her.

"Kutty is a close friend of mine. You are a delight; everyone adores you. And… because I can," she replied merrily.

"My mother should."

"Maybe she can not—mine could not," Rem sighed, and half to herself added, "They are enigmas, mothers. They have a way about them. They show up in fragrances and flowers, sapphires," she glanced at a woman who walked in, "a mother shows up in the shade of another woman's hair; she is always everywhere, even though she is no where at all."

Hebe had never heard Rem so sad; she didn't know what to say, but Rem snapped out of it and gave Hebe an envelope. Inside was her long-awaited passport, Social Security card and a credit card.

"Do not lose them, especially the American Express card; it is money."

Rem had plans with Bob and Philipe, but she did not want Hebe to be alone, so she planned a "girl's night" at the hotel. A car had already been dispatched "to collect and return the Atkinson girl and Bozena" from their respective residences.

"Tomorrow, we will go to The Birches. I want to be there to receive the Medicine man—Rains Fire," she beamed as brightly as a full Hunter's moon which, to Hebe, signaled Bob's arrival. He admired her ornately carved shotgun before he sat next to Rem, and they morphed into sunflowers.

A record player, an ice bucket of sodas and bouquets of fresh flowers awaited her, and a suitcase of her clothes had been delivered and hung in the closet as they had been in New York, and for Rem, probably Paris, Tangiers and anywhere she went. While Hebe contemplated whether Rem was a woman who had no home or one for whom the world was home, she showered, changed and smudged the suite. When Bolek called and canceled on behalf of Bozena who had a stomach bug. She sent well wishes and worried that Anne would not come either and she would be left to battle her dark thoughts alone. Floyd slashed and bleeding on the floor, the iron lung, the Virgin of Guadalupe in her mother's window and the guns aimed at her in Mexico shot into her brain, and she fired back with a shot of rum. She wanted to be upbeat for her last visit with Anne before she returned to Paris. Equally eager to spend as much time as she could with Hebe, she arrived early. They lacquered their nails bright pink, practiced their dance steps and dis-solved into wiggling with a ridiculously unbridled abandon that left them parched.

"Gingerale this time and more ice and ice-cream," Hebe ordered and asked Anne, "What kind?"

"Neapolitan, that way we can have all three." The room service waiter was unexpectedly "so cute," and they concocted reasons to sum-mon him. A bit of hot running water got rid of the ice-cubes.

"We can't find them," Hebe complained on the telephone.

Upon delivering a champagne bucket stacked with ice, he was "ter-ribly sorry," and sincerely and refused their tip with a slight bow which made them feel awful. They hadn't meant to run him around for naught.

"We are two wicked girls," Anne declared mischievously.

They ordered food, to provide another chance to tip him. He rolled in the cart, lifted each lid and raised his eyebrows as he identified the unusual fare to verify their order.

"Anchovy canapé, Welsh rarebit, poussin diable, two vichyssoises, two borsch à la russe, two spaghetti Caruso, mixed olives, celery and two hamburgers. There are extra plates here," he advised. "Will there be anything else?"

Hebe shook her head and palmed him a folded bill. He had the tip. Vindication was theirs. Picking at their mis-matched fare, they shilly-shallied their way through the sundry discoveries and curiosities particular to youth and compared favorites:

What	Hebe	Anne
color	pink	pink
soda	rootbeer	gingerale
alcohol	red wine	liquers
icecream	peach	chocolate
cake	lemon	chocolate
parent	father	father
sport	skeet	tennis

Both liked Elvis Presley's songs, but chose Ricky Nelson as "the dreamiest singer." Playing "have you ever" they discovered they had a good bit in common: had flown in planes, ridden horses, stayed up past midnight, had champagne, swum nude in the ocean and kissed a boy and "seen a UFO," Anne added unexpectedly. Hebe screamed, excited to have someone to discuss Noni's photograph, and the map.

"Cow-e-tom-pá-tim-min," Anne greeted Hebe in the morning.

"Cow-e-tom-pá-tim-min.

The girls exchanged expressions of fondness along with promises of "oodles of letters" and to see one another next summer if they didn't meet in Paris.

Rem's invisible helpers would no doubt pack, so all she had to do was sprinkle tobacco in the pouch she brought as an offering to the medicine man.

Henry reported to Rem that Rains Fire had already been to the Birches and planned to meet them at the hospital because he "Mr. Fire stated he had to see the patient before he could perform his duties here." The Celestial Seven were milling around the grounds at the top of the hill to the hospital when Bob pulled up. Scattered in pairs and groups, they conversed and smoked and waited and waited and waited.

"Maybe he is lost," Noni guessed.

"Or he isn't coming," Holly fretted.

"It's possible. He thinks differently," Hebe explained matter-of-factly.

They wanted to know what that meant.

"I am sure he will be here or he wouldn't have called Henry. I am not sure when. Spirit makes him do stuff, not time. Usually if you ask him to do something, he agrees, 'Nux.' That means yes, but he always adds, 'when the spirit moves me,' so..."

"He is not so different from me then," Philipe noted.

Bob agreed, "'When the spirit moves me.' Translation? When I am good and ready."

They all laughed.

"It's a little deeper than that. Fifteen minutes in Wampanoag is four parts of an hour; 'yauwe chippag and hour.' See? The word hour has to be in English."

"He is here!" Hans yell out from his tree branch lookout.

"Can't be. That's a Duisenberg. Indians don't drive Duisenbergs."

"Sokanuum Nootau does," Hebe corrected.

"Hoh! Hoh! Nuttah!" Púck hollered out from the passenger window as if he hadn't seen her for years, and the driver beeped repeatedly. The staff crowded into the psychiatric hospital windows and a doctor came to the front and whispered, "You might be more comfortable inside." Púck, and Momonchu were out of the car; Sokanum Nootau was not. Momonchu, "he is always on the move," true to his name, perambulated in wide circles. Púck smoked and rubbed his face as he did when he was uncomfortable in a discussion.

"Hub, hub, hub," Púck urged running toward her. "Sokanum Nootau thought *you* were the one sick."

"Does it matter?"

"He doesn't believe our ways work on Cháuquaquock."

She asked them to wait and hurried into the hospital. Only Rem, Bob and Philipe had permission to enter the private intensive care area; the remaining Celestial Seven sat in the lobby smoking. When the phone distracted the attendant at the desk, Hebe slipped into the corridor to locate them. Brass numbers marked the fabulously decorated suites as if it was a hotel rather than a hospital. Philipe leaned woozily against the wall.

"Intensive care? In a psychiatric hospital?" she asked, and he shrugged. Rem and Bob approached, and she stroked Philipe's arm.

"You should have stayed in the lobby."

"Remy I wanted to see Floyd... mais the odor...o la la."

"Alcohol I know, but… Where is the powwáw? Our Floyd is…"

Hebe confirmed Rem's authorization to give him "whatever he wants," and she immediately opened her purse and produced a fistful of cash.

"Not that."

"Je ne comprends pas, Hebe.

"You have to trust me. No questions, Okay?"

Hebe explained what the medicine man requested and then the threesome traipsed curiously with her as she slipped into number twelve. They stayed in the corridor. They heard her rummaging around and Bob raised his eyebrows inquiringly at Rem who shrugged and re-peated the "No questions." A doctor soft-shoed by and they bobbed their heads in acknowledgement. Hebe brought out a luxurious dark brown blanket and pushed it into their arms. Rem opened her mouth and Hebe held her index finger to her lips and ducked quickly in and out of number seven empty handed. From number five, she emerged with a silver-tipped, horn. A wiry rake in dark glasses with too much hair swaggered up.

"Isn't it extraordinary?" Hebe asked Rem to cover her actions.

"Yes. It is," Bob replied.

"We want to offer to buy it but no one is there," Rem explained to the rake.

"Are you with that lot outside?" he asked brazenly fondling the feathers in Hebe's hair.

Moving his hand away, she admitted they were, and he marched into the room and returned with a silvery Indian maiden statue. Impressed, Hebe ogled the detail.

"It's a hood ornament. I'm never going to use it." He took the horn and waved off Rem's dollars. "You took the blanket. They are mohair or cashmere. I did too—my first time here. Good move. Take a fresh one, no bad vibes, you know?"

He directed them to the corner. Philipe opened the cupboard which was stuffed with blankets.

"Some guy donated them."

Rem was relieved to know they weren't stealing. They thanked him. He again fondled Hebe's feather and looked at her over the top of his shades. He had piercing blue eyes.

"That is the coolest barrette I have ever seen."

She slid it off and held it out to him.

"Here. It's awfully nice of you to help."

"Aren't you different," he chuckled. "Keep it. It's only cool because it's in your hair. So you're leaving. Did they cure you?"

"I wasn't here because I am sick."

"I know the feeling."

He took off running down the hall after a doctor.

"Done," Hebe declared in the waiting area. "Not bad for yauwe chippag an hour. I brought tobacco for Sokanuum Nootau, but we didn't bring him a gift for when he makes Floyd better."

"From what I just saw, that would be nothing short of a miracle," Bob remarked and laid his watch on the blanket.

"Are you giving it away?" Philipe asked. "My father has the same. It is tres cher."

"And Bob has a drawer full of them," Rem remarked dryly. "But you don't need them, do you Darling? Bob lives by Indian time."

As soon as Mr. Collins saw Rem, he beamed with obeisance and greeted her, "Ah Mrs. Metternich–Winneburg, to what do we owe the pleasure?"

"That's her," the nurse snarled. "I told her not to..."

Mr. Collins saw Rem and glared at the nurse. "We do not tell Countess Metternich–Winneburg…"

Metternich–Winneburg? Hebe asked herself. *If it isn't a married name, then this is sort of her hospital. Neat.*

Hebe rolled the objects in the blanket and placed them in the car. Momonchu and Púck gamboled toward a girls' volley ball game on the lawn's edge. Beneath the tree stood the mighty Sokanuum Nootau who was rumored to be almost one hundred-years-old. His loose prune-textured skin dropped his eyelids low on his eyes and his jowls on his neck but not in Hebe's eyes. She saw the towering man with the chiseled jaw and virulent good looks that had inspired photographers, which is the image she first saw of him. It was on a cabinet card. He was wearing his big black hat with his two long braids hanging down his jacket front and holding a smudge fan and a club. Wénise found her hypnotized by the card. "He can make animals stare too. That is why he is a medicine man." His powers added to his bear-like bigness. Emitting guttural sounds of approval, he accepted the tobacco.

"Púck and Momonchu did not bring any," he noted to himself out loud, "couple of city Indians. Nuttah, medicine is like religion. Only works for people who believe it. Long, long ago a White doctor came to me and wanted to know how my magic worked," he chuckled. "That's what he called it, 'magic.'" He admitted sometimes he gave 'sugar pills,' but they worked because the patients believed."

Apart from Hans, Hebe was sure the Celestial Seven believed in supernatural medicine because of Rem's Madagascar tale and Noni's nervousness about calling a priest, but she didn't know what Floyd believed, and he was the patient. Traveling beyond the moon was not unusual for him. While he didn't do it when he practiced, he went every time he played his saxophone; she had seen him and knew exactly when he was gone. Whether or not he was a believer, she had heard him say "Abamacho" which she was positive she had "never ever uttered in his presence" on the night he had his "accident," as the Celestial Seven preferred to call what happened.

"Floyd is my friend; they all are, or I would not have asked for your help Sokanuum Nootau."

He closed his eyes, so respectfully waited. A bunny could have eaten a whole carrot before he opened his eyes.

"Kúkkita," he began.

"I am listening. Kukkakittoùs."

"You tell them, no guarantee," he ordered gruffly.

Púck and Momonchu ran up and stopped far enough so as not to interrupt but near enough to eavesdrop.

"Wutaunche~ocouôog. I will tell them."

"I need dark, so I can see," he added which confused her but she didn't want to risk discouraging him with questions. "No one will touch any of my belongings—This is not a side show. No interruptions. First, I need to see the patient and..." he gave the boys his car keys and they grinned from ear to ear. "Go among Floyd's belongings. Be sure the room is lighted. Use eyes only. When Floyd hurt himself, he probably hurt the spirit, made it weak. If it is wounded, it cannot get you, but if you touch it, it will enter you. That is certain."

"What are we looking for?" Púck asked.

"A bone, teeth, fur, animal parts. Do not touch," he stressed.

The Powwáw, Sokanuum Nootau – Rains Fire

They took off. Inside the nurse guided the others to Floyd's room. She promised the reasons for such tight security would be "self-evident" when they saw him, but they didn't see him. In his place was a pale, tortured creature whose spine curved in an arch so high his head hung near his calves; the big toe of his right foot touched the bed and nothing else. His head muscles had contracted revealed his eyeballs sitting in their sockets like boiled eggs with irises. The horror stunned them into total silence until Philipe let out a shriek and left followed by Noni. Holly collapsed onto Hans' chest. In an attempt to soften their anguish, the nurse assured them he had been given "medication for the pain and enough antibiotics to kill the bacteria and possibly him." Hans wanted to know when Floyd would "come down."

Empathy and horror softened her voice. "This is tetanus. The blades must have been dirty. We're doing what we can. Prayers help."

Hebe sat near Floyd's head almost at the foot of the bed, and very quietly introduced Sokanuum Nootau. Barely perceptible acknowledgement and relief shined faintly through Floyd's agony. He used a glass to examine Floyd's skin while curtains to black out the day were tacked up. The nurse handed Rains Fire the phone. It was Púck. When he gave it back, he asked her to "turn it off or take it out. No disruptions."

"Mocenanippeéam."

"Oh," Hebe translated, that means, he'll be back in a bit. He has to get ready."

Holly was checked out by the doctor, and when she was given the okay, they stepped into the hall. A frenzied hullabaloo had broken out near the hospital entrance and two nurses ran by, one screaming hysterically to "call Mr. Collins!"

"What's going on?" Rem asked.

Sokanuum Nootau had returned. He was dressed in his regalia, his great bearskin and assorted animal parts, and he was carrying an abalone shell full of smoking sage. Mr. Collins burst on the scene and waved the all clear. Holly rejoined the Celestial Seven, and they all repaired to the "more civilized environs of the lawn." Rem had arranged with Henry to have picnic baskets delivered from the Birches should they be there past one p.m. Púck and Momonchu who were glad to have arrived in time ate heartily, but worry had stolen the Celestial

Seven's appetite; they had but bits and sips. Hebe had them all sit in a circle.

"People are stronger in a circle. We can direct healing energy toward his window."

Hans did not want to participate in a "séance."

"Séance?" Hebe asked. "It is no such thing, and doing something is better than moping on the lawn, isn't it?"

Heads nodded all around.

Which one is Floyd's?" she asked.

Hans counted, and then announced confidently, "That one."

Momonchu smudged them. Though it was not a tradition Hebe knew of, she had them chant the name of the creator in the southwest, Kautántowwit. Tripping over the unfamiliar name, they repeated it faintly at first and then as a chorus which overtook their minds and obliterated the tragic image of Floyd dangling painfully near death.

The late summer sky darkened to mid-December dusk. A colossal, single charcoal grey cloud billowed into the middle of the Heavens. Vapors fumed from the hospital forming a pale yellow cloud, equal in size, which morphed into a gargantuan Sokanuum Nootau in his regalia. He shot an arrow into the grey cloud. Within an instant, a ferocious, black lion sprang at him roaring so loudly, creatures everywhere scrambled into view. Babbling chipmunks, mice, rabbits and frogs dotted the expanse of the lawn, and birds swarmed in the air as they squeaked, chirped and croaked with dogs barking and horses whinnying. A vicious battle erupted in the sky. The beast and the medicine man shrank to a dot on the horizon and then exploded ten times their size overhead forcing the Celestial Seven to lay flat to avoid being crushed. All of a sudden, the lion was by himself, and they feared the worst.

"Where is he?" Púck asked standing beside Hebe.

"There!" she shouted.

High in the sky, the medicine man's manifestation stood, but it was significantly faded because he had grown tired. The lion shook his mane and bellowed victoriously. The creatures and humans on the lawn watched and waited in fear. Sokanuun Nootau's visibility grew brighter, and he raised his arms over his head. From a dot on the horizon, thundered a bear as big as ten. With a growl, he challenged the lion that reared to confront him. Moments later, the creatures were gone; the sun shined from a clear blue sky. Luminous yellow and orange drops like fire flies rained down on them. Mesmerized, they moved about with upturned palms where a few of them alighted.

"What is it?"

"I don't know Remy," Hans replied in awe. "Wow, its raining fire."

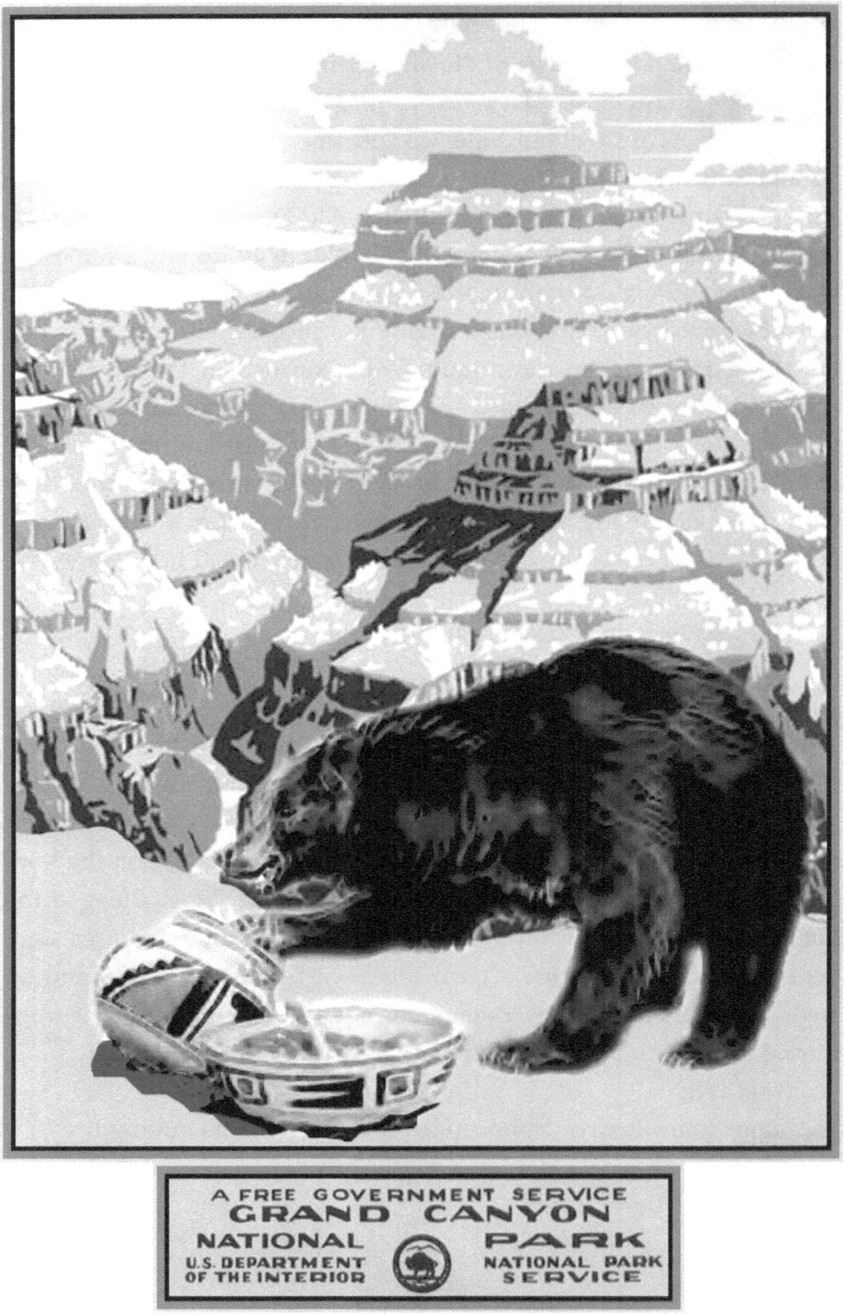
A FREE GOVERNMENT SERVICE
GRAND CANYON
NATIONAL PARK
U.S. DEPARTMENT OF THE INTERIOR
NATIONAL PARK SERVICE

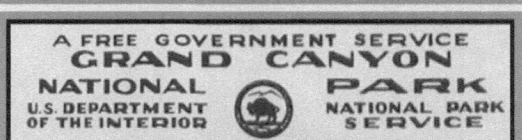

XVI

Spirits

Massachusetts– Nevada – California, Summer, 1958

A few weeks after Sokanum Nootau had made it rain fire, the susurrous trees in red, orange and yellow warmed the cool autumn skies. Hebe was enrolled in the Country Day School but had yet to attend. The headmistress agreed tutors would "catch her up when she returns," and Rem added, "When she is ready."

Why am I going away, when and to where?

The answer to why and when was "a secret surprise, a few weeks from now" as Rem put it, "in the national parks out west," which Bob insisted Rem experience with him and she wanted Hebe to join them. She was relieved and thrilled.

The Celestial Seven had lunch with Rains Fire at the Birches when he delivered Floyd. The survivor of demons, disease or both emerged from the Duisenberg and thrust his sax triumphantly in the air. When Rains Fire didn't budge, Rem urged Hebe to "Tell him to come in. The cook prepared venison and succotash in his honor." He was flattered but wanted to know if any doctors were inside which there were not. At lunch, he explained that three doctors accosted him in the hospital and that one had chased after the car when they drove off. Rem's captivating eyes caught his attention.

"Well of course they did. According to their own no one had recovered, so quickly, even with treatment,

"Quickly? Almost a month?" Noni questioned.

"The invisible aspects had to be addressed as well," Holly added and stroked Floyd's hair.

"And," Nell chimed in, "did you hear? Floyd's roommate in intensive care also got better...completely!"

"Bravo Rains Fire," Rem praised. So of course, the doctors have questions if you..."

"Couple does not exist for doctors. They are scientists, investigators; their lives are inquiry. They ask not for answers but proof, the kind they can see or touch. They will not accept what I say as real answers."

Sokanuum Nootau's wish for privacy led the Celestial Seven to plead ignorance about his whereabouts when the hospital called, and they made a pact never to tell anyone what they had seen or what they knew about the possession which Sokanuum Nootau explained.

"Soon as Púck entered Floyd's space, he saw a fur pillow, made from a kind of wild cat."

"An African lion," Nell interjected. "I know because I bought it in Africa for him.

"That lion's spirit was not freed when it was killed because its life had been taken gruesomely and disrespectfully. He was and before he had left his body completely, he was skinned."

The Celestial Seven's girls gasped in unison.

"And the hunters did not apologize for killing him. They did not eat him. They killed him for pleasure. No animal can do that, only humans. The spirit was filled with disgust and revenge. His plan was to find his own skin and the murderer. He doesn't know from mail that can send his skin anywhere; it could be with anyone. He was too angry to listen."

"Did you bear kill the spirit?" Rem asked.

"Why? The lion made a mistake. He did nothing wrong. He was right. The bear spirit fought him to exhaust the rage, so he could hear the truth, find those who committed this atrocity, punish them correctly."

"And suffer they will!"

Floyd cracked his neck.

"Was the wine not to your liking Rains Fire?" Rem asked, "Perhaps…"

Rains Fire placed a saucer over his glass still brimming with wine.

"Accept my apology. I do not mean to waste. I am sure it is excellent, but…" he swiveled completely around and took Nell's hand, pretty, pale and delicate between his, enormous, brown and gnarled.

She raised her eyes and was instantly spellbound. Hebe again heard Wénise say, "He can make animals stare too," and she was sure Nell had feasted her eyes upon the virile, chisel-jawed, warrior Sokanum Nootau.

"When a maiden bathes me in beauty so rare, so fine, so powerful my heart stops…" Nell turned red, "…my ability to determine whether it is true or a shapeshifter is important. Spirits interfere, so I leave them in their bottles. I had none, so I am positive I sit next to a true girl, and her loveliness brings my eyes very big happiness."

"Try not to faint Nell," Hans muttered flatly.

"Not to worry. I will catch you," Rains Fire promised.

"Dieu. Match point Monsieur Fire," Philipe noted excitedly slapping the table with his napkin and then daubing at the corners of his broad grin.

Everyone turned to Hans who fetched a cigarette from the sideboard and exhaled, "Thank you again Rains Fire. What you did was truly incredible, not just for Floyd, but… I wanted to ask…how did you project the image of yourself and the lion…"

"No questions," Nell reminded him.

"To experience such a phenomenon as a scientist… I have to know, what are those drops of fire made from? We caught them, at least we thought we did, but we had nothing."

Rains Fire sat stone-faced for a moment. Hebe knew he would not reply.

"Nummautanùme, Nuttah."

"Taubot neanawáyean," she said carrying the blanket to him. "It's from all of us."

"I did not ask for anything."

Nell pulled her hand from his, so he could received the blanket in his arms. The shapely, female hood ornament brought out a rare smile.

"That is from me," Nell whispered.

He patted it. Over his shoulder, Philipe eyes the watch."

"That is a real treasure."

"Philipe!" Rem reprimanded.

"We can not be angry at the truth. I never see these in the shops, only jewelry store windows." He slipped it on his wrist. "Looks real good. Thank you."

Bob noticed the watch was upside down, "Rains Fire, I think…"

The old, powwáw repeated, "Thank you," so appreciatively that Bob let it go. "Your deep, rich skin tone compliments it," was all he said.

But Nell removed the watch and put it on correctly.

"See what you do to me?" he told her and chucked her on the chin.

✳✳✳

Hebe and Rem boarded Bob's plane and began the long, noisy, bumpy trip to parts unknown, at least to Hebe. Nausea crept in but she maintained possession of her breakfast. Switching seats with Rem for a better view and the thrill of landing on the lake disrupted her systems tranquility. Hebe was positively green.

"You look ghastly. Did you take whatever it was the Floyd gave you?" Rem asked.

"I don't think it's working."

Bob saw the green tinge to her face and advised, "Use the window," and she thrust her face out to empty her stomach into the sky. "Well, that's one way to feed the wildlife," shouted with a grin dismissing her embarrassment.

Once they were in the lake, they inflated a raft and rowed to the group on shore, an old minister: two doctoral students in anthropology and archaeology, Julie and her husband, Buck and Murphy, their Diné guide.

"It isn't a hunting trip," Julie remarked her when she saw the guns.

"A person in the wild with no weapon, is a fool," Bob defended Hebe, "Besides, she likes to shoot. She is pretty good at it too."

In the brochure about the west, she had read, 'Nature, queen of the world, shamelessly flaunts her largess of natural wonders in the wide-open spaces that are the Grand Canyon, Yellow Stone and Yosemite Parks.' The writer mentioned "breathtaking vistas that stretched to infinity" and mountains that were "awe-inspiring. Nature runs inviting streams through purple shadows along the gorge floor, the foundation of her steep, rugged, golden sides that reach such stupendous height." They would have dwarfed the old oak tree in front of her house in Cambridge. "She daubs entire hills pink with flowers dainty and fragile as snowflakes. Snugly among the tiny petals are occasional stones, smoothed by weather and old enough to recall the ice-cold sensation of the melting glacier that passed their way, yet still strong enough to hold the moose that trod over them in the morning. All around, she places centuries of trees to stand guard; they are mighty and green and humbling."

Hebe drank them in with deliberation to store them in her memory hopefully forever. When she peered into the canyon from atop the donkey, she guessed forever was going to be about three more hours.

"It's a long way down."

He read her face and assured her, "Harry's never dropped anyone yet." He smiled, but she didn't, so he changed the subject. "We don't get many Indian tourists. Who are your people?"

"My father is Wampanoag and Passamaquoddy," she replied truly pleased he had recognized her not as Colored, Italian or Spanish but Indian.

They exchanged tales of bravery about their nations' heroes. Hers featured King Philip's War and British hypocrisy, disrespect and disregard for their own treaties As Wénise and Kutty had told her, and she had herself read, the Indians were willing to share and at first helped the Whites.

"We lent them land on which to grow food. Some say 'sold' but the earth belongs to the creator. Even if it was ours, or anyone's, who would sell it for a few knives and some butter? Those Pilgrims at Plymouth all talked about religion and God, but they were evil doers. After they killed Metacom, King Philip, they ran a spike through his head and put it on display in Plymouth—for twenty-five years—and..." she sniveled,"—and Cotton Mather, climbed up there and ripped the jawbone right from his face, so he couldn't talk from beyond the dead."

"And they called us savages," Murphy added. He dismounted to tighten a buckle on her saddle and added shaking his head, "Same story everywhere, just different names.

"Everything all right?" Rem asked.

Murphy gave her a thumbs up.

"They brutalized our leader too, Narbona. After they shot him, an old man, they scalped him. We Dine, at least 8,000 of us, were forced to *walk* to from a good corner of Arizona down to a bunch of nothing where the Mescalero, Apache was. We fought all those years like you guys, but there was a drought; we were starving. We knew we were doomed one way or another, so we surrendered at Canyon de Chelly and just to make sure we wouldn't want to escape, they burned us out, not they, he—he burned us out."

"He? He who?"

"Who? That son-of-a-bitch Kit Carson."

"Kit Carson! Are you sure?" she asked in disbelief as tears filled her eyes and confused Murphy.

He didn't say another word until he pointed out a chubby bear cub.

"Where do you think her mother is," she whispered.

"Not far, that I promise. We better be careful," Murphy advised, and they ventured on.

At the bottom, her saddle-sore legs refused to straighten up, so she had to hobble to the river where she slipped her legs in the water very briefly to prevent them from becoming popsicles. Murphy gestured for the party to get back, and in a spoken whisper gave them the reason "Bears." The word elicited vociferous noises which he shushed by flapping his arms. Curiosity and caution moved them slowly to various spots near the campsite.

"I don't see Julie. Rem, where is Julie?"

"She had to tinkle and she went …"

"Now? Away from the group? The whole point in having a guide…Never mind," he exhaled with no more than a trace of his voice. The tone was unmistakably serious. "Very important. If you see the bear, do not scream, and do not run."

He shouldered his rifle, and Hebe shouldered hers. Seconds passed into a minute that became two, three, four, and then a scream pitched high on the upper reaches of fear shredded the unnatural silence. Julie had arisen from a thicket of bushes and seen the bear. A chorus of shushes stayed her, and she instinctively ducked back down, but the bear reared up on her hind legs to her full seven feet to investigate.

Murphy and Hebe had no question where she was; from her experience on the shooting range, she estimated her to be was less than a hundred feet away.

"Murphy, we've been spotted."

The mother grizzly charged and closed the gap to fifty.

"Steady Hebe. Steady. That cub is pretty young. Gonna need his mother."

Her knees knocked together. Another cub tumbled into the meadow and joined the first one at their mother's feet.

"Her ears. Wénise told me if they're up like that…"

"Exactly, she's bluffing."

In a calm monotone, as Wénise had, Hebe addressed the bear, "Kúk-kita mosk. Admish, okay? Amdish. Hawúnshech. Hawúnshech."

The bear tipped her head like a dog trying to comprehend. Murphy tossed a bag on the path behind her. She followed the scent as it sailed over her head, dropped down on all fours and lumbered toward it. The two cubs followed. A minute became two, then three and four, and then she led her family away. Rem flew across the dirt to her and hugged Hebe.

"What did you say to her?" Julie asked.

"I asked her to go away is all."

Thus began the first of their days occupied with hiking, shooting and photographing nature. Nights, after Murphy scattered bark around the perimeter of the site, they prepared meals and huddled casually by their makeshift hearth in comfort and companionship, except the ex-traordinarily taciturn minister. He ate, he arose, took a deep breath as if he was about to speak but didn't, and then retired to his tent.

"He gives me the willies."

"Funny power silence has, isn't it Julie? This is his third trip with me. That's just the way he is quiet."

"Has he ever said anything?"

Murphy took a minute and then snapped his fingers.

"You know Hebe, he has. 'The name Grand Canyon makes this Holy land sound empty. The Paiute name Kaibab, Mountain Lying Down is better. It really should be changed.' And that was it."

The graduate students dazzled Hebe with the knowledge they had acquired of people who had lived there thousands of years ago from "evidentiary fetishes."

Twigs in a cliff? How are twigs proof? Maybe a bird was making a nest.

"You don't really know enough to understand, even if we did explain, Buck told her."

Ten days had magically passed and Murphy announced they were approaching their "final destination." Once again, they set up the tents, this time only two for Murphy and the minister and the couple. Hebe, Rem and Bob were to occupy the white adobe dwelling which was charming but so rustic, they were certain it had been abandoned for centuries, thanks to Murphy having had built that way; it was relatively new. Inside the rooms were as grand as a hotel, complete with electricity, fine linens, mirrors, hot running water and little soaps in the bathroom. Gracious as always, Rem offered the shower, but no one took her up on it except Hebe. Showered and on the couch with a cup of tea, she was ready to go home.

That night around the fire, she asked Murphy, "What is that you spread around?"

"Bark. Keeps the Naagloshii away. I put extra just for you."

"For me. Why?"

"Naagloshii go after us, 'specially the young, more than Whites, I wouldn't want anything to happen to you."

Hebe strained her eyes trying to see into the trees past the firelight.

"Like what?"

"Could be anything. Causing pain and suffering is the Naagloshii's entertainment, their reason to live."

"How do we recognize them? What do they look like?"

"Don't know. Don't want to know. If you see them, they will kill you. And they are tricky, shapeshift. You think a wolf is a wolf but..."

Suddenly an owl flew out of a tree, and Hebe screamed and chuckled at her reaction.

"Are you Indian? We heard you're from a Northeast tribe."

"Right there Julie," Murphy said. "Right there's another problem with that Indian-head-buffalo nickel. Whoever put Chief Iron Tail, that old Lakota, on there got everyone to thinking, all Indians got the same features.

"So you're saying the prolonged, ubiquitous dissemination of a five-cent coin gave rise to a multi-nation, psycho-socio identity crisis among American Indians and perpetuated gross misconceptions about their appearance among non-natives," Julie summarized.

"If those are big words for what I just said, then… yup."

He checked with Hebe but giggling she shrugged.

"Anyway, invasion and slaughter aren't good topics for nice customers to hear, especially these two who are here for a very special occasion."

He chucked his chin at Rem and Bob who were cocooned in mutual adoration on a rock, their fingers intertwined. His cheek rested on her hair as they gazed at the stars above the firelight.

There but not there, ran through Hebe's head.

That night, Rem joined her rather than Bob as she usually did; the room positively glowed with Rem's aura. Hebe learned the why of the trip when Rem revealed she wanted to "observe the tradition of the bride and groom sleeping separately." Hebe was over the moon; she squealed and clapped and hugged Rem.

"Why didn't you tell the Celestial Seven?"

"Between us we have six marriages," she crossed her fingers, "which by our calculations makes this lucky number seven. We want it to be just for us, a totally unique ceremony, but one tradition won't hurt."

Unwittingly she had two, for she had donned an old charm bracelet, new white linen slacks, a borrowed white blouse and blue flower Hebe had fashioned into a lei.

Bob wore a shirt he had purchased in the Ukraine from the Cossacks which he told her they wore to demonstrate they were free men.

"That's a strange choice for a wedding."

"No Buck, not when the bride is Rem."

Hebe didn't know how to describe the enchanted expression on Bob's face; it was one she had never seen before.

Someone should hang a sign in a museum that says "true love," and hang a picture of Bob's face there.

The wedding was, as Rem and Bob wished, one of a kind. Unconventionally clad, at a rock altar by a waterfall, they recited vows they had written in French and only they understood. The shot they chose as their official photograph captured wedding crashers who had gone unnoticed, a red bear sow and her cubs, a raccoon in a tree and two deer.

Hebe laid the photograph on the table at the Hotel Del and recalled the flight to San Diego. Luckily, Bob was not only an ardent nature lover and photographer but also a seasoned pilot who had flown the route many times. He directed their attention to rivers, mountains and buildings.

"There is that place. It isn't on any maps. No one knows what it is for way out here."

The buildings were unmistakably laid out in the same formation as those on the map she had retrieved from the air at Horton Fountain, so when Bob asked if anyone was "game to go closer."

Hebe answered, "Let's go."

Down they went. Bob was about to lower his landing gear when she saw several posted signs.

"I see them too." He read, "'Photography prohibited. Restricted area. No trespassing.'"

A call came over the radio warning him he was "not authorized to land," and he must not "under any circumstances."

Ever light-hearted, he quipped, "Must be invitation only."

"Bob. Look out!" Rem cried.

Vehicles drove into their path on the runway.

"Hang on," he ordered and pulled up.

Rem and Bob were stopping over in California on their way to honeymoon in the South Pacific for a yet-to-be-determined length of time. They hoped to meet Gaye-Lee and Art, but they had to catch a commercial flight, and planned for when they "got back."

"Whenever that may be," Bob joked.

"But you are coming back?" Hebe asked skittishly.

"Bien sûr," Rem assured and lamented having to rush. "I do need to talk to your mother. I have called many times. "

Without them as a buffer Hebe confessed, she was going to stay at the Del to reconstitute her psyche for the day she showed up uninvited, unexpected, and in her mind unwanted at her mother's door. As far as Rem was concerned, it was a prudent move, but reminded her the school year had begun and she was expected to come soon.

"If you need anything, contact Henry. He will always know where I am."

They are coming back, they have to; Bob's plane is here.

Through the taxi window, the Del came into view and Hebe heard Art speaking as clearly, as if he was beside her. "'The Del' is not a static structure which represents a particular architectural style. It's as if this building was designed to be started and forever reshaped by the world around it, an adaptable socio-morphic structure. That's what the Hotel Del Coronado is." Famous, Indian-hating former guest and desperately sad, resident ghost aside, Hebe liked it because it was familiar; the Del felt like home. The family's inaugural west coast chapter had begun there, and before Hebe was shipped back east, it became an annex to the Del Mar house; they stayed so often, they had a "usual farthest bungalow." It was a preserve for Gaye-Lee and Art's respectability, the children's' safety and Margarita's peace of mind on special nights.

They enjoyed exclusive clubs dense with privileged regulars guaranteed recognition and sophisticated revelry. Art and Gaye-Lee, the well-heeled architect and his glittering, green-eyed love quaffed part one of a two-part shapeshifting potion. It was served in cut crystal. When their skin flushed and numbed, their speech slurred and their vision blurred, they knew it was time to go. Part two guaranteed their transformation which polite society would not tolerate. So Gaye-Lee would toss a last charmingly coy glance and Art his last jocular remark. With their decorum still intact, the popular, enviable couple, exited smiling, acceptably tipsy and tottering, giving the impression they were destined, as they should have been, for home.

Instead, they sneaked off to unseemly destinations; equally smoky, sparsely occupied with less discerning customers where, any notice they received was to be sized up as "probably slumming." There in those dank, mash-scented lounges blaring jukeboxes they swilled the second part of the potion. It was served in heavy pressed glasses that, no matter how gingerly set, thudded down. On low bar stools, they set sail on boozy seas for a state beyond logic and reality. Art's empty wallet set the closing time for their drunken counterparts who zigzagged across the width of the sidewalks and the street itself. When their hearts were pumping gin to their brains, they did not take different sides of an argument. Completely unawares, they held two unrelated arguments. Gayle-lee insisted, "German Shepherds learn more easily if taught in German," while Art defended the idea that "God named Adam after the adamant, a legendarily hard stone." Gaye-Lee argued, "A tomato is the most useful fruit because it is a vegetable," and Art that "The chair should be called the Wigglesworth," because his great uncle Ainsley Wigglesworth had invented it. When he came out of the coma days later in the hospital, the first thing Gayle-Lee asked him was, "Who is Anne Wiggles worth?"

Whenever possible, Margarita told the truth but when Hebe and Jude awakened with confusion and upset over their missing parents, she decided a little lie was better which was she had no idea where they were. She feigned surprised that they hadn't told them "they went away for a few days, and to their anticipated question, "When will they be back?" she replied, "soon." Suffering from internal bruising and their lacerations dressed in bandages, Gaye-Lee and Art returned to the welcome full of love and relief provided by the kids and Margarita. They were glad to have the Los Angeles hospital bill and police report, to give them the details of the accident that they blamed for their amnesia about everything that happened prior. Why they were in L.A. at 3:00 a.m. no one knew. Margarita arranged to stay while they got back on their feet. The very next day, the excruciating agony accompanying their physical injuries with every move and breath was diminished but not eliminated by drastically self-increased doses of painkillers. Instinct advised them not to take more, but they made the happy discovery that the pills worked better with alcohol. They dressed for a mini-night-in to celebrate having survived, drank, and danced the hours away on the patio. Gaye-Lee opened her cigarette case. Art lit his lighter, and she leaped back and screamed.

"Who are you?!"

Art was stunned. He tried to put his arms around her, but she screamed again and ran to the street.

"Help! Help!" she cried.

He ran after her calling, "Gaye-Lee wait!"

The hubbub aroused Hebe from her sleep and she opened the front door and stepped outside. Art ran by one way, the other way and then he was gone. She sneaked up to the hedges and peered down Sandy Lane where she saw her mother staggering in the street a half a block away. She was crying and a cut on her face was bleeding. The police arrived and while they were walking her toward the beach Art showed up. Hebe wanted to hear what was going on, and just as she was about to tiptoe closer, a voice came from behind her.

"Hi there."

She jumped and acknowledged the officer with a guilty, "Hello."

"You shouldn't be out here by yourself at this time of night."

"Where did you take her, my mother?"

"Over there to talk to her. Says she was having a drink on her patio and this guy came up.

"Guy? That's not a guy. That's my stepfather."

Once the misunderstanding was resolved, Gaye-Lee and Art prevented it from happening again by spending "long nights" at the Del at their "usual farthest bungalow." It was often the beaten path away from police and gossips. It was usually subdued unless there was a big wedding. When Hebe arrived, it was bustling.

Maybe it's the Aztec football Homecoming or the annual Fiesta del Pacifico. They always end up here. She rested her rifle against the reception desk.

"Hello Jeff. "What's going on?"

The clerk leaned over the counter, and in a confidential tone, replied, "They are filming a movie here."

"A movie? How exciting."

"Welcome back. Where have you and your family been Miss Hebe Jeebie? I don't see them. Hot as it is, they must be at the bar?"

"Probably, but not this one. We were on vacation and they sent me back early to 'go to the Del, where it is heavenly and safe.'"

"We do our best. We will take good care of you. What do you have there, a gun?"

"A rifle, for skeet."

"The Wild West Aberdeen Shooting Club is not far from here. We could have a car take you…

"Is their regular driver available? Jose, Jose Evangelista. He wears cowboy boots and… There he is!"

The clerk beckoned to a Filipino man. He had shining black eyes and a slick, polish, even in a chauffeur's uniform. Delight curved his entire almond colored face into a smile when he saw Hebe.

"Wow. You're all grown up. I remember when you were small as a peanut." A hail of reporters' white flashes interrupted him. "She's here," floated dreamily out of Joe's mouth, and stars twinkled in his eyes.

She looked like the woman who had given her a ride to the Garcia's before she went to Mexico. She spotted Hebe and waved ebulliently.

"Do you know her?"

"Not well."

"Do you?"

"Sure. I am her driver here."

The crowd lapped at Marilyn's heels when she minced toward Hebe.

"What are you doing here my sweet little phone pal?"

"A little vacation. This is my…friend, Joe."

"Oh I know Joe. He takes good care of me, don't you Joe?"

She fluffed her shawl end on his face.

"Just doing my job."

"Better than anyone else, so I will see you soon."

Marilyn beamed and swayed across the carpet with the room in her wake.

"And the Duke and Duchess of Ginlee
left the wee princess in the palace by the sea
thinking her tucked in with golden finery,
but setting her adrift on seas so very lonely." Lachlin MacGregor

XVII

Nickómmo & Christmas

Coronado, California Fall/Winter 1958

On the day she went to the club, the mercury had risen to 102; practically unheard of for San Diego in winter; practicing outside was going to be brutal, but she was eager to join. The teenage boy crowned in ill-behaved blonde curls, Dennis according to his brass nametag, blotted his brow, snapped a gratuitous smile in her direction and attended the male clutch in front of his desk leisurely milling about and yammering. Patiently she waited. A grandiose personality trumpeted the room's attention simply by entering. He clipped his speech and rolled his r's, exactly as her grandfather Livingston had. "MacGregor is here," he announced merrily to which the men responded, "Huzzah." He was broader in the shoulder than her grandfather was. An auburn memory ran through the incredibly thick shock of hair framing his old face where flames of childish mischief burned brightly in his blue eyes. Sagging skin drooped over his knobby knees visible below the hem of his kilt. From the moment he reached his friends, he spoke and they chortled and snorted. Assuming they had been loitering in wait for him and they would go to the range, she shouldered her gun tote. They didn't move outside; he lit his pipe and joined in. Dennis sat down.

"Excuse me," she repeated three times before he mechanically sprang into service and thumped the book open.

"How may I help you, Miss?"

"Is this a private facility or may anyone practice here?"

"Both," he replied handing her a glossy brochure. "Give this to you father…."

"My father?"

"…or brother…"

Unwittingly, she employed the mildly haughty, but polite, tone Grandmother Livingston and Rem used when their expectations were not met.

"I am inquiring for me. Is this not where one signs in?"

"It is, but…"

Playfulness rippled into his expression, and then he emitted, a robust guffaw that bent him in two and stamped his foot which jolted the men from their conversation, "Excuse me. Sorry. You got me. Which one of you sent this little girl to sign in?"

Shrugged shoulders and befuddled utterances were his answer.

MacGregor suggested he "Ask the girl. They'll never tell," but the boy stood mute. "What's that then? Y'afraid of a wee lass?" He bent down and asked her directly, "Was it Luk de Menil or John Haskell who…"

"I am here to shoot," she stated and thumbed at her gun cases.

From the men she heard, "Jokes over," and "Run along." "It's not a little girl's game."

"Piffle. Carolina Mandel beat the men in the 20 gauge division in the men's nationals and had almost 100% in 12-gauge."

She set down her American Express card.

"Exception to the rule," a man called out.

"All right girlie, time to go."

One pushed her toward the door.

"Ow! You are hurting me!" she cried in fright greater than pain.

"Ay. Dinnae, Dunderheid," MacGregor bellowed.

The man released her and rejoined the group. The aged Scotsman handed her a handkerchief.

"Excuse me…" she sobbed, "but he scared me."

"He didn't mean to Hebe Nuttah Holmes," he read from her credit card and shot his version of what she said over his shoulder. "Ya hear that Stephen? Ya ugly face put a fright in the bonnie lass," which amused them and dissipated the tension in the air.

MacGregor explained that other than as observers, girls had not come to the range and asked if she really had "guns in that tote."

As she showed him, they conversed privately.

"I remember when I was young I would see this shotgun under my great-grandmother's bed. She used to 'dust the tails' of the four-legged thieves in our vegetable garden...and one time, she had to shoot a fox."

"Killed him, did she?"

"His body; his spirit is all right."

He roared with laughter.

"I took up shooting skeet regularly a year ago. I know how to handle guns well, and I only had to shoot a man once," she lamented and put him on the edge of his seat with the story of how she shot Tom.

"Pure dead brilliant..." he exclaimed, "that means..."

"Really good, and bahooky means fanny. I know a few words. My grandfather, Malcolm Livingston is the sixth Earl of Linlithgow, or so my people tell me."

Amusement sparkled in his eyes. Based on her grandfather's name and her mention of "bahooky," MacGregor pegged her for a Scottish-American.

"Good Scots family; that's where you get your gumption."

Risking rejection and the chance to shoot at the club, she also credited it to her American Indian blood by handing him Twenty-Men's 1873 Winchester. He could not hide his thrill in holding it.

"One of the guns that won the west this... "

"No sir. This is one of the guns that tried to save it."

"You come from fine people all around."

"Thank you. Wampanoag and Passamaquoddy."

"East coast! First casualties on the continent. We Scots are tribes too and that bastard, Monck —sorry my dear—sacked and plundered Dundee, under Cromwell's direction mind you. We know from experience what it is to suffer at the hands of the British, so most of us have a soft spot," he thumped at his heart, "right here for you."

His companions had drifted near, and he introduced her.

"Gents, we shall be plus one. It is my pleasure to introduce Miss Hebe Holmes, granddaughter of the Sixth Earl of Linlithgow..."

"And a Wamp..."

MacGregor's discreet shake of his head held her tongue.

"...a nature's child of this land," he winked at her, "and the lass has royal arms. Show them the Barella Hebe." As they offered high praise, he choked out a laugh and warned, "And you'd better behave lads or she'll dust your tails with her Winchester."

On the range, her sharp skills dispelled them of any notions women could not shoot. MacGregor, the club president, could not allow a child to become a member, but he did give her permission to use the range. In gratitude, she offered a lunch at the Del which he accepted and put on his account then and every time they met, although, subsequent lunches were at a variety of "great spots," enjoyed by him and his wife, Winifred, who joined them. During one lunch, Winifred asked about her mother.

"She is a beauty," Winifred noted when she saw the photo. "Lachlan didn't tell me you were adopted," she added raising his hackles.

"Winifred!" he crowed sharply. "You, my darling, with your flamboyantly, incarmined mass of locks, should know better. He leaned toward Hebe. "She is the only red-head in her whole clan. The rest are like Christmas black buns," he said and took the photo to have a look for himself. He tapped it with his big manicured index finger and said "Oh yes. I..." and then stopped before he let out the words, "She's stunning," He recognized Gaye-Lee, but he kept that in because to admit it was to admit that he too had responded to the irresistible call of loud mash-scented joints. In a voice one would use to begin a fairy tale, he recited.

"And the Duke and Duchess of Ginlee, left the wee princess in the palace by the sea, thinking her tucked in with golden finery, they unwittingly set her adrift on seas so very lonely."

✳✳✳

Rem had called full of disappointment that Hebe had stayed on in San Diego.

"You should have come home by now."

"I have not seen my mother yet, and I got involved in planning an early Nickómmo."

"It had better be early Hebe. You told me those were on the full moon, and this month it's December 26. You are expected to be here before Christmas. Comprends?"

As soon as she acknowledged her, they chatted about the guest list that included Anders, his sister and parents who travelled in Rem's social circles; Joe and his niece, Cynthia, a Taxi-Dancer; the MacGregors and Marilyn. Rem relayed a message to Wénise to call Hebe to go over her recipes.

On the Cape, word that "Hebe is on the telephone," spread, and while Mr. Josephs, Púck and Nini spoke with her, Wohwohkau barked in the background. Wénise's voice lulled away the anxiety with which Hebe was unaware she had been living. She wanted to be there with everyone and blurted impulsively, "I can book a flight and be there the day after tomorrow." Wénise encouraged her to follow through with her see her party.

While shopping for ingredients, Joe asked uncharacteristically shyly if his friend Blakely who worked at the Creole Palace could join them.

"Absolutely. I wish we had more guests."

"Okay, but you know… he works at the Creole Palace."

"I heard you, the Creole Palace. Is that important?"

"I forgot you are not from out here. That means, he is a Negro," he announced to her in the rear view mirror.

"A hungry one I hope. Of course he is welcome. Everyone is."

The helper assigned to her late night cooking spree in the hotel kitchen was Steve, a Kumeyaay Indian who she added to the guests. When they got around to talking, she learned, he had left the reservation to accept a job in town, not to fulfil a hankering to be part of the ever-conquering society but because he had to feed his family.

The same as Kit Carson, that Machemóqussu! She told herself while listening to Steve.

According to her recent reading, Murphy's historical account of Kit Carson and the Diné walk to the Bosque Redondo was 1000 percent correct. It completely broke her heart, caused her to question his sentiments for Indians and left her perplexed by human beings.

So rather than fight their warriors like a warrior, he destroyed their food stores. He destroyed everything, burned them out of house and home and the possibility of return. Women and children too.

She was incredulous. And it seems, Kit had a callous disregard for one of her favorite things in all the world, trees peach trees, ancient, thick trunk, peach trees; he ordered entire orchards chopped and burned too. Tears plopped on the page as she read because the acts, as far as she could comprehend were to get the Diné to do what the government wanted, whatever it wanted. In the vacated overnight hours of a hotel kitchen thousands of miles away from Canyon de Chelly, she bore witness to history repeating itself. The only difference was those who did not comply were not shot; they committed suicide by accepting starvation. She focused on Steve.

"Now I am lost in front of my own face. I am here in this kitchen. No time or place for my family, my people, just cooking and cleaning."

"The government is treating people like mules. Go here. Go there. Work for us. I'm twelve-years-old, and I understand that. Why doesn't anyone do anything?"

"Taking time to protest

Steve asked her to smudge the bungalow as soon as he saw the seashell, and though doing it in front of the others felt like a performance, she did it for him. Worry that the mix of guest was going to result in tensions made her follow Rem's advice and only use names, not titles or occupations in introductions which did not please everyone. Ingalinga, Ander's snooty, pipe cleaner-thin fifteen-year-old sister, added Count and Countess to their parent's names. Rudely, she asked Steve whether he was "an Indian too," and defended her question by adding, "Well he looks Mexican, and I think I saw him working in the restaurant."

"Isn't it just wonderful that the United States has given your people this opportunity?" Winifred said with the unfortunate kindling of ignorance and heartfelt sincerity.

Joe stamped out the potential fire by framing Winifred with his hands as if he was a movie director. He got up from his chair and walked to her seat.

"You just need..." he pulled wisps of hair onto her forehead, "Now, even more gorgeous, right MacGregor?"

"Are you a stylist Mister Evangelista?" Winifred asked.

"Well when Marilyn was here, she consulted with me."

"Did you meet her?" Cynthia and Ingalinga asked Hebe excitedly.

"Meet her? They are friends," Joe said and Hebe blushed. "When they were shooting out there on the sand, she made sure we were right in front, didn't she?"

"Yes."

The rest of the afternoon went smoothly. Upon departing, MacGregor complimented Hebe.

"Winifred adores you. Says you are 'like one of those adventurous story-book girls.' Before we go to Scotland, we are having a Christmas brunch. You must come."

"I can't imagine Mrs. MacGregor in the kitchen.

"Neither can I, not with Ian, our cook. He is a master at his craft. And we shall have a great tree. Come around eleven in the morning. It's the only pink place in Del Mar."

Big and pink in Del Mar? Is Mr. MacGregor big, red Mukker's owner?

San Diegans decked the city in Christmas during a ten-day heat wave. They painted the low, palm-tree interrupted skyline in lights and dappled bright red poinsettias. Hebe stood a cardboard snowman on her porch and imagined herself bundled up in the sparkling snow in the Boston Public Garden; her skin continued to glisten. She hung her head into the warm sea breeze that passed by her balcony and heard a familiar voice. "It's not a diaper. It's a breech cloth. I'm not breaking any laws, just wearing my clothes man." She followed the sound around the bungalow corner behind the shrubs, and there was Skinny Iroquois with two officers. Their handcuffs glinted as brightly as Wénise's knife when she cleaned fish by the river, and she sensed she had better hurry. In an instant, she had thrown her arms and legs around him.

"Keen Natóncks! Skinny!?"

"Nux Nuttah! Nuttah!!"

"Chenock cuppeeyau mis?"

"Maish-Kitummayi."

Their strange language made the policemen uneasy. They stared at them suspiciously.

"Hey, Sammy Seminole, we're taking you in…"

Defiant belligerence crackled through Skinny's torso and straightened his spine. He held his chin up and moved back.

"I am Sedwa'gowa'ne, of the Onondaga Nation, seventh son of a seventh son and a veteran, 45th Infantry Division, Thunderbirds."

Hebe kept her arm around his waist.

"Military eh, so you know all about the stockade," one officer smirked.

Every one of Skinny's facial muscles participated in a scowl, "Stockade?" he scoffed, flapped his vest open, flashed three medals and his temper, "No man. I was too busy slogging and shooting in Europe to save my country. Now here it is Thanksgiving 1958, and you want to throw me in jail for wearing my…"

"It's not like that. Some ladies complained about your clothes, and you can't tell us where you live, so…"

Quietly Hebe said, "Yo commeish, a paupaqúonteg for the bungalow," and poked him with the key which bolstered his confidence.

"Those beach broads showing off their goodies in them skimpy bathing suits are more naked than me. And I told you, I'm staying here," he used his arms to imply Coronado in general."

"That's vagrancy, so…"

Skinny interrupted them with a lungful of laughter and dangled the key to the Del bungalow in front of them.

"Gotcha boys."

Agitated, one of them asked, "Why didn't you say you're a guest here?"

"Thank you officers. Happy Thanksgiving," she wished them over Skinny's shoulder before pulling him along the sand to the bungalow.

"What are you doing here?" he asked.

"I have to see my mother. What about you?"

"Didn't you see the flyers for the multi-national gathering? It's going on Nuttah. Marginalization is just another word for prison. We're gonna bust out, raise awareness of the injustices we're facing… all of us."

Over lemonade, he provided a view of the larger Indian political world spinning around her much smaller eleven-year-old girl's world.

"The New York State Power Authority," he shook his head, "what a name, isn't it? All the land in the state, but they have to flood the Tuscarora Reservation for some hydroelectric bullshit, same as they did in the Dakotas. For some reason their project could only use the arable land the Lakota, Nakota and all they are living on. Our people are getting arrested for fishing on land they been fishing on since the fish first got there. For crying out loud, big as Southern California is, the state decides they have to smother the ancient Indian paths in asphalt to make Highway Eight. Doesn't make sense. They're still trying to kill us all Nuttah. "

"The people I live with back east…"

"People you live with? Nuttah what are you talking about? Túckiu còsh, Kutty? Kah Kókas? Túckiu Kókas? Kunnishishem?

"Nux. N'níshishem, but I'll see my mother soon. I don't know where my father is…."

Seeing her discomfort, he changed the subject by slapping his stomach and declaring, "Neàttup Nuttah."

Lucky for you I just had Nickómmo here."

"Oh yeah? White people?"

She cut him a disapproving squint.

"Mat Nuttah. I know your mother's White, and she's good people. I don't mean…It's just that they don't eat a lot when they go to someone's house, especially the chicks. Didn't you notice?" he asked and she nodded, "So you must have a lot of leftovers, kah beeréwese."

"Máttapsh,"she ordered and pulled out a chair, "I didn't serve beer, but there is sonqui Sangria or…"

"Sonqui Sangria? Cool Sangria, accent on cool," he held out a glass while she continued.

"My—friends," she emphasized, "told me an American Indian painter was supposed to have his work in an exhibit of American Indian art, but he got rejected. The organizers decided it was "too modern."

"A ha ha ha ha. Matta káche! Oppression through censorship, figures. See Nuttah to Whites, an Indian artist is not an Indian who paints but an Indian who paints elders in regalia and our little brown, children in the Goddamn clouds of dust they left after running rough-shod all over our country. An Indian writer is not an Indian who writes but an Indian who writes about our legends, as if any of us would really tell them our secrets. Ha. Indian life, you know, stories about nature or ceremonies, and don't forget the vision quest. Wrapping their heads around the idea that we can grasp the whole world is not beyond them. Art by a noble savage is more marketable if it is primitive. Help the meek. So pulling out some story in simple sentences and displaying primitive paintings, you know buffalo circles with stick legs validates their claim that we needed help, that somehow conquest was good which is what they want the world to believe, and we are smart. I mean shit, còsh's, Kutty's brains are spilling out of his ears. And we learned English, but I don't hear them speaking our languages, like they are worthless; it's oppression through censorship, like I said. I even picked up a little French over there in Europe."

"Vraiment?"

"Sure. Voulez vous couches avec moi?" He grinned mischievously."

"To ask a girl to go to bed with you, that's it?"

Astonished, he thundered his hands together and spun around.

"My baby cousin speaks French too? I am proud of you. Say, what's the artist's name?"

"Oscar Howe, Manzuha Hoshina from the Dakota nation, I think."

"I will remember. I want to see his *modern Indian* stuff."

They smudged, Skinny offered up the prayer, and they ate. He was impressed that she cooked so well.

"You are going to make someone a good weéwo."

"A great wife, weéwo," she corrected and fantasized about her life as his, Mrs. Sedwa'gowa'ne. *Maybe someday, not now.*

She could not break her promise to Rem. One evening in the Canyon, she proposed that Hebe marry Philipe as a favor. To meet the stipulations of their father's will and receive his rightful inheritance he had to be married before his father passed away. Doctors predicted that to be in a few months.

Hebe reminded her, "I just turned twelve…"

"Exactly the age at which a guardian can consent for a girl to marry in Massachusetts. And rest assured no consummating…" she paused to find a different word.

"I know…make sexy," Hebe giggled. "But why me? Why not Nell or someone else?"

"The truth is quite a ruse in this case. We need someone we can trust. And Nell is a friend but she tells her fortune hunting-mother everything."

"Fortune-hunting?" Hebe echoed. "Countess Godelieve?"

"Mais, a singer in a club when the count met her, and everyone knows that, so Nell…"

"Still has to be better than a little American Indian girl who…"

"Is also her mother. And yours, as the daughter of an Earl, a Lady in her own right no matter whom she marries, and you are Lady too,"

"Lady Hebe," she laughed

"As soon as father is gone we will have it annulled. That means it never happened."

Impressed that Rem had not tried to guilt her with mention of what she had done for her or offer her any payment, Hebe agreed. Rem promised to have everything on paper for her to read. The plan was to go to Brookline, select a gown and return to California to see her mother. Effervescing like a fresh bottle of champagne, she thanked her.

"Hebe I am still here. Where are you?" Skinny asked. "Someone is at your door."

She blushed when her eyes fell on Anders glowing brightly blonde on the porch, clad in tennis whites and carrying a racket. She shot Skinny an apologetic smile, joined Anders outside and closed the door.

Skinny teased her when she returned, "Contessa?"

"It's a joke. He is my tennis partner."

"Ahque Nuttah. Race mixing upsets a lot of people."

Going on and on about indigenous politics, Skinny talked the sun out of and part way back into the sky. She could not think fast enough to converse, so she settled for listening.

"I'm not saying we have to do the Christian forgive and forget' thing, or 'let bygones be bygones,' but we have to rise up, create a united front, at least until we get what we need, then we can go back to our tribal disagreements."

Being in the company of another Indian comforted her as much as lying in Wénise's bed. Falling asleep that night, the longing for her, her father and her own people churned the marrow in her bones. She realized if the spirit to see her mother didn't arrive soon, she had to force herself to go. In the morning, Skinny was gone. He left the rally flyer for Native Solidarity in Balboa Park, Sunday, December 14.

Dressing for MacGregor's holiday brunch was not easy. No closet of clothes awaited her at the Del as they had in New York. Fortunately before the "destination unknown" trip with Rem and Bob, she had packed a pale green dress. It was shiny silk, quite fancy; the alternatives were all cotton, so she consulted with Rem. "You carry the clothes, not the other way around. Wear what you want, silk or cotton, feathers..." She wore the silk. Anders and his parents were invited. She was titillated the tip of her head to very ends of her toes.

Joe had no trouble finding the home. He drove up the curved driveway, popped out and held the door for her.

"Did you bring a different jacket?" she asked.

"For what?"

He had sat across from the MacGregors at her Nickómmo, and she assumed he would enter with her.

"Ring the bell," he urged while leaning on the car.

"I am waiting for you."

Shaking his head and grinning, he reminded her that "the help goes in their own door," and when she opened her mouth to protest, he added, "One dinner is not going to change the class system cutie. It's okay. Go on in."

Preferring to protect her privacy, she didn't' mention the house on Sandy Lane. Thus, the MacGregors were flummoxed by their dog Mukker's attention to her. Her explanation was that "Dogs just love me."

The brunch was as lovely as every holiday event scented with cinnamon and rum and wood burning, and it was adorned with holiday fairy lights and tinsel. Lollipop colored Christmas bulbs bigger than oranges hung from the tree, and the house was filled to the rafters with guests. To her relief, the women' glittered and swooshed around in poofy skirt; she fit right in. Several of the men wore tartan wraparound, and they flagged like breech cloths did. After she had gotten an involuntary eyeful of a gent's ukkosue pompuhchái, she deduced kilts were worn without underwear. "Well the girls are trussed up," Anders announced with half-mocked disappointment after he retrieved a fallen napkin. Hebe giggled. When Anders went for sodas, she found herself turning her head each time a man sat or went up the stairs. In the process of discreetly leaning to check, she got a pain in her shoulder. It was a bony finger. The owner was a ghostly pale, wrinkled woman with a long narrow nose.

"Two more of these," she said and held out two empty glasses.

Hebe stared blankly. *How can she think I am a server?*

"Tom, you speak Spanish. Can you tell this girl what we want?"

From the stairs, Anders had sized up the situation and interrupted Tom's best efforts at a few words in Spanish, "Here you are contessa."

The old couple stammered blame at each other. Anders offered Hebe his arm, and they ambled away as closely as propriety would allow because this was their last meeting until either she went to Sweden or he came to Boston. He collected the gift he had secreted in the library for her, and they went to the car limo where she had his. Each gave the other an antique book. She received Longfellow's *Leaves of*

Grass and he *King Philip's War.* At the same time, they said "Thank you," paused and then "Merry Christmas." Mutual attraction drew their lips together and gave her the sensation of being tipsy. They explored each other's bodies until voices reminded them the car was in the driveway. A click of the handle stopped them. It was Joe. He excused himself and chuckled.

"I guess it's fog. I thought the car might be on fire. I'll be out here."

"That's all right. We were just saying good-bye."

Anders joined his parents who were among the guests pouring out and showed him the book. She knew she had made the right choice. Mukker saved her from a sad moment by running to and fro in the direction of the beach trying to lure her along, but she couldn't go. The spirit to see her mother and Jude and her own tree overwhelmed her.

Mother will be pleased about the Country Day School.

All she had were good thoughts, but the mere sight of the street sign Sandy Lane released oppressive memories, running away from her mother wielding scissors or watching her insisting to the police she was Mrs. Holmes. The sweet memory of her little brother's face kept her fighting the urge to go back to the hotel, pack, take the next flight to Boston and forget about seeing them. Joe opened his newspaper while she took a deep breath, and then skipped excitedly to the back where she was most likely to find him. The gate was locked. The pool was covered. The hedges, which her mother preferred manicured, were wildly shaggy as was the front lawn absolutely littered with newspapers.

Inside, mail had drifted into a bank on the floor. Mishquáishim had not made his presence known, but she felt unsafe and propped open the front door with a stone in case she had to leave in a hurry. Art's architectural jewel no longer sparkled brilliantly and moved with the Pacific's blue song but stood morbidly dull and still and mute. The slim palm trees yellowing and drooping from thirst stretched toward the razor of dust-filled sun cutting between the drawn burgundy curtains. The little bulb didn't come on when she opened the refrigerator; it was as empty as it was when it was new. On tentative toes, she investigated the first floor, but the idea of going upstairs struck her as invasive. Clearly, there was no one there. The answer to why was certain to be within *their mail. Their mail* she repeated to herself, though some were addressed to Margarita, and she dumped it into shopping bags, as usual, in the hall closet. Carrying it outside, she repeated, *their mail.* Joe grunted and commented in disbelief that it was "just letters." In the back seat, behind her sunglasses, tears attempted to flood out the sight of the dismally vacated Sandy Lane house, and Joe's banter helped. Oblivious to her frame of mind, he uttered a "When Marilyn asked me to…" phrase that began one of his long accounts of driving the star somewhere.

At home in the bungalow, the crushing despondency brought on by disappointment and abandonment reslid her down the wall and onto the floor. Bereft of strength, she had to cling to the wall to rise to wobbling legs, only capable of dragging her to the mini cave she had made in the closet for her wine. Alone on the shaded balcony overlooking infinity beyond the sea, she downed it and watched the guests frolicking in the sunlit sand.

What are they so happy about? Stupid people.

On her way to the closet where she made her wine cave, she stumbled over her abalone shell, and flung it against the wall; the action unleashed a rampage. In the "usual farthest bungalow," she railed and wailed at the universe, unheard by anyone. Her wounded soul was hemorrhaging spirit, and she did not know how to stem the flow. "Take me," she read on bottle of pills Floyd had given her for sleeping on the plane. It was difficult to open, but she managed and most of them scattered on he floor. After gulping down a few with another bottle of wine, she perched on the table and created a snowfall with the letters. Reading them updated her on where everyone was and what they were doing. Tony's letter to Margarita, from the base in Germany, included an updated picture of the baby who was, as babies are, adorable. Rosalita's was from Mexico where she was trying to find an investor in an acorn cake company. It also stated she would be free to visit Mexico around the holidays since "your parents, the Higgins, are going to Austria." This she learned by translating a July telegram: "Sehr geehrte Gaye-Lee Deine Mutter ist sehr krank. Bitte kommen Sie so bald wie möglich. Onkel Otto." An official envelope postmarked November held for Oma Livingston's death certificate; it shipped her to the bottom of another bottle. Perched atop the table she flung the letters into the air and let them snow down into the room. On her hands and knees, she searched the return addresses for the only one she cared about, the one from her father, but it was not there. A sense of abandonment crushed her lungs and she fled outside for air. She climbed onto her first floor balcony and leaped into the blackness beyond the hotel lights.

From the couch, she watched another beautiful California afternoon reflected in several puddles on the floor. A smattering of bright red pills stood out amid the aftermath of broken glass, and mail strewn from one end of the room to the other. How they got there or the sopping wet blanket was a mystery to her. One of Joe's jackets dripped onto the floor from a chair, and she searched the ceiling for a leak. There was none.

Sterbeurkunde

(Standesamt Wien   Nr. 2075/1958)

Gräfin Brunhilde Livingston geborene Brunhilde Gabrielle Wetter -Tagerfelden
- - -

wohnhaft in Mount Vernon Street, Boston Massachusetts, United States of America

ist am   26, September, 1958   um   23 Uhr   07   Minuten

in Wien, in des Haus Johann Wetter-Tagerfelden - - -   verstorben.

Die   Verstorbene war geboren am   27, Oktober, 1885

in

Verstorbene war - nicht verheiratet

Wien, den   20 ·Nov   1958

Der Beauftragte für Personenstandswesen

Erst Ritter

(Siegel)

Geburt des Verstorbenen

Standesamt   Nr.

Best.-Nr. C 252 Sterbeurkunde   Ag 306/57/DDR 4494/00 13 97 5789 V/4.9 DVE 4265
Vordruck-Leitverlag Erfurt

A few days later, she called Joe to drive her into town. Returning his jacket, she apologized and asked if he saw a hole. He raised his eyes and shook his head while he contemplated his dilemma, to stay or not stay on his side of the invisible line between himself and passengers, this one in particular. Crossing it could mean his job. Not crossing it could mean something much more precious to him, her life. He had grown quite fond of Hebe.

"Is something wrong, Joe?"

He pointed at the ocean.

"The other night, around 1:00 a.m., I was dropping a lady off, and my eyes played a trick on me. Ever have that happen? I saw…"

"That lady who swims in the nude?" she tittered, and he shook his head.

"I got out of the car and went down there."

"Oh no! It wasn't a dog was it? Don't tell me if it was, please?"

"No. It was a person, bobbing around like they were dead."

"Was that was you?" Hebe gasped. "I heard some guests talking about that." She pulled a chair up to the table. "What happened?" After what felt like ten minutes, she begged "Tell me…but not if he was a dog"

"You really don't remember?"

She laughed. "Quit teasing me. What are you talking about Joe?"

"Hebe…the person was you."

Reality kicked her out of her seat. While Joe had solved the mystery of the wet blanket and the puddles, she wanted him to keep what he knew of the blackness beyond the hotel lights to himself.

"You saved my life. I heard one woman say, 'They were certain she was dead. That man brought her back to life…You saved my life. Thank you."

He lit a cigarette to help ward off his tears. He wanted to tell her not to be lonely, that the people she wanted to be there might be away, but not to fret because there are other people. Instead he cleared his throat, held the door open and asked, "Where to?"

In town, she bought Christmas gifts, and she mailed to Warren Street, so she would not have to drag them on the plane. Those for her mother and Art and Jude she left with the concierge at the Del reception where she knew they would eventually get them. In the card, she asked her mother to "Please call." She gave Joe his gift and insisted he open it. The card read, "Thank you for all the good times." The gift was a key chain in the shape of the letter J, and it had a diamond in it.

"No one has ever given me anything like this." He handed her a gift. "I couldn't find your guy, Kit Carson, so…"

"I like this just fine," she beamed when she saw the Roy Rogers & Dale Evans thermos. "I have read a lot about Kit Carson, and I am not so sure he is my favorite anymore anyway."

***

With no more reasons to be in California, she prepared to leave. She left the Japanese housekeeping girls to work their magic. In the hours it took to have a deliberately nourishing breakfast and take a walk on the beach, they restored order to the bungalow. She tipped them well because they did a good job and because it was Christmas. Letters recovered during their cleaning were on the table. Her soul sang when her eyes fell on "Kuttiomp Holmes" in the upper left hand corner of a fat one from Istanbul, Turkey. When she took a full breath, a pang in her sternum made her realize she had not taken one for a long time. In addition to a card, there were two envelopes marked "Gaye-Lee" and "Nuttah" He reported that the driver was unable to stop to let him get off when he saw her in Horton Square, and he was working at a place from which he was only free on weekends. "As soon as possible," he had come to visit, but "your mother said you were out in such a way, I thought you would be back soon. I visited several times, but you were always out. I did see Ahanu. He speaks well. You must be a young lady by now. How quickly time has gone." In her mind, she began to compose a letter to him. There was so much to share: the Grand Canyon, skeet shooting, Floyd, all the Celestial Seven, especially Rem, but she had to finish packing, fire a few last rounds and drop by Balboa Park to see Skinny before her flight. She folded his letter into a small square and placed it along side her cash and passport in a pouch around her neck.

The reception was closed. She heard a shot and strolled onto the range where two members were there taking turns launching targets and shooting. Shotgun loaded, she stepped out. Mishquáishim rubbed her leg and growled, and she paused. Stephen, the man who rushed her out her first day, may have greeted her. His words were so garbled, she didn't understand. Drunks, she discovered, even the most dignified, had a rank odor about them that induced gagging if she had recently been drinking. She kept him at bay by wishing him "Merry Christmas" and fleet footed back to the car while they pleaded with her to stay.

Balboa Park—the Japanese Garden? Is that Where Skinny is? "Look at all the Indians!"

"I think you are home Hebe."

Protest signs shouted about fishing rights, equality, solidarity, education, medical care above a colorful Indian mob assembled on the path.

"Haven't seen that for along time? See the flag?"

"Uh oh. How did they get it upside down?"

"On purpose. That's a distress signal. You know, not to take anything away from you, but we should all be out here, Filipinos, Japanese, Mexicans, Negroes and every colored-body. We are all in distress."

"I am going to do that when I organize a rally like this one the Boston Common."

"That's the way. You gotta walk the walk, but it's getting late."

Hebe was compelled to see Skinny. As she stepped out, a photographer asked if she would join the group photograph "with your gun." She obliged. From behind her, someone was pulling on the barrel and as soon as the flash went off, she warned the person. "That is impolite and dangerous." The sight of Skinny sticking his head up through people quelled her anger. He started talking, but she told him she was pressed for time.

"Time? You're all hung up in the White-man's tick tock, huh? Watch out Nuttah." He patted her back, sent his best to all and held up a megaphone. "Time to rise up and take back what is rightfully ours," he said loudly and drew everyone toward him except Hebe.

Just as she was about to leave, a young child crying out "Mama," in such a trembling, pleading desperate tone, it pierced Hebe's breast and penetrated her heart. She scanned the area. Alone on the field of sunlit grass a little girl pivoted in a circle bawling for her mother.

"Awww. No tears. We'll find her."

The child smiled, and Hebe felt her small heart beat more peacefully. They spotted the woman; relief and gratitude glowed around her, and she ran, almost tripping on her long rawhide skirt. She clutched her child close to her bosom and kissed away her tears. Jude and her mother walked into Hebe's thoughts. Abruptly, she reminded herself it was *Time to go* and she rushed to the car for fear of other emotions adding to the sadness she felt about leaving Joe. Her invitation to him and his niece to her New Year's ball eased their good-bye.

"We will send you tickets. You won't have to worry about anything."

"If you can make that happen, we will be there."

"Plan to stay for a little bit..." she said staring into his eyes. "Maybe back east Cynthia could look for..."

"Yeah. She hates that whole Taxi-Dancer scene." He drew hard on his cigarette. "Me too. I hate it that she does that."

They held each other for a long time, and he kissed her bangs.

XVIII

The Magic Kiehtan Tree

December, 1958

Heavy streamers of cigarette smoke hung lazily above the passengers' heads as the DC7 taxied down the runway. Hebe took out her small abalone shell to smudge the cabin but she felt faint and didn't light it. Instead, she offered a smokeless prayer with tobacco. Unbeknownst to her, tiny fragments of the leaves were straying onto the passenger next to her, a handsome, square-jawed man in a finely tailored suit. He absent-mindedly whisked the tobacco away several times but once he became aware of them, he grew annoyed and glared. Her long hair and the beaded feathers curtained him out. He cleared his throat.

"Nummag ne wuttamauog," I offer this tobacco..."

"Miss?—Excuse me, Miss if you don't mind. You're..."

He saw her eyes were closed when she faced him, put her index finger to her lips and made a soft, "Shhh."

"Nuppeantam Kiehtanit, nummag ne wuttamauog. Ohke, nummag ne wuttamauog. Okummus nepauzshad, nummag ne wuttamauog. .."

She continued, knowing full well, the likelihood of the prayer preventing her from being sick was slim, but she needed all the help she could get to endure the long journey. It was eight hours to a layover in Chicago and then a few hours more to Boston; she was willing to try anything and everything. Despite having swallowed Floyd's pills with two straight shots of vodka before she boarded, she remained awake and nauseous; a bilious repetition of her breakfast soured in the back of her throat. The man attempted to ignore the errant tobacco by lighting a cigarette and dipping into a new magazine. By the time she had finished her prayer, a small drift of leaves had accumulated between them, and the jet engines had elevated them thousands of feet into the air. Their blasting roar settled into an ubiquitous drone. She tucked her pouch back into the top of her dress, settled in and offered the man a polite, "Hello."

The sight of her pretty, young face dissipated his initial displeasure with her messy activity.

"Hello." Eyeing her feather, he guessed, "Are you playing Indian today."

"Playing? No I …" Rethinking the wisdom of admitting to being one, she concluded with, "I am rehearsing for a play."

"An actress? Stage or film?"

"'All the world's a stage and the men and women merely players.'"

I'm Paul."

"I'm Hebe.""

"If one of your parents would like to change seats with me, so you don't have to sit by yourself.…"

"I am not by myself. I am sitting with you."

"Yes but…Well I meant, all alone, so you don't have to sit all alone. It must be scary being on a long flight all alone."

"No. I have protection?"

His eyes widened in disbelief, and his mouth fell open when she slipped her rifle from the floor and stood it on end.

"You sure do," he answered and reached for it.

She pulled the rifle away with a polite, "Please don't touch."

The rare weapon fired up an exchange of pleasantries and led to a conversation comparing skeet and trap shooting. Her need to fill motion-sickness bags kept interrupting them and weakened her, so she stopped talking for a while and dozed off. When she came to, the man was holding a glass of ice water tightly on her tray. The rumble seemed much louder and she could hardly hear him.

"Do you want to have a sip? Just a sip. This is a rough trip, so turbulent."

"It is. Have you ever been in an iron lung?"

Shaking his head he asked, "Have you?"

"Yes. It's just like being in this plane…if it was in a cocktail mixer and the devil was the bartender."

Paul laughed aloud and pointed to a butterfly. "Seems we have a stowaway. He'll keep you company while I go to the lounge."

Hebe watched the memengwe flutter around for a while then snuggled into the seat and her own thoughts.

It must be snowing in Boston. I hope it is. I miss it. I'm gonna sit with Jack Frost in the cloistered garden and catch flakes in my hand. Maybe that frisky chipmunk will be there. Rem said, 'everyone is abroad for Christmas.' It'll be strange there without all the Celestial Seven. Before them, I missed the Garcias and Ahanu and before them, Nosh and Wénise and Hans, and now…Now, I am going to miss, Anders, Joe, the MacGregors, Skinny Iroquois? I am always missing someone. I want to leave a place until I do, and then I want to go back. Best to think about the New Year's Ball, the wedding, my wedding. I never imagined I'd get married this year. Life really does change in the blink of an eye.

The plane juddered violently knocking the stewardess into Paul returning from the bar. She handed him the small supply of bags ice for Hebe and braced herself on the seatbacks.

"Too much turbulence. Have to buckle up," he told Hebe.

Mishquáishim rubbed on her legs, and she buried her fingers in his fur. The plane sputtered, lurched and lunged as if it had morphed into the great bird Wuchowson flapping up the winds. Abruptly it swooped down and the passengers emitted shrill panicked screams. Paul grabbed her hand, and she squeezed it tightly. The entire aircraft vibrated visibly, and then… an eerie silence.

"Everything is okay," Paul reassured himself by telling her.

Their eyes met. The fox leaned his entire weight against her, and ever so slowly, she turned her head from side to side.

"No. No Mr. Paul. I don't think it is."

A crack zigzagged rapidly through the cabin ceiling. Peskhómmin! Boom! Clouds of smoke puffed in and the oxygen masks dropped down. A deafening whir knocked out the lights. Hot tongues of fire lapped at the passenger's and curtains. *Tokish Tokêtuck. Tokish Tokêtuck,* she kept saying. *Wake up! Wake up!* She did not. She could not. Her head hurt so much, she wished it would explode. Peskhómmin! Boom! Her shotgun went off. Peskhómmin! Boom! Her flanks were shredded as she was sucked through the roof and into the freezing blackness outside.

Who told me we leave our bodies under stress, Nosh or Hans? He may be right, but leaving my body and floating around doesn't always bring relief, just like closing my eyes doesn't lead to falling asleep, and falling asleep doesn't lead to dreams. I can't tell. Did I leave my body and fly here. I think I am in the bathroom at the Birches?

Rem was sitting on the bathroom vanity chair envisioning Hebe trying on dresses. She sang softly with the music, "Swing low, sweet chariot, coming for to carry my home..."

"Who chose that music Rem?"

She jumped up as if someone had stuck her with a needle, whipped back the shower curtain and asked "Hebe?"

"Look! The memengwe follow… "

"Butterfly? Hebe Where are you?" Rem asked alarmed, flapped the shower curtain, checked the closet three times and spun around.

"Ici même, right here. You make me smile. Cowammáunsh Rem."

"Je t'aime my dear, sweet girl,"

Hebe watched Rem raise her rifle and aim it at the mirror. "Pow," Rem said and Hebe stared and stared. Rem's reflection was there but not her own. The ground vanished from beneath her and all was dark. Like a snowflake caught in an unruly winter blast, she whirled around the Birches bathroom at the top of the stairs until she was buried in snow. Ululations of the wind blew into the jet's droning rumble and the captain added to the cacophony.

"Good evening ladies and gentlemen. This is your captain speaking. We are about to begin our final descent to Logan airport. Local temperature is a brisk nine degrees. Peek out the window. There's the blizzard. Whiteout conditions and forty-mile an hour winds. Welcome to Boston, we have certainly enjoyed having you on board today. We hope to see you again real soon, and thanks again for flying with us." It repeated; it was a recording. Over and over it played, fading with each repetition until it was gone.

Slowly a gentle zephyr blew quite clearly. Chickadees sang ktgee-gil-lassis-ktsee-gee-gil-lassis. The powerful scent of field flowers and smoke stirred Nuttah. The sky on Cape Cod beamed a summery blue between the dense leaves of her magic Kiehtan tree; she lay with Mishquáishim under her head as a pillow.

"Nuttah? Tokish Tokêtuck."

"We are. I am awake" She pinched herself. "Nux. Thank goodness."

"Do you have any Wuttáhimneash?"

"Strawberries? Mmm. Yummy. No, but let's go find some."

At a familiar bush, they ate their fill and headed to the river to cool off. Twenty-Men strode through the tall grass, a fishing pole wobbled at his side. He shot his arm up into the air and beckoned her vigorously.

"Hub hub hub Nuttah. Wompi Mieúck Askeete just arrived; we have to meet her."

"Wénise is here?!" she squealed excitedly and hurried to catch up.

Credits & Illustrations

Front Cover Art UPPER: Collage by Winchinchala. Author's face as a child, ©Seawolfe 1955. Background illustrated by John Rae American Indian Fairy Tales 1921. Bottom Collage art by Winchinchala.

Back Cover photo: Hotel Del Coronado provided by the hotel, 1998 Bottom-Three dogs. From left to right, the first two © Winchinchala, 2007; Collage Art by Winchinchala ©2012, The Irish Setter by Phillip Schiffman, Germany 2005

0. *Pocahontas has a Headache*, Derivative, The Story of Pocahontas and Captain John Smith, Boyd Smith, 1906, Houghton Mifflin.

5. *The Emancipated Duel* circa 1900, Princess Pauline Clémentine von Metternich-Winneburg zu Beilstein née Countess Pauline Clémentine Marie Walburga Sándor de Szlavnicza and Countess Sophia Kielmannsegg on a hill in Verduz, Liechtenstein, artist unknown.

12. *The Palace,* Cape Cod, Photo Credit: © Seawolfe, 1957

15. *Wénise & Nuttah,* after *Twas the women who in autumn stripped the yellow husks of harvest,* Frederic Sackrider Remington for *Hiawatha* from *The Song of Hiawatha* by Longfellow

18. *Kit Carson & Grass Singing,* collage art by Winchinchala © 2012, Kit Carson's face source, Cabinet Card, © 1864; Grass-Singing face source: After *A Half-Breed Girl* by Paul Cane. No true images of Grass-Singing exist; however, an artist, Hildebrand, created a sketch "after Paul Cane's painting *Half-Breed Cree Girl.* Kit Carson was romantically involved with Grass-Singing, Making-out-Road and Josepha Jarimilla.

26. *The Great Bird Wuchowsen* © Winchinchala 2012, original artwork/graphic, Photo: Bald Eagle by Don Pfitzer-US Fish and Wildlife

35. Buck-Wolf Collage art © Winchinchala 2012, Source

39. *Mishquáishim,* © Winchinchala 2012, collage fox/ artwork/graphic

42. Detail des Gemäldes: Schwangere Maria, Fragment eines Altarflügels aus einer Feldkapelle in Cham (Kanton Zug), um 1505. Schweizerisches Landesmuseum, Zürich

45. *The Pied Piper,* © Winchinchala 2012, Derivative graphic

58. *The Rowboat,* © Winchinchala 2012, collage /graphic, Photo Credit: Winchinchala and friend (heads) © Seawolfe, 1956

63. P*ukwudgies,* © Winchinchala 2012, original graphic art based on Library of Congress image.

68. "The look in Pia's eyes froze her." Collage by Winchinchala

74. *Glooskap & Malsumsis* Mirror 17th century woodcut unnamed.

84. *Hotel Del Coronado*, Derivative of © Library or Congress, 1900

87. *Welcome to California Sign*, original art, Winchinchala 2012,

101. Virgin Guadalupe, Vintage Mexican Post card 1930.

117. *The Map*, CIA files, unclassified.

118. Letter ©Winchinchala

122. Vintage postcards from Mexico, 1954.

125. *Bull Ring by the Sea*, © Winchinchala 2012, Derivative Art /graphic from vintage poster

129. *Daring Border Kiss*, © Winchinchala 2012, Derivative Art /graphic from vintage First Love comic book.

131/132. Mock correspondence based on CIA files, unclassified.

133. *Margarita & Hebe,* © Winchinchala 2012, (Dar, great-grand mother to author and Winchinchala from photographs circa 1900 and 1957) collage /graphic based on Photo: Woods, Turkey from Nevada Aerospace Hall of Fame, used with permission.

134. *Mount Vernon Street,* derivative photo from same, Leslie Jones Collection 1929-02 Courtesy of the Boston Public Library

137. *Brunhilde & Gretel*, Austrian Travel poster Österreichische Bundesbahnen, 1910.

138. *The Iron Lung*, © Winchinchala 2012, collage /graphic Photo: Winchinchala's head, Seawolfe, 1955; Photo: Hospital Ward, Courtesy of Center for Disease Control 1950.

141. *Winter Snow in the Public Garden,* ©2012 Winchinchala derivative; photo: Public Garden at night, Leslie Jones Collection 1929-02 Courtesy of the Boston Public Library.

146. *The Art Show,* Derivative collage/photo art © Winchinchala 2012

148. *Uncle Premestaw*—Black and White of *Jan Krzeptowski by* Walery Eljasz-Radzikowski 1892

151. Indian Myth 1940 post card Hayden Planetarium mural

159. *The High Hat,* Derivative collage/photo art © Winchinchala 2012, based on period matchbook courtesy of Seawolfe.

162. *Copley Plaza post cards,* Derivative collage/photo art © Winchinchala 2012, based on period matchbook courtesy of Seawolfe.

166. *The Birches*, photo art © Winchinchala 2012, her own photo.

174. *Van Cliburn*, May 20, 1958, Neal Boenzi/ Nyt Permissions" NYT Pictures, New York Times Company 229 West bird Street, NYC 10036.

175. *Van Cliburn Program and ticket*, Courtesy of Carnegie Hall

179. *The Wrestlers* by Thomas Eakin, 1899
181. Period announcement of ship sailings Public Domain
182. *Provincetown*, Derivative collage/photo art © Winchinchala 2012
183. "The Heavenly Town" by Alma Martin in Paine Smith, Nancy W. *The Provincetown Book* ©1922, Tolman Print, Inc., Brockton, Mass.
186. UFO Memo, CIA files, unclassified
198. *Maushop the Giant*, original art, Winchinchala 2012 includes three Edward S. Curtis photographs.
201. *Wénise & Twenty Men*, collage/photo art © Winchinchala 2012 author's family members and 1900 French postcard.
203. *Venice Italy*, retouched photograph, Buffalo Bill's Wild West Show in Europe, circa 1900, courtesy of Library of Congress
207. *Banquet*, Society of American Indians incorporates faces of author's paternal ancestors.
215. *The International Horse Show 1911* Derivative art work, Manfield & Sons advertisement; faces of author's maternal great-grandparents.
217. *Flying Saucer* Collage art ©Winchinchala
225. *Lightning*, Derivative art ©Winchinchala, source painting, Whistle Jacket by George Stubbs 1899.
228. *Sokanuum Nootau,* collage & photograph ©Winchinchala, face, Source, after *Red Shirt* an Ogallala Sioux, NARA
239. The Duisenberg Arrives, collage art, ©2012, Winchinchala; Photo of car, Errol Flynn
244. Sokanuun Nootau in Regalia, Manipulated drawing by George Caitlin, 1897.
246. Grand Canyon, poster courtesy of the Library of Congress, Bear by John Rae author of American Indian Stories 1900.
256. Groom Lake © Colonel Charlie Trapp contribution to the Nevada Aerospace Hall of Fame NVAHOF Oral History Archive.
262. Hebe in the Hotel, digital collage, Winchinchala © 2012.
278. Austrian Death Certificate from 1958.
284. Collage by Winchinchala. Face photograph of Winchinchala as a child, ©Seawolfe 1955, Background illustrated by John Rae American Indian Fairy Tales 1921.
286. Collage by Winchinchala. Face photograph of Winchinchala as a child, ©Seawolfe 1955,

Wampanoag-English Glossary

Wampanoag (Wôpanâak) fell into disuse about 150 years ago which could mean death for a language, but it didn't. Linguists say it is sleeping because it is still here on the tongues and in the memories of a few. Asleep, as it were, it had no time to evolve as living languages do, and it is quite impossible to resurrect it and the surviving documentation is four-hundred-years old. Nevertheless, Little Doe, (Jessie Fermino Baird), a Mashpee, Wôpanâak, Julie Jennings PhD, Strong Woman of the Nottaway, and Frank Waabu O'Brien Ph.D. work tirelessly to try. Dr. O'Brien, Abenaki Nation of Missisquoi (St. Francis & Sokoki Bands) has authored half a dozen books on and in Wampanoag, including a book of poetry. Little Doe received the MacArthur Fellow genius grant for her efforts in compiling a vocabulary and attempting a grammar. In 2010, Dr. Julie Jennings, Strong Woman received the "Extraordinary Woman Award, a special congressional recognition from the United States Senate for her outstanding achievements in language and cultural enrichment. She and Frank Waabu O'Brien, in particular, have been most gracious in sharing their knowledge.[9] Creating genuine pronunciation without any native Wampanoag speakers makes the task almost insurmountable, but these individuals have collectively resurrected the vocabulary.

Ironically, the 17th century European missionaries' glossaries[10] are the foundation for this process which presents its own challenges. Notation of the language due to documenters' accents and degrees of education varies widely. Thus, there is no uniformity to spelling. An

---

[9] Dr. Julie Jennings, Strong Woman) & Dr. Frank WAABU O'Brien, Abenaki (1998) *Understanding Algonquian Indian Words in New-England* and Dr. Frank Waabu O' Brien, *New England Algonquian Language Revival,* a compilation of *articles* by (2005).

[10] John Eliot *Indian Bible* (1685) & *Grammar Book* (1666); Roger Williams, *A Key Into the Languages of America* (1666); James Trumbull, *Natick Dictionary (1903);* Goddard & Bragdon, *Native Writings in Massachusett* (1988).

example to represent almost every word is Kiehtan (kay-tan), the creator, a non-gender specific entity with no human form. The name appears as: Kehtannit Ketanëtuwit, Kittanitowet, Ketanitowet, Kitanetuwit, Ketanetuwit, Kihtanutoowet, Ketanutowet, Kautantowit, Kautantowwit, Cautantowwit, Cautantouwit, Kehtannit, Kiehtan, Kiehton, Kehtean, Keihtanit, Kehtanit.

The first lost sailors and invaders to New England were not trained linguists or objective anthropologists sent to observe ancient cultures and mine information. They were explorers and missionaries sent by kings to acquire treasures and churches to convert the peoples. Right after the Pilgrims arrived, they focused on teaching the Wampanoag to write, "yu makohteae wussukquohhonk nen," which means, "This is a land-sale writing.[11]" Puritan minister, Rev. Cotton Mather described Indians as "the veriest ruins of mankind which are to be found anywhere upon the face of the earth.[12]" Their notes reflect their narrow opinions, but there are those who saw us as the human beings we are and took the time to try to know us, to learn our ways and our languages. To them and the scholars who work with their books, we owe a thank you. Here are some words.

abamacho = devil
Adchanan = he hunts
ahquompak = when
ahque = be careful
admish-go away
anéqus = chimpunk
anequsanequussuck = little red squirrel
anùm/anúm =dog, depending on dialect
anúnema = help
aquène = peace
aquìúe kuttúnnan = don't tell (secret)
Ascúmetesímmis? Have you not yet eaten?
assótu/ assóko = a fool
attashshiyyinneat = (hide) tie=in hair feather

---

[11] http://www.pilgrimhall.org/natamdocs.htm#1649%20deed

[12] *The Life and Death of the Reverend John Eliot,* 1694.

ausup/ausuppánuog = racoon/s

cháuquaquock =Whites

Chenock cuppeeyau mis? When did you come?

còsh =your father; nosh = my father; osh= father.

cowammáunsh – I love you

cowetompátimmin = we are friends.

hawúnshech = Bye (farewell)

hub, hub hub =come, come, come

kah = and

mutate wunnetu =you are beautiful.

kautántowwit = The Great Spirit who lives in the Soutwest

Keén netop, Is it you?

keesuck = the heavens

kehchis/og =male elder/s

kehchissqu/ aog =female elder

Kiehtan = the great spirit

keihtán anawat =commands

keihtán auntau = speaks

keihtánit wunniyeu= smiles

kitonekqué =forever

kôgwa = porqupine

ktsee=gee=gil=lassis = chick a dee dee dee

kúkkita = listen to me.

kunám = kunnamâuog – spoon/s

Kunnishishem? Are you alone?

Kuttiomp = young buck or a whole deer

machemóqut = it stinks

Machemóqussu = a vile or stinking person

machit =bad evil

Maish-Kitummayi = Just now.

Mannippèno = Have you no water?

mat/matta =no

Matta káche =no doubt

Máttapsh = sit down

matta nickquéhick = I don't want it

méqua =feather

nukquenauwèhhik = I want.

manito = spirit

matta webe wunne = not only handsome

memengwe = butterfly

mieúckaskeete = meadow

Mishquáishim = red fox spirit speaks

mishquáishim = red fox

mishábneke quock = squirrel/s

minikêsu = strong

momonchu = "he is always moving."

mosunnoquat teag = beautiful thing

mosunnoquat teag = pretty thing

muckquand= wolf spirit

natóncks = cousin

naynayoûmewot = horse sound

Neesneéchag Skeétompauog =twenty=men

neimpâuog= the lighting

Neàttup = I am hungry

Niccawkatone, I am thirstie.

nickómmo = A full moon feast or one to celebrate differnt occasions, in particular one after harvest.

Nipewese= give me some water or beeréwese (reconstruct-ed) Give me some beer.

Nippúckis = smoke bothers me

nish kemeoogish, secret things.

nishkenon = broken rain

nissesè/ê an unckle. my uncle

nìtchwhaw =my mother okásu = a mother; kókas=thy mother; wútchehwaw, her mother

n'níshishem= I am alone.

nnowaúntum = I am sorry.

nni, eiu = it is true.

nock win yab—come in

Nosh = my father

nowepinnátimin = friends

nukquenauwèhhik =I want.

nunnamon = my son

nuttaunesog = daughters

nunnaumonog= my sons

Nuppeantam-I pray

nuppaquóntup = my head.

nuttah = my heart/ kuttah = your heart =wuttah =his heart

nux—yes (nukkie)

Puckissu = smokie

Pauskesu, naked

peawyiogguhsemese = small peasik,
okummus / nokummus wuttookummissin= grandmother

nepauzshad=grandmother moon
powwáw = a medicine man
paukúnnum = darke.
paupaqúonteg = key
pequawus = a gray fox.
peskhómmin! = thunder in the sky or a gun
popowuttáhig = sound of a drum
púck = smoke
puckíssu =smokie
quoshaonat = to vow
skeétomp/auog man=men
sóchepo = snow/ falling/storm
Sonqui = cold (it is)
sokanuum nootau = rains fire
squáws=suck = woman women
strawberries == wuttáhimneash
taúbot neanawáyean – thank you
tatta = I know not.
tinogkukquas =frog
titta = I can not tell (woods)
tocketannántum? what do you think?
tocketeáunchim what news?
tocketuspunnaúmaqūn? Did he hurt you?
tokish, tokeke = wake wake
toneska= Hello -Greetings
tunuppasog –turtle
Túckiu = Where is…
tuckìiuash? where are they?
túnna cowâum?= where did you come from?
tunnati =where
ukkosue pompuhchái = virile organ
uppaquóntup = the head.
wadtunkqusoh = her cousin
wâsick = a husband
weéwo = a wife.'
wenîsuck =`old women.'
wequâi, light.

wequáshim, moon=light.

wéshec =hair

what (interrog.) chagwas, changwas

what? chagwas? toh?

who? howan?

wadtunkqusoh = her cousin

wohsum, he shines

wompi bright

Wohwohkau = onomatopoeia for barking

Skeétompauog men

wuchowson the bird

wunégin = well or good/ wauwunnégachick =very good.

wunnamuhkut= truly

wunnickégannash= hands

wunnohteaonk may peace be in your hearts

wusken boy wuskenin (girl)

wuttónoh noosh my father's daughter

wuttootchìkkìnneasin nippawus, grandfather sun

wuhtokquas = rabbit

wuttáhimneash= strawberries

yauwe chippag hour = ¼ of an hour

Yo commeish, a paupaqúonteg=I will give you this, a key

Traditional Wampanoag Prayer

From Cjegktoonupa (Slow Turtle), Supreme Medicine Man of the Wampanoag Nation (On Page 2, it is used without a tobacco offering.)

Nuppeantam

Kiehtanit, nummag ne wuttamauog

Ohke, nummag ne wuttamauog

Okummus nepauzshad, nummag ne wuttamauog

Wutt∞tchìkkìnneasin nippawus, nummag ne wuttamauog

Taubot neanawayean

Nummag ne wuttamauog adt yau ut nashik ohke:

wompanniyeu

sowanniyeu

pahtatunniyeu

nannummiyeu

Taubot neanawayean newutche wame netomppauog:

neg pamunenutcheg

neg pamompakecheg

puppinashimwog

mehtugquash kah moskehtuash

namohsog

Quttianumoonk weechinnineummoncheg:

ahtuk

mosq

mukquoshim

tunnuppasog

sasasō

Kiehtanit, nummag ne wuttamauog

I pray

Great Spirit, I offer this tobacco
Mother Earth, I offer this tobacco
Grandmother Moon, I offer this tobacco
Grandfather Sun, I offer this tobacco
I thank you
I offer this tobacco to the four directions
to the east
to the south
to the west
to the north
I thank you for all my relations:
the winged nation
creeping and crawling nation
the four-legged nation
the green and growing nation
and all things living in the water
Honoring the clans:
the deer
the bear
the wolf
the turtle
the snipe
Great Spirit, I offer this tobacco.

The Lord's Prayer

N∞shun kesukqut
Wunneetupantamunach k∞wesuonk
Peyaum∞utch kukkeitass∞tam∞onk.
Toh anantaman ne naj okheit, neane kesukqut.
Ásekesukokish petukqunnegash assaminnean yeu kesukok
Ahquontamaiinnean nummatcheseongash,
neane matchenehikqueagig nutahquontamanóunonog.
Ahque sagkompagininnean en qutchhuaonganit,
webe pohquohwussinnan wutch matchitut;
Newutche keitass∞tam∞onk, kutahtauun,
menuhkesuonk, sohsúmóonk michéme kah michéme
Amen.

Our Father which art in Heaven
Hallowed be thy Name
Thy Kingdom come
Thy will be done in Earth, as it is in Heaven
Give us this day our daily bread.
And forgive us our tresspasses,
as we forgive them that tresspass against us.
And lead us not into temptation,
but deliver us from evil.
For thine is the Kingdome,
the Power, the Glory, for ever.
Amen.

(From John Eliot (1669). *The Indian Primer; or, The Way of Training up of our Indian Youth in the good knowledge of God, in the knowledge of the Scriptures and in the ability to Reade.* Cambridge, Massachusetts. Reprinted Edinburgh, Scotland: Andrew Elliot, 1880. [Courtesy of The John Carter Brown Library at Brown University].)

PURCHASING BOOKS & CD'S

Note: First & last name: Winchinchala, Winchinchala

For books with personal inscriptions order from:
http://www.writeronthebrink.blogspot.com

All may be ordered at Barnes & Noble online or other online
bookstores –

Prices subject to change. As of August 2011

*Sexy Solitary Suicide & That Beat Hippie Indian Chick, a Trip
Thru the 50's & 60's to Overcome Depression
(Poetry & Novella)* (Illustrated) ~ *$15.99*
(978-1-889768-34-2)
Only Human Short Stories (Illustrated) ~ *$15.99*
(978-1-889768-35-9)
Seinfeld & Neeneemoosha Sweetheart ~ *$15.99*
(978-1-889768-37-3)
The Life and Loves of Mariner JACKIE VIK ~ *$ 17.99*
(Illustrated) ~ *$17.99* (978-1-889768-31-1)
The Life & Times of a Little City Indian in the 1950's 2012 (Illus-
trated) ~ *$21.99* (978-1-889768-36-6)
Derriere: Premiere Seat to Writing (Illustrated) ~ *$19.99*
(978-1-889768-32-8)

FOR PRESS PUBLICITY INQUIRIES or LECTURE BOOKINGS,

Please email:
                    peoplewithwings (at) gmail.com
                        or voice message
                    People With Wings 617-237-0152

Label subject box, NOTICE: BOOKING

FOR READERS: email is welcome. Due to scheduling, the author may not be able to answer all of your emails, but she does read them and appreciates your kind comments and feedback. Thank you.

                    peoplewithwings (at) gmail.com

PLEASE VISIT US ONLINE:

                http://www.barnesandnoble.com/s/WINCHINCHALA
                    http://www.facebook.com/peoplwithwings [Sic]
                        http://www.twitter.com/Thewinchinchala

301

People With Wings Publishing

Since 1992
*Boston * Denver * Amsterdam * Paris*

www.ingramcontent.com/pod-product-compliance
Lightning Source LLC
Chambersburg PA
CBHW031107030726
47496CB00002BA/418